ORPHANS OF THE STORM

Jess and Nancy, girls from very different backgrounds, are nursing in France during the Great War. They have much in common for both have lost their lovers in the trenches, so when the war is over and they return to nurse in Liverpool, their future seems bleak.

Very soon, however, their paths diverge. Nancy marries an Australian stockman and goes to live on a cattle station in the Outback, while Jess marries a Liverpudlian. Both have children; Nancy's eldest is Pete, and Jess has a daughter, Debbie, yet their lives couldn't be more different.

When the Second World War is declared, Pete joins the Royal Air Force and comes to England, promising his mother that he will visit her old friend. In the thick of the May blitz, with half of Liverpool demolished and thousands dead, Pete arrives in the city to find Jess's home destroyed and her daughter missing. Pete decides that whatever the cost, he must find her...

ORPHANS OF THE STORM

Katie Flynn

WINDSOR
PARAGON

First published 2005
by
William Heinemann
This Large Print edition published 2006
by
BBC Audiobooks Ltd by arrangement with
Random House Group Ltd

Hardcover ISBN 10: 1 4056 1498 6
           ISBN 13: 978 1 405 61498 6
Softcover ISBN 10: 1 4056 1499 4
           ISBN 13: 978 1 405 61499 3

British Library Cataloguing in Publication Data available

Printed and bound in Great Britain by
Antony Rowe Ltd., Chippenham, Wiltshire

CHAPTER ONE

NOVEMBER 1918

Nancy Kerris bent over the young man in the bed and put gentle fingers round his wrist. Odd to feel such a tiny flutter in such a strong brown arm— odd to see that his lips were purplish blue and that the tanned face looked suddenly yellow—almost as yellow as his hair. For one heart-stopping moment she did not know what to do; then previous experience, and her training, told her that she must get help—and quickly. She knew the patient had been badly wounded only a matter of a day or so before the Armistice had been signed and now, with a jolt of horror, she realised he was almost certainly haemorrhaging internally. But the gasp which rose to her lips never left them; if you panicked a patient, Sister Saunders said, he could die from fear. No, what she must do was get help and get it quickly.

She laid his hand down on the bed covers and smiled reassuringly into the bloodless face. 'You'll be fine, soldier, but I think maybe your bandage is loosening,' she said, in her most matter-of-fact voice. 'I'll just fetch Dr Amis . . .'

Nancy moved away from the bed, walking with a gliding, rapid step, which was the next best thing to a run, because Sister did not approve of her nurses running, or not on the wards at any rate. 'If you need help urgently,' she told her staff, 'then run as fast as you like along the corridors but not on the wards themselves; is that understood?'

So now Nancy went out of the tent flap—this was a makeshift emergency hospital from which the wounded men would presently be transferred to proper hospitals in England—and, as soon as she was out of sight of the patients, broke into a fast run. A nurse coming towards her turned in her tracks to accompany her, saying as she did so: 'What's up, Nancy? Can I help?'

It was Jess Williams, her best friend, and Nancy spoke rapidly. 'Tent three, fourth bed from the door, haemorrhaging. I'm going to get a doctor; can you lay up a trolley, fetch instruments and so on?'

She did not wait for a reply, knowing Jess was both skilful and competent, but ran on, hearing her friend's hasty footsteps fading in the opposite direction. Seconds later, she was explaining the problem to Dr Amis and turning to accompany him back to the tent she had just left. Obedient to the strictures laid upon them, both doctor and nurse eased their pace to a steady walk as they entered the ward. Already it was clear that Jess had found a blood match between the patient and the young man in the next bed, and had obtained the necessary equipment to do a transfusion. Dr Amis nodded to Jess and spoke softly to the would-be donor, explaining the procedure he was about to carry out, and the young man nodded. Before Dr Amis could ask, Nancy had leaned across the trolley and handed him the appropriate scalpel, then watched as the doctor inserted the tube into the dying man's wrist. Only after that was satisfactorily in place did he make the long incision in the donor's arm. The boy went white but he grinned at Nancy, then switched his gaze to the

2

tubing through which his blood had begun to run steadily into the pint bottle Jess was holding up. Nancy knew that the bottle contained a measured amount of sodium citrate solution to stop the blood from clotting and saw Jess giving the bottle a little shake every few minutes as the blood ran down the other length of tubing into the patient's arm. The donor lay with his forearm supported on a board, and the doctor gently reminded him to keep opening and closing his fist on the piece of rolled-up bandage in his hand in order to facilitate the blood flow.

The young man nodded. Nancy averted her fascinated gaze from the five-inch slit the doctor had cut in his arm and smoothed the damp hair from his forehead. He was only a boy, probably no more than seventeen or eighteen, yet he had volunteered to help another man without a second's hesitation. As she watched, he turned his eyes up towards her and gave her a beaming smile. 'Look at the feller's face,' he whispered. 'He were yellowy-grey two minutes ago, and to tell you the truth I thought he were a goner. But as soon as the blood started to flow, his colour began to come back. Ain't blood a wonderful thing, nurse?'

Nancy, agreeing that it was, caught Jess's eye and they exchanged smiles. To save a life is always sweet and both girls knew that their prompt action had probably done so on this occasion.

Presently the pair were dismissed and made their way towards their sleeping quarters. They were extremely tired, having just worked a double shift, and Nancy guessed that Jess, too, longed to get what rest they could before they went back on duty. Despite her tiredness, however, Nancy could

3

not help remembering that other young man, the one to whom she had been engaged to be married. He had died two years previously, when transfusing blood had been in its infancy; died in her arms, because no one had realised—until too late—that he, too, was haemorrhaging internally from a bayonet wound. She, who had loved Graham Peters to distraction, had knelt on the floor by his bed and held him in her arms whilst his life ebbed slowly away. He had looked up at her wonderingly out of tired blue eyes and she knew she would never forget his last words. 'You've grown so tiny, my love,' he whispered. 'So tiny that I could hang you on a chain round my neck; then I would have you with me for always.'

Before she could answer him, Graham's head had slumped forward on to his chest and she had felt the faint flutter of his heartbeat simply cease as though it had never been.

'Nancy?' Jess's voice interrupted her thoughts and Nancy saw the understanding in her eyes, the shared pain. 'Look, we need our rest; we'll feel better in the morning. And don't think I don't know what you're going through, because if they had known a bit more about blood transfusions two years ago Graham might still be here today.'

Nancy smiled wearily and gripped her friend's hand for a moment. 'I lost Graham and you lost Barney and it was dreadful for both of us,' she said quietly. 'But at least we had their love while they were alive and we have some beautiful memories. And—and we're still young, Jess. I know you think it won't happen, but we might meet somebody else, get married, have children and be happy. I know Graham wouldn't grudge me happiness and I'm

4

very sure Barney wouldn't grudge it to you either; why, they'd both be glad of it!'

Jess was a pretty girl with a cloud of chestnut hair and large, dark blue eyes, but now her lips tightened and her eyes grew cold. 'I shall never marry,' she said bitterly. 'What chance would I have, stuck in a Liverpool slum with a fat, idle mother who wouldn't give tuppence for any of her kids? I suppose I'll have to put in for a training hospital and try to pass the exams but . . . oh no, I shall never marry. There's only ever been one man in my life and that was Barney. It's different for you; you're younger and you've a nice family.'

Nancy knew that in one way, at least, her friend was right. She was a vicar's daughter, from a parish in Devonshire, with loving parents and two older sisters. The Kerris family lived in a beautiful old vicarage, just outside the tiny village of Exham. True, there would be no work for her locally at home, but whatever she did she knew she would have the support of a close-knit family.

*   *   *

Ten minutes later, the two girls made their way into the sleeping quarters. Nancy unpinned her cap and loosened her long, pale gold hair from its neat coil on the nape of her neck. Then she undid the stiff white collar round her throat and removed her celluloid cuffs before casting off her stained white apron and the rustling cotton dress which afforded little protection against the extreme cold. She fished her thick woollen nightdress out from under her pillow and pulled it on over her underwear, for the tents were draughty and no one undressed

5

completely before climbing into bed. As she slid between the blankets, she wondered about the young soldier who might, with luck, now live. She did not flatter herself that she alone had saved his life—that had been done by Dr Amis helped by herself and Jess—but she was glad she had played some small part in the night's happening. Then she snuggled her face into the pillow and put her hands, palms together, close to her chest. Until she had joined the nursing service, she had knelt every night on the cold linoleum of her bedroom floor and said her prayers properly and respectfully as a vicar's daughter should. Now, in circumstances as different from those at the vicarage as could be imagined, she had long ago informed God, rather tartly, that He would have to forgive her for saying her prayers whilst cuddled down in bed.

But once she began, her prayers followed their usual course. She no longer had to pray that the war would end because it had ended. The Armistice had been signed, Victory Day had come and gone, yet still young men suffered and died for a war which she had long ago ceased to believe in. So now she prayed for the recovery of her patients, and for someone to come along and clean up the awful mess that wars leave in their wake, for both victor and conquered. She added a sort of postscript for the young soldier in tent three, realising as she did so that she did not even know his name, could scarcely recall his face. Then, at last, she slept.

*   *   *

'Well, Jess, we're back in Blighty at last! We've got

6

a fortnight free before we start at the Liverpool Royal. Are you still positive that you want to do the course?'

The two girls were sitting in an uncomfortably crowded train heading for London, where they would part company, since each meant to go home to her people for a couple of weeks' break before they started the intensive training course offered to all the volunteers who wished to take up nursing as their career. However, they intended to have a few days in the capital first so that they might buy themselves some warm clothing to replace their threadbare uniforms.

Jess pulled a face. 'What else is there for me?' she asked plaintively. 'I can't go back to living in a cramped little house in the slums with me mam, four sisters and two brothers; mind, the boys don't live at home any more, and nor do me two oldest sisters . . . but Mam and me never got on. Oh, I suppose I might gerra job in a shop, or even an office, but the only thing I know anything about is nursing, and Sister Saunders said it were a good career with plenty of prospects for a girl who didn't mind hard work. Whilst we train, we'll have a room in the nurses' home, and once we're qualified we'll be able to afford lodgings. So . . . yes, I reckon I'll do it. But why do you ask? I thought we'd decided it betwixt ourselves. We put in to go to the same hospital for our training so's we could be together. Don't say you've changed your perishin' mind, our Nancy!'

Nancy smiled. 'When you mention Liverpool you sound more like a scouser every minute,' she said teasingly. She hesitated, knowing that what she was about to say could easily cause offence, for

7

Jess had changed since the death of her fiancé Barney twelve months before. Any mention of marriage seemed to rub salt into the wound and Jess was apt to answer sharply or, worse, not to answer at all. However, it was no good beating about the bush; better to come straight out with what she was thinking and hope that Jess would at least listen to her proposal. Nancy fished in the pocket of her cloak and produced a cutting from a newspaper, then held it out to her friend. 'I saw this a couple of days ago and it made me think,' she said slowly. 'You and I are old friends, Jess, and we've both lost the men in our lives, but in one way I believe we are quite different. I would still very much like to be married and have a family of my own, whereas you seem to have given up any such idea. Oh, I know we agreed there are going to be very few young men to marry after the carnage of the trenches, so I suppose it seemed sensible to you to plan a career and dismiss all thought of marriage. But then I saw this advertisement . . . well, read it for yourself.'

Jess took the small piece of newsprint and gave her friend a curious look. There was bitterness in that look and a sort of disillusion, but then her eyes fell on the paper she held and she began to read aloud: 'Wanted—wives for two white Australians working in the outback. Return passages paid. Apply Box No. 2046.'

Nancy turned to peer in her friend's face. 'Well? What do you think? This would be as much a business proposition as a career in nursing.'

Jess snorted. 'They're after free housekeepers; someone to cook their meals, mend their clothes and manage their wages,' she said bluntly. 'What's

8

more, it's half a world away. Anyone who goes that far isn't likely to turn round and travel all the way back to Britain again. And it's an awful long journey. You've got to live on whatever they send you for weeks and weeks and weeks. I guess that puts you under an obligation which would make it even more difficult to back out, say you'd made a mistake.' She tossed the newspaper cutting contemptuously into her friend's lap. 'Only a fool would answer that advertisement, Nancy Kerris, and if you want to be a fool I can't stop you.'

Nancy sighed and tucked the advertisement back into her pocket. She had known in her heart what Jess's reaction would be but had hoped against hope that her friend might at least consider going with her. She supposed she could go alone, then dismissed the thought. After all, she had no idea yet what the hospital course would be like and how she and Jess would enjoy nursing in an atmosphere far more restrained and conventional than that of the makeshift hospitals in which they had worked for the past four years. So presently, when Jess said, in a distinctly unfriendly voice: 'Well? Are you going to chuck all our plans out of the window and go off on this wild goose chase?' Nancy replied, in her warmest voice: 'Don't be daft, of course I'm not; it was just an idea. Now let's talk about something else because I don't mean to fall out with my best friend over something which is probably just a leg-pull anyway.'

She saw the look of relief which swept over Jess's face and was sorry she had caused her such misery, for she knew the other girl relied heavily on their friendship and was not anywhere near as self-reliant and independent as Nancy was herself. So she began to talk about the sort of warm winter clothing they would buy in London and the show they would see at the London Palladium. At first, there was constraint between them, but gradually this faded, and by the time Victoria Station was reached normal relations had been resumed.

But later that week, when she was once more in her own little room in her parents' house, Nancy got out the advertisement again, then fished out a photograph of herself which she had taken from the big album on the kitchen dresser. It showed her in her nurse's uniform and had been taken at the start of hostilities, but it was the only one she had so she penned a short, friendly letter, not saying much other than that she had read the advertisement and was interested in the writer's proposition, and popped it into an envelope with the photograph, wondering whether she was being a complete fool, as Jess had said. Next day, after some more heart-searching, she told herself that she was committing herself to nothing, squared her shoulders and sent both letter and photograph winging off to Box No. 2046.

*   *   *

Nancy enjoyed her time at the vicarage, and was sorry to leave at the end of her fortnight. Her eldest sister, Helen, had married her father's curate and had recently given birth to a baby boy, named Paul after his grandfather. Helen was still weak from the baby's birth and was happy to let Nancy take care of little Paul, and Nancy was enchanted by the baby. The warm weight of him in

10

her arms, the sweetness of his smile and the soft, silky skin of him awoke in her a strong desire for a child of her own. She did not envy Helen her husband—she thought Samuel both pompous and boring—but she did envy her the baby.

Anne, the sister next to Nancy in age, had also nursed in France, but had been invalided out in 1917 after a severe bout of pleurisy. Mrs Kerris assured her youngest daughter that Anne had made a good recovery, but Nancy thought her sister languid and weak still, content to carry out small household tasks such as dusting and arranging flowers, but spinning these jobs out so that they took all day. Nancy could not say much in front of the rest of the family, but before she left she persuaded Anne to walk into the village with her and cross-questioned her as to why she had changed so radically. She thought she could probably guess the answer—overwork and stress left a body prey to all sorts of malaises—but in fact she was quite wrong.

'I fell in love with a married man,' Anne said bluntly. 'He made all sorts of promises, said he would divorce his wife, swore he didn't really love her. I—I was every sort of fool, Nancy. I made myself believe him, told myself that divorce wasn't so bad, that love conquers all—that sort of thing, you know. Only then he—he mentioned his children and I knew I couldn't go through with it. So I had to tell him that we mustn't meet, that it was all over so far as I was concerned. He was a senior surgeon at my hospital, which made things difficult. When I was off duty, I tried to get as far away from the hospital as possible. I walked out one afternoon into a snowstorm meaning to go

11

into the nearest village, only I lost my way and got benighted. A peasant family took me in but by then I was soaked to the skin and beginning to be ill.' She smiled tremulously at Nancy. 'The rest you know, as they say. I got bronchitis which turned to pleurisy and was sent home. I tell myself I've recovered from—from my love affair, but my health is poor and somehow nothing seems truly worthwhile any more.'

So Nancy left the vicarage regretfully, wishing that she could comfort Anne with the promise that things would get better as time passed, but she said nothing, because she knew Anne would have to learn this old truth for herself. She rejoined Jess in Liverpool, eager to begin the intensive training they had been promised, but after only a month in her new position at the hospital—a month of being treated both as a nonentity and as a complete beginner—she began to long for something different, where she was not continually criticised or mocked. If only the Australians would reply to her letter! After all, there was no harm in exchanging correspondence, she told herself defensively. Probably a score of girls would have answered the advertisement by now and the Australians might not even bother to respond to her own epistle, although she had made it as lively as she could. However, the very fact that the door had not yet closed on a life seemingly more rewarding than the one she lived at present cheered her immensely, and Jess commented on her friend's occasional bouts of optimism.

'I dunno what's happened, but you're more like the Nancy I first met when we both started nursing,' she said approvingly. 'I know you're

12

feeling the way I do—that the nurses here despise us—but they'll get over it once they see how hard we can work.'

Nancy smiled but said nothing and continued to watch for the arrival of the post every morning. She and Jess shared a room in the nurses' home but were on different wards and frequently on different shifts so they saw little of each other during working hours. Nancy was on a medical ward and Jess on a surgical one so even the staff with whom they worked were different. Jess liked Sister Evans though she was not fond of Sister Page who worked nights, but poor Nancy speedily realised that both Sister Frewin, and the rest of the staff on her ward, regarded her as some sort of threat. This was because Mr Myers, the surgeon in charge, knew her from France, where they had worked together, and was unwise enough to make it clear that he had considerable respect for the lowliest member of the nursing staff. Consequently, Nancy found herself emptying bedpans, scrubbing floors and cleaning the lavatories. The patients liked her, appreciating her cheerful willingness to perform any task and teasing her by referring to her as Cinderella, much to Sister's fury. She was a middle-aged, weasel-faced woman, who disliked most of her nurses on principle, but truly detested Nancy. The older woman had a crush on Mr Myers, following him on his rounds with dog-like devotion, and seeing her idol laughing and at ease with the newest probationer on the ward filled her with spiteful fury so that it seemed to be her aim in life to make Nancy as miserable as possible.

So when in April a letter came bearing an

Australian postmark, Nancy opened it with trembling fingers. Fortunately, she was alone in their room so was able to give her full attention to the missive, but first of all she examined the photograph which fell out of the envelope as she extracted the letter. It was a picture of a very young man in army uniform. It was one of the posed pictures which most of the men sent home and showed him stiffly proud of his new uniform. He was half smiling, and the slouch hat which the Anzacs wore could not quite hide the fact that his hair was as fair as Nancy's own. But this photograph had probably been taken in the early days of the war; Nancy flipped it over and read on the back: *Andrew Sullivan, 12 September 1914.* This was written in ink; beneath it, in pencil, were the words: *I don't have a recent photo but this will give you a rough idea; you will guess I am a good deal changed. Andy.*

Nancy nodded slowly to herself. She turned the photograph back and studied it intently; yes, he would be a good deal changed, as indeed she was herself. She knew that, before the war, a photograph of herself would have shown a conventionally pretty, innocent girl, still on the threshold of life, whereas now the picture would be very different. She was not yet twenty-three but knew she looked a good deal older than girls who had not nursed men from the trenches. But it was impossible to guess from this photograph, over four years old, what sort of man Andrew Sullivan was now. The boy had a nice face with guileless eyes. Still, the very fact that he had admitted he had changed meant he was an honest man who did not mean to deceive her.

14

Having studied the photograph for several more moments, Nancy turned to the letter.

Dear Miss Kerris,

Thank you for writing in answer to the advertisement. It was very brave of you, but then all the nurses I met during the war were brave; they had to be to do such terrible work. I have enclosed a photograph of myself, but I am much changed. No one could go through what we all went through and remain unaltered. However, now I am home again I would like a wife and family of my own but girls are scarce in the outback. I am under-manager of a cattle station, and I have a brother. I am twenty-seven years of age and my brother, Clive, is twenty-four. He works with me at the Walleroo cattle station in Queensland and is single like myself, with no commitments, and he also is looking for a wife.

I have had one other answer to my advertisement but have decided that the lady would not be suitable. I will not deceive you into believing that life on a cattle station is easy for a woman. In summer, the heat can be intense and very trying if one is not accustomed, and in the wet, though it is not cold, it rains constantly and turns the station into a bog. Cattle stations are very large, so one's nearest neighbours are a great way off, which can mean a wife is lonely, though of course we employ a great many native workers. However, the native people do not always understand our ways and a woman in the outback needs a friend, which is why I decided to advertise. The other lady who wrote was very frank. She is a widow, forty-two years old, and has lived in cities all her life. I wrote back and explained how we live and she agreed it would not suit her. But you, Miss Kerris, might find the life almost easy after your work in France. You say in your letter that you have two sisters; would one of them not like to take up our offer also? It would be company for you, both on the long journey and, if we decide we are suited, on Walleroo station.

I expect you can guess that this letter has taken me days and days to compose. I do not mean to give you information which may put you off, nor do I want you to see the outback through rose-coloured spectacles. You say in your letter that you were born and reared in the country and this, more than anything else, leads me to hope we might suit. Horses are our main means of transport, but if you cannot ride you can always drive the pony cart.

Clive and I have agreed between us that we will not urge marriage on anyone who comes over as a result of our advertisement, but will leave it up to you to either stay and marry one of us, or return home. I have not enclosed a money order since, until you reply, I cannot tell whether you will come alone or bring a companion—or whether you will simply decide that the Sullivan brothers, and life in the outback, are not for you. As soon as you let me know, hopefully, that you will give us a chance, I will set things in motion.

I am not a man who writes many letters and this one has taken me a mighty long while. I hope I've said nothing to offend you and shall

16

eagerly await your reply.
  Yours sincerely,
  Andrew Sullivan

Having read the letter through twice and then, very slowly, a third time, Nancy settled back in her chair and thought long and hard. If she took up Mr Sullivan's offer, it would be an adventure indeed, but the more she thought about it the more convinced she became that it would be madness to go alone. She might find herself like a bone between two dogs, which would be very uncomfortable, and even if she discovered, upon arrival, that she did not wish to marry either young man, it would still be a difficult situation. She realised, of course, that this applied equally to the two young men, but even so, she found herself heartily agreeing with Mr Sullivan that two girls would find any situation easier to deal with than one woman alone.

She was still mulling the matter over when the door opened and Jess came into the room, untying her apron as she entered and saying in an exhausted voice: 'Well, thank goodness that's over! I've been assisting Staff Nurse Smith in a dressings round and oh, Nancy, she's so clumsy and slow! But of course I'm not allowed to say anything, and when I told her that she had laid a dressing down on an unsterile surface and shouldn't use it, she was absolutely furious and ordered me off the ward to go and—' She stopped short, staring at her friend. 'What's happened? Who's the letter from? Oh, what a handsome young man!'

Nancy had spread the letter out on the table and propped the photograph against the milk jug. She

17

went to gather the pages together, preparing an evasive reply, then changed her mind. 'The letter's from the fellow who put an advert in the paper weeks and weeks ago; remember, I showed you? And the photograph is the one he sent me.' She handed the pages to her friend. 'Go on, read it. Tell me what you think.'

For a moment, she thought Jess was going to refuse. The other girl's colour heightened and her eyes narrowed dangerously; then she snatched the letter, plonked herself down in the chair opposite Nancy, and began to read. As Nancy had done, she read the entire thing through twice and then a third time, before pushing the now rather crumpled pages back across the table. 'Anyone who takes up an offer like that is mad,' she said bitterly. 'Mad and sex-starved, if you ask me. Oh, I don't mean to insult you, Nancy, because I suppose you answered his advertisement as a joke, but he says one woman actually took him seriously, poor fool. What'll you do now, though? Write and tell him it's not on, I suppose—or you could just not reply; perhaps that would be best, just don't get involved.'

Nancy stared thoughtfully at her friend. Jess had beautiful hair, a pretty face and a neat, though slender, figure. She had been an attractive girl but her looks were spoiled now by the strain in her eyes and the bitter lines about her mouth. Nancy gathered up the pages of the letter and thrust them into her pocket, then picked up the photograph and stared at it, trying to imagine the changes which four years of that most dreadful war must have brought. He had talked about the nurses, which meant he had been wounded at least once.

18

For all she knew, he might be crippled . . . no, of course not; if he were crippled he could not possibly be the under-manager of a large cattle station. Besides, she realised suddenly that she believed him to be an honest man, a straightforward man, the sort who would be likelier to tell the worst rather than the best.

'Well?' Jess's voice was sharp, almost spiteful. 'I'm tellin' you, Nancy, if you go, you'll go alone. And if you ask my opinion, only a shameless hussy would go off into the blue, chasin' after a man she's never even met. So what are you going to do, eh?'

'I'm going to write to him again and I think I shall probably set off for Australia some time in the summer, like the shameless hussy I am,' Nancy said quietly. 'I'm sorry you have such a poor opinion of me, Jess, my love, but I think I've discovered that nursing in peacetime isn't for me. If Graham had lived, I would have married him and borne his children and been perfectly happy. As it is, I'm prepared to settle for something less. Perhaps I'll get to this cattle station and discover I've made a mistake but, oh, Jess, it'll be a new country, a new life! Even if Mr Sullivan and myself decide we aren't—aren't suited, as he put it, there may be somebody else. At any rate, I mean to give it a go. Jess, my love, come with me! I don't believe you're any happier with the present situation than I am. Think of it! A new country, new opportunities and young men; decent young men who want wives and families. Please, Jess, give it a chance. Don't turn your back just because it's a long way off.'

'It's nothing to do with being a long way off,'

19

Jess said, her voice rising. 'I were in love with Barney and I'll never love anyone else, lerralone marry. You may forget Graham, but that's not my way. I'll be true to Barney till the day I die and I won't go chasin' after no bleedin' foreigners.'

'I'm not chasing after anyone, Jess,' Nancy said coldly. 'I may get there and decide Mr Sullivan is not for me and come straight home. Or I may go for work in an Australian hospital, or do something quite different. And . . . I shall never forget Graham, but if he were here and able to speak to me, he'd tell me to seize any chance of happiness. After all, I'm only twenty-two; I might live another fifty years. Why should those fifty years be sterile ones? I told you how I enjoyed helping with my sister's baby whilst I was at home; the truth is, Jess, I would very much like a baby of my own.'

'That's disgusting,' Jess said. 'Girls like us don't get married just to have babies; we know better. Anyway, there's no guarantee that you would have a baby. Lots of people marry and never have kids; what about that, eh?'

'If I can't have a baby of my own, then perhaps I could be a nanny and have charge of someone else's babies,' Nancy said, rather wildly. 'What's wrong with that, Jess?'

Jess snorted. 'You could be a nanny in this country,' she pointed out. She got up from her seat and went round the table, putting an arm round Nancy's shoulders and giving her a quick hug. 'I'm sorry I was horrible but you're me best friend and I can't bear to think of you going so far away. Nancy, just think! If you're ill, or very unhappy, you'll have no one to turn to. Not me, because I'm certainly not going with you, not your family, because they've got their own lives to lead. Why, you've only worked in this hospital for a month but you've half a dozen friends already who would do anything they could to help you.'

'I would hope to make friends wherever I went,' Nancy said. 'Jess, come with me! If there are two of us . . . remember, if I'm your best friend, you're mine! Don't let me down now. Come to Australia as well and I'll make you a promise: if you hate it and want to come home again after giving it a try, then I'll come back with you. Isn't that fair?'

Jess shook her head. 'I'm not going *anywhere*,' she said crossly. 'And nor are you if you've got a ha'p'orth of sense. Oh, Nancy, say you won't go!'

Nancy sighed. She and Jess would be sharing this room and in each other's company for weeks, because she realised it would take time to arrange a passage to the other side of the world. Besides, she might change her mind, decide not to go after all. So she said slowly: 'I'm making no promises, Jess, except that I really will think very carefully before committing myself. I've already got several books about Australia out of the library, and I know a little bit about the heat and the sort of clothing and so on which will be necessary if I do go, but I mean to write back to Mr Sullivan and ask him to paint me a picture of the sort of life a woman would live, and the kinds of opportunities which children would have, because I understand folk on a cattle station can be pretty isolated. But there are some farms on Dartmoor that are pretty isolated, so I'm not really worried by that, but I promise you, Jess, I won't do anything hasty. Will that satisfy you for now?'

'Not really, but I suppose it's the most I can

21

hope for, if you're set on making a change,' Jess said sadly. 'Write back to him if you must, but remember, he wants a wife so he may not tell the truth, the whole truth and nothing but the truth.'

'There would be little point in his lying because, if I go, I shall see for myself what the true state of affairs is,' Nancy said wearily. 'Besides, you've seen his photograph; he looks pretty straightforward to me. Why, you said yourself *What a handsome young man* when you first saw the picture.'

'Handsome is as handsome does,' Jess said, rather obscurely. 'And now let's forget all about it because I've probably already said too much. I'm nippin' out to the shops to buy half a dozen eggs and a new loaf; do you want anything?'

*　　　*　　　*

In the end, it was not until the autumn of 1919 that Nancy finally left the hospital and set sail for what she hoped would be the greatest adventure of her life. She and Andrew Sullivan had exchanged a great many letters, and the more she learned of him, the more she liked the thought of meeting him in person. She thought that she was unlikely to fall in love with anyone, for Graham's face was still clear in her memory, his voice in her inner ear. But Graham had been a generous and loving man and Nancy knew with every fibre of her being that he would want her to be happy.

Despite her hopes, however, Nancy was travelling alone. Not only had Jess proved obdurate, but a week after Nancy had booked her passage they had had the most dreadful row. It was over Nancy's intention to go to Australia, of course, and both girls had said things Nancy was sure they would later regret, though it was Jess who had hurled the most unforgivable insults. It was fortunate that Nancy had handed in her notice at the hospital and was off to spend her last two weeks in England with her parents and sisters, for she did not think she could have so much as met Jess's eyes without remembering the terrible things her friend had said. She stood on the deck of the ship, which would take at least six weeks to reach her destination, and looked back at the coastline, fast disappearing as a light morning mist thickened. A tiny figure waving a white handkerchief was her sister Anne, who had insisted upon accompanying her and seeing her safely aboard. Nancy had hoped that Jess might let bygones be bygones so that at least they could exchange letters, and had written her a conciliatory note, telling her both the port and the hour of her departure. She had scanned the crowds eagerly, but there had been no sign of Jess, and when she had admitted her hopes to Anne, her sister had reminded her that Jess was scarcely likely to be given time off from the hospital merely to wave goodbye to an old friend. Nancy knew that it was true, but she also knew that if Jess had really wanted to make up their quarrel by seeing her off, she would have managed it somehow.

She turned away from the rail and headed for the cramped little cabin she was sharing with three other girls. As yet, she knew nothing but the names of her travelling companions, but she guessed that they would grow to know one another well over the course of the long voyage. She had bought a thick notebook in which she intended to keep a diary of

23

her experiences and now she went and sat on her narrow bunk and fished the book out from her canvas holdall. She was halfway through a description of her tearful parting, first with her family and then with Anne, when another thought occurred to her. She was off on what was undoubtedly going to be an adventure, though whether good or bad she could not yet say, but poor Jess, who had stood by her through thick and thin during the war years, was left behind. The work she was doing was hard and could be satisfying, but it was only work. I'll write her a long, newsy letter, adding a bit each day, and post it as soon as I get the chance, Nancy told herself. Of course I shan't be able to give her an address other than the Sullivan homestead, but I'll tell her to address her letters to the Walleroo station and then her reply will be there to greet me when I arrive. Oh, what a marvellous idea; it will be the next best thing to being met by dear old Jess herself!

*   *   *

Jess had handed in her notice at the hospital a couple of days after Nancy left. She had already obtained a position as private nurse to an old lady of eighty-two, who lived in a large house off Lancaster Avenue, so she had no financial worries for the job was live-in. In fact she would be better off, for her employer, Mrs Bellamy, would provide all her meals and uniform. Despite her age, and the painful rheumatism which made it necessary for her to employ a nurse, she was a lively and intelligent woman and Jess had looked forward to starting her new job.

When she had received Nancy's note begging her to forget their dreadful quarrel and asking, somewhat diffidently, if Jess might like to journey to Southampton to see her off, she had been absolutely furious. How had Nancy dared make such a suggestion! As though she, Jess, would waste her time and money travelling all that way when she had much better and more important things to do. Besides, she told herself that she did not want Nancy's friendship; what was the use of a friend who lived thousands of miles away? Their letters would take a couple of months to reach their destination and Jess knew enough about Nancy to be pretty sure that, having made up her mind to go to Australia, her friend would not turn round and come back to England without giving her new life a real chance. So she had not even replied to the note but had scrumpled it up and thrown it in the waste paper basket.

It was a fine, sunny day in spring. Daffodils danced in Mrs Bellamy's neat garden and Jess, who was growing fonder of her employer with every day that passed, had put a tiny vase of violets on her breakfast tray before carrying it up to her room and placing it tenderly across her knees. 'It's a lovely day, Mrs Bellamy,' she said as she did so. 'If you feel up to it, you might enjoy a ride in the bath chair. You've not been down to Sefton Park since the Cheerfulness narcissus came into bloom and their scent, when the sun is on them, is delightful. So if you feel like an outing . . .'

Mrs Bellamy agreed that it would be lovely to leave the house for an hour or so and Jess hurried downstairs. She was turning into the breakfast parlour when the post came through the letter box. There were four letters for her employer and one for herself which had been forwarded by the hospital and Jess did not even have to glancc at thc handwriting to know it was from Nancy. She thrust it into her pocket as a maid emerged from the kitchen with a tray carrying Jess's own pot of coffee and rack of toast. Jess took the tray, then handed her employer's mail to Gladys and asked her to take it to her mistress. Then she turned into the breakfast parlour, sat down in her usual chair, and pulled out her letter. She was tempted to throw it straight into the fire, but perhaps because she was so happy in her present job, or perhaps because all women are curious, she slit open the envelope and pulled out several sheets covered in Nancy's clear, elegant handwriting.

Nancy's letter began with an account of her voyage and went on to describe several ports which she had visited in company with the three other girls who had shared her cabin. Then she described her excitement over reaching Sydney, the beauty of the big, modern city and her surprise and delight when, descending on to the quayside, she was approached by a tall, fair-haired man who introduced himself as Andrew Sullivan.

He had recognised me from my photograph and had come a great distance to meet me so that I should not feel myself a stranger in a strange land, she wrote. *I know I should have realised what a huge country Australia is—Mr Sullivan had told me so in all his letters—but I had not realised how long it would take us to reach the Walleroo from Sydney. First we had to catch a steamer which took us, extremely slowly, up the coast. Then we caught a train, which was also very slow. Dear Jess, I won't describe the journey to you because, to be honest, a good deal of the scenery, though strange at first, was also very boring. The heat on the train was intense, the food available of the plainest, and we were plagued by flies which descended on us in huge numbers every time the train stopped at a station, which was often. However, Mr Sullivan did his best to entertain me, telling me the names of all the trees, flowers, birds and animals we saw whilst travelling and trying to put me in the picture as regards the homestead and staff at the Walleroo.*

And now, Jess, I must tell you the most important piece of news. Andy—I must call him Andy now—and myself were married before we left Sydney. Truly, Jess, Andy is a good man and I know you would like him. Neither of us pretends to be in love but we like one another very well and I am sure we'll grow even fonder as time goes by. Dear Jess, I can imagine your face, but please don't be cross, or think I acted impetuously, though I suppose I did. But it would have been very difficult to undertake this long journey as an unmarried woman, accompanied only by a bachelor; for Australians are every bit as conventional as English folk and would have expected me to have a female companion. Also, Andy says we would have had to travel all the way back to this town—the one I'm writing from—in order to get married and Andy's brother, Clive, has already been in charge for far too long. Andy is obviously worrying in case his brother can't cope.

Andy manages the cattle station for a Mrs Briggs, who is very old and lives a great way away, down on the coast. She has one daughter, who is not in the least interested in the Walleroo, so the arrangement is that when Mrs Briggs passes on, the daughter will sell the property to Andy and his brother. So you see, dear Jess, that it is vitally important to keep the station in good heart, both for Mrs Briggs's sake and for the Sullivans' future.

Oh dear, I do hope I've made you understand how difficult it would have been to delay our marriage until we reached the cattle station. Andy did not try to persuade me to marry; he simply set out how things were and left me to make up my own mind.

We are, at present, staying in a small hotel before starting on the last leg of our journey. Andy suggested that I should spend the day writing letters home, since if I were to leave it until we reach the cattle station, we would have to wait for the mailman's visit before the letters could be despatched. The mail is delivered once a week and any letters we may have written are collected at the same time. The pack horses cannot deliver parcels, only letters and small packets, so when a parcel arrives, someone from the Walleroo has to drive to the railway station to pick it up, which is almost a hundred miles away!

I am hoping there will be a letter from you waiting for me when we reach the homestead. You are such a generous person, Jess, so I'm sure you will forgive me for my part in our quarrel. I said some dreadful things which I certainly didn't mean, and I long to hear from you.

All my love,
Nancy

Jess propped the letter against the toast rack and poured herself a cup of coffee. It was not fair! If only Barney hadn't died! She did not have Nancy's longing for a baby, but she was beginning to realise that, fond though she was of Mrs Bellamy, she did hunger for a home and a man of her own. But not badly enough to go to the other end of the earth, she reminded herself. She was not that desperate. Mrs Bellamy often suggested that she should take an evening off and go out with her friends from the hospital, but so far Jess had not done so. Slowly, she reached for a round of toast, spread it with butter and marmalade, and began to eat. No, it wasn't fair. Nancy was married to a man of some importance, who would eventually be the owner of an enormous cattle station. She would be mistress of the Walleroo homestead; the word homestead had already conjured up a picture in her mind's eye. It would be a long, low building, whitewashed and roofed with cheerful red tiles. There would be roses round the door and the house would be set amidst trees and rolling hills. Every window would be framed by pretty curtains, the floors would be luxuriously carpeted, and there would be servants who would run to do Nancy's bidding and adore their beautiful intelligent mistress, with her ash-blonde hair and big blue eyes. Yes, Nancy had landed on her feet, there was no doubt of that.

If she, Jess, should do as Mrs Bellamy suggested and go to a dance, or some other social event, what sort of young man was she likely to meet? The war had left everyone weary and dispirited. Jobs were difficult to find—as were unmarried men—and money was short. And anyway, she told herself briskly, you had a chance of a better life in Australia, the same as Nancy, but she took it and you didn't. You said you'd never forget Barney, never love another. You really ought to eat your words, tell Nancy you're sorry for the things you said. But she knew she would not. Nancy had abandoned her, left her to loneliness and spinsterhood; she would never forgive her old friend for that, not if she lived to be a hundred.

*   *   *

'Well, Nancy, there it is! Not bad, eh? The boys knew what time the train would arrive and how long it would take Abel to drive back from the station, so they'll have gathered in the yard to meet you. Yup, I can just about see them from here.' Andy chuckled and squeezed Nancy's hand. 'They're that excited, you'd think they'd never seen a white woman before, though of course Mrs Delaney is white. See her? She's standin' right by the front door.'

Nancy murmured that she could indeed see Mrs Delaney and smiled inwardly at Andy's feeling he had to point her out for, in the sea of faces, only one woman was white. Nancy guessed that the tall young man with the gingery hair must be Clive, her new brother-in-law, and that the elderly man with the seamed sunburnt face and stooping shoulders was Tom, who had been manager here but had retired several years previously, staying on as a helper when needed.

The buckboard, an uncomfortable springless vehicle with no canopy to shield one from the burning sun, skidded to a halt in the middle of the yard, and everyone surged forward. 'This is my new wife and your mistress,' Andy shouted to the assembled company, as he helped Nancy down from her seat. 'You must tell her your names when she serves out your wages on Sunday morning. Now you'd best go about your business. Supper may be a little late but I dare say you realised that.' He turned to Nancy. 'There's only one of the gins works in the house and that's Violet . . .' He indicated a fat black woman, with an enormous white grin and tiny bright eyes, who bobbed a half-curtsy whilst grinning broadly at Nancy. 'She helps Mrs Delaney with the cooking and cleaning. There's a deal of cooking because, obviously, we feed the entire staff and their families.'

As the staff began to scatter, Mrs Delaney, who was leaving that day to go and live with her married daughter in Cairns, moved forward and held out a strong, workworn hand. 'How do you do, missus,' she said gruffly, in a broad Irish accent. 'I reckon you'll be wore out after your journeyings so I've made so bold as to set out some fresh clothes on your bed and to cook a tasty dish for supper. The shower is charged up, so if you'd like to come wi' me, I'll take you to your room.'

Nancy murmured something conventional whilst her eyes roved with disbelief across the homestead. It was built of corrugated iron and looked more

31

like a gigantic garden shed than a house. It was a single-storey building, built on a slight rise, and completely surrounded by hard-packed earth and fenced-off paddocks, though the paddocks themselves, at this time of year, were bare of grass. She looked wildly up into Andy's face and saw, with astonishment, that there was pride in his eyes.

'Go inside, hon,' he urged. 'We've done all sorts to make you feel at home—whitewashed the walls, put some mats down, prettied the place up a bit. But see what you think. I'll let Mrs Delaney show you round while I get a report from Clive; learn what's been going on.'

Cautiously, Nancy went in through the front door and entered a large room with a tiny, uncurtained window. It was floored by some sort of cement upon which two large rush rugs had been spread. There were four easy chairs, all obviously homemade, a long wooden table and two benches, and an enormous sideboard upon which stood a motley assortment of china and glass. Nancy looked round her rather helplessly. Despite the fact that evening was coming on, the room was stifling. What was more, when she looked up, she could see the wooden beams upon which the corrugated iron roof was set, and the lack of a ceiling, she guessed, made the heat worse.

'Nice, ain't it? We were going to put a ceiling in here, like what we done in your bedroom, but there hasn't been time. Still, I dare say you can do it in the wet, when there'll be more help about the house,' Mrs Delaney said. She opened a creaking door and indicated another room. 'This here's your bedroom. What do you think?'

Another rush mat lay on the floor and a big

brass bedstead stood in the middle of the room. The bedding looked clean and fresh and the one chair, roughly fashioned from planks of wood, held a kerosene lamp and a Bible. 'Like the ceiling?' Mrs Delaney asked, rather anxiously. 'It's cooler in here, wouldn't you say?'

Nancy, looking up at the lengths of white calico material nailed to the beams, agreed faintly that it was a great improvement. 'But I would dearly like a shower,' she said, and followed Mrs Delaney out of the house and across the yard to a small, corrugated iron shack. Mrs Delaney instructed her in the art of taking a shower in the outback. You removed your clothes and hung them on a hook on the back of the door, stood directly under the large bucket balanced on beams above your head, and then pulled the piece of rope which dangled almost to floor level. Nancy sighed. She might have guessed how it would be, she told herself ruefully; this was the outback, after all, and Andy had told her over and over that life in the bush was hard, not like life in the city. Only, of course, she had not been able to even imagine that conditions would be like this. And next time I take a shower, I shall wrap myself in a big towel and come across the yard like that, she told herself, removing her clothing as she had been bidden. Presently, she pulled the rope just sufficiently to get thoroughly wet, then used the rough bar of soap, pulled the rope again to rinse herself off, and rubbed herself dry on the coarse towel hanging beside her clothing on the back of the door.

She emerged from the shower feeling a good deal cooler and followed Mrs Delaney back across the yard, observing as she did so that she did not remember seeing a door leading to the kitchen. Mrs Delaney shot her a surprised glance. 'Kitchen's separate,' she said briefly. 'It gets real hot in there; you wouldn't want the kitchen in the house, missus. Remember, you'll be cooking for fifty or sixty people, not just for the bosses.' She led the way across to another corrugated iron building which contained wooden work benches round three sides and an enormous cooking range in the centre. It was even hotter in the kitchen than it had been in the house and when Mrs Delaney explained that, except in the wet, the family would eat on the veranda which ran along the whole length of the house front, Nancy was not surprised, though considerably relieved. 'And I dare say it'll be Violet who does most of the cooking,' she added, as they turned from the kitchen. 'My husband introduced her as the cook.'

Once more, Mrs Delaney looked doubtful. 'She'll mebbe help but I don't know as she's ever done anything but camp-fire cooking,' she said. 'However, I've no doubt you'll learn to manage. What's your bread like?'

It was Nancy's turn to look doubtful. 'Bread? I don't quite . . . oh, if you mean can I cook bread, no I can't, but surely Violet . . .'

'Violet's never handled yeast in her life,' Mrs Delaney said positively. She turned to stare at her companion, her eyes going slowly from the crown of Nancy's head to her toes, in their smart black boots. 'But you'll soon find your way around, missus. You were nursing in France, the boss told us, and you've come all the way from England not knowing what were before you, so you've got courage. Oh aye, you'll pick it all up soon enough.'

They had skirted the house and were heading for a third corrugated iron shed. 'Storeroom,' Mrs Delaney said briefly. 'We orders up six months at a time, which is why . . .' She produced a large key from somewhere and unlocked the door, opening it just enough for Nancy to get a glimpse of the interior, which looked more like the stockroom of a shop than anything else. Sacks, bottles, jars and boxes filled every shelf. Drums of kerosene and cooking oil stood on the ground, and Nancy saw that all the windows were bolted on the inside. 'Have to keep it locked or the boys would help themselves. And of course, it's the first place the wild blacks make for if they're on a raid,' the older woman said. 'Now next, there's the meat house . . .'

Nancy dutifully inspected the meat house, which had large windows covered in gauze, and was also locked though Mrs Delaney said that no one was likely to try to steal meat when it was on the hoof all around them. Then, upon Nancy's delicately requesting to be shown the . . . er . . . facilities, Mrs Delaney led her a hundred yards away from the house to where yet another corrugated iron shack, surrounded by hatefully buzzing flies, was perched over a deep and noisome ditch. 'This here's what you might call a moveable feast,' Mrs Delaney said bluntly. 'Every now and again, the boss gets the boys to fill in this trench and move the shack mebbe twenty yards further off. Now, is there anything else I can show you?'

She turned as she spoke and began to walk briskly towards the house. Nancy clutched her arm, drawing her to a halt. 'No, there's nothing else,' she said rather breathlessly. 'Except . . . could you

35

possibly stay for a little longer, say a week? Or even a couple of days? I fear I simply don't have the knowledge ? . . . cooking for fifty or sixty people . . . Mr Sullivan seemed to think Violet . . .'

'Can't be done,' Mrs Delaney said briefly. 'Not for a week, that is, but I can manage a couple of days . . . I might manage three, if that would be any help.'

Nancy could have kissed her, but instead she said humbly: 'Thank you, Mrs Delaney, that would be wonderful. I am sure you can teach me an awful lot in three days and perhaps Violet might learn something too.'

That night, after thoroughly enjoying the supper Mrs Delaney had cooked, Andy and Nancy retired to the big brass bedstead and Andy asked her, with just a shade of anxiety, how she thought she would settle into her new life.

'I guess I'll get along just fine, though I hadn't bargained on having to cook for such a large number of people,' Nancy said, with a confidence she was actually far from feeling. 'But Mrs Delaney is going to stay over to teach me and I mean to see that Violet learns as well so she can be a real help to me. But Andy, I asked Mrs Delaney where our fresh fruit and vegetables came from and she stared at me for a moment without saying a word, and then she said: "From tins, of course," which set me back on my heels, rather.'

Andy laughed and reached out a long arm, drawing her close. 'You can have fresh fruit and vegetables, only you have to grow 'em,' he said comfortingly. 'Pretty soon now the rains will start, and soon after that the river will flood. Then, after Easter, the floods will recede and the ground near

36

the river will be that rich that anything you plant will thrive. Of course, it's also when we muster the cattle for sale, because they're in good shape. Vegetables aren't the only things that thrive at that time of year; the grass fairly shoots up.' He stroked her cheek gently, running his fingers down her neck to cup her shoulder. 'The fellers, and myself and Clive of course, will be gone for weeks, but you'll have the gins to help you, and old Tom too. And now we'd best get some sleep, because tomorrow you'll be baking your first batch of bread.' He chuckled deep in his throat. 'I always swore I'd never marry a woman who couldn't bake a good loaf. What's the use of a pretty face? That won't fill a man's belly, I used to say. And here I am, married to a girl fair as a lily, who's never cooked so much as a pancake in her whole life.'

Nancy dug him in the ribs with a clenched fist. 'How do you think we lived in the nurses' home?' she asked indignantly. 'Why, I'm a dab hand with boiled eggs and bread and butter soldiers; it's just the thought of cooking for fifty which daunts me a bit.'

'Bread and butter soldiers?' Andy said dreamily. 'Is that what you called us? If so, young lady . . .' He made a mock growling noise and grabbed her, nuzzling her neck.

But Nancy pulled away, very conscious of Mrs Delaney, sleeping in the tiny bedroom only separated from their own by a thickness of corrugated iron. 'Haven't you heard of boiled eggs and a round of bread and butter cut into fingers to dip into the yolk?'

'All the eggs I eat are hard all through, like bullets,' Andy said, his voice already slurring with sleep. 'And you won't get no eggs here. The boys ate all the chickens while I was out of the way.'

'We'll buy some more,' Nancy said sleepily. 'Day-old chicks, little round balls of yellow fluff. My mother kept chickens in our orchard. I know about chickens.'

Against her neck, she felt him smile. 'You'll have to watch the crocs,' he said indistinctly. 'They come pretty well up to the house in the wet and they'll eat anything smaller than themselves. Still, you could mebbe fence off a bit of the veranda.' His voice died away and, presently, he slept.

CHAPTER TWO

Jess had not replied to either of the letters Nancy had written since her marriage, but when a third letter arrived, after a considerable time lapse in which Nancy said that she had given birth to a boy, and that she and Andy had agreed to call him Peter, Jess decided that it would be downright churlish not to congratulate her old friend. Also, she had news of her own to impart. Mrs Bellamy sometimes went to Southport to visit her son Claud and his wife Veronica, and on these occasions she hired a car from a well-known local firm. She was not fond of her daughter-in-law, an overbearing self-satisfied woman, so she usually only stayed a day or so, and always insisted that Jess should accompany her. 'My daughter-in-law says that her servants could look after me perfectly well, but I remember when I visited her four years ago and said I needed help with dressing how she grumbled and told poor Claud I was a burden and should be forced to do more for myself.'

Jess always enjoyed their visits to Southport, especially after her employer took to insisting that they should be driven by Mr Ryan, a neat young chauffeur employed by the car-hire firm. Mrs Bellamy hired the car for the length of her stay, so that she might visit Southport and other resorts along the coast, with the result that Jess and Mr Ryan were often in one another's company. After several such meetings, Mr Ryan asked Jess to go dancing with him and a delightful friendship ensued. Now she and Ken Ryan were engaged to be married, though both knew it would be at least two years before they were in a financial position to tie the knot.

So when the letter arrived with the news of the baby's birth, Jess decided to write back for the first time, passing on her own exciting news. After all, why not? She still envied Nancy the wonderful home which she believed her friend owned, and the life she led, for in her second letter Nancy had talked of the number of black servants they employed though she had not described the homestead, or its surroundings, in any sort of detail. Naturally, therefore, when Nancy talked of baking bread, making soap, and harvesting the vegetables from her garden, Jess assumed that Nancy merely supervised, whilst her servants did the work.

What was more, in the letter telling Jess of Peter's birth, Nancy had asked, anxiously, whether Jess was so unhappy that she could not bring herself to reply to her letters and had also suggested that she might reconsider coming to

Australia, saying that Clive was a really delightful man, and still not married.

So it was partly to scotch any such hopes and partly to boast of her fianc8E that Jess took pen and paper one evening, when her employer was safely tucked up in bed, and began to write to her old friend.

She decided she must first apologise for allowing the rift between them to widen, and once she had done that she found that words came easily.

How delightful that you have a little boy; I wish I could see him. As soon as I got your letter, I began to knit a blue matinée jacket with matching bootees, which I shall despatch as soon as they are complete. I took some advice from Mrs Bellamy and have knitted in cotton instead of wool, since she seems to think that Queensland is pretty hot all the year round. Anyway, I hope you will find them useful.

And now for my own news. I am engaged to be married! His name is Ken Ryan and he works as a chauffeur for a car-hire firm. He has dark hair, brown eyes and a nice, square chin, and he looks very dashing in his chauffeur's uniform, which is a navy suit, pale blue shirt, navy tie with a silver stripe, and a smart peaked cap. We are both saving every penny we can but I think it will be a couple of years before we can afford to actually marry. Oh, Nancy, my dear, I am so happy! I truly never expected to fall in love again but now that I've done so, I can understand completely why you went to Australia and why you married your Andy. You

40

sound blissfully happy and I am sure Ken and myself will be blissfully happy too. I'm afraid I'm not a good correspondent—I find writing letters very hard—but I will do my best to keep in touch,
*   Your old friend,*
*   Jess*
*   PS How awful I am! I completely forgot to tell you that, soon after you left for Australia, I got a job as a private nurse to an elderly lady (Mrs Bellamy). We live at Lancaster Avenue; it's a lovely house and I couldn't be happier. She is very good to me, treats me more like a daughter than an employee, so it will be a wrench to leave her when Ken and I marry. The hospital have redirected your letters but that will no longer be necessary since you can write to me here.*
*   Much love,*
*   J.*

*   *   *

It was a Sunday afternoon in May when Nancy heard the clatter of approaching packhorses as she was putting the finishing touches to what would presently become their main evening meal. She straightened up, put a hand to the small of her back for a moment, then brushed the sweat off her brow and went into the yard. Jimmy Bullwhip, the mailman, so called because of his boasted ability to take a fly off a packhorse's ear with his whip without causing the animal to bolt, was handing Andy the Sullivans' post plus a number of newspapers and a couple of small packages. Both

41

men greeted her cheerfully, Jimmy sniffing appreciatively at the good smell of beef stew which followed Nancy out of the kitchen. He was a tall, rangy man, who wore a thick black beard and side whiskers, though since he never removed his large bush hat, even at mealtimes, Nancy had no idea whether his hair was as black as his beard or whether, in fact, he was as bald as a coot.

Both men had turned at her approach and now Jimmy said: 'Somethin' smells good; I allus likes bringin' your post, missus, 'cos I reckon the food you produce is a good deal better'n what I get at other stations. And I've grown kind o' fond of settin' me bedroll down in that little cabin of yourn right agin the creek.' He grinned at Andy. 'Kind o' handy, that creek.'

Andy grinned back though Nancy pretended not to know what he meant. Because of the long distances between stations, Jimmy always overnighted at the Walleroo before going on to his next drop, and since he was a man with a good thirst he enjoyed several mugs of Nancy's homebrew with his evening meal. She guessed that the trek to the lavatory was probably too much trouble and that he used the creek, though at this time of year it was already only a trickle between its high banks.

'Two for you, honey; both packages,' Andy said. He turned to the mailman. 'Ever since the kid arrived, we've been getting packages from England; real nice stuff some of it . . .' Nancy could see his lurking grin and understood the reason, for some of the baby clothes would have been suitable for Little Lord Fauntleroy and were of small use to Pete Sullivan.

42

'It's the thought that counts,' Nancy said firmly, however, taking both packages from him. 'And the reason you think my beef stew is tastier than the stuff served on other stations is thanks to my garden. Onions, carrots, swedes and beans would grow just as well on the Clitheroe and McGuire stations if someone bothered to plant them.'

'You forgot to say our beef cattle's the best as well,' Andy said reproachfully, as the mailman went to his horses' heads and began to lead them to the paddock where they would be rubbed down, fed and watered by one of the hands. 'Or mebbe you'll say the beef is tender because you cook it for hours in the bake oven and not because it's the best.'

Nancy laughed. 'What does it matter who does what, so long as it tastes good?' she asked. 'Ah, this package is from Anne. It'll be those rubber knickers she talked about; we'll be the first people in Australia to have them. And the other one's from Jess; she said she was making a matinée jacket and matching bootees. She knits beautifully; I just hope these will fit little Pete because he's shooting up like—like a corn stalk in the wet.'

She began to rip at the package and Andy put an arm round her shoulders to steer her back into the house. Even as they entered the living room, they heard the baby begin to mutter, the sound rising to a hiccuping roar the moment his parents bent over the large rush cradle in which he lay. 'He's outgrowing the cradle already,' Nancy said, ripping open the package as Andy picked up his son and laid him across his shoulder in a very professional manner. 'Oh, what beautiful work Jess does. Everything will fit him—he can wear them next time we go to town.' She held up the pale blue matiné e jacket, admiring the intricate pattern, so faultlessly knitted, and the lace collar crocheted around the neck. 'Sensible Jess—she said she'd used cotton, so he won't get too hot, poor little fellow. But I'd better feed him before I do anything else, or he'll start bawling and you won't like that.'

'I don't mind him bawling,' Andy protested, but he handed the baby over and followed Nancy into their bedroom. She laid the baby on the end of the bed and began to remove his nappy whilst Andy went over to the chest of drawers which Ben, the carpenter, had made, and took out a clean towelling square, folding it expertly whilst Nancy dropped the wet nappy into the bucket of water beneath the washstand. She took the clean nappy from him, then glanced up with a teasing smile. 'No one's watching, so you can put the nappy on just as soon as I've wiped him down and spread zinc and castor oil ointment on his little bits and pieces,' she said, smiling up at the tall, suntanned man beside her. 'Go on, Andy. If I was ever taken ill someone else would have to change his nappy, and if Violet wasn't around . . . well, I wouldn't trust any of the other gins to do it.'

'I'm an old hand with nappies,' Andy said loftily. 'Look, I'll put it on while you open the other package. And this evening I'll help with the chores and rustle up a couple of the gins to give me a hand—or the boys, come to that—so that you can write nice thank-you letters to Jess and Anne for Jimmy to take to the post when he leaves in the morning.'

Nancy stood on tiptoe and kissed her husband's jaw just beneath his ear. He knew how important

44

her friendship with Jess was to her and how dearly she loved her sister, and she was aware, not for the first time, how very lucky she was. She and Andy did not talk much about their unconventional meeting and marriage, but she had known for a long time now that he loved her with a depth and sincerity for which she had not dared even to hope. It was partly because she had simply accepted the hardships which were a part of life on a cattle station. Every week, she tackled the mammoth task of breadmaking for fifty or sixty people. It took her two whole days; days spent in the sweltering heat of the corrugated iron kitchen whilst she constantly fed the fire with great logs and watched for the moment when perfect loaves could be stood on the window sills to cool. Last year, after the floods went down, she had performed the back-breaking task of planting her garden. In theory the gins or even some of the hands were supposed to help her, but in practice they were not much use. They either buried the seeds so deep that they were more likely to come up in England than in Australia, or they planted them so shallowly that birds or animals ate them before they had even begun to sprout. Then there was soap-making. Before Nancy came to the station, she had thought soap came in pretty packets from Pears, scented with sweet geranium, lily-of-the-valley, or her own personal favourite, rose. Now she knew better. Every so often, she tipped five pounds of caustic soda into a large kerosene can of water, added melted fat, and simmered the concoction over the open range until it thickened and became soap. She then commandeered three or four hands to tip the cooling substance into large trays to set, and

45

then, when it was hard, she cut it into squares. Since it was the only soap available she and Andy had to use it, as did the staff, but the smell was not pleasant and when she opened Anne's parcel and found it contained, as well as a hand-embroidered nightdress for Peter and several pairs of rubber knickers, two bars of her favourite scented soap, her eyes filled with tears at her sister's percipience. Wordlessly, she held out the fragrant packets, and Andy bent and kissed her cheek.

'I know,' he said softly. 'I know, my dear love.'

Nancy felt ashamed, then, that she could not answer him in kind, but she was too honest to do so, for she had never felt for Andy the vivid sparkling love which she and Graham had shared. She was fond of him, appreciated his many good points and enjoyed his love-making, but she was not in love with him. As for Peter—Pete they called him—she only had to feel his warm silken skin against her cheek to know such a sense of love and fulfilment that it brought tears to her eyes. But this was foolishness, and as Andy finished pinning his son's nappy neatly into place she sat down in the cushioned rocking chair which Andy had caused to be made for her, unbuttoned her blouse and held out her arms for the baby, who snuggled joyfully against her and began to suck with a lustiness which proved, at any rate, that there was nothing wrong with his appetite. Nancy sighed with contentment and settled herself more comfortably against the cushions. This one small but essential task gave her more satisfaction than anything else she did. Happily sitting down for the first time for many hours, she let her mind wander to the letters she would write after supper, leaving the clearing

46

of the tables, the washing and wiping of the dishes, and the other multitudinous tasks of the evening in Andy's capable hands. The staff, of course, provided their own tin plates and eating implements and she suspected that these were almost never washed up, thinking with grim humour that when the crust of stews, roasts, fruit pies and custards grew thick enough the natives would simply bang the dishes on some hard surface until the dried debris cracked off, and return to the yard to hold out the 'clean' plates for the next helping of food.

*   *   *

Jess was in the kitchen, preparing a tea tray for Mrs Bellamy. It was a fine August day; a day which had followed a week of rain and high winds, so the old lady had seized the opportunity to take an outing. She in her bath chair, and Jess pushing it, had spent a delightful afternoon in Prince's Park. They had watched some children playing games on the grass whilst others sailed homemade boats on the lake. They had brought buns in a brown paper bag and fed them to the ducks. They had even walked through to Sefton Park and visited the aviary where Jess had exchanged remarks with a large white bird whose head was capped with bright yellow feathers. 'It's a sulphur-crested cockatoo,' Jess had told her employer, reading the information on the card affixed to the cage. 'It comes from Australia . . . that's where my friend is! Isn't it odd, Mrs Bellamy, to think that whilst we're looking at these birds in a quiet, green English park, my friend Nancy may be watching one fly

47

across her vegetable garden, or perched on her linen line, and never think it strange.'

Mrs Bellamy had laughed. 'How long has your friend been in Australia?' she had asked teasingly. 'I seem to remember you came to work for me around the time your friend went there, and that's no more than two years ago. Surely she can't have grown accustomed to tropical birds in her back garden in a mere two years?'

Jess had giggled. 'I suppose you're right,' she had admitted. 'And, of course, they won't talk, because wild birds don't. But this chap does, don't you, Cocky?'

'Doncher, Cocky?' the bird had croaked, then did a little dance on his perch, pushing his big curved beak against the bars. Jess had put a cautious finger through the wire and begun to rub his head, and the bird had made a small trilling noise and let his grey lids slide up to mask, for a moment, the round bright eyes.

But that had been earlier in the day, and Mrs Bellamy was having a late tea because both she and Jess had been tired after their expedition. 'I think I'll have a little nap, so if you don't mind, my dear, you can help me into bed now and then bring my afternoon tea up at about five o'clock,' Mrs Bellamy had said. 'I'll just have a pot of China tea, some thin slices of lemon and a round of bread and butter.'

'Cook has made a beautifully light sponge cake,' Jess had said enticingly. 'Couldn't you manage a very small slice of that? She's filled it with her own homemade raspberry jelly. Can I put a tiny piece on your tray? Only we don't want to hurt her feelings, do we?'

The cook had been with them three months and was good at her job, and Mrs Bellamy already valued her, so she had smiled and told Jess to include a piece of cake on the tray. 'Though you may have to eat it yourself,' she had said warningly. 'For I don't feel at all hungry, and I am very tired.'

So now Jess carefully cut a slice of the deliciously light cake, placed it on a pink plate, and added it to the tray. Gladys was washing up at the sink and Cook was having five minutes with her feet up, sitting outside the kitchen door in the sunshine whilst a batch of scones baked in the oven. Jess glanced at the clock above the kitchen mantelpiece. It lacked only a couple of minutes to five o'clock so she would take the tray up now. She had already warned Cook to put dinner back by an hour so that was all right.

Jess went quickly up the stairs and across the landing. She tapped on Mrs Bellamy's door, not waiting for a reply but going straight in. She had half drawn the curtains across the windows but the room was still very light and her employer was sitting up with a book spread out in front of her, her reading glasses perched on her nose. She smiled at Jess and began to speak, and then, to Jess's horror, her voice trailed away and she fell forward, giving a little groan as she did so. Jess put the tray down with a crash, heedless of the delicate china, and rushed forward. Gently, she moved Mrs Bellamy back until she was once more resting on her pillows, but there was something in the way her head sagged, something in the almost papery whiteness of her face and blueness of her lips, that told their own dreadful story. Jess did not need to put her fingers round Mrs Bellamy's thin old wrist

49

to know that she was dead.

*   *   *

'It was a massive heart attack, but very sudden and quick; she was actually speaking to me when it happened,' Jess told Ken tearfully, when she met him that evening. 'I couldn't have had a better employer, or a better friend, for that matter, so I'm glad she went quickly without suffering. But oh, Ken, whatever will I do?'

'You'll have to get another job, of course,' Ken said slowly. The two of them were sitting in the garden because it was the only place, just now, where they could have any sort of private conversation. 'Her son seems a pleasant enough gentleman. I'm sure he'll give you a good reference if you ask.'

'Ye-es, so long as he doesn't consider that a reference for a nurse might come better from his wife,' Jess said, a trifle doubtfully. 'But there aren't all that many opportunities for a private nurse, you know. And I don't mean to go back into hospital nursing, if I can possibly help it. Well, I don't believe they'd take me, because I've been off the wards two years, and I never did complete the training course I started after the war.' She looked up at Ken, loving the strong planes of his face, seeing the troubled look in his eyes and knowing that he was worried for her, for their future together.

'You'll get a job, and a good one, too,' Ken said comfortingly. 'But if you don't, we'll simply have to get married and scrape by somehow. We've both saved a bit, enough to buy a bed and a couple of chairs. I'm sure when my mam and dad married, they didn't have two farthings to rub together.' He grinned down at her, his face suddenly looking boyish, mischievous. 'Well, to tell the truth, I were on the way so they didn't have much choice, like. But they got by somehow, and at least if we marry there'll only be two mouths to feed, not three.'

Jess had to smile at this. 'But if we marry, you know, we're almost bound to have a baby quite quickly. Dr Marie Stopes might have opened her birth-control clinic, but she's down in London and local doctors and nurses won't even discuss it, let alone advise one.'

'Well, I reckon we'd manage somehow,' Ken said obstinately. 'I know we said that we wouldn't rush into anything and that two years would soon pass, but it would be grand to get married right away.'

'I know it,' Jess said, giving his hand a rueful squeeze. They were sitting on a small curved seat set into the wall of the garden, but now she got reluctantly to her feet. 'I'd best go in now, Ken, my love, because there's going to be an awful lot of arranging to do. Poor Mr Bellamy was astonished when he heard the news, though of course I suppose he should have been prepared for it—she was eighty-four, after all.'

'He was already here when I arrived,' Ken remarked, as they walked round the side of the house and out into the road where Ken had left the car. 'He must have got a move on.'

'Well, not really; it was a coincidence that he had decided to come and talk to his mother about a business matter . . . he rang the bell about ten minutes after the doctor had arrived. I'm really glad he's here, though, because he's handling all the funeral arrangements and says none of the staff are to worry because our jobs are safe until the end of the month at least. He's going to employ Cook himself, and possibly Gladys as well, but of course he won't be needing a nurse.'

'And I wouldn't want you working in Southport,' Ken said at once. 'Look, my darling, I dare say things will sort themselves out over the next few days, but whatever you do, don't *worry*. I'm never far away.' Ken looked around him, then bent and kissed her gently on the mouth before turning to climb into the car.

Jess waved until he was out of sight, then returned reluctantly to the house, feeling tears gather in her eyes as she crossed the familiar hall and glanced towards the drawing room where, she knew, Mr Bellamy was closeted. She would miss the old lady so much! Indeed, she realised now that she had allowed most of her old friendships to lapse because a live-in job made socialising somewhat difficult. However, it was no use wishing now that she had not cut herself off from her nursing friends.

Resolutely, she went across to the kitchen where she found Cook making up a tray of sandwiches and scones. The other woman looked up and smiled as Jess entered the room. 'The doctor has left and Mr Bellamy asked for a light supper to be delivered to the breakfast parlour,' she said. 'I've made a big tureen of leek and potato soup and I've popped some of my bread rolls into the bake oven to warm, but I've sent young Gladys to bed.' She sniffed scornfully. 'I know the gal were fond of Mrs Bellamy—well, we all were—but that's no excuse for high-strikes, I told her.' She smiled hopefully at Jess. 'So in the circumstances, Miss Williams, I wonder if you'd carry in a tray for me, bein' as I've only got the one pair of hands.'

Jess agreed readily and presently went to the drawing room to tell Mr Bellamy that a light supper awaited him in the breakfast parlour. She saw that he was looking pale and red-eyed and guessed that he was suffering from shock as well as grief. It was all very well telling oneself that Mrs Bellamy had had a long and happy life; shock and sorrow were inevitable after any death.

'Thank you, nurse,' Mr Bellamy said. 'I hope you've had something to eat yourself? I feel we must all keep our strength up because there will be a deal of work to be done in the next few weeks. I shall have to sell this house and most of the furniture and fittings, and there are arrangements to be sorted out . . . oh, could you ask Gladys to make up the bed in the guest room? I've telephoned to my wife to let her know I shall be staying here for a while and advising her not to come rushing over until the date of the funeral is fixed.'

'The bed is kept made up, sir, but I'll put a couple of hot water bottles between the sheets just in case they're cold,' Jess said. 'Gladys has gone to bed—she's not feeling too well—but Cook and I will see to everything.'

'Thank you; I know I can rely on you, nurse,' Mr Bellamy said gratefully. As they talked, they had been crossing the hall, and now he entered the breakfast parlour, closing the door gently behind him, and Jess returned to the kitchen.

Cook had laid the table with two places, and two

bowls of her delicious leek and potato soup stood waiting whilst a steak and kidney pie steamed gently beside the stove. Jess's mouth watered as she slipped into her chair and lifted her soup spoon. 'Mrs Fielding, you're a marvel,' she said, as the older woman sat down opposite her and raised her own spoon. 'I'm afraid the next few days are going to be very trying, but I'm sure, between us, we will cope.'

* * *

Ten days later, Jess let herself out of the front door and almost ran to the bus stop on Croxteth Road. The Bellamy house was on the telephone so she had rung Mendelssohn Motors, Ken's employers, and left a message asking that Ken should meet her that evening outside his place of work. A helpful recept ionist had looked in the diary and told her that Mr Ryan would be leaving work at eight o'clock, so Jess had finished the tasks she had been set by Mr Bellamy—at present, she was cataloguing Mrs Bellamy's books—and had set off to catch a No. 15 tram which would take her practically to the door of Mendelssohn Motors.

When she reached her destination, Ken was already waiting for her, which was fortunate since Jess was in such a hurry to get off the tram that she tripped and fell, and it was only Ken's quickness in scooping her up that prevented her from a painful fall.

'Hey, hey, hey, what's the rush?' Ken said, setting her on her feet and kissing her cheek. 'Don't say something else has happened! I've managed to get the day off tomorrow so I can support you at the funeral; is that what you wanted to ask me?'

'No, no, no, it's more important . . . different . . . oh, Ken, we can get married as soon as you like,' Jess gabbled, feeling her cheeks burn with excitement. 'They had the Will reading this morning, and all the family came, and of course Cook and I were rushed off our feet because everyone stayed for lunch so we were far too busy to wonder about the Will. We were pretty sure that young Mr Bellamy would inherit everything but this afternoon he came into the kitchen and told the three of us, Cook, Gladys and myself, that we had each been left a small sum of money and a keepsake. I have got the most beautiful amethyst necklace, Gladys has a silver bangle set with very pretty crystals, and Cook has the dragonfly brooch which Mrs Bellamy wore pinned to her best coat when she went to church on Sundays. I remember she once said she meant to leave it to her daughter-in-law, because it's such a pretty thing, but then young Mrs Bellamy said only a woman with no taste would wear such a gaudy brooch and Mrs Bellamy heard and must have changed her Will.'

'Well, how good of her to remember the servants! I always said she was a right 'un,' Ken said warmly. 'But . . . are you thinking of selling the necklace, queen? Only I'd rather you kept it, because I'm sure that's what Mrs Bellamy intended.'

'Of course I'd never sell it, not if I was starving,' Jess said vehemently. 'But I won't need to; oh, Ken, she's left me *two hundred pounds*! Cook's got a hundred, and so has Gladys, and it was so kind of

55

her to include Cook because she's only been with us a short time.' She looked up at Ken with shining eyes. 'What do you think of *that*, Ken Ryan?'

*   *   *

Despite their hopes, it was after Christmas before Jess and Ken actually got married. For one thing, Mr Bellamy had asked Jess to stay on so that she could supervise the cataloguing of all the contents of the house in order that they might be auctioned. Everything was to go: carpets, curtains, furniture, even Mrs Bellamy's much loved collection of Dresden figurines and the Sèvres tea set which had graced the china cabinet in the drawing room. Young Mrs Bellamy had come to the house one day and informed Jess, coldly, that her husband had told her to stick a label on anything she wished to have for herself. Jess had accompanied her round so that she would know which objects should not be included in the catalogue, but it had hardly proved necessary. Young Mrs Bellamy had seemed to despise all her mother-in-law's possessions and apart from the grandfather clock in the hall, and an oil painting of a rural scene, had told Jess that everything might be sold.

'Would—would it be all right, Mrs Bellamy, if I bought some of the kitchen equipment?' Jess had asked timidly. 'I would bid for it at the auction but I'm afraid I shall probably be in another job by then and unable to get time off. I'd pay whatever you considered fair,' she had added hastily, as Mrs Bellamy's cold and fishy eyes stared down at her.

The other woman had hesitated and then said

56

grudgingly, 'Well, I suppose it would be all right. I don't suppose the kitchen equipment would fetch much, but you'd best ask my husband what you should pay.'

Jess had thanked her but thought crossly that she had probably been silly to mention it. After all, Mrs Bellamy had not wanted any of the stuff, and her interest had been so cursory that the staff could have walked off with half the contents of the house had they been dishonest. As it was, she and Cook put to one side things that they particularly wanted, though they took care not to choose anything of value. Pots and pans, sieves, wooden spoons, ladles and good sharp knives were, she felt, acceptable, but the beautiful solid silver cutlery, lying on its bed of velvet and polished weekly by Gladys, would fetch a decent price and so could not be included. Jess was amused to see, amongst Mrs Fielding's treasures, the kitchen knife with a bone handle and only half a blade which the three of them always tried to grab when preparing vegetables.

And in the end, as Jess had suspected he would, Mr Bellamy simply told them to put the stuff in their own rooms and refused to charge them anything. 'He's a nice feller, nearly as nice as his ma,' Cook said appreciatively. 'Wish I'd took more now, but there you are. I dare say I shouldn't be greedy.'

When Jess had explained to Ken that the house and its contents were to be sold and that Mr Bellamy had asked her if she would take charge of the place until the sale was completed, he was very understanding, even though he had hoped for an earlier wedding.

'I know you've got that two hundred pounds, which is an awful lot of money, but I guess Mr Bellamy will pay you pretty well for being in charge,' he had said. 'And it would be grand if we could put your inheritance away as a sort of nest egg, like. Anyway, you were that fond of old Mrs B. that I guess you'll want to do right by the son, even if his wife is a nasty piece of work. So you stick to your post, love, and we'll marry when all the business is settled.'

Jess had agreed that this was fair, and, indeed, she had quite enjoyed this new twist to her work. Like most nurses, she was neat and methodical, and got a good deal of satisfaction from making order out of chaos. Within a month of Mrs Bellamy's death, Cook had moved up to Southport, but Gladys had agreed to stay on and the two of them rather enjoyed managing for themselves. Jess had little experience as a cook, but Gladys had watched Mrs Fielding closely as she worked, often assisting in simple tasks such as mixing pastry, preparing meat and vegetables and making gravy or custard. Now Gladys taught Jess all she knew, and when necessary Jess took down one of the well-thumbed and food-bespattered cookery books and consulted its pages. Very soon, she and Gladys were not only eating well themselves, but could serve up a tasty dinner for Mr Bellamy when he spent the day in the house.

'It's all good training for when we do get married, because, before, my cooking skills were distinctly limited,' Jess had told Ken. 'But now I can make you a delicious meal without spending an awful lot of money, or a positive feast if it's some sort of celebration. And there's other things. When

58

I was in nursing, our uniforms were laundered, so I never knew how to starch a collar, or sides to middle sheets, though I was a dab hand at darning because some of my black stockings were more darn than anything else. But now Gladys and I have had to learn to do all sorts. Oh aye, whoever gets me for a wife is a lucky feller!'

They had been strolling in Prince's Park enjoying the late October sunshine, and now Ken, grinning, bent and gave her a quick kiss. 'I'd be a lucky feller even if you couldn't boil water,' he had assured her. 'I'm marrying Jess Williams, not a cook, or a cleaner, or a laundry worker, and don't you forget it.' He sighed. 'What chance of a wedding before Christmas, do you suppose?'

'Oh, I should think we'll be finished before then,' Jess had said hopefully. 'Tell you what, Ken, it might be best if we decide on a firm date some way ahead, and tell Mr Bellamy. I don't think it's occurred to him that I have plans of my own, but if he knows I shan't be available—well, say after Christmas—then I'm sure he'll get things moving. The last thing he wants is to have to organise things himself.'

This was true, for she and Gladys had noted, some while since, that Mr Bellamy was no organiser, and when, later that same day, she had told him she and Ken had decided on a Christmas wedding, she saw by his suddenly widening eyes that he did not relish the prospect of losing her. He had told her, hastily, that the auctioneers had been pestering him for a definite date, and asked when she thought this date should be.

'Well, we don't want to marry on Christmas Day . . . indeed, I don't think it's allowable . . . but Ken did suggest the twenty-seventh, the Tuesday after Christmas,' Jess had said hopefully. 'If everything could be completed by, say, the seventeenth, including the sale of the house itself, then it would give me time to get my wedding, and my future, sorted out.'

Mr Bellamy had agreed that this seemed reasonable and the very next day had telephoned her, from his office in Southport, to say that the sale of all goods and effects would take place on 15 December, which would leave the house empty. 'Apparently, it's easier to sell an empty house than one half full of old-fashioned furniture and carpets,' he had said. 'So if that date would suit you, Miss Williams . . .' Jess had assured him that it would be fine and she and Gladys began to plan their futures.

Gladys had been lucky and had got a good job as cook/housekeeper to a small family of four living quite near the park. Mr Bellamy had given her an excellent reference, extolling her abilities as a cook and assuring her prospective employer that she was very honest and a hard worker. Jess, on the other hand, did not attempt to get another job since she and Ken had decided to see how they went on as a married couple. Ken's wages should be adequate for most of their expenses—they had considered buying a property but in the end had decided against it. 'If we decide to buy later, then it's an easy matter to give a landlord a week's notice and move out,' Ken had said. 'But we neither of us know a darned thing about property. We could easily splash out our gelt on a house and then discover the roof leaked like a sieve, or the drains smelt bad or the beams had worm, and then where would we be? No; I reckon we'll leave owning property till we've had more experience.'

Jess had agreed, and after having viewed a number of rented properties they took a small terraced house in a side turning off Heyworth Street. It had a parlour and a kitchen and scullery on the ground floor. There was a large brass cold-water tap over the kitchen sink and another smaller one in the scullery. Upstairs, there were two decent-sized bedrooms, and up a further flight two tiny attic rooms. There was a back yard with a wood shed and a lavatory, and this last particularly pleased Jess since, when she had lived at home in a court off Vauxhall Road, there had been a communal lavatory which was shared by all ten houses, and a communal water tap from which the householders filled numerous buckets, morning and night. She had said nothing of this to Ken, knowing that his parents had been far more affluent than her own, but had simply agreed with him that the house would do very well for a start.

She had told Gladys, who was to be her bridesmaid, that it would be a quiet wedding. 'Ken's parents are dead and me mam's as poor as a church mouse, so the cost is going to fall on us and we'll have enough expense without adding a huge wedding,' she had explained. 'My very best friend, the person closer to me than a sister, lives in Australia and couldn't possibly come home. But I've other friends, of course, girls I nursed with. I may invite some of them.'

And despite Jess's fears that something would occur to ruin their plans, everything had gone forward smoothly. The sale of the household goods and personal effects had taken place on the date selected, and Gladys had moved into her new post, whilst Jess, laden with bulging bags, had taken up residence in a small lodging house. The weather had been cold and crisp and Jess was fully occupied with Christmas coming on. She had written a long letter to Nancy and had spent the rest of the time either helping her landlady with the preparations for Christmas, or cleaning their future home from top to bottom. Over Christmas itself, she and Ken had whitewashed all the walls and ceilings and moved what little furniture they owned into place. Ken had ordered coal and logs but said they were not to be delivered until 28 December, for though the neighbours seemed pleasant enough there was a jigger behind the back yard and it would have been easy for anyone who knew the house was vacant to nip over the wall into the yard of No. 4, break open the rickety door of the shed, and help themselves.

On the evening of the twenty-sixth, tired from the pleasant Christmas they had enjoyed, but excited by the prospect of the wedding next day, Ken and Jess had taken themselves off for a walk through the frosty streets. 'It'll be a grand day, because we've planned it all so carefully,' Ken had said contentedly, squeezing her hand. 'I know Christmas isn't a good time for flowers but chrysanthemums is real pretty—colourful, like. And Mrs Clarke has done wonders with the money we gave her to get food for the reception. Oh, aye, it'll all go like clockwork, you'll see.'

'And after the reception, we're having a real honeymoon,' Jess had breathed ecstatically. Ken had booked two whole days in Blackpool, a place she had only ever visited once, and she had never before stayed in a real hotel—a hotel, furthermore, which would provide them with three meals a day. 'Oh, Ken, it's going to be wonderful, I know it is.'

As they had turned and walked back towards her lodgings Jess had thought that, if she were honest, the thought of being married was even more exciting than staying in a hotel. But she could scarcely say so; nice girls never mentioned such things. One was supposed to be nervous, anxious even, not all lit up and longing for the feel of Ken's arms round her and his body close to hers.

She had looked up at Ken as they reached the front door, and he had taken her in his arms. Was he worried, or anxious? Would the responsibility of having a wife trouble him? But then their eyes had locked and she saw the smile and the little flame of desire in his, before their lips met. And she had known, suddenly, that it would be all right, that they were meant for each other. Slowly, they had drawn apart and Ken had turned, reluctantly, back towards the tram stop. Jess had waved him out of sight, and slipped into the house.

*   *   *

It was February and when Nancy woke that morning, it had been to the steady clattering of rain on the iron roof. She lay still for a moment, remembering that Andy lay beside her, that it was Sunday, and that breakfast could be late, for once. There were definite advantages to the wet, though there were disadvantages, too. Lying there, with the sound of the rain deafeningly loud, she considered the day ahead. She ought to seize the opportunity of a quiet day to write to her parents

. . . and Jess, too. Her friend had been married to Ken now for . . . goodness, fourteen months . . . and she had only written twice. She really should have a letter-writing session this very afternoon, tell Jess and the Kerris family all her news.

Moving cautiously, so as not to wake Andy, she rolled on to her back and looked up at the mosquito netting which shrouded the bed and saw, with revulsion, a positively enormous beetle, a scorpion and a number of other ugly and hateful insects suspended in the gauzy material almost directly above her head. Thank God for the netting, she told herself. She had been stung by a scorpion in the previous wet season and Andy had cut the small wound and sucked out the poison, but even so the sting had been horribly painful.

Beside her, Andy stirred, then woke. Nancy pointed to the scorpion and Andy groaned and sat up. 'I'll deal with it,' he said, knowing that she hated the things so much that even killing them worried her. Not that it stopped her dealing with the creatures when Andy was away, mustering cattle; she and Violet had once killed thirty or forty intruders, including several small snakes, during a bad thunderstorm. But Andy, of course, was used to such things. He had been born and bred in Queensland and took it for granted that, during the wet, they would be invaded by every sort of animal and insect that desired to get out of the rain and under a roof. Snakes and scorpions hid themselves in any convenient corner, and great care had to be exercised, since the dark clouds decreased visibility. Nancy had learned to be very cautious when crossing a room or going out to the kitchen to make a meal.

Andy disentangled himself from the mosquito netting and got out of bed. He picked up the book he had been reading the previous evening, flipped the scorpion on to the floor and disposed of it, then carefully surveyed the room before yawning, stretching and reaching for his clothes, which he shook vigorously before beginning to dress. 'Might as well get up, I suppose,' he remarked, tipping his boots upside down and examining them carefully before putting them on. 'C'mon, old girl, and I'll help you cook the breakfast.' As he spoke, he was shaking her clothing and upending her shoes, a task he performed every morning when he was not away mustering cattle.

'Right you are,' Nancy said, climbing reluctantly out from beneath the thin sheet which was all the covering they ever needed, for even in the wet the sullen heat did not lift and the humidity was worse. Besides, she was pregnant again, and every movement was an effort.

'What are you doing today?' she asked, as the two of them left the bedroom. 'I'm going to bake, but once the first batch is in the oven I mean to write some letters. I feel awfully guilty because I've barely been in touch with Jess since her wedding and that was more than a year ago. Somehow I'm always too busy.' She looked down at the mound of her stomach, patting it thoughtfully. 'I wonder if she's expecting yet? It would be lovely if Jess and I had a baby at about the same time.'

'Well, you aren't likely to hear about it even if she is,' Andy observed. 'I reckon we're in for another month of rain and the river will soon be so high and the floods so deep that Bullwhip won't be able to get through. Which means no mail in either

65

direction, of course,' he ended.

Nancy sighed. She hated being cut off from the rest of the world, as they always were in the wet, yet she loved waking up each morning to find Andy beside her. When the finer weather came, he would be away for weeks at a time, mustering the cattle for sale, because when the floods subsided grass, sweet and good, grew up almost overnight and the fattened cattle fetched their best price. During the wet, however, both Andy and Clive slept each night in the homestead and worked at repairing the yards and buildings. Occasionally, they went further afield, but this was the exception rather than the rule, and they nearly always got home at night since sleeping out in the wet was impossible.

'So you're baking, eh?' Andy said, opening the door and stepping out on to the duckboard walk which he had constructed between the house and the kitchen. 'Well, I'm going on an egg hunt, and you aren't to worry. I'm always careful, particularly in the wet. I'll take Clive with me and half a dozen of the blacks. I'll probably be out all day, because finding the nests isn't always easy, but I'll be home for dinner.' He cocked a hopeful eye at her. 'Are there any spuds left? There's tinned peas, I know, in the store, and if you're baking . . . well, how about a steak and kidney pudding, with mashed potatoes and peas? Or a pie, for that matter?'

'I'll make one or the other, I promise,' Nancy said, trying to keep her voice steady. Of all the frightening things on the Walleroo, the creatures which scared her most were the great crocodiles. They could grow up to twenty feet in length and they were remorseless and cunning killers. She had seen a strong young stockman taken by a crocodile last year, when the river had been in flood, and she knew she would never forget it. The man had been fishing, standing on a rock only a foot or two from the shore, and she had been staring at him as he wound in his line. There had been a splash, the beginnings of a scream, a turbulence in the swirling water, and then . . . nothing. Other men fishing had fled for the bank and it had been one of them who had answered her frantic queries. 'It were crocodile, missus,' he had said, grabbing her arm urgently. 'Come away from river, missus, in case there are others . . .'

So now Nancy knew what Andy meant when he said he was going egg hunting. The big crocodiles came ashore in the wet and dug themselves 'nests' in the mud which fringed the lagoons formed by the flood water. They laid their eggs there, and although the floods would have begun to recede by the time the eggs hatched and the baby crocodiles emerged, there would still be plenty of water for the young crocodiles to make their way back to the river. Andy and the other men would visit the places where they knew the crocodiles lay up to smash the eggs and kill any young already around. If they had not, life on the Walleroo would have been more dangerous than it already was, but even so, Nancy hated it when the men went egg hunting. Andy had assured her many times that crocodiles had no motherly instincts; they simply laid their eggs and then went back to the river, never to return, but she always had the nasty, niggling feeling that one day a furious mother crocodile would come back to examine her brood and discover Andy, Clive and the others in their

67

destructive work. But it would never do to say so; instead, she asked him if bacon and beans would do for breakfast since the hens laid almost no eggs in the wet. Andy said that bacon and beans would be fine and he hitched himself on to one of the work counters and began wielding the opener on a can of beans whilst Nancy cut half a dozen thick rashers off the joint.

She was just beginning to fry them in the big iron pan when she felt the first warning stab of pain in the small of her back. She said nothing, but she must have stiffened because Andy said at once: 'What's the matter, hon? Did you splash yourself with hot fat? If so, I'll watch the pan while you dip the burn in a bucket of water.'

I must have jumped as well, Nancy thought remorsefully, turning to assure Andy that she was just fine. There was no point in alerting him yet. He needed to destroy the crocodile eggs and the pain might be a false alarm. She began to lay the cooked rashers on a dinner plate, then tipped the can of beans into another pan and put that over the heat. 'I wonder if Pete's awake yet?' she asked idly, gently stirring the beans so that they did not stick to the bottom of the pan. 'If so, I'll put some porridge on.'

'I reckon he'll be up and doing,' Andy said, as Nancy tipped the beans on to his plate. 'You start the porridge off and I'll take this across to the living room and check on Pete and Aggie for you.'

Aggie was a healthy young Aboriginal woman who was a great comfort to Nancy. She had a small daughter of her own named Nellie, but her husband had gone off on walkabout when Nellie, now eight, had been a year old, and had never

68

returned. Aggie was strong and attractive, but she had never wanted another man in her life and was happy to look after little Pete and to help Nancy in the house. She and Nellie shared Pete's room, as would the new baby when it arrived, and Nancy trusted the younger woman completely, knowing Aggie would die in defence of the two children, should danger threaten them.

'Missus! The boss says to tell you Aggie and Pete is up an' doing.'

Nancy swung round and smiled at the big woman almost blocking the doorway. Violet was about fifty years old—none of the Aborigines knew their exact ages—and was another trusted member of the Sullivans' extended family. Until Nancy's arrival, the only sort of cooking she knew was camp cooking over an open fire, but because she enjoyed the fruits of Nancy's labour—the bread, cakes, pies, stews and roasts produced on the kitchen range—she had professed herself willing to learn how to do these things. Nancy was overjoyed to have an assistant and now Violet could be trusted to do a good deal of the baking, though Nancy still preferred to make the great loaves of bread herself since Violet was impatient and hated waiting for the dough to prove.

'Thanks, Violet; then if you'll make the porridge and put more bacon in the pan, I'll take my own breakfast across and eat it with the boss,' Nancy said. 'I'll send Aggie over to fetch the porridge in about ten minutes, all right?'

Violet said that that would be just fine and Nancy escaped from the heat of the kitchen, paddled across the yard and entered the living room just as Andy was about to leave it. He took

69

her by the shoulders and dropped a quick kiss on the tip of her nose before telling her not to worry about anything but to send for him if she needed to do so. 'You know where I'll be; down by the lagoons,' he reminded her. 'Now hear me. Take care of yourself; February is the worst time we could have picked for a baby to come but I guess you can't plan nature. I don't know that I'm much of a hand as a midwife, but Violet told me the other day she'd helped many of the gins to deliver.' He shot her a shrewd glance. 'Any more pains?'

Nancy wagged her finger at him reprovingly but could not help laughing. So he had guessed! 'You're quite right. I did get a stab back in the kitchen, but I haven't had one since,' she assured him. 'And if I do go into labour, you may be sure I'll send for you at once. Now off with you and make the river a safer place for our little Sullivans.'

As she had said she would, Nancy worked in the kitchen all morning, and in the afternoon settled down to write to Jess and to her parents and sisters. She had not yet replied to Jess's last letter. The trouble was, Jess was a poor correspondent, and even with the excitement of her wedding and her new little house to write about, the letter had only consisted of about half a page. Nancy, with many more correspondents to satisfy, always wrote at length. She described a little of her life on the station but not the hardships because, to be honest, she did not want to worry her family, or to let people think that Australia was a dreadful, dangerous place. She wrote of the beauties of the river in the dry, when the families picnicked on the banks and the children swam in the shallows. She told of corroborees when the workers had

70

something to celebrate and of her occasional, exciting trips to the nearest town. She was still keen to persuade Anne to come and visit her too, so she had no desire to frighten her sister off. Anne might come, if only for a holiday, and Nancy honestly believed that if she did so, her sister would fall for Clive's many charms and would, as Nancy had, grow accustomed to life in the outback.

Of necessity, her letters to her sisters and to Jess were somewhat similar, as she wrote of the impending birth of her second child. Without meaning to deceive, she spoke of Violet as though she were a professional midwife, and of Aggie as though she were the sort of nursemaid that the Kerris family had employed when the girls were small.

She had finished a long letter to her parents, another to her elder sister, and was halfway through the letter to Anne, when she felt another skewer of pain in the small of her back. This time it was so sharp that she could not prevent herself from gasping, and she decided that before continuing with her letter she would get Aggie or Violet to make her a nice cup of tea. After all, it might be only indigestion, and a hot drink could soon cure that. Nancy gave a shout and Aggie's head popped round the door. She had Pete on her hip and he grinned at his mother with a great display of little pearly teeth. He was almost two and a half now and beginning to talk quite nicely. But Nancy guessed from the flush on his cheeks and the way his yellow fluffy hair stood on end that he had just awoken from sleep, for he usually had a nap after his lunch. 'Hello, Mammy,' the child said cheerfully. 'I want Aggie to take me to the river

71

so's I can find my daddy, but she says not now. Tell her she must take me now, Mammy!'

'Certainly not; you aren't the boss man yet,' Nancy said teasingly, for when Andy was away from the homestead Pete always said that he was the boss man now. 'I called Aggie through to ask her to make me a cup of tea, so you can stay with me while I finish my letter. Tell you what, Pete, you can draw a picture for your Auntie Anne while I write.'

Pete accepted a stub of pencil and a sheet of paper with joy and began to scribble, but Nancy found she was restless and could not settle to the long and chatty letter she had planned. Instead, she put Anne's letter to one side, took another sheet and decided, rather crossly, that she would serve Jess with her own medicine. She would write a short, uninformative letter, merely telling her friend that she was expecting a baby and that, because of the heavy rain, she would probably be unable to post anything after this for several weeks.

She finished the letter feeling slightly ashamed of its abruptness, folded the sheet and pushed it into an envelope. Then she stood up, suddenly realising that whilst she had been writing the rain had ceased and a watery sun had appeared. Pete, sitting on the floor, looked hopefully up at her. 'I done with this bit of paper,' he said, and Nancy saw that he had indeed scribbled over every inch of it. 'Can you take me to the river, Mammy? Aggie says Daddy's smashing croc eggs, and I want to *see*!'

Nancy was about to tell her small son that she did not mean to traipse down to the river bank when she hesitated, and even as she did so another pain shot through her back, this time accompanied by a cramping sensation in her lower stomach. Abruptly, she made up her mind. She would walk down to the river and take Pete with her. They would stroll quietly along the bank, in the pale sunshine, until they found Andy, and if she had any more pains she would tell him, because someone had to look after Pete while Violet and Aggie helped to deliver the baby. So she stood up and held out a hand, which her small son eagerly grasped. 'I don't mean to carry you because I'm not too well at present,' she explained as they left the house. 'But you're a big boy now; you can walk as far as the river and then along the bank. Only, if your legs get tired, you mustn't expect Mammy to pick you up; understood?'

Pete said, contentedly, that he did indeed understand, and the two of them set out for the river. As they went, Nancy considered her situation. In the outback, a man had to face up to doing things which were normally women's work, and she knew Andy would not hesitate to help with the delivery of her baby if she needed him. However, she still felt it would be more appropriate for Violet and Aggie to bring the baby into the world, as they had done when Pete was born, leaving Andy to look after their son. It was a pity that they could not have hired a proper nurse for a few weeks, but it did not particularly bother her. Already she was proud of being an outback wife who could cope with anything. And she had great faith in Andy and was fond of him, though she had never known with him the heady excitement which the mere touch of Graham's hand on her arm had aroused.

As she walked along the river bank the pains came again, a little closer this time, and she began to hurry. Ahead of her, something bobbed in the water, and she pulled Pete closer to her and further from the shore. Was it a crocodile? She peered at the object, then gave a hoarse scream, dropped Pete's hand, and began to run. At first, she had thought it was just a tree trunk, but now that she was closer she could see that something was trapped in it; a head . . . a man's head? She could see light-coloured hair, a closed and flaccid eye . . . Andy! It must be Andy! . . .

It was Andy! And suddenly Nancy knew that she did love her husband, loved him much more than she had ever loved Graham, though in a very different way. Graham had been her first love, but now she knew that what she felt for Andy was real love: the sort that never falters, never dies.

Andy was her reason for living, and if he were dead, she wanted to die too. Desperately, she pushed little Pete away from her, telling him to go home, to get help, because his daddy had fallen into the river.

Then, heedless of crocodiles, water snakes, currents, she plunged into the swirling waters and grabbed for the roots of the tree which had trapped her husband, knowing that she must get to him before the trunk got into midstream and out of her reach. But even as she stretched out her hands, another pain clutched her and she missed her step and tumbled forward into the turgid water. For one moment, she fought to regain her footing, then darkness overcame her.

*   *   *

74

Nancy came round to find herself staring, muzzily, at a patch of muddy grass under her nose. There was pressure on her shoulders, then a voice she knew and loved said briskly: 'She'll be good now. I squeezed the water out of her quite easy . . . I saw her fall so she weren't in the flood long. Don't cry, Pete, your mammy's gonna be just fine.' Nancy felt herself being rolled on to her back and, opening her wet eyelids, saw Andy's strong familiar face above her, smiling reassuringly down. When he saw her eyes open, he bent and kissed her quickly and softly on her forehead, then addressed someone standing behind him. 'Lucky we were making our way home when Pete started to scream, otherwise . . . but it don't do to think about what might have happened. Can you sit up, darling? Only you'd be best in the house where we can get the mud off and find some clean clothing.'

With his help, Nancy struggled to her feet. Immediately, two of the stockmen came across, offering help, but Andy shook his head. 'Thanks, fellers, but I reckon I can carry her. You bring Pete along; he's a hero, my son is. Saved his mammy's life, I reckon. He's a bonza boy.'

As he spoke, he scooped Nancy up in his arms and she leaned her head thankfully against his shoulder, puzzlement and joy blending as she remembered her reason for charging into the river. 'Andy, I thought . . . I was sure . . . this great tree came down on the flood and there was a man's head . . .' She shuddered, burying her face in his shoulder for a moment, then emerging to say shakily: ?'. . . I honestly thought it was you. Oh, Andy, I never told you before—I don't think I even knew myself—but I love you more than anyone else in the whole world, and if it had been you . . .'

He was striding towards the house, carrying her as though she weighed no more than little Pete, but at her words he paused for a moment to let the others get ahead. Then he spoke quietly. 'You've been telling me you love me by your actions these past two years and more, and as for thinking it were me trapped in the branches of that tree— well, I'm insulted! It were a bloody sheep off McGuire's place, I suspect. Still an' all, I reckon I fished you out before there was much harm done.'

'A sheep?' Nancy began to giggle weakly. 'It was the hair . . . the fur . . . the wool, I mean. It was a blond sheep. No, I don't mean that . . . you're a blond man . . . Ouch!'

By this time they had reached the house and Andy laid her on the sofa in the living room, looking down at her with concern. 'Did I hurt you? Pete, run and get Violet and tell her to make your mammy a nice hot cup of tea with plenty of sugar in it. Tell her Mammy fell into the water . . .' He looked down at his wife's face and what he saw there seemed to make up his mind, for without questioning Nancy further he added: 'Tell her I reckon the new baby's on its way. Oh, and get Aggie to come as well.'

Little Pete nodded importantly. 'Tell Violet tea and new baby, tell Aggie to come bloody fast,' he said. 'I'll tell 'em.'

When the child had gone, Nancy tried to swing her legs off the sofa, but Andy immediately pushed them back. 'No you don't,' he said firmly. 'For once in your life, you're going to do as you're told, Nancy Sullivan. You've had one helluva shock,

76

what with thinkin' you'd married a sheep an' damn near drownin' in the river. When you've had a cup of tea, I'm going to clean you up and get you into your nightdress and pop you into bed.'

Nancy immediately began to protest, to say that she was fine, that she would get on with her chores as soon as she'd had that cup of tea, but even as she spoke another pain arrowed through her back and this time she was in no doubt. The baby was coming and there was nothing she could do about it, so she might as well give in gracefully. 'All right, Andy, darling,' she said submissively. 'Only I don't think we'd better wait for the tea; the pains are coming every two or three minutes now.'

Andy nodded as though satisfied and within ten minutes Nancy was in bed, clean, and dressed in her best nightgown, her damp hair tied back from her face with a blue ribbon. Andy sat on the bed holding her hands and timing the pains on the big gunmetal watch he kept in the top pocket of his shirt. When the urge to push overcame her, he stayed beside her, giving her every encouragement as she struggled to birth the baby, whilst Violet and Aggie scurried about fetching hot water, bringing the cradle through, and glancing with admiration at their master as he wiped his wife's face with a flannel dipped in cold water and soothed her between pains with promises that her task was nearly done.

*   *   *

Pete was outside in the yard playing mud pies with three of the stockmen's children when he heard his father give a shout. Immediately, he sat up and

77

stared towards the house, while his companions, well used to birth, continued to mould the mud into strange shapes. Pete hesitated, then got to his feet, wiping his filthy hands on the seat of his small cotton breeches. Then he went towards the house at a gallop, running full tilt into his father as Andy emerged from the bedroom.

'Daddy, Daddy!' Pete squeaked. 'Is the new baby here? Can I see it? I watched for a stork 'cos Mammy said them big white birds bring babies, but I never see'd 'im.'

His father sighed. 'Where did Smiler's little brother come from?' he asked gently. 'Did the stork bring him?'

'Nah,' Pete said scornfully. 'He come out of his mammy's belly. All the fellers' babies do.'

'And why should your mammy be any different?' his father asked, taking Pete's small hand in his large one and leading him towards the bedroom. 'The stork is just a fairy tale for English kids.'

'Oh,' Pete said, digesting this. 'But Father Christmas is real, isn't he?'

His father did not answer directly but threw open the bedroom door. 'Pete's come to say hello to his new brother,' he said loudly. 'Storks, indeed! This young feller-me-lad has watched cows calving, horses foaling, pigs farrowing, chicks hatching . . .'

Pete looked doubtfully at his mother, then saw with relief that she was smiling, saw also that she held a white-wrapped, pink-faced, blond-haired baby in the crook of her arm. 'Hello, Pete,' she said gently.

Pete stole forward. A brother! He had always wanted a brother, had hoped that the new baby would be a boy and not a silly girl. He put out a tentative, and very grubby, finger and touched the baby's cheek. 'Hello, baby,' he said softly. 'I'm your brother, big Pete. And you're my little frog.'

'Frog?' his mother queried. 'Why frog? Oh, I know!' She turned to smile at her husband over the top of Pete's head. 'Don't you remember? I was reading *The Jungle Book* to him a couple of nights ago, and that's what Mother Wolf calls Mowgli— her little frog.' She turned back towards her small son. 'Only Daddy and I thought we'd call him Jamie; that's short for James, you know.'

Pete compressed his lips. 'Jamie,' he said firmly. 'I like Jamie. It's a nice name.'

'Well, it's better than Mowgli,' his father said.

CHAPTER THREE

JUNE 1931

'But Mammy, it's my birthday. You said when I was five I could do all sorts of things, and Ella's mammy wants to take us to the beach at New Brighton and then on the fun fair. We'll have our dinners at a beautiful restaurant on the promenade and maybe have ice creams as well. Do, do say I can go.'

Jess, standing at the sink scraping potatoes, sighed, popped the last one into a pan of cold water and turned to dry her hands on the roller towel behind the kitchen door. Then she looked fondly at her only child. Deborah Anne Ryan was a pretty thing with Jess's chestnut hair and wide blue eyes, and she had been born when Jess and Ken had quite given up hope of ever having a child. There was Nancy, having what seemed like a baby every year to her envious friend, yet she, Jess, had been married over four years when Debbie (as they called her) came along. The pregnancy had been a wonderful surprise, though it had meant she had had to give up a rather good job as an appointments clerk at the Stanley Hospital. But neither she nor Ken had grudged the loss of income, for they adored little Debbie and Jess really enjoyed being a full-time housewife and mother. Besides, after a couple of years she had augmented their income by working for their doctor two or three days a week.

'Mammy? Can I go? Oh please, please, please, please, please!'

Jess smiled at her small daughter, though inwardly she was cursing the fact that Debbie and her friend Ella had been born on the very same day, which meant that the treat which Mrs Markham had planned for the two little girls was a birthday present, and if she refused the invitation she would be spoiling Ella's day as well as Debbie's. Yet a birthday was special; this year it fell on a Saturday and she and Ken had planned to take a picnic and go over to Eastham near Birkenhead. Jess had pictured them sitting on the grass beside a tumbling brook, whilst Debbie paddled, fished for tiddlers, and generally enjoyed herself. She supposed now, rather doubtfully, that they could take Debbie to New Brighton themselves, but the fun fair cost money and the woods were free, and besides, it would look horribly ungracious if she were to refuse Mrs Markham's invitation and then come face to face with her on the beach.

'Darling, I'll have to think about it,' she said now. 'Daddy and I had planned a birthday treat for you. When he comes home I'll see what he says.'

'Oh, but Mammy, Mrs Markham wants to know now. If you won't let me go, I expect they'll ask that horrible Betty-Ann; she's the one with blonde curls and a silly laugh. Ella doesn't really like her, not the way she likes me, but if her mammy says she must ask Betty-Ann of course she will. Oh, Mammy, do let me go.'

Jess was just thinking, ruefully, that she was putty in her child's hands when the back door opened and Ken came into the kitchen, whistling cheerfully. He was still wearing his chauffeur's uniform and threw his cap on to the kitchen table as Debbie dived for his legs. 'Watch out, queen, you nearly had me over then,' he said gaily, picking Debbie up and swinging her into his arms. 'I'm not really home, love,' he added, addressing his wife. 'But I've got a job in this neighbourhood—I'm driving an old feller out to his daughter's place on the Wirral—so I've just popped in to tell you I'm liable to be late for tea tonight.'

Jess hurried over and gave him a peck on the cheek, then kissed Debbie for good measure. 'Thanks, Ken, you are so thoughtful,' she said gratefully. 'I was going to prepare lamb chops, new potatoes and some peas, but now I know you'll be late I'll do a casserole instead. Look, have you got a moment, only there's a bit of a problem. Mrs Markham has asked Debbie to go to New Brighton with them tomorrow, but as you know we've made—well, different plans.'

Ken looked surprised. 'What's the problem?' he

81

asked breezily. 'If the Markhams are going to the beach tomorrow, then why shouldn't we take the birthday girl out on Sunday? Come to that, it would be a nice gesture to ask young Ella to come along with us as well.'

He grinned and set Debbie down carefully as she gave a whoop of joy. She began to dance around the kitchen, chanting: 'Two treats for Ella and me, two treats for Ella and me.'

Jess sighed. The Markhams were a great deal better off than the Ryans, for—though Jess would never have admitted it to the other woman—it stretched the Ryans' budget to its fullest extent to pay the fees of the small private school the two little girls attended. Ella and Debbie were good friends but Jess secretly resented the fact that her daughter was always keen to play at the other girl's house instead of at her own, and would come home with tales of wonderful toys, a whole library of children's books and a garden complete with swing, slide and a sandpit.

Jess had hoped that Debbie would make friends with children whose circumstances resembled her own, but the truth was that no one else in Debbie's class had parents who struggled to make ends meet. Anyway, children, like adults, choose their friends for themselves and she knew Debbie would resent any attempt to make her play with the less fortunate children who attended the local council schools. Because they lived near Prince's Park Debbie met such children there but never so much as glanced at them, even when they were playing a game in which she might have wanted to join. Instead, she would search for a child from her own school and then beg her mother for pennies to take a boat out on the lake, or for money to buy stale buns from the café so that she might feed the ducks.

Ken must have noticed his wife's hesitation for he swung the back door open and shooed Debbie into the garden, telling her to play on her own little swing whilst he and Mammy had a talk. Then he turned to Jess, raising his eyebrows at her. 'Not a good idea?' he asked. 'I know we were thinking of going as a family to the woods, but Deb would have much more fun if her pal's there, you know. And we've got each other. I know you aren't too fond of Mrs Markham and you think Ella's a spoilt little madam, but from what you've told me Mr Markham isn't much of a companion for either his wife or his daughter, being so wrapped up in his business. I'd take a bet that he won't go to the beach with them, for a start. So be generous, queen, and let young Ella share our family fun.'

'Yes, of course I will,' Jess said, feeling her cheeks go hot. 'You've put me to shame, Ken. You're always so generous.' She reached up and put both arms round his neck. 'I'm the luckiest woman in the world to have such a wonderful husband,' she said, just before their lips met. 'Debbie shall go to New Brighton and I'll send her with some money for ice creams—though I can't imagine Mrs Markham licking a cornet.'

'Well, if you're the luckiest woman I'm the luckiest feller,' Ken said, walking across the kitchen and picking up his cap to set it at a jaunty angle on his smooth dark hair. 'See you later, love!'

*   *   *

83

Jess hummed to herself as she laid the kitchen table for supper, reflecting as she did so that Ken was indeed late, for it was almost half past eight and Debbie had been in bed for an hour and a half already. The child adored her father and always tried to stay awake so that he could read her a story when he came home, but she had had a full day at school and was excited at the prospect of visiting New Brighton on the morrow and had fallen asleep within moments of her head's touching the pillow.

Jess took the cooked potatoes off the stove and carried them over to the sink to drain off the water. She would put them in the bottom of the oven to stay hot. Surely Ken would be in soon? The June evenings were long and light but his boss liked the men to be off duty by nine o'clock at the latest, preferably earlier, for though he did not pay extra for overtime work he always put a little something into the wage packet for what he would have called 'out-of-hours driving'. If he stays out much longer we'll be able to afford a trip to the cinema, Jess thought, if I can get Mrs Rudd next door to give an eye to Debbie.

Glancing round the kitchen and seeing that everything was ready for Ken's return, Jess got out her writing case and the last letter from Nancy. They were both busy mothers now, Jess thought contentedly, spreading out her friend's last epistle. The lapse in their friendship, which Jess knew had been partly because she had been so jealous of Nancy, was a thing of the past. Now the two women had a comfortable relationship, writing probably no more than three times a year, but making sure that each letter was full of news and snippets of information about husbands and families. Nancy's eldest boy would be eleven in October and her youngest was only a year older than Debbie, and Nancy had declared, with what seemed like confidence, that three sons was quite sufficient, and she and Andy had decided not to have any more children. Jess and Ken would dearly have loved another baby and Ken had smiled at the assumption that one could regulate one's family at will, but Jess knew that Nancy had been interested in Dr Marie Stopes's theories of birth control and guessed that she was putting them into practice. Jess thoroughly approved; when she had been nursing, she had seen too much of the misery of women whose health and vitality had been drained by the birth and upbringing of a dozen or more children. She would have liked to have one more child herself, but realised that she and Ken were fortunate, for every child you produce means money you have to spend and, as it was, the three of them managed pretty well on Ken's salary and the money she earned in the doctor's surgery.

Jess had kept most of Nancy's letters and now she reread the most recent. Her friend was delighted to tell her that her sister Anne had yielded to her blandishments and come out to Australia. She had spent six months on the Walleroo station and to Nancy's joy had fallen for Andy's brother Clive. The two had married and then moved out to manage a cattle station not far from Cairns. Jess was delighted, because she thought that, full though her life was, Nancy must often long for female companionship. After all, her friend had worked in hospitals for years, had slept in dormitories with thirty other girls, had grown

85

used to sharing both triumphs and trials with her sister nurses. To be suddenly transported into a world of men with only the Aboriginal women to talk to must have been hard indeed. To be sure, Anne was some way off, but Jess did not doubt that they would manage to visit one another's homes a couple of times a month.

Nancy, however, never grumbled or said she was lonely. She wrote of her thriving kitchen garden, which provided the family with delicious vegetables from June to October. She spoke of the wonderful fish which were pulled out of the river during the wet and of making delicious bread, cakes and pies using flour made from grinding the corn which they grew on the river banks. She talked of parties, usually given in May or June, where one travelled a hundred miles or more to see one's neighbours. Naturally, such parties were rare, but they were much appreciated.

Jess thought of her own life and guessed it must seem dull to Nancy, but knew that she would not swap with her friend for anything. I suppose I was always timid, frightened to take risks or seize chances, she told herself, settling down with the inkpot close to hand. Nancy was always the daring one, but how lucky we both are! We adore our husbands, love our children deeply and would not exchange places for any money in the world. Of course I wish Ken and I could have another baby because I can see that it would be easy to spoil Debbie, but if it's not to be then it's not to be, and we are a happy little family.

She dipped her pen in the ink but had only written *Dearest Nancy* when there was a knock on the front door. Jess laid down her pen with an inward sigh and crossed the kitchen and then the small hall. It was a nice house and Penny Lane was in a nice area. She and Ken had rented the house when she was first pregnant, still meaning to buy property at some stage, but Ken had decided against it. They had put the money Jess had inherited away in an account where it grew a little larger each year. Ken always called it 'your nest egg' and refused to allow her to use it because he said it was there for a rainy day and English weather was so uncertain. So the house had been furnished gradually, over the years, and now it was beginning to repay their care. The walls of the hall were cream washed, the boards were shiny, and the strip of red and blue carpet which covered the stairs matched the rug upon the floor.

Upstairs in her small room, Debbie slumbered under a pink and white chequered counterpane with matching curtains at the windows and a rose-coloured carpet on the floor. There was a bathroom, a luxury almost unknown to householders in the area where Jess had been brought up, a spare bedroom, and the master bedroom overlooking the street, which Jess had carpeted in blue Wilton, with curtains of a paler blue at the windows, and a matching bedspread.

Now she crossed the hall and opened the front door, expecting to see Mrs Rudd, or perhaps the vicar, for Ken always came round the back. She eased the door back carefully and saw that the man outside was a policeman. He had a round and rosy face, and at first she smiled at him brightly, thinking he was going to tell her that he was collecting for some good cause, or perhaps warn her that the water would be turned off next day.

Then she read his expression, the strained and anxious look, the almost apologetic way he was turning his helmet between his hands. She grabbed at the door jamb, feeling suddenly dizzy and sick. She managed to say: 'Ken? Is it—is it my husband? Is he . . . has he . . . ?'

The policeman looked supremely uncomfortable. 'There's been a motor accident,' he mumbled. 'I think it would be best if I were to come in, Mrs Ryan. Then you could sit down and mebbe I could put the kettle on and we could . . .'

But Jess heard no more. She saw the policeman's face tip crazily sideways and the hall carpet come rushing up to meet her. Then she plunged into darkness.

*   *   *

It was weeks and weeks later before Jess felt strong enough to continue the letter to Nancy which she had begun on that frightful evening when the constable had come to tell her that Ken had been killed. He had been driving the old gentleman home when an approaching driver, in a lorry, lost control of his vehicle and ploughed into the hire car. Ken and the lorry driver had been killed instantly, yet the old gentleman, sitting in the back seat, had escaped with only minor injuries, and this had seemed to Jess the most unfair thing of all, for Ken was young and had a family to support. However, by the time she picked up her pen to write to Nancy once more, autumn was bringing the leaves down from the trees in Prince's Park and there was a nippy wind which had driven Debbie to play indoors. Jess was still devastated by Ken's death, knew she would miss him as long as she lived, but she was beginning to be far too busy to spend time simply bewailing her loss. At first, she had been tempted to break into her nest egg, but had decided not to take an action which would have grieved Ken deeply. The trouble was, of course, that the little family had been reliant upon Ken's wages for such things as the rent, the electricity and gas bills, and Jess's housekeeping allowance. The money she earned from Dr Foster had simply enabled them to pay for the odd treat, and because she had been too grief-stricken to continue with her job immediately after Ken's death Dr Foster had engaged another nurse, and no longer needed her services.

Her widow's pension would not even have paid the rent, let alone Debbie's school fees, and when September had arrived, Jess had reluctantly withdrawn her daughter from the small private school she had attended, and had made a big decision. She would have to work and the only work she knew was nursing and all the hospitals were in, or near, the city centre, and not out by Prince's Park. But she might get shared accommodation, or possibly even lodgings, which would mean she could take on full-time work, yet not have to worry about Debbie's being left alone in the house. So she had pulled herself together as much for the child's sake as for her own and had begun to look for work. She had gained a nursing post in the Stanley Hospital and had then scoured the neighbourhood for suitable housing, ending up with a flat share on the Scotland Road over a bicycle sales and repair shop. To Jess's intense relief, one of the other sharers had a small boy, only a few months older than Debbie, which meant that her child was not considered an impediment to flat sharing.

Having sorted out both a job and accommodation, Jess had handed in her notice to her landlord three weeks ago and had tearfully begun selling off the furniture which she and Ken had chosen and she had lovingly polished two or three times a week. It was worth a fair amount of money and any move, she was discovering, cost more than one could have credited. However, one of her mam's favourite sayings had been 'Necessity is the mother of invention', and this was certainly true in Jess's case. She had taken Debbie along to the Daisy Street school, almost opposite the Stanley Hospital, and had enrolled her as a pupil. She had then asked the teacher if she could recommend someone who would walk Debbie home to the flat after school each day. Miss Grant had advised her to try a Mrs Monk in Harebell Street and Jess and Debbie had gone round to the old woman's house that very afternoon. Mrs Monk was a chatty, friendly little soul, talking brightly of her eight grandchildren and two great-grandchildren, and had professed herself happy to 'help Mrs Ryan out', as she put it. Fortunately, Debbie took to the little woman at once, though as they walked back to the tram stop she informed her mother that Mrs Monk's house smelled funny, as did Mrs Monk herself.

'Well, you won't be visiting her house, my love, because the arrangement is that she will meet you out of school and walk with you back to the flat. Then I suppose she'll just walk home again,' Jess finished, rather lamely.

She waited for Debbie to make some comment but the child merely nodded. 'I shall miss Ella an awful lot, especially her beautiful toys and her lovely garden,' she said, ingenuously. 'But I expect I shall soon make new friends and I did like Miss Grant, didn't you, Mam? It will be nice to have a young teacher instead of old Miss Charlotte and Miss Abigail. They were too old to play games and I always thought Miss Abigail must suck sweets—those little purple ones—all day long because when she leaned over your desk she smelled of violets. Ugh!'

Jess laughed. The small school which her daughter had attended had been run by two elderly spinster sisters, and having seen the Daisy Street school Jess had realised that the education Debbie would receive there was likely to be a good deal broader than that which the Misses Grainger had offered. It was nice to know that, in moving her daughter away from the neighbourhood in which the child had been born and brought up, she would probably be doing her a good turn; Daisy Street School—and Miss Grant—had impressed Jess very much. Now that she came to think of it, she remembered that Ken had been doubtful over her choice of the little private school. 'I know it's nearby and you say the girls are taught to be little ladies, but one of these days Debbie may need qualifications of some sort . . .' he had begun, but Jess had just laughed and told him that the most important thing right now was to make sure that Debbie learned to speak nicely and have good manners. Ken had bowed to her superior knowledge of female education, but having been conducted over the Daisy Street school Jess saw his point of view and was glad, in one way at least, of the move she was about to make.

But now she must write to Nancy explaining what had happened to Ken and how it had affected her life. She would give Nancy her new address and promise to write regularly whilst warning her old friend that because she would be in full-time work her letters might be even shorter than of old.

Having made up her mind to start, Jess took a deep breath, dipped her pen in the ink, and began the painful task.

*   *   *

Pete was alone in the house, unless you counted Aggie, who was making up the beds, cleaning the rooms and shouting remarks every now and then to the other women also engaged in house cleaning. At this time of the morning, his mother was usually in the kitchen or one of the storerooms, planning and preparing the meals for the day, while his father and the men were out bringing in sick cattle for doctoring.

Generally, Jamie and his youngest brother Jacko would have been with Pete because mornings were when they were supposed to do the schoolwork which was delivered regularly by the mailman. Today, however, was different. Jamie and Jacko, lucky little beggars, had been invited to a neighbouring station, the owners of which had hired a lady teacher for a whole week to instruct younger children in the art of basic first aid, mathematics and joined-up writing. Last year, Pete had done the course when it had been held at the Walleroo and it had been great fun. Other children had come to the station with their bed rolls and they had all mucked in together. His ma had excelled herself, cooking delicious meals, and every evening they had had a corroboree in the yard, for then the course had been held during the dry. However, this year the dry season was still some weeks off and Pete could not help thinking that any corroboree might easily get ruined by rain, and that the adventure of sleeping on the floor with a great many other lads could be spoiled by the insects and small animals which would invade any dry area should a heavy downpour start.

What was more, he was enjoying having his mother's company to himself, for with his brothers away she had more time for him. Early that morning there had been an extremely large snake curled up in the bathtub and he had swelled with pride when she had shrieked for him to 'Take it away, Pete; *please* get rid of it! Ugh, ugh, ugh, I nearly stepped on it!'

He had looked into the tub with a little trepidation, for there were sufficient deadly snakes in the outback to make him cautious, but it was all right. The snake was not a venomous one. It was certainly very large, but Pete had not spent the last half dozen or so years trapping snakes with a forked stick for nothing. It wasn't easy because the prongs of the stick simply clattered on the galvanised tin bath and did not dig in, but with a quick flip he managed to extract the creature from its refuge. Then he pinned it to the earth floor, seized it behind the neck so that it was unable to turn and bite him, and carried it outdoors. Had it been poisonous, he would have had to kill it, but as it was he simply carried it a good way from the house and released it into long, wet grass, thinking as it turned to give him one last look, before wriggling out of sight, that there had been gratitude in the golden eyes.

'Pete, my love, you're a brick,' his mother had said when he returned to the house, giving him a hug. 'Thank God you did your first-aid training last year, because you know how odd the women can be about snakes. If it hadn't been for you I should have had to tackle it myself . . .' she shuddered, 'and if I had, it would have sensed how scared I was and turned round and bitten me. And don't tell me it wasn't poisonous, because you know what your pa says: a bite from a wild animal can infect you with all sorts . . . rabies, septicaemia . . . oh, anything. So thanks, Pete. You're a son to be proud of.'

Right now, Pete was working out a sheet of mathematics and thoroughly enjoying himself. He loved the simple logic of figures and was already doing work two years more advanced than that normally given to his age group. His teacher in far-off Perth wanted him to take his School Certificate in a couple of years, though should he do so he would have to swot up on other subjects. And what good, he reasoned, were languages or history to a feller who meant to become either an engineer or a pilot in the air force?

He was just settling down to the very last problem on the page when there was a commotion outside and Bo burst into the room. He was a stockman's son, the same age as Pete, and one of his closest friends. The boys rode together, swam in the river together, hunted together. In fact, the only thing they did not share was lessons, for Bo considered his education complete when he could read a bit and write his own name; mathematics left him cold.

He skidded to a halt beside Pete, and thumped him vigorously on the shoulder. 'Get your pa's gun, Pete,' he shouted urgently, 'quick, quick! Harry and the littl'un were splashing in and out of the big pool by the river . . . and there's a croc. I seen him, honest to God I did, and he's *huge*; the biggest one I ever seen. I screamed at the kids to get out o' the water, then I come runnin' for you. Hurry, Pete, hurry!'

Pete needed no second urging. He dashed across the room and into his father's study, seized the gun from the rack and came out again at a gallop. He was seething with excitement, and with fear, too, for he had gone on a crocodile hunt with his father not so long ago and had been amazed—and terrified—by the speed with which the enormous reptiles could act. Once he had seen a croc, completely hidden but for its eyes in a shallow lagoon, leap out of the water, grab a big bull by the nose, and drag it under all in one movement. He had waited for the fight, the crash, the explosion . . . but there was nothing. The croc had drowned the beast without allowing it to give so much as one sound, one splash, and had then, he presumed, towed it into deeper water and devoured it.

But there was no time for such recollections now; no time for anything but speed, if the kids were to be saved. He and Bo ran, not for their own lives but for the lives of Bo's two little brothers, and Pete told himself briskly not to think; no time. Just remember everything his pa had ever told him about crocs and guns. Be steady, aim between the eyes, fall back if you have to but keep an eye on the terrain behind you because you can't afford even one little mistake when it's a croc in your sights.

The two boys saw the kids, running, screaming . . . the pool behind them was quiet, the water smooth, reflecting the pale blue of the morning sky. Pete began to relax, to think that he was not to be put to the test after all; the croc must have given up on them, returned to the river . . .

It had not. It had quit the pool and was coming after the kids, moving with a swiftness and a smoothness which terrified Pete, for the kids were no longer running all out. Harry glanced back, did not appear to see the beast on his heels, actually waved to his brother and Pete as they continued to tear across the muddy ground between them. Then the reptile seemed to see Pete and Bo, and it was as though that tiny, agile brain said, 'Bigger game!' It swerved towards them, coming on at a waddling run, its snout elevated, its mouth opening to show the rows of hideous yellow teeth. Pete and Bo skidded to a stop. Pete was trembling all over but he knew he must keep cool. *Between the eyes*, his father had instructed him, *aim between the eyes because that way you stand the best chance of getting him in the brain*. Waveringly, he lifted the rifle barrel; so little time, so little time! But Pete felt cooler now, more in command, with the rifle stock cuddled against his shoulder and the barrel pointing steadily at his enemy. God, but Bo had been right; it was *huge*. He could see the cold gold of the crocodile's eyes, even see the liquid running from them, running down the great scaly face . . . crocodile tears. Then he squeezed the trigger, heard the explosion . . . but still the beast came on. Thanking God it was a repeater rifle, Pete fired again, again, again. The beast was so near he could smell the fetid stench of it, feel its hot breath. He longed to run but knew that if he tried to do so on the slippery mud, it could easily be the end of him.

Then Bo was punching his shoulder, trying to pull the gun from his grasp, jumping up and down in front of him, shouting, 'You done it man, you done it! Clean between the bloody eyes, dead as a dodo! Biggest one I ever did see! Wait till your daddy gets home. Why, it had to be a big 'un to get over that wall the fellers made so's the kids could play in the pool.'

Pete was shaking; he was shaking so much he was afraid Bo might notice and think him cowardly. Well, he had been frightened; anyone would have been. The croc had seemed gigantic when he looked at it along the smooth-backed gun barrel, but then it had been head on. Now he and Bo paced it out, both keeping well clear of the wicked teeth and claws, though no crocodile had ever been deader than this one, with the top half of its head blown away. Having satisfied themselves that the creature was at least thirty feet long, and maybe more, Bo shouted to Harry and his brother to come back and see for themselves what had been chasing them up from the pool. They came, eyes round with astonish ment in their shining black faces, clutching each other, shuddering and exclaiming.

'Good thing I'm not a trophy hunter, eh, Bo?' Pete said, indicating the bloody mess of the reptile's head.

'Yeah, but I reckon we'd best get ropes round it

and tow it back to the river,' Bo said, 'else the predators will be attracted by the smell of blood and we'll end up worse off'n we started. I'll go up to the camp and fetch most everyone down here. You go up to the house and get ropes and your ma. Reckon she oughta see it.'

'Right,' Pete said, and presently returned with ropes, accompanied by his mother who looked with astonishment at the enormous creature.

'I heard shots and thought your pa and the men were back,' she said. 'I wish Andy could see this, but Bo's right: it'll attract more attention than we want or need. Hold on a moment, though, and I'll fetch my measuring tape. Then at least we can tell your pa exactly how big it was . . . oh, my lor', look at those kids!'

Pete followed the direction of her pointing finger. Already, Harry and the little one were back in the water, shouting and splashing one another, without a thought of danger.

*   *   *

Jess was teaching Debbie how to make poached eggs on toast when Nancy's letter popped through the door. Debbie had browned the toast nicely and was hanging over the poacher, watching the transparent white gradually grow filmy and then solid, so Jess read the letter aloud to her as her daughter took the pan off the heat and began to butter the toast. When Jess reached the description of Pete shooting the crocodile she gasped, and Debbie, who was carefully scooping the eggs out of the poacher, glanced questioningly across at her. 'What's up, Mam? Oh, don't say the

98

horrible crocodile got one of the little boys! Gosh, crocodiles are horrible, aren't they? Remember the one in Peter Pan, the one who had an alarm clock in his tummy and ate up Captain Hook?'

'No . . . I know Nancy said it chased the children but I don't think they can run on dry land. No, the reason I gasped is because she said Peter shot it, but that can't possibly be right; he's only eleven or twelve, not old enough to hold a gun, lerralone fire it. I expect she was in such a hurry to write that she meant to say Andy, but put Pete by mistake.'

'Crocodiles can run on land; I read it in a book somewhere,' Debbie said. 'And boys of eleven are pretty strong, Mam. I bet it wasn't a mistake. I bet it really was Pete who shot the crocodile.'

'Oh well, I s'pose anything's possible in that barbarous land,' Jess said dismissively. 'Poor Nancy, stuck out there with hardly any women and no dear little daughter to give her a hand. My, queen, those poached eggs look delicious.'

After the meal, Jess left the room to change into her uniform, and as soon as she had gone Debbie dived on the letter. She adored Aunt Nancy's letters and always read them as soon as she could decently do so, and now she perused this one eagerly, putting it back on the table only when she had read it through twice.

Of course it had been Pete who had slain the crocodile—why on earth should Aunt Nancy be so pleased and excited if it had been her husband who had done the killing? He and his men went on crocodile hunts regularly when the wet was at its height, but Pete . . . well, he was only a boy when all was said and done.

But what a boy! One who picked a snake out of

the bath and then coolly killed a huge crocodile! Debbie wished that she could go to Australia and meet this hero amongst men, this eleven-year-old boy who could shoot a crocodile without thinking twice!

CHAPTER FOUR

SUMMER 1938

It was the first day of the summer holidays and Jess was doing the eight till eight shift on Geriatric under the eagle eye of Sister Thomas. Because she and the sister had never got on—Sister Thomas was heartily disliked by almost all of the staff and definitely all of the patients—Jess was determined to be early, so she bundled her porridge plate and mug into the sink and decided it was time to wake her daughter. She crossed the kitchen and stood at the foot of the stairs looking contentedly about her. She and Debbie had moved out of the flat above the cycle shop some years ago because life there had become unbearable for both of them. At first, it had only been Debbie who had suffered, for Sam Platt, the son of one of the nurses who had shared the flat with Jess, had hated Debbie on sight and had made her life a misery by constant bullying and taunts—though never, of course, when adults were present. The trouble was, the two children had often been left to their own devices, and though Debbie had grown adept at slipping out of the flat whenever she and Sam were alone, there had always been the odd occasion

100

when she could not do so. Because the flat share had been cheap and she knew her mother was hard up, Debbie had not complained about Sam until the dreadful day when he had pushed her downstairs, causing her to break an arm and crack two ribs. Then, of course, it had all come out and Nurse Platt, when confronted, had actually said it was all Debbie's fault, that she had taunted and bullied Sam until he had been forced to give her a little shove in self-defence.

Despite being almost of an age, Sam was twice Debbie's size: a hulking great brute of a boy with little intelligence but plenty of muscle, and the thought of Debbie's giving him a push was almost laughable. Jess had said so and Nurse Platt, using language so obscene that it had taken Jess's breath away, had announced that she would get her feller to come round one dark night and teach snooty Nurse Ryan a thing or two.

After this, the atmosphere in the flat had become difficult, to say the least; not that it had ever been easy. Three women sharing one kitchen is never a good idea but when they also shared a communal lavatory in the back yard, and a rather poky living room, small differences began to seem very large and tempers frequently flared.

Jess had done her best to pretend her nest egg did not exist, but during the years they had lived in the flat various things had happened which had forced her to dig into her savings. Twice she had had a recurrence of the sepsis which she had caught from wounded soldiers during the war years, through dressing septic and gangrenous wounds when the skin on her own hands was broken by small cuts or cracking chilblains. When her hands were really bad she could not work, for her fingers were too stiff to allow her to pick up so much as a teaspoon, quite apart from the danger of infecting others as she had been infected. On these occasions she was not paid, and was grateful for Ken's good sense in not allowing her to spend the money on new furniture or even on a home of their own. She and Debbie had got by on as little as they possibly could but her share of the rent still had to be paid and she and Debbie had had to eat.

Nevertheless, when things had come to a head, she still had a little left of her inheritance, and she had decided that they must move out of the flat. If she could manage the rent of a small house, then she might take lodgers, and she had sounded out Nurses Pennymore and Barker to discover whether they would be willing to leave the nurses' home and move in with her should she be fortunate enough to find a small house in the district.

Nurse Pennymore was a fat and jolly woman in her mid-thirties, sweet-tempered and friendly. She had agreed at once that she would be happy to take a room in Nurse Ryan's house, should she find one to rent, and as soon as the question had been put to Nurse Barker she, too, had hailed the idea with enthusiasm.

Jess loved working on the geriatric ward, finding many of the old ladies under her care to be women of great character, and it had been one of these, a Mrs Dawson, who had suggested that she might try the street directly behind the Stanley Hospital. 'When my husband were alive it were handy for his work at Ogden's tobacco factory,' she had explained, 'but I'm moving in wi' me daughter Mollie, so I shan't be goin' back no more; I give me landlord notice only two days ago. It's a grand little house in Wykeham Street; why don't you go after it? I doubt Mr Potts will have let it yet.'

Jess had loved the house from the first, though it had needed completely redecorating, and when Mrs Dawson had offered to sell her, for a very small sum, most of her furniture, Jess had accepted gladly, knowing that this would help the old woman and would also mean that she and Debbie could move in at once, though it had been several weeks before the house had been ready to receive Pennymore and Barker.

Jess had looked at the small sum of money left in her savings account, had taken a deep breath, and had withdrawn enough to buy some decent curtains and four almost new beds. These had been necessary because Mrs Dawson's ancient feather mattresses had gone lumpy and in the damp of an unoccupied house had turned mouldy as well.

Now, however, Jess was well content with their little home. Whenever she could afford it, and saw something she liked, she would buy another item of furniture to replace the old items she had bought from Mrs Dawson. Now the house was growing downright respectable and Jess knew that, should either of her lodgers decide to move on, she would have a queue of nurses at the door, eager to take their rooms.

She had been standing in the hall, glancing contentedly at the gleaming brown linoleum on the floor and the strip of blue carpet which led up the stairs, when she remembered abruptly that she had come out to shout to Debbie. Had her lodgers been in, she would have run up the stairs and woken Debbie quietly, but Pennymore and Barker were both on nights this week and would not return home for another half hour or so. Accordingly, Jess shouted. 'Debbie! Debbie? Are you awake, queen? I've left your porridge in the black enamel saucepan on the back of the stove, but there's a good wind out today so the fire's blazing up. If you leave it too long the porridge may burn on the bottom of the pan, and you know you hate burnt porridge.'

Jess waited and heard the thump as her daughter's feet hit the floorboards before padding across the room. The door creaked open and presently Jess saw Debbie's tousled head and sleepy eyes appear round the corner of the newel post at the top of the stairs. 'Wharrisit, Mam? Have you forgot it's the first day of the holidays? I meant to have a lie-in today, 'cos me and Gwen's goin' out later to try to find ourselves jobs. We're sick of havin' no money and Gwen says there's heaps of folk what'll employ a bright girl for the summer hols, so they can give their own workers a bit of time off.' She yawned hugely, then knuckled her eyes and ran her hands through her shining bob of hair. So like mine used to be, Jess thought sadly, before Ken's death and the hardships that followed began to turn me grey. Debbie has inherited my colouring, though she's like Ken in lots of ways. She's got his grit and courage. If it had been me who had been bullied by Sam, I'd have told my mam straight off, but Debbie never complained. Ken was just like that; he never wanted to worry me, always kept fears and bad news to himself if he could, and Debbie takes after him, so she does.

'Mam, are you listening? Me an' Gwen's goin' job hunting. Ain't you goin' to wish us luck?'

'Sorry, queen, I wasn't really attending,' Jess said apologetically. 'But I can't see any shopkeeper employing a couple of twelve-year-olds, not even on a temporary basis. There's an awful lot of unemployment in Liverpool right now—the Depression isn't over yet, even though things are looking up. But before you go off job hunting, you will do the washing up and clear away the crocks, won't you? No need to do anything for Pennymore and Barker; if they're hungry they'll make themselves something. But they may go straight to bed; I always do when I'm on nights. Oh, and peel a pan of spuds for supper, would you? And I've left you a list of messages, and the housekeeping purse, on the kitchen table. All right?' Jess gave a rueful laugh and pushed a strand of hair behind her ear. 'If you *do* get a job, heaven knows how we'll manage, because you work so hard for me. You get all me messages as well as seeing that the lodgers are fed when I'm not here. Still an' all, we'll tackle that problem if it arises. And in the meantime, I know you'll do everything I asked you like the good girl you are.'

Debbie yawned again, then nodded so vigorously that her mop of hair bounced. 'All right, Mam,' she agreed. 'I'll get the meal. What's it to be, anyroad?'

'Lamb chops if you can get 'em, and spuds, carrots and peas,' Jess said rapidly. 'And a marmalade roll for pudding; I cooked it after I got in last night, but you'll have to warm it through. Okay?'

'Yeah, fine,' Debbie said. She licked her lips. 'I

105

just love marmalade roll. I wish I could get a job in one of the big posh restaurants, waiting on. Then they'd have to feed me and I'd have marmalade roll every day . . . twice a day!'

Jess laughed, and turned back to the kitchen. Sister Thomas was a tartar; she did not simply take it out on you if you were late, she took it out on the patients too, slamming around, insisting that truly sick patients were dragged from their beds and made to walk through to the ablutions, refusing to fetch bedpans unless the old ladies were desperate. 'Got to run,' she shouted over her shoulder. 'It's Sister Thomas today, so . . .'

'So you're going to ask for a transfer . . . I don't think,' Debbie shouted, tauntingly, after her. 'You may hate Sister Thomas, but you love your old ladies, even when they're gaga. See you later, Mam!'

*   *   *

An hour later, Debbie and her best friend, Gwen Soames, were walking up the Scotland Road, their arms round each other's waists, gazing hopefully into every shop window that they passed. Cash, as usual, was short, and neither Mrs Ryan nor Mrs Soames was in a position to hand out money to her offspring. Gwen's mother had been widowed four years ago, when her husband, a seaman, had been killed in a drunken brawl, and since Gwen had three younger sisters and two brothers Mrs Soames was, if anything, worse off than the Ryans. The girls were of an age to yearn for pretty clothes, hair ribbons, a trip to the cinema and similar things, all of which had to be paid for, and their growing

106

sense of independence made them long for a wage packet of their own, however small.

In the past, Debbie and Gwen had been happy enough to earn a few pennies running messages for neighbours, or keeping an eye on younger child ren, but such small tasks no longer satisfied them. It was boring work for a start, and badly paid, when they considered what they might earn as relief workers during the summer holiday, so they had determined to spend as long as it took in the search for decently paid work.

Suddenly Gwen slipped her arm out of her friend's and pointed at a small card in a window. 'Look! That'll be a job, I bet!'

It was a job—a sales assistant was needed—and after some giggling and pushing the two girls went in together. They came out very promptly, however, the proprietress having looked them up and down scathingly before saying that she was already suited and had meant to remove the card earlier that day.

'Lying old biddy,' Gwen said scornfully, as soon as the shop door clanged shut behind them. 'Why didn't she just say we was too young? Still, at least we tried.'

'And I don't think she was a lying old biddy, because she did say she wanted someone full time,' Debbie said, a trifle reproachfully. 'I were listening to Pennymore and Barker talking a couple of nights ago . . . you know, about this here war they keep saying is going to come, and they said there will be well-paid jobs at some of the big factories, making uniforms and guns and that. They said that girls in them factories earn more than shop girls and that means that shop girls will be applying for jobs in factories. It's no use us doing that because we're too young, but it made me think someone might be glad to employ us in a shop during the summer holidays. But there isn't going to be a war, is there? It's too soon after the last lot, my mam says. But if there really is a war, she doesn't want me to go nursing, like she did, so I might as well get some experience of shop work if I can.'

'Well, I dunno,' Gwen said doubtfully, and Debbie realised that her friend had been somewhat shaken by the proprietress's instant dismissal. 'I don't reckon they'll give us work in a posh gown shop like that one, even if they're desperate. Women working in shops like that have their hair permed and they wear smart black dresses and high-heeled pumps.'

'There's deliveries,' Gwen said hopefully. 'Shops will pay girls to deliver dresses 'n' that because girls aren't so careless as boys. As for your mam worrying about who'll get the messages, that's one good thing about living in Ogden's. There's dozens of kids what'll carry any amount of stuff for a penny or two.'

Debbie nodded abstractedly. She knew that the flower streets close to her own Wykeham Street were known as Ogden's because of the number of people who worked at Ogden's tobacco factory who lived there, but she didn't comment because just then they were passing the Dining Rooms frequented by a good many office workers and she was remembering her conversation with her mother that morning. 'There's no sign in the window but there's no harm in trying,' she said to her friend.

*   *   *

Jess was bustling back and forth, doing the bedpan round which, on the geriatric ward, sometimes seemed to go on all day and most of the night. She and Nurse Wardle swished curtains back and forth, stood either side of the beds to assist the occupants to get on and off the big bedpans, then shoved the used utensils on to the trolley and wheeled it to the next cubicle. It was tiring work, for though some of the old ladies were feather light others were very heavy indeed and it took the combined strength of both nurses to move them up and down the beds. What was more, the doctor would be doing his rounds in ten minutes and heaven help the patient who wanted a bedpan when a doctor was on the ward!

Accordingly, Jess and Wardle hurried round the ward, and then Jess left Wardle emptying bedpans in the sluice whilst she returned to tidy the patients. Sister Thomas was prowling up and down the aisle, much like a sergeant on parade. Two little probationers, both of whom were terrified of the sister, scuttled back and forth, doing her bidding. They took old Mrs Brown's knitting away and pushed it into her bedside locker. They folded another patient's newspaper and popped it into her bedside drawer, tidied away glasses and jugs and made sure that, even beneath the beds, there was not so much as a speck of dust on display. Sister Thomas swept regally down to the door, then stopped short, her head swivelling sharply to the left. She stared accusingly at the patient in the nearest bed and Miss McTaggart, a retired head teacher, stared equally accusingly back. 'Yes,

Sister?' she asked. 'Is anything wrong?'

Sister pointed a trembling finger at Miss McTaggart's bed. There was a neat pile of papers upon the coverlet and Miss McTaggart, pen in hand, was writing on the topmost. 'What is that?' Sister Thomas enquired, her voice trembling with annoyance. 'All beds should be completely cleared for Doctor's rounds.' She marched across the small intervening space and seized the papers just as Miss McTaggart also grabbed them. 'I shall confiscate these,' she said grimly, 'until Doctor has left. And you should think yourself lucky that I don't throw them in the nearest rubbish bin.'

She tugged impatiently, but Miss McTaggart hung on, her thin old cheeks reddening. 'Kindly take your hands off my papers, Sister,' she said, with only the tiniest quaver in her voice. 'I am employed to mark examination papers and these are my most recent batch. I'm afraid no one may look at them . . . and that includes you. However, if you'd like to place them in my locker, then I'll not work on them whilst the doctor is present. But I cannot allow you to—'

Sister tugged; Miss McTaggart tugged. And then, with astonishing suddenness, the sister released her hold on the papers and before anyone could stop her she had slapped Miss McTaggart so hard across the face that the old woman nearly fell out of bed. Even so, she retained her grasp on the examination papers, though her hands were trembling so violently that the papers shook like leaves in a gale.

Naturally, the whole ward had been riveted by the drama, and now Jess acted without a second thought. Sister was reaching out to snatch the papers with her left hand, her right hand coming up as though she intended to strike the old woman again. Jess seized the upraised arm and twisted it up behind Sister's back in a half nelson, causing the older woman to give a muffled shriek and release her hold on the papers, which fluttered to the floor. Jess jerked her head at the nearest probationer. 'Pick up those examination papers— don't look at them—and return them to Miss McTaggart, please,' she said authoritatively. 'If the patient gives her permission, then you may put them in her locker until the doctor's round is over.' She released Sister and turned to Miss McTaggart. 'I'm so sorry that you should have been—er— reprimanded for doing your duty,' she said gently. 'I'm sure Sister acted in the heat of the moment and will be happy to apologise . . .'

But by now, Sister Thomas had regained her equilibrium. She tossed her head and gave Jess a glance so full of malevolence that Jess flinched back, half expecting the older woman to strike her as she had struck Miss McTaggart. However, the sister merely addressed her through thinning lips.

'Go to my office, Ryan,' she said. 'I'll deal with you there.'

As Jess moved along the central aisle, she saw that every face she passed was smiling and thought that her treatment of the sister was being greeted with approval. Most of the patients on the ward were long term and all had suffered both from Sister's rough handling and from her bitter tongue. Seeing the hated despot brought low, if only for a moment, must have given them a good deal of pleasure, and as she got nearer to the end of the ward Jess could hear the comments: 'Well done,

111

queen! You showed her, nurse . . . you're a good gal, you are . . . why didn't you break her arm while you were about it?'—this last from a patient who had suffered continually from Sister Thomas's spite since she was very overweight and was thus a butt for the sister's nastier remarks. As she pushed through the swing doors, Jess saw the doctor and his team approaching along the corridor. She hesitated, wondering whether she should tell them of the fracas which had just taken place, but it was too like tale-clatting, so she merely smiled politely and continued on her way. After all, she had seen the scarlet weals on Miss McTaggart's cheek and no doubt the doctors would notice them too. Indeed, she hoped they would, because it would serve Sister right after the way she had treated the patient, Jess thought grimly as she pushed open the office door. And what could Sister Thomas do to her, after all? She could scarcely complain of the way she had been treated without revealing the reason for her nurse's action.

So Jess picked up a copy of a nursing paper and began to read.

*   *   *

Debbie approached the flat triumphantly, having struggled round the markets and done all her mother's messages after finishing work. It was not the glamorous job for which she had hoped, but she had been taken on as a washer-upper and general dogsbody for a large Dining Rooms on the Scotland Road to start that very day, though she had been allowed to leave early after explaining to the manager that she had messages to run for her

112

mother and must be home in time to cook a meal for their lodgers.

'But you said you'd be willing to work eight till eight,' her employer had pointed out. 'I can do wi'out a gal what skives off every time she fancies a break.' He was a weaselly little man with thinning hair carefully arranged over a pointed, pink head, a tiny toothbrush moustache and eyes which darted about even while he was speaking to you. Debbie had explained again that this would not happen once her mother knew about her job and he had appeared to accept her assurance, though he had not admitted it. 'We'll see how you shape,' he had said grudgingly, as she had taken off the enormous overall in which she had been swathed and reached her coat down from the pegs which decorated the office wall. 'And don't you be late in the mornin' or you'll find yourself out on the street, pronto. This place is busy from the moment we open until well after closing time, and we don't suffer lazy layabouts—can't afford to, 'cos their work gets purron the rest of the staff.'

Debbie had murmured that she would be in on time, though she was beginning to wonder whether she had done the right thing in taking the job. For hour after hour she had stood before the great stone sink, cleaning the debris off hundreds of greasy dinner plates, knives, forks and spoons. When the water had grown cold—and thick with bits—she pulled the plug, cleaned the sink and filled it afresh with water from the big brass tap which was fed by a temperamental gas geyser on the draining board. Then she had added soda and begun all over again. Another girl, Polly, was supposed to scrape the remaining food off the

113

plates before piling them up on the left-hand draining board, but she was careless, not bothering to check the underneath of the plates, so that Debbie had often found herself washing up in water that resembled vegetable soup. Now and then, she had taken a tea towel from the rack above their heads and dried huge quantities of dishes, cups, saucers and cutlery, though this was really Polly's job. But the other girl was slow, and it had been easier to do it herself rather than allow the dishes to pile up.

Now, walking rather slowly towards Wykeham Street, for her marketing bag was heavy, Debbie wondered how Gwen was getting on. They had had little chance to compare notes, meeting only briefly at staff dinnertime. They had both been employed by the Dining Rooms but Gwen had been put in the dreadful smelly scullery, preparing meat and vegetables for cooking, and she had no excuse for leaving early so she would still be at it, chopping and grating, peeling and slicing. As a washer-upper, Debbie thought she was really well paid; she had been promised seven and six a week to start with and ten shillings if she proved to be satisfactory after a couple of weeks, but Gwen had been made no such promises. She would be paid seven and six a week all right, but there had been no mention of an increase in money should she prove satisfactory. But if she's good at the job, I'm sure they'll increase her wages, same as mine, Debbie told herself optimistically, as she turned into Wykeham Street. The manager had understood that she and Gwen were schoolgirls but had said, bitterly, that because of the sudden upsurge of jobs for women in munitions and

114

uniform factories he was having difficulty not only in employing holiday cover staff, but also in persuading women to work long hours. 'So if youse works well, then I'll mebbe employ you from four to eight during term time, an' all day Sat'days,' he had said to Debbie. 'See how it goes.'

Debbie went down the jigger and approached the house across the small yard. The key was hidden under a flowerpot to the left of the door, so she stood her marketing bag down, picked the key up, and let herself into the house, dumping the bag on the kitchen table with a sigh of relief. Then she jumped. The house should be empty—Pennymore and Barker always went out after seven or eight hours' sleep—but she was pretty sure she had heard a floorboard creak in the room overhead. Burglars? But what was there to burgle? She glanced towards the mantelpiece where the housekeeping purse was kept, then remembered that she had taken it out with her and it now reposed, considerably thinner than it had been this morning, in the bottom of the marketing bag. Swiftly, she glanced round the kitchen; nothing missing that she could tell. She checked the parlour where her mother's walnut bureau stood— Jess's most prized possession—and was relieved to see it was still there. She went slowly back into the kitchen, then stopped short. Someone had crossed the landing above her head, making no pretence of quietness, and was descending the stairs. Debbie edged towards the back door, though she was almost certain, now, that the intruder was no intruder at all but someone with every right to be in the house. Probably either Pennymore or Barker had come home early to prepare for the next shift.

115

So it was all the more of a shock when the kitchen door opened and a man entered. He was very tall with frizzy close-cropped hair and a long, rather lugubrious face. He was clad in a blue shirt and navy trousers, and had a navy jacket slung over one shoulder, and when he saw her he smiled ingratiatingly, with a great show of long, yellow teeth. Debbie was opening her mouth to ask him just what he was doing in her house when her mother entered the room close behind him, saying reassuringly: 'It's all right, queen . . . goodness, what a fright we must have given you! This is Mr Bottomley; he's—he's come to take a look at a room.'

Debbie opened her mouth to say that all their bedrooms were taken and then saw her mother, behind Mr Bottomley, shaking her head. 'Oh, I see,' she said feebly. She returned the elderly man's smile. 'Sorry, Mr Bottomley; I thought for a moment you was an intruder.'

Mr Bottomley laughed so heartily at this idea that he nearly choked himself. As soon as he was able to speak, he said, 'Well now, that ain't likely! I's a big feller, too big to slither through that letter box of yourn.' He looked, appraisingly, round the kitchen. 'Cosy, real cosy. Nice an' clean, too—youse could eat your dinner off that floor.'

Debbie considered making a sharp retort, saying something clever like 'We've never been reduced to doing that yet', then thought better of it and moved over to the table, beginning to unload the shopping. She half listened to her mother talking to the stranger, telling him that she would write to him at his place of work. 'I can't say too much now, not until I know how things stand,' Jess said,

116

opening the back door as a clear indication, to Debbie at any rate, that she wished her caller to leave. 'But I should know by tomorrow, or the day after . . . I'll drop you a line.'

Mr Bottomley, however, was not to be so easily ejected. He ignored the open back door and proceeded to look curiously about him whilst chattering amiably about the convenience of living so near the Stanley Road, with trams constantly passing and repassing, so that one was within easy reach of the city centre. 'And I'd be much obliged, missus, if you could let me know by tomorrer at the latest,' he said, in a rather aggrieved tone, as Jess, losing patience, walked into the yard herself and beckoned him to follow. 'I told you me landlady needs me room 'cos her eldest daughter's comin' down from Glasgow to have her baby under her mother's roof, and when you mentioned you was lookin' for a lodger you never said nothin' about seein' how things stood. I thought it were all cut and dried and that if I liked the room—which I does—then I could move in immediate.'

Debbie saw her mother's back stiffen and could imagine the expression of annoyance on her face, but she only said, coolly: 'I'm sorry if I gave you the wrong impression, Mr Bottomley, but I'm sure I never meant to do so. The fact is, I've two lodgers at present, both nurses. One of them told me this morning that a friend had offered her a flat share and she will probably take it, but I don't know when she'll be moving out, so you see . . .'

Mr Bottomley, halfway across the yard, stopped short. 'If I'd knowed that . . .' he started belligerently, then paused and heaved a sigh. 'Look, missus, if you want the truth, I'm pretty

117

damn desperate. I'm out on me ear at the weekend and your place would suit me down to the ground. I'm norra difficult feller; you'll find I'll fit in right well with your family and I'll pay reg'lar as clockwork. If you'll give me a definite promise then I'll move into a doss house until your room's free. I can't say fairer than that, can I?'

Jess turned away, saying coldly as she did so: 'I said I'd let you know, Mr Bottomley, but perhaps I'd better say at once that I don't think we should suit.' She re-entered the kitchen and shut the door smartly behind her. 'Phew!' she said, her face pink with annoyance. 'Of all the cheek! I've never met anyone so—'

The kitchen door crashed open and Mr Bottomley surged back into the room. He looked furiously angry, and dangerous, too, and he began haranguing them at once, saying that he had been unfairly treated, that he had come to view the room at Mrs Ryan's request.

Debbie quailed but Jess faced up to the man without any sign of fear. 'Get out of my house or I'll call the police,' she said brusquely. Without moving her eyes from Mr Bottomley's, she added: 'Debbie, run round to number seventeen and see if Constable Bullock is in. Or you can go on to Stanley Road and find a policeman somewhere. I refuse to be bullied in my own home.'

Debbie shot across to the back door but her mother's threat seemed to have done the trick, for Mr Bottomley turned, left the kitchen, and almost ran across the yard, mouthing obscenities as he did so. Jess slammed the door and locked it, then collapsed on a kitchen chair. 'My God, I wonder if you should really go round to number seventeen?'

118

she said, her voice shaky. She looked apologetically across at her daughter. 'He seemed such a nice quiet man, but . . . look, put the kettle on, queen, because it's a long story and you'll want to know exactly what's gone on since we both left the house this morning.'

'You're right there,' Debbie said fervently. 'But is it true that one of the nurses is moving out?'

'Yes, it's true,' Jess said, wearily. She stared towards the back door as though half expecting Mr Bottomley to start hammering on it, then gave a rather watery giggle and relaxed. 'I dare say the poor old feller had a point and I was a bit unfair. You see, love, I've had an absolutely awful day. It started when Sister Thomas . . .'

'Gosh! But Sister Thomas deserved everything she got. How dared she hit the patient,' Debbie said, when her mother paused for breath. 'Only I expect she managed to blame you, didn't she?'

'Yes, she did, and I was given my cards,' Jess said, rather bitterly. 'Matron admitted that Sister Thomas had been wrong to strike a patient, but of course Sister had said the patient had hit her first. There's going to be an enquiry and maybe at the end of it I'll be reinstated, but quite honestly, love, we can't hang around waiting. I'll have to get another job, and this time it won't be in nursing. Naturally, when Pennymore told me she was moving out—and I'd just been sacked—I was in despair. Losing my salary was bad enough, without losing a lodger as well. So I nipped out to Protheroe's corner shop, to put a card in the window, advertising the room, and there was Mr Bottomley putting a card in the window as well, asking for lodgings. It—well, it seemed like the

119

answer to a prayer. Perhaps I should have made an appointment for him to come and view the room when we were all at home, but he was very insistent that he should see it right away. It was all right at first; he liked the house and the situation, liked the room very much indeed, but the more I thought about it the less I liked the idea of sharing a house with a man like him. He's very opinionated, laid down the law, kept telling me how things should be done, so by the time we came into the kitchen I'd already decided that I would have to turn him down.' She heaved a deep sigh and rose to her feet to fetch two mugs from the dresser as the kettle began to boil. Debbie fetched the caddy from its shelf and began to make a pot of tea. 'But I never thought he'd turn violent the way he did. And his language! He told me he worked at Lime Street station but he swore more like a docker than a railway porter.'

Debbie, pouring the tea, laughed. 'I expect railway porters can swear just as well as dockers when they let themselves go,' she observed. 'But Mam, surely you can get another nurse to replace Pennymore. It's a shame, because we've got on so well, the four of us, but I dare say there are other nice nurses eager to get lodgings near the hospital.'

Jess shook her head glumly. 'Unfortunately, nurses aren't well paid so we've always let them have the rooms cheap,' she said. 'That didn't matter when I was earning, but it may well matter now. And I don't imagine that nurses will be exactly keen to share a house with someone who has been sacked. So things may be difficult, for a while at least. In fact, you could say our future looks rather bleak.'

120

Debbie set the mugs of tea carefully down on the table, then suddenly remembered her own news. She leaned across and clasped her mother's hands. 'Oh, Mam, I am a fool. I'll forget me own head next! Our future isn't that bleak, 'cos I got meself a job, just like I said I would. I'm working at Deakin's Dining Rooms as a kitchen helper. I'll get two hot meals a day and seven and six a week to start, which goes up to ten bob if I give satisfaction. It's a long day, eight till eight, but I don't mind that.'

Jess beamed at her daughter. 'Well done, queen,' she said. 'It may not be a fortune, but every little helps . . .'

'. . . as the mermaid said when she wee'd in the sea,' Debbie cut in, and was pleased to see her mother smile. 'Look, Ma, you're not to worry. You're a fully trained nurse with heaps of experience, so you're bound to get a job, and a well-paid one too. Everyone keeps saying that factories are paying good money so you could try there, for a start.'

'I can't imagine what working in a factory is like, or whether I'd be any good at it,' Jess said, rather doubtfully. 'Nursing has been my whole life, ever since I left school, though of course when your father was alive I didn't have to work. But when I think of the unfair treatment I've received from Matron . . . well, I believe I wouldn't go back if they paid me double. I was thinking of having more lodgers and charging them much more, as well, because I'd be at home all day and able to make cheap, nourishing meals, but I can see it wouldn't do. If there's one thing Mr Bottomley has taught me, it's that male lodgers can cause a deal of trouble, and we can do without that, so I'll start job hunting tomorrow. Right now—when I've finished my cup of tea, that is—I'll go back to the corner shop and put another advert in for a lodger, only this time I'll specify that it must be a female.'

*   *   *

Debbie was wandering along the Scotland Road with a large canvas bag in either hand. It was bitterly cold but she was feeling at peace with the world for it was Christmas Eve and she had just spent an enjoyable couple of hours not only getting her mother's messages, but also buying Christmas presents for those she loved best. She had had, perforce, to finish her summer job on her return to school, though they had kept her on from four o'clock till eight o'clock on Thursdays and Fridays and all day on Saturdays. But when December came the Dining Rooms were so busy that she had been promoted to waitressing, and this—oh joy— meant that in addition to her wages she got a great many tips. Debbie loved being a waitress. She enjoyed the customers' cheerful banter and the air of excited anticipation which was almost palpable as Christmas drew nearer. And, of course, she enjoyed the increase in her take-home pay. She had asked the manager, rather shyly, if she might do some waitressing even after Christmas, in order to keep her hand in, so to speak, and, to her secret astonishment, he had agreed, adding the rider that she had worked longer as a washer-up than any other girl he had employed and so deserved the reward of more congenial work when it was available.

So now Debbie loitered outside the brightly lit shops, for though it was nine o'clock at night few had yet put up their shutters and customers thronged the pavements, spilling out into the roadway and clustering round the tram stops like bees round a honey pot. Despite Mr Chamberlain's 'Peace for our time' speech, there were still mutterings of war, but just now everyone was in a festive mood. Debbie was pondering the advisability of spending some of her tip money on a second-hand winter coat as she passed the front of Paddy's Market. She saw customers gathered round Mrs Finnigan's stall, which was where she usually bought decent, part-worn clothing, but decided that she could scarcely give coat buying her full attention without setting down her marketing bags, so turned once more for home. Her mother would be in the kitchen, no doubt preparing something delicious for the late supper they always shared when Debbie was working. Even though she had enjoyed a good meal at Deakin's, the thought of an appetising mutton stew or beef casserole made her step out a little faster.

As she walked, she thought about the extraordinary events of the last five months. None of her mother's fears of being penniless, or having to leave the house in Wykeham Street, had come to pass. In July, when her mother had lost her job and Nurse Pennymore had given in her notice, their future had looked bleak indeed. But Jess had got a job in a large chemist's shop, just off the Scotland Road. At first, she had worked as an ordinary assistant and money had been short, but then customers had begun to come in with various medical problems and since the pharmacist was an elderly man who wanted to retire such problems were passed straight to Jess. Very soon, Mr Jarvis asked her if she would be willing to take the job of deputy manager and deal with medical enquiries when he himself was not present. Jess had agreed and was much in demand, though she never interfered with the commercial side of the business.

She had told her daughter, with a twinkle, that Mr Jarvis had said his rivals were very envious of the fact that he employed a real live nurse, and added that this was perfectly true, for her colleagues had admitted that business had doubled since Jess had joined them.

Then, of course, there were the lodgers. Pennymore had moved out and despite her mother's fears two other nurses—the Fletcher cousins from a village on the Wirral—had moved into her room, announcing that they were happy to share. Jess had asked for the same rent from each of them as Pennymore had paid, and the young women had agreed willingly.

Then, after only a month, Pennymore had come round one evening, asking hopefully if her room was still vacant. It transpired that she and her flat share had fallen out and she wished to return to Wykeham Street just as soon as there was a room for her. Debbie had expected to be asked to sleep on the sofa in the parlour but instead Jess had told Barker that she could no longer afford to let one whole room so cheaply and Barker had agreed to share with Pennymore, for the two girls were old friends.

Then Debbie remembered the horrible affair of the detestable Mr Bottomley who had tried to bully them; he had come back several times over the course of the following weeks, until Jess had finally acted on her threat to tell the police, whereupon he had disappeared. However, it now seemed to Debbie that even Mr Bottomley had had his uses; her mother had resolutely refused to consider any male lodgers and seemed to distrust men in general. Once, Debbie had secretly worried that Jess might marry again, for men were attracted by her brisk self-confidence and pretty looks. Now she only went out with the nurses, or colleagues from work, relieving Debbie's mind of the fear of being asked to accept a stepfather in the place of her own beloved daddy.

'Debbie! Debbie, will you hang on a tick.' Debbie swung round at the sound of her name and smiled as her friend Gwen came panting up beside her. 'God, girl, you must be deaf as any post. I've been shrieking your name ever since I spotted you passing the market entrance.' She peered, curiously, at Debbie's shopping. 'Wharr've you got there? And why's you shoppin' so late? Oh, I forgot; I s'pose, since it's the Christmas hols, you're back at Deakin's.' She sniffed disparagingly. 'Rather you than me.'

'Yes, that's right,' Debbie said placidly. Gwen had left the Dining Rooms at the end of her first week when she had been offered a job by one of her many uncles. He had a fish stall in the Charlotte Street market, and though the work was really no easier than preparing vegetables at least it meant that Gwen was not shut away in the smelly scullery, with no company except for occasional visits by the cook or one of his minions, come to collect the trimmed meat and to grumble that

125

Gwen was slow.

Furthermore, Gwen's Uncle Percy, though he did not pay as much as Deakin's, saw that she took home any fish left over at the end of the day's trading and usually managed to persuade other stallholders, in the nearby St John's vegetable market, to bag up weary vegetables and bruised fruit for his niece. Unfortunately, the job had finished when the autumn term had started and by then the job at Deakin's had been given to someone else, so Gwen was at a loose end for the time being.

'Here, give me one of them bags. No point in you carryin' them both all the way home,' Gwen said, taking one of the carriers from her friend. 'Tell me about Deakin's; is it still as 'orrible as ever?'

'It never was horrible, only you didn't stick it long enough to find out how friendly everyone is,' Debbie protested. 'And it's grand now that I'm waitressing, though I do help with washing up when the restaurant is quiet, which ain't often. And today I asked the manager if I could waitress again after Christmas, to keep my hand in, like. And you'll never guess what he said!'

'He said, "No you can't, you're a dirty little washer-upper,"' Gwen said, grinning. 'Well, it's what he would have said to me, anyroad. He never did like either of us, I don't think.'

'Wrong, wrong, wrong,' Debbie chanted triumphantly. 'Well, he may not have liked me at first, but he must quite like me now because he said I've worked hard and he had appreciated it and I could work as a waitress in the New Year so long as I was prepared to wash up when Ivy was

126

away; Ivy's ever so old and ever so fat, and normally she just helps out when we're terribly busy. But she took over the washing-up earlier in the month, when I started waiting on, and now she's permanent. Good, ain't it?'

'Ye-es. Perhaps I should have stuck to it meself,' Gwen said, rather dolefully. 'Money's always short in our house, and if there's any goin' spare the younger kids gerrit. And, a'course, Uncle Percy don't need me in the Christmas hols because there ain't much fish sold at this time o' year. Nor much caught, for that matter,' she ended. Then she handed Debbie her heavy bag and turned into Daisy Street, calling back over her shoulder that she might come round the following morning, just to see what sort of presents Debbie had been given. 'Because you're bound to get stuff from your lodgers,' she shouted over her shoulder. 'And I'll show you me prezzies from me uncles 'n' aunts.'

'Okay,' Debbie shouted back as she crossed the busy main road. She hurried along Fountains Road and turned down into Wykeham Street. Rattling on the front door, since she had no desire to lug her heavy marketing bags all the way along the jigger, she thought, a trifle enviously, that no one would expect Gwen to buy presents for her uncles and aunts whereas she, since she was earning, had had to buy presents for all her mother's lodgers. She had wondered what on earth to get them but her mother had solved the problem for her. At Christmas Mr Jarvis bought in a supply of bath salts, talcum powder and scented soap, which always sold very well, and he offered his staff a discount if they purchased such things from the shop. Debbie had taken advantage of the offer and had bought lily-of-the-valley soap for all the nurses and a tiny bottle of Evening in Paris perfume for her mother and some thick woolly gloves for Gwen. Some of the staff at Deakin's had exchanged presents but, fortunately, they had realised that Debbie was in no position to reciprocate. 'But you'll gerra bonus after you've worked the full twelve months next year, chuck,' Ethel, the senior waitress, had assured her. 'Now have a good Christmas; see you on the twenty-seventh.'

The front door shot open and Jess was there, with her reading glasses perched on the end of her nose and a letter in one hand. She swooped on the marketing bags and took them from her daughter, saying that they were too heavy for one person. Then she led the way down the hall into the kitchen. 'Sit yourself down, queen, and I'll dish up,' she announced. 'I reckon you'll be hungry after doing so much shopping . . . my goodness, it's past ten o'clock. Never mind; you can have a nice lie-in tomorrow.' As Debbie took off her coat, her mother added: 'And I've got my Christmas treat right here; it's a lovely long letter from your Aunt Nancy. Want me to read it to you after I've dished up?'

When she was small, Debbie had been fascinated by the Sullivans and their lives in Australia. Nancy had written of monstrous crocodiles, of water snakes and of enormous spiders whose bites were poisonous. But she also wrote of pleasanter things: watching the young boys, when the river was in flood, coming down the torrent on homemade rafts; and corroborees, which seemed to be some sort of party, starting in the late afternoon and continuing long into the night. And of the pleasure she got from cultivating her kitchen garden on the banks of the river, of gathering in her crops . . . and even of her experiments with a flower garden which, as she grew more experienced, provided fresh flowers for the house for weeks at a time.

There had been many other things, all intriguing to the young Debbie, who thought the cattle station sounded wonderfully romantic. She imagined the homestead as a low white building, creeper covered, with the family sitting out on a wooden veranda, enjoying a meal in the cool of the evening. She knew Aunt Nancy had a number of sons but they were so far away and their lives were so different from her own that they seemed more like story-book heroes than real people.

The meal was a beef casserole with floury potatoes, and Debbie did full justice to her food whilst her mother read the letter aloud. It seemed that the Sullivans were prospering, for Andy and his men had added another wing to the homestead and the eldest boy was taking flying lessons. Nancy explained that the station covered many, many miles, so a light plane which could get quickly from one side of it to the other would be a great advantage. Debbie stared, open-mouthed, at her mother. Did that mean that the Sullivans were going to buy an aeroplane? It seemed unlikely, and, as the letter ended with good wishes for Christmas, she put it out of her mind. The Sullivans might be doing very well but so were the Ryans. Her mother was putting money away regularly and hoped to be able to buy a house, instead of renting one, one of these days. Purchasing the house in Wykeham Street might not be possible since the landlord seemed to have no desire to sell, but there were other properties which could be bought. Provided one was within easy reach of the city centre, lodgers were not difficult to come by, and though Jess was happy working for her chemist, Debbie knew her mother would have liked to stay in her own home instead of having to go off to the shop each day. But that was for the future; for the present, they could not have been happier. Debbie knew that their lodgers were comfortably settled and had no intention of deserting such a cosy billet and that when she left school the Dining Rooms would be pleased to employ her, though her mother had made it plain that she thought Debbie should aim higher than waitressing when she wanted full-time work.

And tomorrow is Christmas Day! All in a moment, Debbie felt she could see into the future and it was good. I wouldn't change places with the Queen of England, she told herself. She may be eating roast peacock and drinking champagne but beef stew and a nice hot cup of tea will do me fine.

She said as much to her mother who smiled gently. 'And peace,' she reminded her daughter. 'All those dreadful rumours that there was to be a war, all the awful stories coming out of Czechoslovakia and Yugoslavia and Poland, must have been simply stories, tales made up to frighten children. Mr Chamberlain, bless him, has got a written treaty from the German High Command that there will be no war, and I thank God for it.' She smiled affectionately at her daughter. 'I feel now we can get on with our lives and stop worrying about tomorrow.'

Debbie smiled back at her but a tiny little trickle

130

of cold doubt ran down her spine. Tales to frighten children? There must be more to it than that, but her mother read the papers, listened to the wireless, knew what she was talking about, whereas Debbie had little or no interest in current affairs. So she took a sip of her tea, then set the cup down carefully. 'Tomorrow's Christmas Day,' she said, voicing her thoughts. 'Do you remember telling me about that Christmas in the trenches, Mam, when the men had a football match, Germans against British, and exchanged little presents and talked to each other, as friends do? That was wonderful, wasn't it? If only everyone had acted like that, then thousands of lives would have been saved.'

Jess sighed and stood up. 'Aye, you're right, but next day they were killing each other, same as before,' she said bitterly. 'Men are all alike; they enjoy war and fighting. If it were left to us women . . .'

'But Mr Chamberlain's a man and I suppose the German High Command are men as well,' Debbie remarked, carrying the dirty crockery over to the sink. 'And they seem to want peace or they wouldn't have signed Mr Chamberlain's piece of paper.'

Jess had been finishing off her own food, but suddenly she pushed her chair back from the table and stood up. 'I don't want to talk about it,' she said abruptly. 'It's time we were both in bed, queen. Tomorrow's another day and you may be sure it'll be a busy one.'

She turned and left the kitchen and did not hear Debbie murmur: 'Tomorrow never comes,' as she, in her turn, made her way up to bed.

131

CHAPTER FIVE

OCTOBER 1939

Debbie and Jess were sitting in the kitchen because it was the only room, so far, that they had been able to fit with blackout blinds. Debbie had been occupying herself working out mathematical problems whilst Jess was industriously knitting for, ever since 3 September, women had been urged to help the war effort by producing socks, gloves and balaclavas for men in the forces. Despite promises, Hitler's storm troopers, aided by the Russians, had marched into Poland, spreading death and destruction as they went, and all Jess's worst fears had been realised. The tales made up to frighten children had proved to be anything but fiction.

Because she was thirteen, Debbie had refused to be evacuated when the younger children at Daisy Street School were marched off to places of safety. She was still too young to take a regular job and had expected, gleefully, to enjoy herself mightily with no school and no teachers to bother about. However, she had reckoned without the strenuous efforts to keep the country safe which had closed all places of public entertainment and made life difficult for ordinary people. Instead of wandering the streets with Gwen and her other friends, she had spent countless hours trying to buy blackout material so that they would not show a light, and longer hours in the search for brown paper. This was supposed to be cut into strips and stuck over window panes so that the glass would not shatter if bombs fell. It was not too bad during daylight hours, but what with unlit streets and unlit vehicles it was downright dangerous to venture out of an evening. The newspapers reported heavy casualties as a result of the blackout, though they were unable to quote actual numbers from the Ministry of Information since it was feared that such reports might be used by the enemy.

'Finished, Mam,' Debbie said, putting down her pencil. 'Did the school give you the answers or just the problems? Only, if you've gorra work them out, who's to say whether my answer or yours is right?'

Jess laughed. 'Who's to say our answers won't be the same?' she countered. 'But the teacher did give me the answers, as it happens. It was kind of Miss Rogers to give you some work, even if you don't appreciate it.'

'Well, I don't,' Debbie retorted, though this was not entirely true. She found she was often bored, for already shortages were beginning to bite and she seemed to spend hours standing in queues. Of course she grumbled about being given work to do at home but at least it gave her something to think about other than the war. It was all very well for her mother: Jess was now managing the chemist's shop full time, for Mr Jarvis had retired, and she had also joined the Local Defence Volunteers, which meant that she was out on official business two or three nights a week. If I were a boy, I could be a messenger and have a bicycle, Debbie thought longingly, pushing the sheet of mathematical problems across the table. If I were a bit older, if I were already fourteen, then I could get a job at one of the big factories out on Long Lane. I'd have proper money then and pals to talk to; I reckon it 'ud be grand to work in a factory. Her job at Deakin's had finished with the start of the war, for customer numbers had shrunk as men were called up and those remaining had less money to spare. Debbie had looked desultorily for another job, but so far had been unable to find one.

Jess produced a piece of paper from her pocket and compared it with her daughter's answers, then smiled encouragingly. 'You've gorr'em all right,' she said. 'It just goes to show that you've not forgotten all you were taught. And now, how about that essay? What was the subject again?'

Debbie's sigh came all the way up from her boots. ' "Careless talk costs lives",' she said bitterly. 'What sort of a subject is that? I'm just about sick to death of being told "Tittle tattle lost the battle" and "Kill that rumour—it's helping Hitler". You'd think there was a Nazi spy in every household, hiding under the kitchen table.'

'Never mind, queen. English is your best subject so I'm sure you'll be able to produce something really good. Miss Rogers said to hand all the work to her next time we're passing, so if you start writing at once I'll drop it off tomorrow on my way to work.'

'All right, Ma,' Debbie said. She reached for the pencil and flipped open her exercise book. 'By the way, old Mrs Finnigan said she'd found up some good stiff paper and a small tin of black gloss paint. She said we could paint the paper black and make blinds for the front parlour; the bedrooms, too, if we'd a mind. I wasn't sure whether you'd have managed to get proper material from somewhere so I didn't say we'd take it; what do you think?'

'If it weren't for the bleedin' blackout, I'd go round to the market right now and pay whatever she's asking,' Jess said fervently. 'But then I suppose the market is shut, which at least means she can't sell the stuff to anyone else. So if you'll go round tomorrow morning, as soon as we've finished breakfast . . . oh, and best get some drawing pins, or nails or something, to put the blinds up with when we've made 'em.'

Debbie was scribbling busily away, but she nodded abstractedly as her mother finished speaking. 'Yes, I'll do that,' she said. 'Then I'll call for Gwen and we can start searching the shops for bits and pieces which are in short supply. After all, Christmas is only a couple of months away and you'll be wanting to make your Christmas cake in plenty of time, I expect.'

Jess nodded, picked up her knitting and squinted anxiously at the pattern she was following. This had been issued by the government and was consequently standardised, but Jess, remembering Ken who had had large hands and feet, always added a few extra rows when making gloves and socks. 'Good girl. You're quite right about the Christmas cake, because once everyone begins to bake there won't be a currant or a sultana for miles and we'll be thanking heaven for dried eggs, I dare say.'

Debbie pulled a face. 'Why don't we keep a few chickens, Mam?' she asked eagerly. 'We've gorra decent sized backyard and the shed where I keep my bicycle could house a dozen or so hens easily. And I'd look after 'em, honest I would. I'd clean 'em out an'all that. I know you've never let me have a dog because you said it were another mouth

135

to feed and you didn't think I'd bother to exercise it when I came home late after working at Deakin's, but hens is different and one thing I do have is plenty of spare time.'

Debbie half expected her mother to scoff at the idea, but instead Jess agreed at once. 'Only you'll have to buy 'em and find out from whoever sells them to you what you'll need to rear 'em,' she said. 'You might get some advice from the Hudsons in Harebell Street. Mr Hudson used to keep hens and a pig on his allotment, so he'll know what you should do.'

Debbie agreed that she would consult Mr Hudson before parting with her money, and immediately after breakfast next morning she rushed to Paddy's Market to get the stiff paper and the black paint from Mrs Finnigan, returned to the house with her booty, and then went round to Harebell Street.

When Mrs Hudson led Debbie into the kitchen, Mr Hudson was trying on a tin hat in front of the cracked piece of mirror on the mantelpiece, and he peered, toothlessly, at their visitor. 'I've joined the Local Defence Volunteers 'cos they say I'm too old for the forces,' he announced, grinning at her through the mirror. 'Hang on a minute whilst I put me teeth in.' There was a sharp chink and a crunch, which made Debbie wince, then the old man turned and grinned at her, his dentures gleaming. 'Oh, it's you, young Debbie. How's your mam? An' what can I do for you? Alfie from next door is doin' us messages if you're after a job.'

Debbie assured him that it was only information she was after and presently left the house with reams of advice still ringing in her ears. He had

136

suggested that she buy what he called 'in-lay' pullets, since such birds, though a deal more expensive than the day-old chicks she had thought to acquire, would start producing eggs very much sooner. He gave her the name of a farmer who would sell her such pullets, advised her what price to pay, and told her to buy a sack of meal since it came cheaper that way, a small amount of grain, and to add leftover food—cabbage leaves, potato peelings and such—to the meal, which must be mixed with hot water before being fed to her new charges.

By the time Jess came home that evening, the pullets were shut in the shed and Debbie, helped by Mick from down the road, had made them a run from a roll of wire netting and some pieces of wood which she had begged from a nearby timber yard. Debbie led her mother out to the shed and together they peered through the tiny window, though in truth they could see almost nothing of the interior. 'I bought some straw from the pet shop for the floor,' Debbie explained, following her mother back to the house, 'only Mick says poultry likes to perch so he's rigged up a couple of old yard brooms. They're wedged in the window frame one side and he's nailed them in place the other side.' She beamed up at her mother as they re-entered the kitchen. 'I told him he can have the first dozen eggs when the birds start laying,' she finished.

'You've done marvels,' Jess said, but her daughter thought she sounded absent-minded. 'Mind you, if I'd known you were going to buy quite elderly birds—I thought you were getting day-old chicks—then I don't know as how I'd have

137

said get a dozen.'

'Mam, I didn't get a dozen, I only got six,' Debbie said, feeling hurt. 'And I did what you telled me; I went round to the Hudsons' to get advice and Mr Hudson said not to buy day-olds. And when I'd got 'em I could see at a glance that they wouldn't settle down inside the shed but needed more space. Then Mick came round to see if I'd like to go down the Scottie to the market and he saw the hens—pullets, I mean—and said what they needed was a run. I dare say you couldn't see much in the dark but he helped me make it, and it's pretty strong, honest to God. He says it won't only keep the hens in, it'll keep cats and such out, so you see, between us we've thought of everything. I bought a sack of meal and some grain but I couldn't leave them in the shed so they're in the boot cupboard under the sink.'

'That's fine; you've done very well,' Jess said, but Debbie thought again that her mind was not on the pullets. 'Queen, the Fletcher cousins have given me notice, both of them. They're going to be land girls . . . they made enquiries after an uncle told them that he was looking for girls to replace the farmhands who have joined up. They go at the end of the week.'

'Gosh!' Debbie said blankly. She liked all four of their lodgers and had not even considered that the girls might want to leave. 'What about Barker and Pennymore? But I suppose they'll stick to what they know 'cos they're a lot older than the cousins.'

'I expect you're right,' Jess said. 'I suppose I ought to advertise their room but I don't think there's much point. With so many parents either

138

being evacuated with their children or simply having their children's rooms free, it might be really hard to find lodgers, and we can manage pretty well now that my job is so much better paid.'

'And I'll be able to get a job when I leave school, maybe in one of the big factories out at Long Lane,' Debbie said eagerly. 'It'll seem strange without the Fletchers at first, but I'm sure we'll manage.'

*   *   *

By the time spring arrived, however, the Ryans were the only occupants of the house in Wykeham Street. Barker and Pennymore had joined the Queen Alexandra's Nursing Service and gone off to Southampton to nurse wounded sailors, and though Jess had asked around at the hospital for potential lodgers they were actually short of staff and had rooms to spare in the nurses' home. However, Debbie now had a job in a large factory, assembling wireless parts, and although she and Jess would be glad of the extra rent money should a lodger come their way, they could manage very well on their joint earnings.

One sunny morning in early May, while mother and daughter sat in the kitchen eating toast before leaving for work, Jess cocked her head at a sound from the hall. 'Have you nearly finished, queen? Only I reckon that was the post.'

Debbie crammed the last piece of toast into her mouth, jumped to her feet and hurried down the hallway. Sure enough, there were letters on the mat. She scooped them up and returned to the kitchen, remarking as she did so: 'One is a government thing, probably telling you they're going to ration something else, then there's one from Nancy . . .' she fingered the envelope thoughtfully, 'not a very thick one this time, it only feels like one sheet. And the last one . . . well, I don't know who it's from, but it's ordinary handwriting, not typewritten.'

Jess took the letters eagerly, opening the government one first. It proved to be a gas bill. The letter from Nancy was quite short and she read it aloud to her daughter.

Dear Jess,

I fear you are having a horrid time of it back in dear old England. I told you in my last letter that my eldest son has joined the Royal Air Force and has gone to South Africa to learn to fly war planes—he can already fly the other sort, which has gone a long way to getting him accepted, I imagine. We are all well and wish we could help but there is little we can do, being so far away. I am knitting for victory and buying war bonds, but that is about it. Dear Andy would love to join up but, thank God, they will not accept him; too old, and besides, he's needed here. As you know, Clive moved to work on another station after his marriage, and with my eldest boy gone all the hard work lands on Andy.

I've told Pete that if he ever gets to England he must look you up, so if a strange young man comes calling, I know you'll make him welcome.

Take care of yourself, my dear, and of your little girl.

140

Much love,
Nancy

Debbie gave a derisive snort as her mother laid the letter down on the table. 'Little girl! Who does she think she's calling a little girl?' she demanded. 'Doesn't she know I'm a working woman, bringing in a proper wage? How old is that Pete, anyway?'

Jess laughed. 'It seems like only yesterday that I was writing to congratulate Nancy on his birth,' she admitted. 'I expect it's the same for her. I sent her a photograph when you started school but that was . . . goodness, nearly ten years ago! And now let's read the last letter.'

She slit open the envelope, pulled out the single closely written sheet it contained and began to read. After a moment, Debbie said impatiently: 'Well, go on, Mam, who's this one from, eh? Looks like there's a deal more information than your pal Nancy saw fit to purron paper.'

'It's from your Uncle Max,' Jess said joyfully. 'Well, he isn't your uncle really because he's my cousin, not my brother, but we were always close, me and Max.' She sighed, patting the letter affect ionately. 'He's ten years older than me but he was awful good with us children, never grudged spending a bit of money to give us a treat, went out of his way to walk us up to school or give us a ride on the ferry. Why, the very first time I went to New Brighton was with Max. I thought the world of him.'

'Why have you never mentioned him before?' Debbie asked, surprised. 'It sounds as though you thought the sun shone out of him, Mam. Did something happen to him?'

141

'His wife ran off with a sailor after they'd been married half a dozen years, and has never been heard of since, as far as I know,' Jess explained. 'After she left we hardly saw Max any more—I think he were ashamed, felt he'd brought disgrace on the family. He moved down to London, and this is the first time I've heard from him since before you were born, though I've tried to get in touch with him once or twice. I remember I wrote to him when I started working at the Stanley—that must be how he got this address.'

'So why's he writing now?' Debbie asked. 'I s'pose he wants something. You say men are only nice when they want something.'

Jess had turned the page over and was reading the rest of the letter. She finished it and, after a moment's hesitation, handed it to her daughter. 'You're right in a way,' she admitted. 'He's too old to join the armed forces, of course, but he's in some rather important job with the Ministry of Supply. He's been working in London but his whole department is being moved to Liverpool. He says he'll be given a generous lodging allowance, and since he'd rather family benefited than strangers he wonders if we could offer him accommodation.'

'Well, you won't have him, of course,' Debbie said, with a wicked glint in her eyes. 'I know how you've always refused to consider a male lodger, so obviously you'll have to turn him down. After all, you've always said one's principles . . .' She had been scanning the letter as she spoke and now she broke off, giving a low whistle. 'Gosh, Mam, it's a huge amount of money to turn down. What'll you do?'

'I'll write straight away and say he'll be very welcome,' Jess said, plucking her coat and hat from the peg on the back of the door. 'After all, he is family; it's not as if he were a complete stranger. And I know you'll like him.' She glanced up at the mantelpiece as she spoke and gave a muffled shriek. 'Heavens! Look at the time! You're going to have to run like a rabbit if you mean to catch your tram!'

*   *   *

Debbie enjoyed her work in the factory for she was neat fingered and quick, which meant she was popular with other workers and supervisors alike. At first, she had found the long hours of standing at her bench trying, and suffered from backache and cramp in her legs and feet. But gradually she learned to move her feet gently as she worked and to take every opportunity to sit down. Then she was moved from simple assembly to the more complicated job of fitting together tiny parts, and for this she was perched on a high stool under a strong light and was soon so accustomed to the task that she could talk and laugh and listen to the wireless set playing music and comedy shows without stopping her work for a moment.

When she had gone for the interview, Gwen had accompanied her, equally eager for a job. Fortunately, both girls had been diligent pupils at the Daisy Street school and had been given excellent references by the teaching staff, so the factory management had had no hesitation in employing them for a trial period, at the end of which both girls were confirmed in their new jobs.

143

So Debbie and Gwen caught the same tram each morning, sat side by side at the long bench, and ate their sandwiches perched on the wall which fronted the factory building. The older members of staff preferred to stay in the workers' rest room, but unless it was wet the younger ones usually congregated on the wall, chattering like sparrows, and commenting on any man who had the temerity to walk past.

Right now, however, Debbie glanced up at the big clock at the end of the room, and even as she did so the hooter went signalling the end of their shift. Debbie knew that in other departments girls would simply turn away from the benches and rush to get their coats. But here, in Assembly, that would never do. She finished the delicate task upon which she had embarked and sat back to watch Gwen doing the same. Then the two girls turned in the direction of the cloakroom, not hurrying because they had learned, from bitter experience, that the scrum at the tram stop did not begin to ease until shift end was ten or fifteen minutes distant.

'You doing anything nice this evening, queen?' Gwen asked, as the two girls stood at adjacent basins, thoroughly washing their hands, for the work made their fingers greasy and grease was fatally easy to overlook until you saw the marks on your only winter coat.

'No, not that I know of; it's up to me mam, really,' Debbie said. 'Life's a lot easier at home, now there's only Mam and me and no lodgers. But Mam's gone into spring cleaning mode now because her cousin Max has written to say he'll be with us in a couple of days. Mam was ever so keen on him when she were a kid, and from the fuss she's making you'd think he were the King of England. It's scrub the kitchen floor, help me to lay a new roll of lino in the big spare room, iron them pillow cases, run out and buy a white tablecloth 'cos she don't want Uncle Max sitting down to our old gingham one. Why? Gorrany ideas?'

'I thought we might see a flick,' Gwen said, rather wistfully. 'There's a good one on at the Commodore.' As she spoke, they emerged from the factory building into the soft May sunshine and saw a tram trundling towards them. Gwen gave a squeak. 'Quick, queen, if we run . . .'

Breathlessly, the two girls charged up the road and leapt on to the tram just as it began to move off. The conductor shouted at them but he was trapped at the far end of the vehicle by the sheer number of passengers, and by the time they reached their stop he had forgotten their abrupt arrival and merely took their fares. The girls got off the tram, and as they did so Gwen pointed at a fly sheet. 'Look at that!' she said. 'Who's Churchill, anyway?'

Debbie followed the direction of her friend's pointing finger: *Chamberlain resigns, Churchill to form new Gov't.*

Debbie gasped. Ever since the war had started, she and her mother had made a point of listening to the news broadcasts on their small wireless set, so she was familiar with both Churchill's name and his reputation. 'I'd best get a paper,' she said excitedly. 'It's wonderful news, Gwen. Everyone's been saying for weeks and weeks that Chamberlain's too old and weak to govern a

145

country at war, but Mr Churchill's just grand.' As she spoke, she was proffering her pennies and taking a paper from the newsvendor.

Gwen, who could have told you the exact amount of butter, sugar and bacon one was allowed per ration book, but had far less interest in the running of the country than her friend, craned her neck to read the headlines. 'What's a coalition?' she asked. 'And what difference will it make, anyhow? I don't reckon it'll affect us.'

Debbie sighed. She knew that the Soames family did not possess a wireless set, so Gwen's ignorance was understandable, but she did not feel up to lecturing her on current affairs just now. 'Come home wi' me and we'll listen to the six o'clock news,' she suggested. 'And if we do decide to go to the flicks, then you can jolly well pay attention during the Pathé News instead of chattering the way you usually do. Honestly, Gwen, this war will affect us whichever way it goes, so it's time we both took an interest.'

When they burst into the kitchen, Debbie waving the newspaper, Jess's enthusiastic interest quite made up for Gwen's ignorance. 'Churchill's a great man and he understands the Nazis in a way poor Mr Chamberlain never did,' she informed the two girls. 'He was a reporter in the Boer War, so he knows a thing or two, and he started warning the country that Hitler was a dangerous maniac years ago, only no one would listen. Now he's been proved right and he'll lead us to victory, you see if he doesn't.' Jess turned and smiled at Gwen. 'Are you going to stay to tea, chuck? I made a sausagemeat pie and there's a treacle sponge for afters.'

'Thank you, Mrs Ryan, that 'ud be grand,' Gwen said gratefully. 'We thought we might go to a flick later, if that's all right by you.'

'A good idea; if you're going to the Commodore then I think I'll come with you,' Jess said, to her daughter's surprise. 'I expect Debbie's told you that her Uncle Max is moving in the day after tomorrow, so I guess I shan't have much time for trips to the cinema after that.' She smiled reminiscently. 'I shall have to start cooking big meals again—men eat much more than women— and he'll probably expect me to be home of an evening until he begins to make friends of his own.'

Debbie stared at her mother. 'But lodgers never stopped you from having a trip to the cinema or a bus ride out into the country before,' she observed. 'Why should things be different just because it's Uncle Max? I should have thought things would be easier since he's a relative an' all.'

She was watching her mother's face as she spoke and saw a tide of pink creep up her cheeks. 'Things will be easier once Uncle Max settles in,' Jess said, rather defensively. 'But remember, queen, there was no rationing before the war. Now, putting a decent meal on the table takes a lot of work. So many things simply aren't available even though they're not rationed yet. Now be a good girl and lay the table while I check that the pie is cooked.'

The three of them bustled around, Gwen pouring large mugs of tea, whilst Debbie laid the table and Jess dished up. They listened attentively to the six o'clock news as they ate, and when they had all finished Jess glanced at the clock. 'We'd best get a move on if we're not to miss the beginning of the big film,' she said. 'Only another

147

couple of days and Max will be here and then, Debbie, you'll see for yourself why I'm so anxious to make my cousin feel at home. I'm sure you'll love him as much as I do.'

*   *   *

Debbie had not quite known whether to look forward to Uncle Max's arrival or to dread it, since her mother was making such a fuss, but she did expect to like this new relative since her mother thought so highly of him. He arrived at teatime on the day appointed and Debbie let him in. They greeted each other warily and then he followed her into the kitchen carrying a very large suitcase in one hand and a very small bunch of flowers in the other. He was a tall, heavily built man, with a mop of light brown hair, rather small blue eyes and a mouth partly hidden by a large, drooping moustache. He entered, crashed the suitcase on to the kitchen tiles, dropped the flowers on the draining board, and crossed the room in a couple of strides to take Jess in his arms and plonk a smacking kiss on her flushed cheek. 'Hello, 'ello, 'ello, if it ain't my pretty little cousin grown into a beautiful woman!' he shouted boisterously. 'Eh, the old town ain't changed a dot since I were last here. Same old trams, same old buildings, same old folk throngin' the streets. I dunno what I expected but I'm glad it's the same—makes me feel at home like.' He stopped hugging Jess and beamed, broadly, at Debbie, showing a great many sparklingly white teeth. 'And this is your little girl who just let me in—only she ain't so little.' He held out a large red hand. 'I was going to pick you up

148

and give you a kiss but now I see you're a young lady and won't fancy being treated like a child, so what say we shake hands and make friends, eh?'

Debbie, who had felt her hackles rising when Uncle Max grabbed her mother, held out her own hand, saying rather stiffly as his huge palm engulfed it: 'How do you do, Uncle Max? I hope you had a pleasant journey . . .'

The big man laughed heartily. 'You call me Max, young lady,' he said, pumping her hand up and down with great energy. 'I ain't your uncle and there's no point in usin' two words when one will do. I'm just plain old Max, and though my work will keep me pretty busy I mean to see that you and your mam have some fun.' Debbie began to say that she and her mother had fun anyway, but Jess cut across her words.

'I'm sure you will and it will be wonderful to have you living here,' she said breathlessly. 'But at the minute you must be hungry as a hunter, so take off your coat and sit down. I'm afraid it's only meat and potato pie, but as you know, rationing has made things difficult. Or would you rather see your room first?'

'I'd best do that and get some of the grime of me journey off,' the big man said, picking up his suitcase and heading for the stairs. 'No need for you to come up; just tell me which door to open.'

Jess, however, shook her head chidingly at him. 'Don't be so silly, Max. I'll bring a jug of hot water up and show you to your room. Then when you've washed, you can come down and have a meal.'

Max consented to wait and Jess poured hot water from the kettle into an enamel jug and followed him out of the room, leaving Debbie

149

sitting at the table and staring resentfully at the closed kitchen door. Far from liking the newcomer, she found everything about him objectionable: his size, his loud voice, his whole attitude. He had scarcely been in the kitchen five minutes, but in that time he had contrived to intimate that she and her mother were a dreary couple whose lives would be brightened up by his mere presence. Debbie sighed and picked up her knitting. Her mother had abandoned her work but Debbie saw no reason why she should do likewise. She decided that after they had eaten she would go straight round to Gwen's house, where she knew her friend would be simply longing to hear what their new lodger was really like.

However, this intention was foiled by her mother's speedy return to the kitchen. She was pink-faced and smiling and clearly assumed that Debbie shared her own enthusiasm for the newcomer. 'Isn't he nice, queen?' she hissed. 'Of course he's changed, but he's still a real breath of fresh air, full of fun and jokes. We shan't be dull for one moment with Max in the house.'

'We shan't be able to hear ourselves think for a start, because he's got a voice like a foghorn,' Debbie muttered. Aloud, she said: 'How long's he going to stay for, Mam?'

If Jess had heard the first part of her daughter's remark she gave no sign, merely turning away from the stove and raising her eyebrows. 'How long? Well, for as long as the war lasts, I suppose. He's doing important work. He wouldn't tell me much about it because it's very hush-hush, as they say nowadays, but I don't imagine they'll move him again.'

150

Debbie would have liked to say that people who put two and two together often made five, but she did not want to upset Jess and told herself, philosophically, that her mother would soon begin to realise that, however delightful Max had been thirty-odd years before, he was now noisy and self-opinionated; definitely not the ideal lodger. But she realised that the less she said the better, and closed her lips firmly over the critical remarks she longed to make. Instead, she said: 'Oh, I see. Will it be all right if I go round to Gwen's when we've finished supper, Mam? Only I want to tell her that Uncle Max has arrived.'

'Don't you think it's rather rude to Max to go off out on his very first evening here?' Jess asked. 'I don't want him to feel that he's not welcome as a member of the family.'

Debbie sighed but capitulated; she had guessed how it would be, for her mother was a stickler for good manners, and though she herself might not care for Max good manners decreed that she should remain at least until the washing and wiping up was done. After that, however, she saw no reason why she should not go round to Gwen's.

In a remarkably short time, Max joined them in the kitchen once more. He had changed out of his navy blue suit and now wore an open-necked shirt and flannels, with a pair of old carpet slippers on his feet. Debbie's heart gave a jolt of dismay as she took in the slippers, for no one donned slippers in another person's house. They were a sign, so far as she was concerned, that the wretched man was here to stay—or thought he was. But when Mam realises how he's changed, I'm sure she'll ask him to move on, Debbie told herself, though with

151

waning confidence. Think of Mr Bottomley; we got rid of him though it took some doing.

'Here we are, here we are, here we are again,' Max carolled, taking his place at the head of the table and thus fuelling Debbie's resentment a little more. 'Bring on the meat and potato pie; it'll be the first time I've eaten anything cooked by me baby cousin Jessie.'

Debbie looked hopefully across at her mother. If there was one thing Jess hated, it was being called Jessie. But there was no outburst; Jess merely put a large plateful of food in front of Max and then slid a tiny piece of pie on to her daughter's plate and another small piece on to her own. She gave Debbie a significant look which Debbie had no trouble in interpreting. It meant: *Eat slowly to keep our guest company and I'll do the same.*

The pie was delicious and Debbie began to eat it slowly, as she had been bidden, but it turned out there was no need. Max crammed his capacious mouth so full that he was soon wiping a piece of bread round his empty plate and saying, with a satisfied sigh: 'Well, now, that were a bit of awright, it were. Any more where that come from?'

Jess looked astonished, as well she might, Debbie considered, for, what with rationing and shortages, second helpings had become a thing of the past, but Max's huge frame obviously needed more fuel than most and Jess dished up the last slice of pie and the last three potatoes, explaining that since there was a treacle pudding to follow she had not perhaps heaped his plate as she would otherwise have done. Max nodded, but his mouth was already too full to reply, and presently Debbie had to watch as two-thirds of the treacle pudding was placed before their guest, whilst the remainder was divided between herself and her mother. Max made short work of the pudding as well, then drank two mugs of tea whilst Jess and her daughter cleared the table, washed and wiped up the crocks, shook the tablecloth outside the back door, and started to make preparations for next day's breakfast.

'Debbie and myself have to be in work early— Debbie starts at eight and I have to be in the shop by half past,' Jess explained, almost apologetically. 'We don't have a big breakfast during the week, just porridge and toast, and we usually save our bacon ration so that we can have egg and bacon pie as a main meal. But we keep hens, which makes things easier. If you leave the house after us—and I imagine you will since you're in an office job— then I'm afraid neither of us will be here to cook your breakfast. But I'll leave the porridge pan on the back of the stove and I dare say you can make yourself a cup of tea?'

'Aye, I can manage that,' Max said. 'I'm usually in work by nine. But wharrabout hot water for washing?'

'Oh, one of us will bring you up a jugful before we leave,' Jess said at once. 'Now, is there anything else? Only Debbie wants to nip round to her friend Gwen's house, and we're never late to bed on a weekday because we're early risers. Do you fancy a stroll round the neighbourhood, Max? Oh, and I'll be needing your ration book.'

Max immediately dug into his trouser pocket and produced the small beige book which was so important to everyone these days. 'There you are, queen,' he said, flinging it down on the table. 'Aye, I'd like a stroll before I go to me bed. You can point out the best pubs and the best shops and so on; and it 'ud be useful to know where you work, just in case I need to gerrin touch with you during the day.' He turned to Debbie. 'Why don't you come wi' us, lass? I know you ain't at school no more, but I seem to remember there were a school in these parts. You might like to point it out to me.'

'Mam will show you everything,' Debbie said immediately. She unslung her mother's coat from the kitchen door and helped the older woman into it. Then the three of them made for the back door and Debbie, hurrying across the yard, called over her shoulder: 'Enjoy your walk!' feeling like an escaping prisoner as she did so.

Gwen greeted Debbie eagerly when she came to the door. 'Has he come?' she demanded. 'What's he look like? He's your mam's cousin, ain't he? My mam says some o' that family had bright ginger hair, but she couldn't remember whether Max did.'

'No, it's light brown with a bit of grey at the temples,' Debbie said. 'I won't describe him because you're bound to meet him soon enough. Come to that, you can't miss him; he's the size of a perishin' house and he makes so much noise that you can't think straight while he's talking.' She peered past her friend and saw that the kitchen was, as usual, crowded with the younger members of the family, all of whom had been evacuated the previous September but, in the absence of bombings of major cities, invasions of paratroopers dressed as nuns, or battles on the beaches, had returned in time for Christmas. Hastily, she jerked her head towards the back gate. 'We can't talk in

154

there. You know what kids is like for repeating your every word just when it does most harm,' she whispered. 'Let's go for a walk; if we go down by the docks, we ain't likely to run into Mam and Max.'

'No, we could go on the overhead railway, then we can take a look at the shipping as we're going past,' Gwen said. 'It's always really interesting to see what's come in. We can get off at the Pier Head and take a look at the ferries before coming back home.'

Debbie agreed enthusiastically, for she had always enjoyed a trip on the overhead railway. It was not expensive and it was interesting. 'Good idea,' she said approvingly. 'And we aren't likely to meet Mam and Max down there; he wants to be shown the best pubs and shops and that.'

They had crossed the yard and were walking along the jigger towards Commercial Road, but at these words Gwen stopped short, her eyes rounding. 'But how would your mam know anything about the pubs?' she asked. 'I don't reckon she's so much as stepped inside one, lerralone had a drink.'

'No; well, but men—most men—go to the pub of an evening,' Debbie said fair-mindedly. She had heard her mother complaining that it was the drink that filled Casualty on a Saturday night, but she did not want Gwen thinking that her relative was a hard drinking man. Indeed, she had no reason to suspect that he was. Men who worked in hush-hush jobs, jobs which paid excellent money, were scarcely likely to be heavy drinkers.

The two girls crossed Commercial Road and headed for Huskisson Dock station, threading through the narrow streets until they reached their destination. Debbie gave her friend a blow by blow account of Max's arrival and consequent behaviour, but Gwen refused to believe that Jess could like someone who sounded so unpleasant.

'Mebbe he's just shy so he talks loud to pretend he's at his ease,' she said, as they climbed aboard the train and settled themselves on the comfortable leatherette seats, realising that they had entered a first class carriage by mistake, but deciding to remain there until they were turfed out, for the train was half empty. If it had been the rush hour it might have been different, but with so few passengers Debbie thought the guard was unlikely to come along checking tickets, so she and Gwen sank back in their seats to enjoy both the view and a good gossip.

At the Pier Head, the girls descended from the train and went and had a cup of tea at a nearby refreshment room, and Gwen gave her friend what was probably excellent advice. 'You took agin that Max of yours because he gave your mother a great big hug and a kiss, and because he shouted a bit, but you didn't take into account the fact that he were probably shy and a bit ill at ease,' she observed. 'You don't want to make quick decisions about folk, queen, because it's always a mistake. Remember how you hated Mr Gladstone when you were first moved up into his class? But after a few weeks, he were pretty well your favourite teacher. You've gorra give this Max a chance for your mam's sake, because it sounds to me as though she's mortal fond of him.' She gazed, shrewdly, at her friend. 'Suppose your mam married again? Cousins can marry, you know, and you say she

156

always liked him. If you've decided to hate him, it 'ud be a poor outlook for you.'

'*Marry?* Why, Mam would never marry anyone again, no matter what,' Debbie said, trying to sound shocked though it was her secret fear. 'Besides, she's not met him for years. They're strangers, just about.' She turned angrily on her friend. 'Gwen Soames, you've—you've got a really horrible, evil mind; as if my mam would look twice at any man after living with me dad. You didn't know him, but he were—oh, just wonderful! He were kind and loving and he thought Mam was the most beautiful person in the world; he would have done anything for her, I'm telling you. What's more, his voice was soft and gentle, and though Mam said he were a wonderful driver he never boasted or told us how good he was. No, there's lots of things I do worry about, but Mam marrying again isn't one of them.'

'All right, all right,' Gwen said soothingly, clearly taken aback by her friend's outburst. 'I'm sure your dad were one of the best, same as my dad, and neither of our mams would dream of marrying again. But for your own sake, queen, give old Max a chance. It don't do to make snap decisions, particularly when you're sharin' a house with someone. Tell you what, I'll come round to your place tomorrow after work—get your mam to invite me for tea—then I can see for meself.'

Debbie agreed to this, and presently the two of them boarded the train whose destination board read 'Seaforth Sands', well content with their evening.

'I really love the overhead railway, especially now that the docks are so crowded,' Debbie said contentedly as they got down once more at Huskisson Dock station and headed for home. 'It was a grand idea of yours to use the Dockers' Umbrella, because now I've shared my feelings I don't feel nearly so cross. Tell you what, why don't we take the round trip all the way from Seaforth Sands to Dingle and back, next time we're at a loose end? It's only ninepence, a good deal cheaper than the flicks, and there's such a lot to see. I'm sure we didn't take half of it in because we were talking all the time, but if we do the round trip we'll both bag a window seat and take a good look at all the shipping and forget our troubles.'

'By the time we've saved up our pennies our troubles—or rather your troubles—may well have disappeared; you might even ask this Max to come with us,' Gwen said with a chuckle. 'No, don't shake your head and scowl at me. Wait and see, that's my motto.'

CHAPTER SIX

Despite her hopes Debbie continued to find Max objectionable, though she seemed to be the only one. Gwen and her mother both liked the large and generally cheerful man and Jess did not seem to mind his authoritative announcements on every aspect of the war; she simply said that he was in a position to know what he was talking about whereas she and Debbie could only repeat what they had read in the papers or heard on the wireless.

In early June, when the evacuation of troops of

the British Expeditionary Force, who had been fighting in France, was under way, the streets seemed to be full of gaunt, hollow-eyed young men with frightening stories to tell, though each and every one of them was pathetically grateful for the help given to them to get home, both by the little boats and by the ships of the Royal Navy. Any craft which was available to make the crossing had steamed across the Channel to 'bring our boys back' and along with everyone else Jess and Debbie had read of the graveyard of ships which had made it to the French coast only to be sunk by the Luftwaffe, sometimes with a full complement of rescued men, before they could even begin the voyage home.

Liverpool men had played their part in droves, many of them boys who had been at school with Debbie and Gwen. Both girls were distressed to realise that some of their old school mates had never come home again, and perhaps this made Max's attitude to the returning forces more difficult to swallow. He seemed to regard them as having failed in some way, but Debbie thought they had been let down by their continental allies. Max said they should have been forced to fight it out; Debbie thought this downright ridiculous. She had helped the WVS distribute tea and sandwiches to the men getting off the trains at Lime Street station, and they had talked of the immeasurably strong and well-armed forces ranged against them and of the German air supremacy. 'Retreat's always hard but it was the only thing to do and it's a bloody miracle so many of us got back,' a young officer had told Debbie. 'You see, it's given us a chance to prove ourselves. We can re-form, re-arm

159

and retrain, and God knows we can do with retraining and with something a bit more modern than the weapons we were issued with. Then, maybe, we'll teach the Jerries a thing or two.'

But Uncle Max had not agreed. Despite his wish to be called 'Max' Debbie had decided that she would stick to 'Uncle' and for once her mother not only agreed with her, but had backed her up. 'Debbie's over thirty years younger than you, Max, and it's disrespectful for her to use your Christian name,' she had said gently. 'I would much prefer that she continued to call you Uncle; it's what I've always taught her to do anyway.'

So Uncle Max he remained, though this did not make him one whit more acceptable to Debbie. She was furious when she had heard him telling Jess that invasion was now a certainty and advising her mother to start storing supplies bought on the black market, since when the Germans landed, as he believed they would, everything, even ration food, would be fought over in the streets.

'That's defeatist talk, Uncle Max; you sound like Lord Haw-Haw,' Debbie had said coldly. 'Didn't you listen to Mr Churchill the other night?' She had lowered her voice to a growly imitation of the Prime Minister's: '. . . *we shall fight on the beaches, we shall fight on the landing grounds, we shall fight in the fields and in the streets, we shall fight in the hills; we shall never surrender* . . . Oh, I know he was talking about the possibility of invasion, but he made it pretty clear that if such a thing happened it would fail, because we would resist.'

For once, Uncle Max had looked taken aback, even a trifle ashamed. The three of them had been sitting in the kitchen at the time, having just

160

finished a meal, waiting for the kettle to boil. Uncle Max had shifted uneasily in his chair and stared, rather fixedly, down at his feet. 'Out o' the mouths of babes and sucklings,' he had quoted, almost quietly. 'You're right, queen, mebbe I shouldn't have said it. But you know, I'm worried for your mam . . . concerned for her, that is to say. I can't bear to think of her—and yourself of course—going hungry when a little forethought could prevent it.'

Receiving a glare from her mother, Debbie had not pointed out that, since Uncle Max devoured three times the amount she and her mother ate between them, it must be fear of going short himself which had led him to advise black market purchasing. Instead, she had said: 'Sorry, Uncle Max. Ah, the kettle's boiling. I'll make the tea.'

When August arrived and they were told in every wireless bulletin and all the headlines that the Battle of Britain was being fought daily in the skies across southern England, invasion still had not happened, and far from worrying over the possibility that the man queueing for the telephone box behind you might be a Nazi spy, folk began to relax.

One Friday evening Gwen and Debbie were strolling along in the hot sunshine, planning a trip into the country the following day. 'There are plums for sale in the markets, so I bet, if we catch the ferry, and then get a bus into the real country, the farmers might let us pick some for a few pence,' Gwen said enthusiastically. 'We could take a picnic; and what do you say if I bring the kids along? It 'ud be a real treat for them and they's good at fruit picking; remember all them

161

strawberries we picked up just after Dunkirk? Me mam bought sugar from everyone who was prepared to sell and made jars and jars of strawberry jam. She had to beg the jars from everyone, mind, but she sold the jam at a real good profit.'

'I'd love a day in the country, if the weather holds. In the old days, Mam would have come along with us—she's the quickest fruit picker I ever saw—but now I doubt she'd leave Uncle Max on a Sat'day, when he's home. Still, it 'ud get me out of their way, which will probably please them as much as it will please me,' Debbie said.

'Your Uncle Max might come along as well,' Gwen said brightly. 'Last time he saw us playing with the kids in the Kirkdale rec, he gave us a bag of bulls-eyes—remember?'

'Yes, I remember,' Debbie said wearily. She could not deny that Uncle Max flashed his money around and was generous with such things as sweets and cakes. But she did not intend to say so to Gwen. 'Did you ever wonder where he got them bulls-eyes from?' she asked truculently. 'I bet he bought them on the black market.'

'Who cares?' Gwen said airily. 'Besides, if he's got the money why shouldn't he spend it on bulls-eyes for kids? It's all very well for you, Debbie Ryan, but you're an only child. Why, your mam bought three jars of my mam's strawberry jam—three whole jars! Us Soameses only had one jar between the lot of us.'

'Sorry, sorry, sorry,' Debbie said repentantly. She flipped open the lid of her gas mask case, rooted around for a moment, and then produced two boiled sweets and a small lipstick. She handed

162

one of the sweets and the lipstick to her friend. 'Here, you poor, hard-done-by creature, have a lipstick. I went into Woolies yesterday and Patty Ross—remember her, she were in our class at school—slipped me this when no one were looking. She said it were the last one so I took it for you 'cos I've still got a good half of mine left.'

Gwen had been looking rather cross but as she took the lipstick her face lit up, for make-up was almost impossible to obtain. 'Oh, Debbie, are you sure?' she breathed. 'I do love a bit of make-up, particularly lipstick. Mam rubs geranium petals on her cheeks instead of rouge and I know she uses lamp-black on her eyelashes when she goes to a dance, but all you can do for lipstick is to keep biting your lips to make them red, and that's painful work.'

'Lamp-black? But don't it come off all over her face if she rubs her eyes?' Debbie asked curiously. Her own mother occasionally powdered her nose but seemed to manage very well without other aids to beauty. 'And suppose her eyes water, or she cries? And if she got some in her eye, the pain must be awful.'

Gwen giggled. 'That's probably why she don't go out very often,' she said wisely. 'In fact, she only goes when her sister—that's me Aunt Minnie—asks her along. Minnie isn't married but she don't like going to dances by herself so she gets Mam to go with her for company, like.'

'Oh, right,' Debbie said, rather awkwardly. Uncle Max sometimes took her mother dancing at the Rialto or the Daulby Hall and Jess had made biting comments about middle-aged women who went to dances to try to meet men. Debbie had

163

looked at her with astonishment; did her mother not realise that she herself was a middle-aged woman? The fact that she was with Uncle Max would not be common knowledge to others at the dance who might well think that Jess, too, was hunting for a man. After all, no one would think a woman would voluntarily take up with hulking Max Williams if they could meet anyone else.

'If the weather does change and we have rain, what say we take the kids to the Saturday Rush at the Broadway?' Gwen suggested. 'They're showing a Tarzan film with Johnny Weissmuller, I think. I know we'd have to do the messages in the afternoon but at least it 'ud keep the kids from under my mam's feet for an hour or two.'

Debbie thought this a good idea, though looking up at the brilliant blue of the sky she found it difficult to even imagine a rainy day. At this point, the two girls said their goodbyes and Gwen turned down Daisy Street whilst Debbie continued on her way. When she reached her back yard, she walked over to the hen run. The scrawny pullets of almost a year before were now fat hens and highly regarded by Debbie and Jess since they provided eggs regularly, and always rushed to the wire making hopeful clucking sounds whenever a human being approached. Now, Debbie ferreted in her coat pocket and produced a handful of crusts from the sandwiches her mother had made for her carry-out. She did not just throw them into the run but fed them to each hen separately, poking the pieces of crust through the wire and talking to the hens as though they understood every word. 'A piece for you, Blackie, now a piece for you, Goldie, now one for you, Speckles, another for Henny

Penny, and one for Snowy . . . it's all right, Fluff, I've not forgotten you, and kindly don't take my fingers off in your eagerness.' The hens continued to look hopefully at Debbie as she stood up and turned towards the house. Her mother had warned against making pets of the birds, saying that when they ceased to lay they would have to be somebody's Sunday dinner, but Debbie had been unable to resist naming them. Once they were named, though, she realised it would be difficult, if not impossible, to even consider making a meal of them.

'Debbie!' Debbie turned her head and saw Jess framed in the kitchen doorway. 'Why are you always late on a Friday? Or perhaps you aren't, and it's just that Friday is my night out so I try to get back that bit earlier. Stop spoiling the hens and come along in, do. Uncle Max means to take both of us out tonight. There's a concert in the park, so hurry.'

Debbie entered the kitchen, shrugging off her jacket. 'But Friday isn't *my* night out,' she reminded her mother, 'and I don't want to go to a concert; not if Uncle Max is going, at any rate.'

'Hush,' Jess said nervously, glancing round as though she suspected that her cousin was hiding beneath the kitchen table or behind the pantry door. 'You really are rude, queen, and I simply can't understand it. Why do you dislike Uncle Max so much? He's awful kind to both of us, but probably to you more than me. He's always slipping you the odd bob so you can go to the cinema or have a ride on the overhead railway. He brings you back little treats and if there's anything amusing going on he makes sure you're not left

165

out.'

Debbie sniffed. 'He's mortal fond of sweets himself,' she pointed out. 'He buys on the black market, so when he give me two ounces of aniseed balls or a stick of nougat he's not going short himself.'

'Debbie! That was a really nasty, spiteful remark,' Jess said reproachfully. 'Whatever *is* the matter with you? Don't say you're jealous of Uncle Max because you've no cause to be. I'm very, very fond of him but if you think it's anything but sisterly affection, you're wrong. I know folk gossip; that nasty old Mrs Shipham from down the road actually had the cheek to ask me when I were going to change my name back to Williams. Horrid old cat. I couldn't think what she meant at first, and when I realised she was hinting that I was going to marry Max, I was absolutely livid. I wiped the floor with her, I'm telling you. Why, I've known Max since I were two or three years old; he was always like a brother to me, which means that no matter how fond I am of him neither of us would dream of marrying the other.' She looked earnestly at her daughter, then took Debbie's hands in her own, shaking them slightly. 'Have you been listening to gossip, queen? Is that why you're so against poor Max? If so, I'm prepared to swear on the Bible that I don't mean to marry again, not anyone, least of all my cousin.'

'Well, I never thought you would,' Debbie said untruthfully. 'The trouble is that Uncle Max and me are totally different. We don't like each other . . .'

Jess broke in. 'That's not true, darling. Uncle Max loves you dearly; he'd do anything for you.

166

I'm afraid all the dislike is on your side.'

Debbie stared desperately at her mother. Should she tell her the truth? But if she did, it might make life impossible for all of them. She took a deep, steadying breath and said quietly: 'He—he crowds me, Mam. Maybe it's because he senses that I don't like him so he tries too hard. Couldn't you . . . well, couldn't you ask him to back off a little?'

'But I don't understand,' Jess said helplessly. 'You hardly ever come out with the two of us and you certainly don't go out with him by yourself. You're away from the house most weekends, and if you aren't, Max and I are. You usually manage to leave the table before your uncle has finished his pudding . . . I don't see what you mean.'

Debbie sighed. For some weeks, Uncle Max had been positively pursuing her. Oh, never in a manner so obvious that her mother would notice, but she felt he was pursuing her nevertheless. He lurked outside her bedroom door in the mornings in order to grab her and give her a quick cuddle, and lately he had taken to popping, unasked and unexpected, into her bedroom, crossing to the bedside and giving her a kiss on the forehead, or the cheek. This was always accompanied by his saying in a bluff voice: 'Night, night, sleep tight, let's hope the bugs don't bite,' as he let himself out of the room. 'See you at breakfast, queen.'

Once, he had caught her in the back yard when she had been shutting up the hens. He had come out ostensibly to visit the privy, but had seized the opportunity of putting a heavy arm about her waist and giving her a wet and slobbery kiss. If it had not been for her quick reaction in jerking away from

167

him, Debbie thought that the kiss would have landed on her mouth, and the mere suggestion of such a horrible fate sent cold shivers down her spine. Yet if she told her mother how her beloved cousin behaved, would she be believed? Everyone who knew Max seemed to like him, with the exception of herself; even Gwen liked him, but then Gwen wasn't being constantly ambushed since they did not live under the same roof. Oh, Gwen came in for the odd cuddle, the rough and tumble when he insisted upon playing relievio or blind man's buff with the youngsters, but Gwen took it in her stride. She thought Debbie was being over-sensitive, said that Uncle Max was an affectionate man who wanted children of his own, which was why he was so fond of the Soames kids. 'I suppose he thinks of you and me as children, even though we aren't, and that's why he likes to hug us and give us sweets and biscuits,' she had said wisely, when Debbie had complained about Uncle Max's habits of squeezing and cuddling. 'He don't mean no harm; I expect he thinks you like it.'

Debbie had opened her mouth to say scornfully: 'Like it? When he comes into my bedroom without so much as a knock, hoping to catch me in me knickers?' But somehow she could not bear to reveal, even to Gwen, the lengths to which Uncle Max had already gone in their relationship. She told herself she was not afraid of the dirty old man, would give him a good kick in the bread basket if he persisted in annoying her, but she was realising more and more that the situation was fraught with danger and was beginning to fear that, if she spoke out, she would not be believed. Jess really adored Uncle Max and would hesitate to believe any ill of

168

him. What was more, she was pretty certain Max would totally deny everything, say she was trying to make trouble, insinuate she was jealous of his warm friendship with Jess herself. And if she told Gwen, she was afraid her friend might either make light of it or insist that she tell Jess.

So now, standing in the kitchen with her mother's warm hands clasping her own, she decided that her best, her only course was to speak privately to Uncle Max. She would tell him that she was not a child but a young woman, and did not relish his trying to caress her. She would also buy a small bolt for her bedroom door, and if her mother demanded to be told the reason for this action she would say that now she was getting older she needed a bit more privacy. Having made her decision, Debbie smiled brightly at her mother and withdrew her hands. 'I'm glad you're not going to marry him, Mam, and it truly isn't jealousy; it's just that I don't like him, though I've tried to hide how I feel,' she said. 'As for tonight, I suppose I could come to the concert, only Gwen, meself and the kids are going into the country tomorrow to pick plums, leaving early in the morning, so I don't want to be out late tonight.'

'We won't be late, honest, queen,' her mother said coaxingly. 'Only after what Mrs Shipham said, I'd rather you came along. Max is the dearest feller and when I told him there was talk he just laughed and said "Women's gossip", but just for a while I'd prefer to stick to family outings. You'll do it for me, won't you?'

'Yes, of course,' Debbie said gloomily. 'Do you want to come plum picking with us, then? Only otherwise, I dare say Uncle Max will want to take you out tomorrow as well.'

Jess looked triumphant. 'No thanks, queen, my Saturday is already planned,' she assured her daughter. 'Apparently, Max has met an old friend, and he asked me if it would be all right to invite him to supper when they both come back from the football match. The Saturday girls will have to manage in the shop, because it will take me all morning to do my messages; then I'll have the afternoon to get the house into shape, and after that there'll be three of us here, not two, so you can stay out as long as you like.'

'Oh, that's marvellous,' Debbie said, very relieved. 'I've often wondered why he doesn't bring friends home. I wonder what this one's like?'

'If he's a friend of your uncle's, I'm sure he'll be delightful,' Jess said earnestly. 'Apparently, they were great pals in the old days and met up quite by chance, probably in a pub or the snooker hall, or somewhere like that. Now, what time do you think you'll be home tomorrow? Your uncle has managed to get hold of a very nice piece of pork which I'm going to roast; I wouldn't like you to miss out on that.'

'Nor me,' Debbie said fervently. 'I expect the younger kids will get tired by about four, so I'll make sure we're home by six. Then I can help you prepare the meal and we can use the fruit we've picked to make a plum pie to follow the pork.'

At this point, the back door burst open and Max surged into the room, an enormous beam almost splitting his face in two. 'Hello, 'ello, 'ello, ain't I a lucky feller to find me two favourite women eagerly awaiting me return from work?' he bellowed. 'Lookin' forward to the concert, are we?

170

And I dare say there'll be a nice little box of chocolates to eat during the interval.' He leered at Debbie. 'Give your mam a thrill and say you'll come with us,' he said. 'There's been a deal of foolish talk . . .'

'Yes, Debbie's coming with us,' Jess said hastily, as though secretly afraid that her daughter might change her mind. 'I'm afraid there's only blind scouse for supper tonight but I got some marrow bones from Short's, so the gravy will be really good.'

'Everything you cook is really good, sweetheart,' Max bawled, taking off his navy blazer and hanging it on the back of the kitchen door. 'I told me pal Herbert that he were invited back for a meal after the footie tomorrow, and he's delighted to accept. He's gorran old aunt what lives out Great Sutton way and he says next time she gives him a rabbit he'll skin it and joint it and bring it round so's you can make a rabbit pie.' He turned to Debbie. 'What do you think of that, eh? He's a generous feller, my friend Herbert.'

Debbie mumbled something and left the room, running up the stairs at top speed. She had had a brilliant thought. Until she bought a bolt for her door, she would wedge her bedroom chair under the handle. Uncle Max would have some explaining to do if the chair crumbled to matchwood beneath his violent onslaught.

*   *   *

On Saturday morning Debbie woke when somebody started rattling and banging on her bedroom door. Irritated, and still half asleep, she

171

shouted: 'Oh, come in, do!' before sitting up and seeing the chair still wedged under the door handle.

Guiltily, she jumped out of bed and ran across the room, pulling the chair hastily away from the door and opening it. Her mother came into the room carrying an enamel jug of hot water and put it down on the washstand. 'I dunno what was the matter with your door, but I couldn't seem to get the handle to work,' she said, rather crossly. 'And there was I, bringing up your hot water to save you having to come down for it since I thought you wanted to get a move on this morning.'

'Thanks, Mam,' Debbie said humbly. She picked up the jug of hot water and began to pour it into the round china bowl. 'What's the time? Me and Gwen and the kids, meant to catch an early tram down to the Pier Head and go across on the ferry . . . is it awful late? I don't mind missing me breakfast if it is, because I dare say you'll want to get off to work.'

Jess tutted. 'You've got a head like a sieve, queen! I told you yesterday that I'm not going in this morning. As for the time, it's not too late, barely seven o'clock. Now don't you forget you promised to be home by six.'

Debbie was so relieved that her mother had not enquired more closely into the reason for her door's jamming that she shot through her usual routine of washing and dressing and hurried downstairs. When she got to the kitchen, her breakfast porridge was already on the table, along with a neat pile of sandwiches wrapped in greaseproof paper, half a dozen boiled eggs and a wedge of her mother's famous carrot cake.

172

Delighted, Debbie flung her arms round Jess's neck and kissed her cheek. 'You're the best mother in the world, Mam,' she said fervently, sliding into her seat and beginning to demolish her porridge. 'Look, I'll be back as soon as I can to give you a hand, honest I will, and I'll bring back a grosh of plums and anything else we can buy cheap from the farms.'

*   *   *

Debbie was as good as her word. After a glorious day in the countryside, the young people made their way back home again with their canvas bags full of plums, carrots and onions, their faces and arms flushed from the sun and their stomachs comfortably full, for they had augmented their picnic with great golden gooseberries from some old bushes which the farmer's wife told them they might strip of the remainder of their fruit. They had paddled in the river, helped one farmer to load four squealing pigs into a small trailer, burrowed into a haystack when no one was looking and swung from the ropes tied high in a beech tree. Jess was delighted with the fruit and vegetables Debbie presented her with, and advised her daughter to hurry up to her room so that she might wash and change before their guest arrived. Debbie was only too happy to do as she was told for she had seen herself in the kitchen mirror, with hayseeds in her hair and a dust-smeared face, and did not want to make a bad impression, even though she could not imagine anyone nice being pally with Uncle Max. She was still upstairs, struggling into a clean gingham dress, when she

173

heard sounds of arrival, and then Uncle Max's great voice going on and on, occasionally interspersed with murmurs from her mother. By the time she reached the head of the stairs, she had decided that Herbert was either a very quiet man indeed, or a very noisy one whose voice was identical to that of Uncle Max. She entered the kitchen with some trepidation, then stopped short in the doorway, her eyes widening with a mixture of astonishment and horror. There was Uncle Max, sprawled in his usual chair, and opposite him, horror of horrors, sat Mr Bottomley. He was grinning from ear to ear but Debbie, quick to pick up an atmosphere, realised that he was not as comfortable as he was trying to appear and Uncle Max, though recounting at the top of his voice an event that had occurred at the match, kept darting puzzled looks, first at Jess and then at his friend Herbert.

Debbie could not help feeling a thrill of triumph. She had thought that any friend of Uncle Max's was bound to be horrid and now she had been proved right. Debbie knew full well that Jess had not only disliked Mr Bottomley, she had been a little bit afraid of him. Now, surely, she would have to admit that Uncle Max was not perfect—anything but perfect, in fact. Debbie hoped, fervently, that once a tiny seed of doubt had sprouted in her mother's mind it would lead to other doubts. Perhaps it might even make Jess realise that, as she had been wrong about Max's friend, so she might also be wrong about Max.

Uncle Max looked up as she entered the room; he also looked relieved, no doubt thinking that her arrival would dissipate the tension he had picked

174

up between his cousin and his friend. However, Debbie did not mean to miss such an opportunity. 'Hello, Mr Bottomley; so we meet again,' she said coolly. 'I never thought to see you sitting at our table, but there's no . . .'

She had been going to say 'no accounting for taste', but her mother cut across the sentence before she could complete it. 'Mr Bottomley is your uncle's friend, and our guest,' Jess said firmly. She turned to Max. 'You never gave me a chance to explain that Mr Bottomley and I had met before. It was some time ago, when I lost my job at the hospital and decided to take in paying guests. I wanted ladies but Mr Bottomley was desperate, having been given notice by his landlady. He came round and looked at the room—it's the one you're in now, Max—but we decided we wouldn't suit. And now I think we should bury the past and have our meal.'

The table was already laid, and Jess took the warmed plates out of the bottom oven, then brought forth the sizzling pork joint whilst Debbie began to dish up vegetables. Max usually sat at ease until his food was put before him, but now he took his place at the head of the table and began to carve the pork and pass it round, saying heartily as he did so: 'Well, well, well, ain't it a small world? I'm telling you, Herbert, this is a pretty good billet, but I'm sure you'll be welcome here as me mate, even if my cousin felt more at ease with lady lodgers.' He gave his friend a very obvious wink. 'Reckon you didn't know I were a lady, did you, old pal? But Jess and meself is old bezzies as well as cousins so I guess I were more acceptable than some strange feller wantin' to find lodgings.'

Mr Bottomley muttered something and Jess turned to him politely. 'Well, Mr Bottomley, and where are you lodging now? I trust you found somewhere satisfactory.'

'I were in Great Nelson Street with a Mrs Halton,' Mr Bottomley said. 'Only her daughter was living in London and she's been bombed out so she's coming back to live at home, which means I've gorrer move on.' He looked hopefully at Max. 'So me old pal 'ere said as there were a spare room in his lodgings—a'course, I didn't know it were your place, missus—and his landlady might let me take it.'

Debbie glanced at her mother, horrified at the mere suggestion. To be sure, Mr Bottomley had not shouted at all since he had entered the house, but that was because Uncle Max had done all the shouting for him. She was sure that as soon as he got his feet under the table he would out-boom even Uncle Max, and the thought of having to live with two such overpowering people made Debbie go cold. But Jess was speaking and Debbie, with a forkful of food halfway to her mouth, paused to listen.

'I'm afraid I couldn't possibly manage another lodger, not even a woman,' Jess was saying firmly. 'You see, I am now in full-time employment as manager of a busy chemist's shop, and Debbie here works in a factory out on Long Lane, assembling wireless parts. So you see, we simply don't have enough spare time to cope with lodgers.' She looked across at Max and smiled, and Debbie was alarmed at the depth of affection in her mother's eyes. 'Max is different, of course, being family.'

176

'But suppose I say I'll take on board any extra work,' Max said eagerly. 'I'm a dab hand at burnin' porridge and boiling eggs till they's like stones. Honest to God, Jess, old Herbert here won't be no trouble and I'm sure a bit of extra money wouldn't come amiss.'

'It's not as if I were suggestin' a permanent thing,' Herbert Bottomley pointed out righteously. 'It 'ud only be until I found somewhere else . . . somewhere I'd be made welcome,' he added, with unconcealed bitterness. This time Jess did not even bother to reply, and Debbie thought her mother must remember, all too clearly, how difficult it had been to dislodge Mr Bottomley on their previous encounter. Instead, Jess looked round the table, eyebrows rising. 'Would anyone like some more vegetables or gravy? I'm saving the rest of the pork, which we'll have cold tomorrow, but if someone doesn't eat the potatoes they'll go to waste.'

'Oh no they won't, the hens will enjoy them . . . and the cauliflower too,' Debbie said cheerfully, since her mother's remark appeared to have fallen on deaf ears. Mr Bottomley looked sulky and Max was beginning to scowl. Debbie turned to him. 'Go on, Uncle Max, you're always saying how you love roast potatoes; well, now's your chance to prove it.'

Max leaned across and helped himself to three of the six potatoes in the tureen, then added a good quantity of cauliflower which he splashed liberally with gravy. Then, after a moment's hesitation, he plunged the spoon into the dish again and put the last three potatoes and the rest of the cauliflower on to his friend's plate. 'You might as well have yourself a good meal, Herbie,

177

'cos me cousin's a prime cook even if she ain't as hospitable as I'd hoped,' he said gruffly. Then he turned to Jess. 'What's for pudden, queen?'

*   *   *

Debbie had half expected Uncle Max to return to the attack but the days passed and no more mention was made of Mr Bottomley. Debbie, however, kept her eyes open and was not pleased to discover that Mr Bottomley was lodging with an old widow in Crocus Street. She was sure Mrs O'Brien would soon get tired of him and invent some excuse to get him to move on, but for the moment at least the old lady seemed quite happy with her lodger, and because the two friends now lived so close Uncle Max did not pester Jess to take the other man in. But very soon, in fact, Debbie noticed despairingly, Mr Bottomley was spending as much time in Wykeham Street as he did in his own lodgings. He came round as soon as he finished his evening meal, often complaining that Mrs O'Brien was a poor cook and did not manage to fill him up at mealtimes. When Max had provided Jess with unrationed food, she felt it incumbent upon her to offer Mr Bottomley a slice of cake or a piece of pie, but at other times she simply pretended not to hear.

Debbie was always glad when Uncle Max took his cap and jacket off the back of the door and the two men sallied forth to the nearest pub, because it meant that she and her mother might have a quiet evening. They would sit in the kitchen, knitting away, with the wireless playing softly in the background. Often, they would go to bed before

Max returned, though they invariably heard him arrive home since it seemed he could not so much as move across a room quietly, let alone close a door without slamming it.

What did please Debbie was the fact that Max never came into her room any more. A few days after her picnic on the Wirral, Jess had asked her curiously what she had done to the chair in her bedroom. 'There are some odd scratches on the back,' she had said. 'And I remember someone once saying that you could wedge a door shut if you jammed the back of a chair under the handle.'

She had been eyeing Debbie steadily as she spoke and Debbie felt she simply had to come clean. 'I wedged it,' she had admitted. 'I didn't like to say anything, Mam, because it were too like tale-clatting, but Uncle Max don't knock before he barges into my room to say goodnight and—and I'm not a child, Mam. I was going to buy a bolt but I didn't want to keep you out . . .'

For a moment, Debbie had seen that her mother's face had grown stern and cold. Now I'm for it, she thought apprehensively. Jess, she knew, would never believe ill of her beloved cousin Max. But instead of berating her, Jess put an arm round her and gave a quick squeeze. 'I'll have a word,' she had said softly. 'He don't mean any harm. I guess he thinks of you as a little girl, but it won't do. Leave it wi' me, queen.'

And never, since that day, had Uncle Max entered her room, though he was still apt to give her a cuddle if he caught her alone.

CHAPTER SEVEN

AUGUST 1940

Nancy was making bread in the kitchen when she heard Bullwhip arrive, or rather she heard the thunder of his horses' hooves and the jingle of their harness as they clattered across the iron-hard earth, for there had been no rain for weeks. She glanced at the oven, but the loaves needed another twenty minutes, so she left them where they were and hurried through the doorway of the kitchen just as Bullwhip shouted 'G'day' as he caught sight of her. 'Eight letters for you, missus—well, for you and Andy—and a couple of parcels for young Jacko.'

'Yes, Jack is fifteen in a couple of days so I expect one of the parcels is from Pete and the other from Jamie. And I hope there are letters from them as well.'

'Aye, there's a letter here from Pete; I reckernise the writing,' Bullwhip said, handing over the missive. 'It's a thick one; plenty of news in there, I guess. Where is he now, anyway? I know he's in the Royal Air Force, and I know he's abroad, but that's about all I do know.'

'He was in South Africa being trained to fly bombers,' Nancy told him, ripping open the letter from her eldest son. She scanned it briefly. 'He's eager to start active service and he doesn't think it will be long before he and his mates set out for England. But come along in and I'll make you a cup of tea and a bite to eat.'

Nancy went back to the kitchen and pulled a kettle over the heat, whilst Bullwhip made his way to the veranda, and presently she carried a big pot of tea over to the waiting man and set it down on a small table. Then she went and fetched the jug of milk, which was never brought into the kitchen where it would speedily have turned sour in the heat but was kept in the coolest place they could find, a man-made lagoon close to the nearby river, where it stayed good for the best part of a day. Returning, she smiled at the picture Bullwhip made, sprawled at his ease on a long cane chair, his dust-caked boots resting on a small table, weary eyelids drooping over his bright eyes. She mounted the steps, poured milk and tea into the two mugs which stood ready, then added two heaped spoonfuls of sugar to Bullwhip's mug. She handed him his drink and raised her brows. 'Bacon and eggs, Bullwhip? I just baked, so the bread's really fresh, but if you'd rather have something cold . . .' Bullwhip looked quite shocked; no working man ever refused a hot meal in favour of a cold one, Nancy thought, amused, but she said enticingly: 'How about a helping of trifle? Or some junket? It 'ud cool you down.'

'Reckon I'll stick to bacon and eggs, missus, with a good thick slice of your homemade bread,' Bullwhip said gruffly. 'I reckon hot food gives you a nice sweat and a nice sweat cools a feller down.'

Nancy sipped her own tea and felt perspiration pop out on her forehead as the hot liquid slid down her throat. 'Okay, Bullwhip; bacon and eggs coming up,' she said, getting to her feet. 'You staying over?'

Bullwhip stretched and yawned hugely before

replying. 'Guess I'd better do one more call,' he said regretfully. 'I've a fair amount of post for the McGuires; when that's delivered I can start my return trip.'

'Right you are,' Nancy said equably. She was longing to read her letters but etiquette demanded that she should feed Bullwhip first. However, jiggling the big black frying pan, crowded with thick slices of home-cured bacon and four hissing, spitting eggs, she spread out the pages of the letter from Pete which she had already opened, and read as she cooked. Pete was exultant. His course was finished; he and the rest of the lads had passed all tests with flying colours, and expected to be off to England any day. He was full of news, mainly about the kindness of their South African hosts, whose lives seemed to consist of receptions, parties and balls, to which the young air force personnel were always invited. Pete was a good boy, Nancy reflected, for he had not forgotten her asking him—how long ago it seemed!—to visit her old friend Jess when he reached England.

Of course I've no idea whereabouts in England I shall be posted, he wrote, but I guess wherever I am I can't be too far away from Liverpool. It's a small island, after all, and though I may not get leave for some weeks, I'm bound to get some eventually. I guess public transport will be better out there than at home since you can't forbid people to drive their cars and ration petrol so severely without providing an alternative. The only thing is, Ma, you'll have to write to me again giving me Aunt Jessie's surname and address, since I seem to have lost the bit of

182

*paper I'd written it down on. No use writing to
me here, by the way, because by the time you get
this letter I may have moved on, but I'll write
again just as soon as I'm settled. I had a letter
from Jamie a couple of days ago; he thinks
Sydney is wonderful and college first rate. He
always was clever but he says that as soon as he
is old enough he'll put his degree on hold and
join up. Got to go now—we're off to a beach
barbecue; lots of red snapper, lobsters and
crabs, to say nothing of champagne. It's made
in South Africa, not France, but it's still pretty
damn good!*
    Your loving son,
    Pete

Nancy scooped the pages up and shoved them
into the pocket of her calico apron, then she
dished up the eggs and bacon and cut, with some
difficulty, a thick slice off the loaf she had taken
from the oven. Then she cut another slice which
she fried crisp in the remaining fat before carrying
the laden plate back to the veranda. Bullwhip was
actually asleep, she could tell by the angle of his
lolling head, but he awoke as she stood the plate
down on the table and reached for it, grinning his
appreciation. 'That sure looks bonza, missus,' he
said gleefully. 'All it needs to make it just perfect
is . . .'
    '. . . tomato ketchup,' Nancy finished for him. 'I
know how fond you fellows are of my tomato
ketchup so I made a barrel of the stuff. I'll fetch
some out . . . want some mustard as well?'
    'That 'ud be beaut,' Bullwhip conceded, and
when she returned to the veranda he splashed both

condiments liberally over the food. He took a big mouthful, chewed, swallowed, then grinned across at her. 'You can leave me now, missus, and go off somewhere to read your mail,' he suggested. He gestured to the plate with his fork. 'This'll keep me busy for a while yet.'

Nancy smiled but shook her head and reached for the pile of letters, slitting open the one from her second son. 'It's all right, Bullwhip, I can read them out here,' she said. 'To tell you the truth, it's too bloody hot indoors for comfort.'

Jamie was well and enthusiastic about Sydney. It was a light-hearted letter but, like his brother, Jamie was longing to be a part of the action. Nancy laid down his letter and picked up the one in Jess's familiar handwriting. Dear Jess! Her facility with a pen had increased over the years and now her letters were always interesting to read and full of little anecdotes about the war and her life. This one had been written back in June, after the evacuation of the BEF from Dunkirk. Naturally, Jess had been delighted when Churchill had formed a coalition government and she had carefully written down his inaugural speech, which was included in the letter. As if I'd not heard it on the wireless myself, Nancy thought, amused. But of course, the Walleroo was a world away from Wykeham Street, and it might not have occurred to Jess that they had anything so civilised as a wireless set, though Nancy always tried to draw a pleasant picture of her home. Indeed, she thought now, looking around her, it was scarcely recognisable as the corrugated iron shack to which she had come as a bride. Now, the walls were timber and there were screen doors and windows too, to keep out mosquitoes and other flying insects. The windows were curtained, the mud floors were covered with bright linoleum and the kitchen contained a good many labour-saving appliances which had been unknown to homesteaders twenty years ago. Outside, there was a flower garden near the house, an orchard on the river bank, and an enormous kitchen garden.

At first, Nancy had despaired of ever teaching the Aborigines to plant, tend and harvest the huge quantity of vegetables and fruit the homestead needed, because it was foreign to their nature. Left to their own devices they would hunt, fish and forage but they had no conception of agriculture. It had been the women who had begun to help in the garden first and they had teased and cajoled the men into doing some of the harder work such as digging and carting water. Now, many of the women had begun to cultivate small gardens of their own outside their humpies, for though they still had all their meals provided it was nice for the children to be able to have fresh fruit and vegetables on tap, so to speak. Furthermore, Nancy was aware that it stopped them from taking such things from the homestead garden.

'Everything all right?' Bullwhip said, through a mouthful of bread and egg. 'Kids are always a worry and sometimes a nuisance, but when they're away . . . well, I reckon it's hard on the women left behind.'

'It is,' Nancy agreed, 'but every generation has to leave home some time and the war was as good an excuse as any. And anyway, Jacko's still at home.' Bullwhip scraped the last piece of fried bread round the plate, gave an enormous belch,

185

and lay back in his chair; already, his eyes were beginning to close. Nancy waited until a gentle snore emanated from her guest and then began to read her letter once more.

We're all so relieved to have our brave boys back home, Jess had written. *I'm sure bringing them back was the right thing to do because it has heartened the country wonderfully. We are all pulling together, which was not perhaps the case before. Rationing is a fearful nuisance but we get by better than most. I expect you remember my speaking of my cousin, Max, who was so good to me when I was a small girl. He has been lodging with us for quite a while and the money does come in useful. I never buy on the black market myself, but Debbie says Max does, and I suspect she may be right. However, he is a huge man with a huge appetite, and quite frankly I shouldn't know how to satisfy him if it were not for the extras he brings in from time to time. He has contacts with farms on the Wirral and buys pork or bacon when a pig is killed, and sometimes even a joint of mutton. The meat ration is ridiculous—you can only spend 1/10d per week for each adult, and 11d for a child, so as you can imagine, a meat and potato pie is mainly potato, and a roast joint just isn't possible.*

Still, I mustn't grumble. Things could be a great deal worse. Clothes are not yet rationed, though they say on the wireless it will have to come, but, as I believe I told you, Blackler's had a half price sale just before the war started and Debbie and I went mad. We both bought thick winter coats, a couple of warm nightgowns each at 2/9d apiece, and some stockings.

We've had a couple of air-raid warnings, which was very frightening, but I suspect was just a practice because folk in the LDV warned us something was going on and told us we'd be in trouble if we were found in the streets without our gas masks. It's bound to come, however— the bombing, I mean—though of course we all pray it won't.

And now for more cheerful news. Cinemas, theatres and even restaurants are doing a roaring trade, so Max took me to see Gone With the Wind *with Vivien Leigh and Clark Gable. It was wonderful. I cried buckets, especially at the end when Rhett Butler is no longer under her spell . . . but I won't say any more because you won't have seen it yet, and I wouldn't want to spoil it for you.*

I know that letters often go astray in wartime, so I tend to repeat myself, but what I am going to do in future is number every letter. Then if you get 9 and 11 you will know that poor 10 was in a ship which was sunk by some horrible U-boat. Dear Nancy, I have never been more grateful that my baby was a little girl and feel for you over your lovely boys. I am sure, if petitions to God have any influence, they will come through all right because Debbie and I include them in our prayers each night. You said Pete would visit us when he arrives in England, and when he does we shall make a great fuss of him and have what you'd call a corroboree to introduce him to all our friends. I expect he will want to go down to Devonshire to

187

*meet the Kerris clan, which is only natural, but
do persuade him to come to us just as soon as
he can. It would be wonderful to meet your son
even though you and I seem destined to live a
world away from each other.*

*Must go now; we women are all knitting for
victory and I am halfway through a seaman's
sock for some lucky sailor. And then I must
start preparing a rabbit stew (rabbit is not
rationed!) for Max and Debbie when they come
home from work. I am still manager of Jarvis's
Chemist but I get Thursday afternoons off,
hence the letter.*

Bye for now,
Jess

Nancy put down her letter with a satisfied sigh.
The thought of Jess managing her little household,
cooking the meals, going to and from her chemist's
shop and visiting the cinema filled her with
pleasurable nostalgia. She had never known
Liverpool well but she could still remember it quite
distinctly, the big busy hospital, the cinemas and
theatres, the constant bustle in the streets and the
huge stores selling every imaginable luxury. Now,
her life was very different. Shopping was a rare
event and not a particularly pleasant one at that,
she thought, remembering the small, fly-ridden
stores and the scarcity of almost everything. Oh,
they never went short and whatever they
ordered—so far at any rate—always arrived in the
end, but there was little choice between one brand
and another; one simply accepted what one was
sent.

Things were getting better, however. Beef was

188

fetching a steady price, and as they grew increasingly prosperous the station owners began to get together more. There was a fortnightly picture show at a cattle station less than eighty miles away and Andy always insisted that they should attend, because it gave him a chance to talk to other cattlemen and he thought it was good for his family to enjoy a film now and then. There were dances, too, invitations to weddings, birthday parties and similar events, and there was wireless, which meant that the stations could keep in touch with one another and call on medical help in an emergency. The radio also broadcast a school session for children and a 'natter' hour when anyone who wanted to chat, or listen to others doing so, had the freedom of the airwaves. Nancy often spoke to her sister Anne during these 'galah' sessions, though they were always aware that other ears were listening, drinking in every word.

Now she glanced across at her visitor, then got quietly to her feet and stole off the veranda. The steps creaked, but Bullwhip did not wake. As she was crossing the yard, she saw Aggie coming towards her with her arms full of vegetables, for the women had been hard at work harvesting a bumper crop of sweetcorn. Aggie was heading for the vegetable store but stopped when Nancy called her. 'Yes'm?' she said interrogatively. 'I were just going to put these here cobs in the veggie store.'

'Good. When you've done that, come into the kitchen and give me a hand getting the loaves out,' Nancy said. She sighed. 'Then I reckon you'd best fetch Violet from the house—she's cleaning the bedrooms today—and we'll start dinner.'

                    *   *   *

'Oh, gawd, look at that, will you? When I gorrup
this morning the sky were clear, and I were certain
the fine weather were goin' to last. Me mam told
me to take a brolly 'cos she said September were a
tricky sort of month. But did I listen? Did I hell as
like! So now I've gorrer make me way to Bootle in
a bleedin' downpour.' The speaker, a tall, heavily
built girl with frizzy blonde hair combed up into a
huge pompadour, turned hopefully towards
Debbie and Gwen, as the three of them peered at
the driving rain through the open factory door. 'I
ain't even gorra scarf to keep me 'air dry. Any
chance I can borrer something off of you?'

Debbie sighed. Ethel Catnip was the dizziest girl
in their department. If she remembered her brolly
then she forgot her butties and had to beg or
borrow from everyone around her—which, with
rationing tightening its grip, was unpopular to say
the least. If she remembered her butties, then she
forgot her overall and had to borrow one of the
spares kept in the department's cupboard. If she
remembered her overall, then she would have put
her card back in the wrong slot and would hold up
the whole queue whilst she feverishly searched.
Nevertheless, she was well liked because she was
generous and hard-working and sympathised with
the woes of others, having so many herself.

So Debbie turned to Gwen. 'If I lend my brolly
to Ethel, can I share yours? I'll walk with you to
Ogden's and then hang on to it until I get home, if
that's all right?'

'Sure,' Gwen said readily. She erected her
umbrella and the two girls huddled beneath it

190

whilst Ethel beamed her thanks and turned to Debbie. 'I'll bring it back tomorrer, honest to God I will, queen. And if me mam's baked them oatmeal biscuits you liked I'll bring you a couple, sangwiched together with margarine and a bit o' jam.'

Debbie laughed. 'You don't have to do that,' she said. 'Only I would like the brolly back. They're scarce as flippin' hens' teeth and I reckon I'll need it once the winter comes.'

Ethel promised fervently that this time she would not forget and the girls splashed through the downpour to the nearest tram stop, squeezing on to the first vehicle to come along. It was a No. 36 which would take them all the way home, though there was no opportunity to talk since the racket made by other passengers rendered conversation impossible.

When they neared their destination, Debbie reminded Ethel that she had boarded the tram complete with umbrella, since she had seen the other girl shove it down beside her seat. However, when they disembarked on Commercial Road, leaving Ethel aboard, she made the thumbs up sign and Debbie presumed from this that their scatterbrained friend had retrieved the umbrella, though the rain was beginning to ease.

'Mam had an interview at the Stanley yesterday,' Debbie told Gwen as the two of them set off towards Ogden's. 'She was offered the job and she told me she was really happy to accept because she had felt guilty because of the shortage of nurses . . . working in the chemist's shop is all very well but I think she secretly felt she was wasting her training when she could be using it to help the war effort.'

191

'So what about the chemist's, left in the lurch without a manager?' Gwen said rather plaintively.

Debbie grinned; she suspected her friend was thinking of the advance warning they had been given when make-up or scented soap came into the chemist's shop. However, it would not do to say so. 'Didn't I tell you? Because of the war, Mr Jarvis has come out of retirement. The new pharmacist was called up, you know, and the shop isn't as busy as it was, what with shortages and everything. He was ever so apologetic but he explained that he couldn't pay a manager and work himself, so Mam could either stay there as an ordinary shop assistant, or find something else. Well, Matron had actually visited the shop and had told Mam that, should she wish to return to the wards, she would be employed at once with the salary of a senior staff nurse. She and Uncle Max had talked it over—he wanted Mam to take Horrible Herbert in as a second lodger to make up for the drop in wages, but she said she'd rather be a nurse, doing important work for which she had been trained, because anyone can be a landlady.'

'With all three of you earning so much you should do all right,' Gwen said. 'In fact I suppose you could even manage without your uncle's contribution.' She glanced slyly at her friend but though Debbie laughed, she shook her head.

'It wouldn't be that easy; I know we earn a lot but prices have gone up, so I suppose I'll have to put up with the nasty old brute for a while longer.'

'But you've got used to him now, haven't you? I believe you quite like him,' Gwen said, pushing open her yard gate. She handed her umbrella to her friend. 'Don't forget now, bring me brolly in tomorrow even if the sun's cracking the pavin' stones.'

Debbie assured her that her umbrella would be restored to her next day, and did not add that her feelings for Uncle Max remained obstinately the same. She did her best to hide it, but the touch of his hand made her flesh creep and she tried to avoid him whenever she could. No use telling Gwen, though; Gwen was completely taken in by Uncle Max's generosity and jolly ways, as were a good many others.

Now, Debbie saw Gwen into the kitchen and then turned and retraced her steps. She wondered whether her mother would be working shifts. Whilst Jess had worked at the chemist's, she had always been the first to get home in the evening, so that Debbie and Max came back to a warm house which smelled deliciously of baking bread, or pies, or a nice scouse. If her mother worked shifts, then it might be she, Debbie, who prepared the evening meal and did a number of chores. Suddenly, she realised that she and Uncle Max would be the sole occupants of the house until her mother returned and this thought really horrified her. She could imagine all too clearly the groping and grabbing which would result, and wondered how she could convey her fears to her mother without upsetting her. There was a war on, after all. Uncle Max was her own problem and she must, she supposed, learn to deal with him without troubling Jess too much.

She splashed round the corner into Wykeham Street, hurried along the jigger and across the yard, and entered the kitchen. Her mother was stirring a large pan of what smelt like scouse, and

193

turned to beam at her daughter. 'Mr Jarvis has been awfully good. He's paying me up to the end of the week but he said not to come in because he can manage. So I start work on Women's Surgical at eight o'clock on Monday morning. I'm going over tomorrow to be fitted for my uniform and I shall be working with Sister McPherson, who was plain old Staff Nurse Dolly McPherson when I worked there last. I'm jolly glad now that I kept up my friendship with her because I shall need to take things slowly at first. Things will have moved on since I left, but Dolly will see I don't make any bad mistakes.'

'Oh, Mam, I'm so glad for you,' Debbie said. She hesitated, and then said, 'But what about the shift system? Will you be working nights? Only I don't know that I fancy being alone in the house with Uncle Max whilst you're away.'

Jess stared at her. 'I've told you before, love, that Uncle Max doesn't mean any harm. He's just . . . friendly. But as it happens, I warned Matron that I didn't want to do nights—I'm a fire-watcher, after all—and she said that was all right. I'll probably be working eight till six, mostly, which is similar to my hours at Jarvis's.'

'Oh, I see,' Debbie said, considerably relieved. Her own work finished at six, but Long Lane was a good way off so she was unlikely to be in first, though past experience told her there would undoubtedly be occasions when Jess would work a double shift, or be called to another ward to fill in for somebody else. Aloud, she said: 'That's all right then. But, Mam, if you are likely to be away from the house at night, I'll ask Mrs Soames if I can share with Gwen—or she can come home and

194

share with me. I'd rather do that if you don't mind.'

Jess began to speak, then stopped and shook her head ruefully. 'You're right, of course. Emergencies do arise, particularly in wartime. And tongues wag, and gossips gossip, so I reckon you're right and I'll do my best to give you plenty of warning if I'm working over. But you'll make Uncle Max's evening meal before you flit off, I trust?'

Debbie was glad that her mother had not taken offence. 'Of course I will; and I'll come down first thing to get his breakfast and polish his bleedin' shoes,' she said cheerfully. 'And with you working full time at the hospital, at least we won't have to have Horrible Herbert lodging with us.'

'Sshhhh; your Uncle Max is upstairs having a wash,' her mother said. 'I'm afraid he—he's sulking.'

'Sulking? Why?' Debbie asked, puzzled. Uncle Max had many faults—many, many faults—but sulking was not usually one of them.

'He isn't too pleased that I'll be working at the hospital full time,' Jess said vaguely, picking up a fork and stabbing a potato with it. 'Yes, these are done and the table's laid, so if you'll just run your hands under the tap, you'd best call Uncle Max. The thing is, he thinks that my working as a nurse might well be inconvenient for him because I couldn't guarantee I'd be here to cook his evening meal. I pointed out that nurses were desperately needed and he said so were good landladies . . . I could have smacked him!'

Debbie giggled. 'Is he upstairs packing?' she asked hopefully, but though Jess laughed, a little self-consciously, she shook her head.

'No, no, he wasn't unreasonable when I explained how important it was for me to get back to the work I know and love,' she said earnestly. Footsteps began to descend the stairs, and she raised her voice. 'So I bought two pounds of cooking apples and I've made an apple tart, and apple pudding, and . . .' The door's opening cut the sentence short and both mother and daughter turned and smiled as Max entered the room. 'Ah, here you are, Max; then we'll dish up at once,' Jess said. 'Three potatoes or four, Max?'

*   *   *

Debbie, the Soameses and the rest of the occupants of the underground shelter made their way up the steps and into the crisp cold of the December morning. They had been below ground for many hours whilst mayhem raged outside, for it seemed that the Luftwaffe had got into their stride at last. Debbie glanced round her anxiously, expecting to see ruined buildings on every side, but despite the fearful din the only sign of bomb damage came when she turned to look towards the docks. They had been hit all right; she could see flames, gaps where warehouses had once stood, and a thick pall of black smoke overhanging the area.

'Cor, wharra night, eh?' Gwen said, following her friend's gaze. 'Your mam was working, wasn't she, and since I can see the Stanley from here and it don't look damaged, I dare say she's safe and sound. Want to come back to Daisy Street for a spot of breakfast? Only bombs or no bombs, I've gorrer do me Christmas shopping today or the kids

196

won't have so much as a cracker to pull.'

'Thanks, Gwen, but I'll have to go home. Uncle Max was fire-watching and, as you say, Mam was working on the wards, so the least I can do is cook breakfast for them. But I'll come round to yours as soon as I've done that and we'll do our shopping— if there are any shops left standing, that is, and anything left to buy in them,' she finished grimly.

'Fair enough,' Gwen said cheerfully, turning to help heave Mrs Soames up the concrete steps. The older woman had put on a good deal of weight since the war started and blamed rationing, since she said she now had to fill up the chinks with bread and potatoes. 'Will you come round to Daisy Street or shall I come over to Wykeham?'

'I'll come to you, because I won't be able to leave until Mam's made a list of the messages she wants done,' Debbie explained. 'She was doing a double shift so she had no chance to shop yesterday and will probably go straight to bed as soon as she's had her breakfast. See you later, then!' The city had been bombed before, she reflected, as she crossed the main road, but never so badly. The inhabitants of the shelter had heard the steady thrum of hundreds of planes passing overhead, and the whoosh and crump of falling bombs, and had speculated on the destruction that must have resulted.

Even on Stanley Road the air was dusty, presumably as a result of fallen buildings, but Debbie could see no actual signs of destruction. She walked down Fountains Road in the slowly strengthening light and made her way back to Wykeham Street.

An ARP warden, making his weary way home

197

along the Fountains Road, told her that the canal had been hit, releasing millions of gallons of water which had poured into the Canada Dock railway station. 'My brother works there, but he were at home last night, thank gawd,' he said gruffly. 'The overhead railway's been hit, though, and the shipping's in a right shambles. Eh, we've been that sorry for poor old London, and now we know what it's like ourselves.'

Debbie still had several yards to go before she reached her gate when her mother emerged from the house, coated and hatted and white as a sheet. She saw her daughter and gave a little shriek, then began to run. She flung her arms round Debbie, giving her a hard hug. 'Oh, my love,' she gasped, and Debbie felt her mother's tears wet on her own cheeks. 'Oh, my love, I've been so worried. It said on the wireless that the docks had been bombed and the shelter isn't that far from the docks. You're so sensible, I knew you'd go down the shelter as soon as Moaning Minnie started, only even shelters can't guarantee complete safety.'

'It's all right, Mam. So far as I could see, it really was mainly the docks and the railway,' Debbie said reassuringly, just as she saw, past her mother's shoulder, the large figure of Uncle Max erupt from the front door and begin to roll along the pavement towards them. He was red-faced and beaming, and, somewhat to her surprise, he looked honestly delighted to see her. Debbie, who always treated him rather coolly, felt a stab of guilt. If only he would keep his hands to himself, he wouldn't be a bad sort of fellow, she supposed. The trouble was, he was the type of person who always stood close and had to touch. Indeed, right now, he was

198

giving her and her mother a hearty hug whilst saying over and over how glad he was to see that Debbie was obviously unhurt and in good spirits.

'As y'know, I'm a fire-watcher when I ain't on duty in my own job,' he said. 'Last night I was seconded to one o' the tallest buildings in the city so I had what you might call a bird's-eye view of everything. When the raid was finished and I came home, I was able to assure your mam that the Stanley Road area was clear, but of course she just had to see for herself.' He cocked a quizzical eye at Debbie. 'I'll be bound you was every bit as worried that the hospital might have gorra packet, but we were lucky.'

'Yes, I was worried,' Debbie admitted, as the three of them turned back towards the house. She looked hopefully at her mother as they entered the kitchen. 'Have you and Uncle Max had your breakfast yet? Only I'm just about starving.'

'You poor thing,' Jess said mockingly. 'No, we've not eaten yet, though I did make Max a big jam butty when he came back; then I set out to find you, queen,' she went on, heading for the pantry. 'I think we all deserve something nice and hot, so I'll do porridge first and then scrambled eggs on toast.'

By two o'clock that afternoon, Debbie and Gwen were ensconced in the Lyons restaurant on Church Street, eating beans on toast and discussing the raid. 'Well, it could have been worse,' Gwen said philosophically. 'I know some people got killed when there was a direct hit on the railway viaduct, but apart from that it really was mainly warehouses and docks, wasn't it?'

Debbie nodded, her mouth full. 'But it won't

199

half disrupt things,' she said, as soon as she could speak. 'The Dockers' Umbrella stops at Canada Dock now and someone said some of the other stations had been hit, though Lime Street is still okay.'

'I know, and I expect there'll be more on the news tonight,' Gwen said, nodding wisely. 'I'm going to listen to old Haw-Haw on the new set; I bet he'll have a gloat about it.' She imitated his well-known and much hated voice. 'Garmany calling, Garmany calling. He's always telling us our "Empah" is crumbling; now he can crow over all the shipping the bloody Luftwaffe sank last night, though a good few of 'em came from foreign countries who aren't even in the war.'

'We shouldn't listen to him, I suppose, but he's good for a laugh,' Debbie said. 'Uncle Max hates him and so does Mam, but they usually listen in. He's got it into his head—Lord Haw-Haw, I mean—that he can stir up rebellion in India by pretending we're as good as beaten, but Uncle Max says he's barking up the wrong tree there.'

'I thought you hated your Uncle Max,' Gwen said slyly. 'I thought you said he knew nothing about the war and was just a big show-off.'

Debbie grinned rather sheepishly. 'I'm trying much harder to see his good points,' she said gruffly. 'I haven't said anything before, Gwenny, but I used to have a bit of a problem with Uncle Max. He would march into my bedroom when I was getting ready for bed, and if I wasn't fully dressed he'd get awfully excited and red in the face, and keep sort of grabbing at me. I hated it, but he doesn't do it now, though he still tries to give me a cuddle if we're in the house alone or if

200

Mam's upstairs and we're down.'

Gwen's eyes rounded and her fork stopped halfway to her mouth. 'Why didn't you never tell me before?' she breathed. 'That's awful, queen; no wonder you didn't like him much. You should have told your mam, you know; I would have.'

'I did tell her about his coming into my bedroom,' Debbie admitted. 'She said she'd speak to him and she must have done so, because after that he did steer clear. But he still cuddles in corners, if you know what I mean. Mam says it's because he thinks of me as a child, but I don't think a man of his age should cuddle anyone when they make it plain they don't like it. I got terribly worried when Mam first told me she was going back to the hospital, because Uncle Max and I would have been alone in the house morning and evening. But then your mam said I could stay at your place when my mam was on nights . . .'

Gwen interrupted, a slow smile stealing across her face. 'So that was why you started coming to us,' she said triumphantly. 'I thought you might be trying to avoid that Herbert bloke, but it didn't seem likely. It's a pity him and your Uncle Max don't take a house on their own account, then you and your mam could have your place to yourselves, but there's fat chance of that happening. I've yet to meet a feller who can cook and clean, get the messages, peel the spuds and light the fires of a morning.'

'Do you know, I've never thought of it like that,' Debbie said, awed by her friend's remarks. 'When you think, my mam does all those things and has a full-time job nursing at the hospital, and takes a turn at fire-watching or giving a hand at the WVS canteen . . . well, it does show you which is the weaker sex, doesn't it?'

Gwen giggled. 'You're right there,' she agreed, then set down her knife and fork with a regretful sigh. 'That were really good. Now let's stop gossiping and get down to brass tacks. How many presents have you bought this morning and how many have you still got to get?'

Debbie sighed but fished out her list. 'I've got everything except something for Uncle Max. I'd like to get him a cigarette lighter if I could find one cheap enough, because he's always reaching for a fag and he's one of those fellers who strikes a match, uses it to light up and then puts it back into the box. Then, of course, when you reach down the matchbox from the mantelpiece, you have to root through all the old dead matches to find a live one. It fairly drives me mad and even Mam said the other day that it annoyed her. She chucks her used matches in the fire or in the bin, same as I do, but when she moaned to Uncle Max he said she was wasteful and didn't she know there was a war on.'

Gwen laughed. 'Silly old fool; does he think you can make a warship or a Spitfire out of matchsticks?' she asked derisively. 'So all you want is a lighter for your uncle; is that right?'

'Not quite; Mam's old purse is so worn that any day now it's going to give way and she'll be chasing pennies and ha'pennies across the pavement,' Debbie said. 'I know I said I were going to give her that pretty headsquare with the orange and lemon pattern all over it which we got off Paddy's Market, but I'd feel a bit mean just giving her that. It was second hand, after all, so a nice new purse would be really useful. Oh, and I want to buy your mam

202

something; she's invited me to come to yours on Boxing Day, 'cos Mam's working and Uncle Max is going to the footie with Horrible Herbert.'

'But you said you were making up bags of toffee for each of the kids,' Gwen protested. 'Mam will be that thrilled, because your mam's toffee is the nicest we've ever tasted, and she'll say you shouldn't go wasting your money on her what with the war 'n'all.'

Debbie got to her feet, scooped up the bill and joined the queue at the cash desk. As Gwen came and stood beside her, she said decisively: 'I'm really grateful to your mam, Gwen. So what do you think she'd like, then?'

'She could do with a new umbrella,' Gwen said, with a promptitude that told Debbie that Gwen had decided to protest no more. 'I see'd a real smart one in Bunney's but I dare say there'll be one on Paddy's Market if we look around.'

At this point, the girls reached the head of the queue and paid for their meal, then set off into the cold December afternoon. 'I'm pretty flush at the moment so she shall have the one in Bunney's,' Debbie said grandly, as they traversed Church Street. She also meant to buy her mother's purse at the popular shop. She knew that if she went to Lewis's or Blackler's she might buy quality goods but she would pay quality prices, whereas Bunney's catered for folk like themselves, who liked nice things but could not afford to throw their money about.

They reached Whitechapel and plunged straight into the department store, emerging as the early dusk was beginning to fall not only with the umbrella and a purse, but with a small metal lighter. 'And now we'll nip into St John's Market and see what's going cheap,' Gwen said. 'I shouldn't think there'll be another raid, not two nights running.'

Debbie, however, looked up at the sky, in which she could just see stars beginning to twinkle. 'The planes always come over on a clear night,' she observed, 'but it takes them a while to get here so we can still do St John's Market and be home before a raid starts, if there is one. Mam will be that pleased with any extras we may find; c'mon.'

The two girls had a successful trip to the market, each coming away with a bag of eating apples, some pears and a mixed assortment of vegetables, all being sold off cheaply since the stallholders wanted to get home before darkness fell. They were lucky enough to catch a tram almost as soon as they left the market so Debbie emptied her fruit and vegetables out on the kitchen table scarcely twenty minutes after purchasing them. She hurried the rest of her shopping up to her room, and when she came down her mother was laying the table for supper whilst Uncle Max got himself ready to fire-watch should there be another raid.

Jess smiled at her daughter and gestured at the vegetables now neatly piled on the draining board. 'Thanks, queen, you're a grand girl, so you are,' she said, beginning to dish up. 'I'm not on duty tonight, thank goodness, so I thought we'd go to bed as soon as we've finished our meal. I'm hoping there won't be another raid, but if there is, we'll have had an hour or two's sleep before it starts.'

'There will be another raid, Jessie,' Max said grimly. 'It's a clear night and the Luftwaffe have got their eye in now and know exactly where we are. The docks took a fair pounding last night so I reckon they'll come back tonight to finish us off.'

'Well they won't bloody well succeed,' Debbie said quickly. 'Our fighters weren't around last night, someone told me, because they didn't know where the German planes were heading, but they know now. Oh aye, they'll be out in force tonight. And did you hear our ack-ack batteries? They make a good old racket, don't they?'

Uncle Max grinned at her, settled himself at the table and began to eat the food which Jess set before him. 'I dare say you're right, young 'un,' he said, rather thickly. 'And your mam's right, too. We should get what sleep we can before Moaning Minnie starts to wail.' He turned to Jess. 'Any chance of a few sandwiches so's I can keep body and soul together if I'm fire-watching till dawn? These winter nights are too bleedin' long an' I get rare starving by two in the mornin'.'

Jess assured him that she would pack him up a carry-out, and presently they made their way to their beds, though they were not there for long. The siren sounded and almost immediately the three of them left the house. Uncle Max hurried to his post whilst Jess and Debbie joined the crowd making their way to the big public shelter. They carried with them a bag containing a loaf, a square of margarine, half a pot of jam and a flask of tea, as well as blankets and pillows, for though the shelter was provided with army issue blankets and hard little bunks, there were never enough to go round.

Everyone did their best to sleep but this raid was even heavier than the previous night's and sleep was almost impossible, for the noise was incessant.

205

This time, the All Clear did not sound until almost eleven hours had passed, and Jess and Debbie re-entered their house as dawn was breaking, almost astonished that it was still standing. They heard on the wireless, later that morning, that many of the bombs had fallen in Cheshire as well as on the docks.

'Thank God it's Sunday,' Jess said fervently, as Max joined them for a hasty breakfast. 'At least we can all get a good day's sleep—and if last night was anything to go by, we'd better make the most of it.'

CHAPTER EIGHT

Pete arrived in England on a sunny, blowy day in March. As the plane in which he was a passenger flew steadily onward, he looked down at the country about which he had heard so much and marvelled at the greenness of it; the gentle hills and valleys, the shining blue rivers and lakes. He had spent the intervening months since his South African experience in Texas and had grown accustomed to flying over vast areas of desert and great plains where wheat was grown in enormous quantities. In Texas he had been training other men to fly, but at last his request for active service had been granted and he was on his way to an airfield in Norfolk, whence he would fly sorties over enemy country, bombing their military installations, airfields and armaments factories, and trying to keep the Channel clear of enemy shipping. His first task when he landed would be to choose his crew, who would then fly together,

206

possibly for the rest of their active service, so it behoved him to choose carefully. And then, when he was able, he meant to gratify his mother—and his Aunt Anne—by visiting the vicarage in the west country, where his grandparents and his Aunt Helen and Uncle Samuel lived. He had three cousins, two boys and a girl, but he did not expect to meet them since Paul and Matthew were in the Navy and little Nancy, named for his own mother but always known as Nan, was a land girl in Cornwall which, for all he knew, might be a hundred miles away.

The aircraft they were in was a lumbering old transport. He had fretted at its slow progress and the number of refuelling stops it needed when they had first set out, but now he was glad of it because it gave him more time to gaze down at England and to wonder about his new posting. His work in Texas had allowed him almost no free time and besides, the airfield had been many miles from the nearest town, so they had met scarcely any Texan civilians. It had been different in South Africa and he hoped it would be different in England. His mother always maintained that English people were very friendly, though she had hinted at a certain reserve. He smiled at the thought because his Aunt Anne, with her soft fair hair and rose-petal complexion, had always seemed to him typically English. She blushed upon meeting strangers or folks she did not know well, stammered when she talked on the wireless, and had never lost her English accent, though her children had picked up the Australian way of talking, probably from the stockmen and other children on the big cattle station near Cairns which his Uncle Clive managed.

The man sitting next to Pete was Sammy Wells and Pete was already determined to bag Sammy for his crew, if he possibly could. Sammy had ginger hair, pale green eyes and a lot of freckles. He had a loud voice and was a great practical joker, but he was also a very good wireless operator, and he and Pete had been together in South Africa and had always got on well. Now, Sammy jerked his elbow. 'Where's that, mate? I mean that great town we're passing over. It looks a bonza place.'

Pete peered over his shoulder. 'I dunno,' he said doubtfully. 'It isn't London, that's for sure—not big enough—and the only other big town I've heard much about is Liverpool.' He peered again. 'No, I don't reckon it's Liverpool because I know that's a port, and in her last letter my mam said they'd been heavily bombed.'

'Well, that place hasn't been bombed,' Sammy said decisively. 'I've seen photographs in the paper of bomb damage and I reckon you wouldn't be able to miss it.' He glanced curiously at Pete. 'How come you know about Liverpool, anyway? I thought your folks came from Devon.'

'They do,' Pete admitted. 'But I think I told you that Ma nursed all through the First World War. Well, she had a great friend, Jess Williams, who worked with her and when the war ended they got jobs in a big hospital in Liverpool. Ma hated it; the regimentation, the way senior staff looked down on girls who had only had war experience. So she quit after a few months, came over to Australia, met my pa and married him. But she and Nurse Williams kept up a correspondence over the years—kept their friendship green you could say. Nurse Williams married and had a kid, but her husband died and she never remarried. I promised my ma I'd visit her while I'm in England, see how she's getting along,' he finished.

'Well, you'd better choose a nice cloudy night to go visiting Liverpool, since you say it's a port and the bloody Luftwaffe know that ports are the lifeblood of a country at war,' Sammy told him. 'I guess we'll be bombing German ports just as soon as we're on active service.'

Pete nodded, pushing his cap to the back of his thick white-blond hair and thinking that he would have to get a haircut as soon as he landed. He wondered if there would be a barber on the station, or whether he would have to make his way to the nearest town or village. But it didn't really matter; on the cattle station, the blacksmith had cut everyone's hair whenever his father felt it was necessary and his mother was a pretty good hand with the shears as well, which probably meant that if he had to he could chip away at his own fair locks. He was grinning at the thought when he became aware that the plane was losing height and he and Sammy, amongst others, got to their feet and crowded close to the windows. They could see trees, mostly still bare-branched, which seemed strange to Pete, used to the perennial foliage of the bush, and large areas of grass, criss-crossed by concrete runways. In the shade of the trees there were buildings, though he could not see what they were made of or how big they were from this angle. The plane banked sharply and he saw what must be a village, probably no more than four or five miles from the airfield. Then the aircraft righted itself and came smoothly into land, only bumping a little as the tyres met the runway and slowed to a stop. Pete picked up his rucksack and bedroll and the holdall in which he kept those of his possessions which would not fit into the rucksack. Then he and Sammy joined the queue waiting to get out on to the grass. They were the only Australians on this particular flight, probably the only passengers who had never touched down on English soil before, but the excitement after the long and wearying journey seemed to have affected everyone. There was a buzz of conversation; men laughed and joked, anticipating the meal they would presently be enjoying, for they had taken off early that morning and had been given only bottles of water and small packets of sandwiches to sustain them on the flight. Everyone crowded to the exit, jumping on to the ground and heading for the buildings which they could see in the distance. Before they had gone far, however, a large and elderly-looking bus, camouflaged in green and brown, drew up beside them and the driver, an exceedingly pretty little WAAF, with a peaked cap perched at a rakish angle on her cropped brown curls, invited them all to get aboard. 'The Winco says he wants a word and then I'm to take you straight to the cookhouse,' she said cheerfully. 'It's bangers and mash followed by treacle pud . . . you lucky people.'

Everyone laughed, even Sammy and Pete, since Tommy Trinder's catchphrase must be known, Pete thought, to the whole of the English speaking world. 'But what's "bangers and mash"?' he hissed in Sammy's ear.

'Dunno, but it ain't steak and chips, worse luck,'

Sammy was beginning, when another voice cut in.

'It's sausages and mashed spuds, of course,' the man behind them said, giving them a lurking grin. 'Where was you brung up, you higgerant savages?'

'As if you didn't know, Hedgy,' Pete said. Flight Lieutenant Bland had been given his nickname because of his hair, which grew in spikes all over his head, like a hedgehog's bristles; no matter how much Brylcreem he smeared on it, it never lay flat for long. 'And I'll thank you not to call me a higgerant savage; my ma is a Britisher and old Sammy here is Winston Churchill's nephew.'

Hedgy grinned unrepentantly. 'You're a lyin' old sod, Blondie, but then you colonials are all the same,' he said. 'You'll be asking what treacle pud is next.' They were crowding into the bus as he spoke and he lowered his voice, glancing towards the front of the vehicle. 'Nice welcome, eh? I've always fancied them neat little WAAFs and that one's pretty as a picture. Wonder what they call her?'

'No doubt you'll find out soon enough,' Pete said, as the bus lurched to a stop in front of a red brick building and the men began to pile out and to file in through the green-painted doorway. He just hoped that the Winco would not keep them too long; sausages and mash, followed by treacle pudding, suddenly sounded extremely attractive. And there would be tea; he had not tasted tea whilst in Texas and found himself looking forward to a large mug of what he understood to be the national drink.

As they were ushered into a large room full of benches, Hedgy shook his shoulder. 'When you choose your crew, don't forget your old pal,' he said urgently. 'I know I shouldn't blow my own

211

trumpet but if you have me for a navigator I'll guarantee to get you out and home again, no trouble. And Solly Parr is a bloody good gunner. How about it?'

'I'll do my best,' Pete promised. He liked Hedgy, who was a Londoner, and knew that little Solly Parr was a Londoner, too. But picking crews would come later; no point in jumping the gun at this stage. The three of them squeezed on to a bench and presently a tall, fair-haired man with a toothbrush moustache came and stood behind the desk and began to speak.

Life on an English air force station was about to begin.

*   *   *

Pete soon settled into his new life, both on the station and in the cockpit of his Wellington bomber. The Wimpeys (as the men called them) were steady, reliable aircraft and Pete's crew soon proved to be both efficient and friendly. They even hung about together when they weren't flying, which was always a good sign.

Pete intended to visit his relatives at the first possible opportunity. His chance came when Katie, as they called their kite, was hit by flak as they circled their target. They had limped home, and when the ground crew examined her they found damage severe enough to make replacement parts necessary.

Accordingly, the crew were told that they might go on leave for five days, and Pete instantly decided to go down to Devon to see his family and to take Sammy with him. The rest of the men were

212

all British and had relatives or friends of their own to visit during their leave, but Sammy had no one, coming as he did from the city of Melbourne on the opposite side of the world.

The two men set off on a sunny morning at the end of April, travelling by train through the brilliant and beautiful countryside. They were both awed by the scenery through which they passed, and they had plenty of time to observe it, for the train travelled slowly. They were equally delighted when they arrived at their destination. The vicarage was a rambling old building, built of rosy red brick, set amidst beautiful rolling hills and surrounded by a wonderful garden, part of which was walled so that the fruit and vegetables which flourished there were sheltered from any but the strongest wind.

The vicar and his wife welcomed their grandson and his friend warmly. They were both in their seventies, white-haired and, at first glance, apparently frail, but Pete soon discovered that the latter was an illusion. For a start, they had eight evacuees billeted upon them, ranging in age from three to thirteen, as well as one feckless young mother who was supposed to help with the children but spent most of her time mooning about the village on the look-out for young men. Mrs Kerris, however, dealt with all matters concerning the evacuees. She cooked and mended for her temporary family, scolded them when they did wrong, handed out treats when any were available, and took them on long rambling walks through the countryside, naming every wild flower, every crop in the field and every creature they observed. She told Pete she was determined that these young

213

cockneys, from the heart of London, should go home with a very real knowledge and love of country ways. She accompanied her charges to school every morning and met them in the afternoons so that there should be no truancy amongst them, and Pete thought that she treated the child ren as she must once have treated her three daughters, with love, humour and firmness.

His grandfather, slightly the older of the two at seventy-five, was equally busy. In addition to his work as vicar of the parish, he organised the older evacuees—there were three of them—to help him in the garden, where he grew all the vegetables needed for his large household, as well as a considerable surplus which he sold to a firm of wholesalers, using the money to fund a Christmas party for the children, and a pleasure trip by coach to the seaside in the summer.

The work in the garden was hard but the old man took it in his stride. 'I've been fond of gardening ever since my father gave me a little plot of land to cultivate when I was no more than eight,' he said, in his soft Devonshire burr, one bright morning at the beginning of Pete's leave. 'Ever since then, I've worked on the land every day of my life, so I reckon what may seem hard to a younger man who is new to cultivation comes easy to me.' He smiled up at his grandson, his faded blue eyes twinkling. 'As soon as my girls were five or six, I marked out a little plot of land for each of them, gave them a few seeds, and left them to it. Very soon, they were a real help to me. Your Uncle Samuel was never a keen gardener, but your Aunt Helen used to grow wonderful flowers in her little patch. Now, of course, she grows vegetables, and

214

very fine ones too. Well, you ate her early potatoes for dinner last night; delicious, weren't they?'

Pete agreed that the potatoes had been delicious and told his grandfather that his own mother, and subsequently her whole family, had profited from the old man's early teaching. 'When Ma came to the Walleroo there was nothing in the way of green stuff, no fruit trees or cultivated land near the homestead,' he said. 'But Ma could see how fertile the land near the river was when the floods went down. My father had grown maize for cattle feed but it hadn't occurred to him to grow his own vegetables; probably he simply didn't have the time. By the time I was three or four, Ma hadn't just made a large vegetable garden, but she had planted a flourishing orchard. I remember her saying how she and her sisters had helped their mother to make jam and to bottle fruit and vegetables, so of course she sent away for jars with sealed caps, and within a year or two we had all the fruit and vegetables we could desire.'

'Yes, I remember her first letters, how bleak and strange the place seemed to her and yet how determined she was to make a go of it,' his grandfather said reminiscently. 'We've kept all her letters, you know, and I like to think she shared most of her experiences with us. At first, as you say, life was incredibly tough, and when your father was away mustering the cattle I know she was dreadfully lonely and often very frightened. But that did not mean she ever considered for one moment giving up. Of course, she loved your father very deeply, but it wasn't just that. Very soon she began to love the life and to be proud of their achievements. And now she has everything the way

215

she always wanted it, though I'm sure she misses her sons.'

'Of course, but not as much as Pa does, I bet,' Pete said, with an inward grin. The price of beef had risen because of the war, so he knew his father was trying to produce even more cattle for the overseas market. Jacko at sixteen was some help but the Walleroo was not his greatest interest as it had been Pete's. Andy would be hard pressed, but as Pete and his brothers had grown up and moved away, so the sons of the stockmen had also grown up. Only they had not gone away, but stayed to help his father with every aspect of station life, as their young wives were no doubt helping his mother in her prolific garden and her productive kitchen, making jam, bottling fruit and, now, using her new canning machine to can vegetables.

'Do you have any plans for today?' his grandfather asked. He bent over a well-grown currant bush, for they were in the netted-off enclosure where he grew soft fruits, then straightened. 'It'll be a while before my blackcurrants begin to turn, but when they do I'll send you a box of them, by rail. They travel better than strawberries and raspberries . . . now, what was I saying?'

'You were asking if Sammy and I had any plans for today,' Pete said. 'We'd like to see a bit more of the country . . . I did wonder about visiting Aunt Helen, but Gran said the bus only goes three times a week and it's a fair distance to walk.'

'Ah, that reminds me of what I was going to suggest,' the old man said. 'Your grandmother and I used to do a great deal of cycling, and even now we use our machines once or twice a week. They

216

are in good order, though rather heavy and old-fashioned. If you would like to borrow them to ride over to your aunt's place, then you could save me a journey. Farmer Muswell killed a pig last week and whenever someone in the area has a pig, we share the meat around. I have a big parcel for Helen and Samuel, so if you could deliver it . . .'

Pete said he would be glad to do so and, presently, he and Sammy set off on their ten-mile journey through the deep Devonshire lanes. Birds sang overhead, and the trees which grew on top of the banks cast a dappled shade over the two riders, whilst on every side they saw wild flowers and tiny ferns.

They arrived at their destination, a delightful thatched cottage with whitewashed walls and a heavy oak door. Their knock was answered by a tall, thin man with a long, serious face, who peered at them over a pair of tiny half-moon glasses. Pete began to introduce himself, but his uncle-in-law stopped him with a wave of his hand. 'I know who you are; you're my nephew Peter, and this will be your pal. Another Samuel, I believe, though I understand he's always called Sammy.' He smiled delightedly at them both. 'Don't ask me how I know because it's incredibly complicated, but news travels fast in small communities. I dare say I heard of your arrival within half an hour of your getting off the train. You see, the inspector who clipped your tickets is brother-in-law to Miss Briggs, who runs our local post office; need I say more?'

As he spoke, he had been ushering them into the cottage, where they were joined by a tall, fair woman whose likeness to his mother was so

217

pronounced that if left Pete in no doubt that this was his Aunt Helen. Much exclaiming and talk followed. Pete handed over the parcel of meat and his aunt bade the visitors sit down at the kitchen table whilst she set the kettle on the Aga and began to butter newly baked scones.

'How kind of you to come and see us when I know you will have to be back on your airfield in a couple of days,' Uncle Samuel said presently, when they had drunk two cups of strong tea and eaten the scones. 'I must show you round our little cottage, which was almost derelict when we moved in ten years ago. Before then, we had lived in a great draughty vicarage on the outskirts of the village, which needed so much money spending on it that the Parochial Church Council decided it would be cheaper to rehouse us and to pull the old place down. They wanted to build a neat, modern villa in the grounds of the old vicarage, but Helen had seen this cottage for sale and fallen in love with it, so we persuaded the powers-that-be to buy it—it was very cheap—and said that we would make the place habitable if they would pay for the materials needed. They agreed, and Paul and Matthew and myself set to work whilst Nan and your Aunt Helen slaved in the garden. Why, they even built a respectable pigsty in the orchard, as well as a grand hen house.' He had been leading the visitors up the steep little stairs as he spoke and now flung open the first door on the small, square landing. 'Our bedroom, mine and Helen's; I always tell myself that we have a sea view, and I'm certain, sometimes, that there is a line on the horizon, far, far away, which really must be the ocean.' He passed to the next door. 'Nan's room.' Alongside

218

that was the boys' bedroom, but it was the last room that brought the broadest smile to his face. 'It's a proper bathroom, with a WC and a hot water geyser over the bath,' he said proudly. 'It took the boys and myself over a year to complete but now, of course, Helen and I have our bath once a week—four inches of water only—and can wash in hot water at the turn of a tap. And now we'd best go back downstairs as I'm sure Helen is longing to show you the garden.'

After they had examined the garden, the hen house and the pigsty, they were given a delicious lunch, then sped on their way home with a bag containing Aunt Helen's all butter shortbread. 'We keep a house cow on the meadow which abuts our orchard,' Helen told the two young men. 'When the children were young, we had an old pony on which they learned to ride, and when we moved here we brought old Trooper with us. He was a grand little gelding and we missed him sadly when he died five years ago, but then we got Blossom. She's a pure bred Hereford, and she's not only a charming creature, she provides us with the means to make our own butter and cheese, and gallons of milk as well.' She sighed wistfully. 'I *wish* you could have met Paul and Matthew—and Nan of course— but perhaps next time . . .'

Pete and Sammy took their leave as the sun began to sink and discussed the delightful cottage most of the way home. Samuel had told them that it had, in fact, been two dwellings, farm workers' cottages he presumed, but to the two young Australians it had seemed just about perfect. For both of them, it was their first visit to an English house, other than the vicarage, which was scarcely typical; their first chance to become familiar with the sort of place that Pete's relatives occupied, and they were mightily impressed. Pete had expected to feel cramped, to miss the wide open spaces of his home country, but, so far at least, he had not done so. Indeed, why should he? Neither his uncle and aunt's house nor that of his grandparents was surrounded by other dwellings; both had beautiful countryside all about them and an air of permanence which Pete found strangely attractive. Both the tiny church of which Samuel was rector and the larger one in which Pete's grandfather preached were very old indeed. Yet their antiquity was completely taken for granted, not even remarked upon.

'I never expected a cottage to be so roomy and comfortable,' Pete said as they cycled along. 'And the old folks' vicarage is a grand house as well. My ma and pa have worked wonders at the Walleroo homestead, but it's not anything like the house in which my ma was brought up. She must have missed it dreadfully—the vicarage, I mean. I can't understand what made her go off in the first place.'

Sammy grinned. 'Birds fly the nest,' he pointed out. 'I bet your Aunt Helen's kids won't go back to live there after the war. Well, do you mean to go back to the Walleroo?'

Pete said that of course he would go home. It was a hard life but a grand one, he told himself, and it was the one he had been born into. He remembered with pleasure his mother's wonderful vegetable garden, the picture shows at the neighbouring homestead, the big fan which his mother had installed on the veranda. Of course there were drawbacks: the fearful heat and humidity, the relentless downpours in the wet, and the long burning days of drought that followed it. Then there were the insects. When the water began to recede from the flood plain by the river, dangerous mosquitoes swarmed around the homestead. In the wet, snakes, scorpions and enormous spiders shared one's house.

He looked round at the cool green shade of the lane along which they were cycling. It was beautiful all right, but it . . . oh, it enclosed him, almost smothered him. He thought of the freedom, the sheer emptiness of Queensland and knew it was the place he most wanted to be. He grinned at his friend. 'What about you, Sam?'

'I shan't live at home again,' Sammy said immediately. 'Though I dare say there are jobs in Melbourne which would suit me. My dad works in a grocery store and my ma has her own little hairdressing place, so it ain't as if I've a family business to go back to. When I first left school, I worked in a factory making wireless parts, which is why when I joined the RAF I put in to train as a wireless operator. I couldn't go back into a factory, it 'ud drive me mad, but I reckon I'll go back to Australia. It's a grand country, you know.'

'Yeah, I'm with you there, cobber,' Pete said at once. 'But, you know, I like flying. Oh, I don't mean I like bombing Germany, or dodging the flak, or risking all our lives every time I take Katie Kite off the ground; I like the actual flying. When the war's over, I reckon I'll stay in the air force for a bit before going home. I was talking to Johnny the other day and he was saying that after the war he thinks commercial flying will really take off.' Sammy spluttered and Pete, grinning, said: 'Yes, I know, but that was what our revered squadron leader said. He thinks that folk will want to see the world when it's not at war and flying is a lot quicker and more convenient than going by sea. If he's right, then there may be jobs with commercial airlines for those who want them.'

By this time, the two young men were cycling up the lane which led to the vicarage, and as they dismounted and pushed their bikes round the corner of the house Pete said regretfully: 'Only another couple of days and then it'll be back to the station once more. Oh well, all good things come to an end, but this little break has meant a lot to me. I guess I feel more a part of things. Before, I was fighting Hitler because he's evil, but now . . . aw, hell, how can I explain it?'

'You don't have to,' Sammy said equably. 'I know just what you mean. Now, you're fighting to protect a way of life. You've seen how your ma's family live, their homes, their gardens, the way they're looking after them kids who aren't even related to 'em.' He shot a quick glance at his friend. 'I know they ain't my relatives, but, d'you know, I feel the same? Spendin' time with your folks has given the war a whole new meaning.'

Pete was beginning to reply when they reached the old stable where the bicycles were kept, and as they did so the kitchen door opened and his grandmother emerged. 'I thought I heard someone talking; come along in, supper's ready,' she called. 'Did you find your aunt and uncle at home? I thought afterwards they might have taken themselves off into Barnstaple to do some shopping, it being such a lovely day.'

Pete assured her that they had found the

Warwicks at home and had been royally entertained by them. 'They gave us a great high tea,' he admitted, as they were ushered into the big kitchen which smelt deliciously of cooking. 'I doubt we could eat another morsel. But I expect the kids will clear up anything we can't manage,' he concluded, glancing at the evacuees already seated round the huge kitchen table.

'Oh, I dare say you'll find you've got room for a piece of my pork and apple pie,' his grandmother said serenely, placing a huge dish in the middle of the table and gesturing to the two young men to sit down. She began to cut the pie into slices whilst Mrs Grundy, who helped out at the vicarage a couple of times a week, served steaming potatoes on to each plate. Gran turned to her husband. 'Say grace, my dear, and then we can all begin.'

*   *   *

Debbie and Gwen came out of the factory both feeling worn out, for Merseyside had been heavily targeted by the Luftwaffe for nights and nights and they were not only exhausted from lack of sleep—for it was hard to drop off in the dank and crowded shelter—but also stale and dispirited. 'It seems a lifetime since we went to a flick or a dance hall, or did anything which was fun,' Debbie grumbled, as they began to walk towards Ogden's. There was little point in waiting for a bus or a tram because the public services were in terrible disarray; it would be much quicker to walk. 'But we're off tomorrow, praise be. I suppose we could have a long lie-in but that doesn't appeal to me; it's no use letting the Luftwaffe ruin our daytimes as well as

223

our nights. What are the chances of getting out into the real country, do you suppose? I know we're going to spend another night in that bleeding shelter and I know we may not get very much sleep,' she added plaintively, 'but I'd like to go somewhere tomorrow. I'm just about sick of hanging round at home, week after week. It's all right when the weather's lousy, but when it's fine like it was today it's such a waste! May is blossom time; we could go to the woods and see the cherry trees in bloom.' The factory had gone on to seven day working, so the girls could no longer rely on a weekend off but had to follow the shift system, which meant that sometimes their 'Sunday' was the middle of the week.

Gwen looked doubtful. 'The trouble is, so many stations and railway lines have been hit that it's difficult to get away from the city,' she said. 'Mind, I suppose we could catch a bus, only because of the bombing we'd likely spend half the day getting there and the other half getting back. Tell you what, though, we could take a picnic to Sefton Park; it's like country there.'

'Well, I suppose we could,' Debbie said. 'It may not be much of a picnic, what with rationing and shortages, but I dare say we can scratch up a few sandwiches and a bottle of tea each.' Because of the almost constant bombing, Mrs Soames had sent the children back into Wales where they were comfortably situated in a small village deep in Snowdonia. Debbie knew that Mrs Soames had set out to visit her family that morning and would not return for at least a week, for she, too, was exhausted by the raids and felt she needed a break. It would have been nice had Gwen been able to accompany her, but as the factory was so busy time off was at a premium, and Gwen had had to remain at her post.

'I don't care so much about the picnic as getting out of all the soot and the mess and the brick dust,' Gwen said frankly. 'Besides, knowing she were leaving me alone for a time, Mam made some of her delicious rock buns and a Woolton pie. I'll bring some of that. I wish the bloody Nazis didn't keep hitting the shippin' and the warehouses though,' she added as they trudged along. 'Old Mr Huxtable—he's next door but two to us—says them buggers in the Luftwaffe know what they're doin'; they're goin' to starve us out. Every time a warehouse or a ship loaded with grub gets hit, our rations get tighter. Still, our mam says the country folk are doin' a grand job. They don't grow flowers no more and their lawns is all rooted up an' put down to spuds, so that's a help, I reckon.'

'I wish the people in the country grew acres and acres of onions,' Debbie said, as they turned into Walton Lane. She wrinkled her nose as a strong stench of sewage assailed her nostrils. 'Phew, it 'ud be a relief just to get away from the horrible smells as well as the muck and the rubbish. I dunno why there are no onions in the shops. You can't say they come from abroad because my mam says any fool can grow onions, and the English ones are lovely, much stronger than the French ones the fellers in berets used to bring over from Brittany. And a stew ain't the same without onions,' she ended wistfully.

Gwen nodded. 'We don't understand it either,' she admitted. 'My Uncle Frank what lives in Seaforth has got an allotment and he grows all sorts, but he says when thieves climb over the fence it's the onions they're after. He says he's goin' to keep a night watch over the allotment when his crops are almost ready and he'll shoot any bugger what climbs the fence and starts on his onions.'

Debbie made a derisive noise. 'What's he going to shoot them with, a peashooter?' she asked. 'And where'll he get the peas from, come to that?'

Gwen giggled. 'He were in the First World War and he kept his old rifle,' she explained. 'Eh, I'm not looking forward to getting home to an empty house. What shift's your mam on? If it's nights you can come and stay with me, an' if it's days I'll come and stay with you. Not that we're liable to be in our beds for long, but at least I won't be alone in the house either way.'

Debbie frowned. 'I keep losing track,' she admitted. 'At least our shifts remain pretty much the same, but Mam fills in here and does a double shift there until she hardly knows which way up she is. But I *think* she's on nights, so if you don't mind I'll come to your place.'

'Sure; that'll be grand,' Gwen said eagerly. 'But I bet we end up in the shelter again; I can't see the perishin' Luftwaffe givin' us a night off, can you?'

'Not really,' Debbie admitted. 'Then it's agreed, I take it? We go to Sefton Park tomorrow, if the weather's fine of course, and take a picnic. I'll have to go home in the morning to make Uncle Max's breakfast, but if it's a nice hot day we'll head straight for the park after that and get ourselves a couple of deckchairs. We might even snooze a little if the raid's been really noisy and we've not had much sleep in the shelter.'

'Right. And if we feel like it, we might go to

a flick in the evening,' Gwen said eagerly. 'Wharrabout this evening, though? Will your mam be at home to make you a meal, or do you want to come straight to mine?'

'You come round to ours, Gwen,' Debbie said at once. 'You can have your tea with us, because whether or not Mam is in she'll have left something ready for cooking.' She tilted her head back to gaze at the blue sky above. 'Isn't it awful to feel afraid just because the sky is clear? But never mind, we'll have a real day out tomorrow.'

*   *   *

Next morning, the girls set out for Sefton Park with their picnic, for the day was as bright and sunny as anyone could wish, though the fires still burned in the docks and the air was thick with the dust from buildings which had been hit during the previous night's raid. However, both their homes were still standing, undamaged, and Jess had applauded their decision to have a day away from the carnage. 'I'd come with you if I wasn't so horribly tired,' she said, and Debbie could see that her mother's face was strained and pale, and her eyes seemed to have sunk into her head. 'I was on the children's ward last night—poor little things, they're so cheerful even when they must be scared out of their wits— and when the siren sounded we had to rush them to the basement, all among the files. If it wasn't for the noise, they might have got some sleep, but even with concrete all round us you could still hear the ack-ack batteries blazing away.'

'Why don't you come with us anyway, Mam?' Debbie asked hopefully. 'We're going to hire a couple of deckchairs and have a sleep in the sun when we reach the park. You could follow suit.'

Jess had smiled but shaken her head. 'No, love, I'm going straight to bed and I shall sleep the clock round,' she had declared. 'I've got two more night shifts and then I'm back on days. So I'd best get a proper rest while I can. I'm afraid I probably won't be here when you get home, but I'll leave you something cold for your tea.'

'We thought we might see a flick, just to round our day off nicely, you know,' Debbie had said. 'That means we may not be home in time to get Uncle Max his tea, but if it's cold, surely he can get his own? It's ages since we went to the cinema,' she finished, rather wistfully.

Jess had laughed and pinched her cheek. 'You deserve a really nice day out so I'll tell Max he'll be on his own for tea this evening,' she had said. 'If he wants company, he can ask Mr Bottomley to share his meal. Have a lovely time!'

Now, they were walking along the pavement, occasionally having to move into the roadway to avoid the rubble of bombed buildings. Everywhere, people were working to clear the roads, and there was very little traffic about, but presently a van stopped just ahead of them and a young man jumped out and walked towards them, grinning cheerfully. 'Gwenny? I come past your house just now so I guessed you and your family was all right, same as us. But what's you doin' here? Ain't you at work today? Youse goin' in the wrong direction if you're headin' for Long Lane!'

Debbie glanced interrogatively at her friend and saw Gwen's cheeks beginning to flush pink. 'It's me cousin Bert's pal, Dicky; he's ever so nice. He's put

228

in to join the air force, but till then he's driving a delivery van for Matheson's,' Gwen hissed beneath her breath. She raised her voice. 'How ya doing, wack? Me an' me pal's off to Sefton Park, only there ain't no buses runnin'—or none have passed us—so it looks as though we'll spend most of our day off footin' it.'

'Footin' it? Nonsense. Ain't we all told to help one another in this bleedin' war?' Dicky said genially. He swung open the passenger door as they reached the van. 'I don't mean to see me favourite girl walking her feet down to the ankles, so just you hop in.' The girls squeezed on to the narrow bench seat. 'I've got two more deliveries which won't take above five minutes apiece and then I might as well drive past Seffy as not.' He grinned down at them. 'Is that a picnic you've got there? I might even join you for half an hour if it'll stretch to a third person.'

'We'd be glad to share our food in return for the lift,' Debbie said, seeing that her friend was almost overcome; clearly, Gwen had a crush on this young man. Debbie turned to her. 'That's right, isn't it, Gwen?'

'Of course it is,' Gwen mumbled. 'Only we shan't eat straight away; we're going to try to get some shut-eye 'cos it were that noisy last night we hardly slept at all.'

'You and the whole of Liverpool,' Dicky said. 'Still, it can't last for ever and they say a barrage balloon accounted for one of the enemy last night and the ack-ack fellers brought down two more.' He put the van into gear and moved forward. 'Tell you what, I'll drop you off and go back to me depot, then I'll come back around five. Save me

229

some grub and I'll give you a lift home.'

Gwen began to murmur her thanks but Debbie cut in. 'We'll be glad of a lift but we're going to a flick this evening,' she said. 'This is the first real day out we've had for ages and we want it to be a good one, so could you drop us off at any cinema which hasn't been bombed flat?'

'Course I could,' Dicky said obligingly. 'Well, young Gwen. How's the family?'

*   *   *

'Well, I can't think when I've enjoyed a day more,' Gwen breathed, as they walked up the Scotland Road on their way home. 'Oh, and wasn't that the most romantic film you've ever seen? I just love Clark Gable. And isn't Dicky grand? Why, even going to the trouble of finding out what the various picture houses were showing. I like him better'n any other feller I know.'

'Yes, he's really nice,' Debbie agreed. 'I remember you mentioned him once before . . . didn't he come to that party at your aunt's house the Christmas after war was declared.'

'That's right,' Gwen said. 'It's a pity he couldn't come to the cinema with us but since he lives out at Crosby I suppose it's reasonable that he wanted to get home before dark. Still, walking home from here is nothing to the walking we'd have had to do if Dicky hadn't took pity on us.'

'True,' Debbie said. She took her friend's arm. 'I've got my torch. The battery's not a new one but it'll serve to stop us walking straight into a big hole or a pile of rubble. We'd best get a move on or we shan't reach the shelter before—' A familiar sound

230

cut across her words; Moaning Minnie was in good voice tonight and giving advance warning that the raiders were crossing the Irish Sea, doubtless on their way to deliver another stunning blow to the docks. Debbie stopped short, a hand flying to her mouth. 'Oh damn, damn, damn! We're still a good way from home . . . I wonder whether we can make it if we run?'

But it was already too late. The road was full of scurrying figures, clearly making for the nearest shelter, and when the two girls would have hurried on by, an ARP warden, tin-hatted and uniformed, barred their way. 'Shelter's fifty yards ahead, on your left, young ladies,' he said briskly. 'You just come along o' me and I'll see you safely stowed.'

'Oh, but mam will worry dreadfully if we don't get home, or at least into the shelter up by the Stanley,' Debbie said immediately. 'We'll run all the way, honest to God we will.'

She tried to get past him but the warden grabbed hold of Gwen and shook his head chidingly at Debbie. 'No you don't; you've got younger ears than mine, and I can hear the engines overhead,' he said grimly. 'Better safe than sorry, queens. Now step lively.'

Debbie and Gwen found themselves descending a steep and narrow set of concrete steps and emerging into a long, dank-smelling public shelter. They saw, without much surprise, that the bunks were already taken but there were long narrow benches and a pile of grey blankets by the door, so they took a blanket each and squeezed on to one of the benches. Clearly, this was a shelter used by people who did not live in the area but were visiting the places of entertainment by which it was

231

surrounded. Locals had taken the bunks, but the rest of the inhabitants did not seem to know one another and were strangely polite, and quieter, on the whole, than those in neighbourhood shelters.

Debbie glanced curiously about her. One end of the shelter was curtained off with what looked like rough sacking and she guessed that this would hide the buckets half full of earth, or sand, which were the best the shelter marshals could manage in the way of toilets. Against one wall there were a couple of primus stoves and several tall enamel jugs which probably contained water. There were shelves upon which various goods were set out, but she thought with a pang which was almost homesickness that it was not as well provisioned as their own shelter. No one could leave anything of value in a shelter, of course, but back on the Stanley Road they had evolved a very good system. Someone would take care of the tea, the conny-onny, and a bottle of Camp coffee. Someone else would be given a big bag of broken biscuits which would be passed among the children when the noise of the raid was at its height. Others would look after pillows because these were too bulky to be brought to and from the shelter when one had children in one's charge.

Gwen nudged Debbie, glancing around her. 'It ain't exactly a home from home, is it?' she said. 'It seems odd to be amongst strangers . . . over the weeks we've kind o' got used to each other at the Stanley Road shelter, haven't we? I wonder if there'll be a sing-song later, or if anyone has brung spare food? I wish we'd not eaten all our sandwiches and Mam's pie and cakes. It's funny, isn't it? If we was at home in our own beds we

232

wouldn't dream of getting up for a sandwich and a drink, but when you're stuck down in a miserable bloody shelter it's different. D'you reckon they'll light them primuses and boil up some water for tea?'

'I dunno,' Debbie said. Outside, it was a warm night, but in this place the cold combined with a sort of stuffiness which was most unpleasant. 'But they won't do anything until the shelter's full and they've closed the fire curtain. Gosh, how many folk are they going to cram in?' A large, untidy woman with a baby in her arms had entered the shelter just as the fire curtain was drawn across, indicating that no one else could come in. She was looking round her in a rather helpless manner and Debbie nudged Gwen. 'Shove up,' she muttered. 'That old lady's holding a baby; she's got to sit down.' Both girls shunted along as she spoke and Debbie tugged at the woman's filthy black skirt. 'Sit next to me,' she whispered. 'If the marshal sees you're standing, he might tell you to move on.'

The woman sat down hastily and the baby began to mutter. It was not a tiny new baby but looked to Debbie to be about six months old, and when it started to whimper she addressed the woman. 'Have you a bottle for your baby? It might find a bottle soothing. I don't know much about babies, but I do know they have to be fed every four or five hours.'

'I ain't got nothing for it,' the old woman said crossly. She turned and glared at Debbie out of small black eyes, beady as boot buttons, and Debbie took a good look at her face. She was clearly very old, but her skin was tanned and leathery and, Debbie thought, extremely dirty. She

233

had a large hooked nose and a thin-lipped mouth, and when she spoke Debbie saw that she was toothless. She turned back to the baby for a moment, shifting it uncomfortably in her arms, as though she were not used to holding a child. Then she turned back to Debbie. 'Know me agin?' she asked nastily.

Debbie felt her cheeks grow hot. She knew the old woman was right and she had, indeed, been staring. She looked away quickly. 'Sorry, it's—it's just that you obviously aren't the baby's mother. I just wondered . . .' She abandoned what she had been about to say, changing it to: 'I'm sure if you ask the shelter marshal, he'll find some milk or something for the baby. They're very good as a rule and often have something hidden away for an emergency.' The old woman sniffed, but presently the baby began to cry in earnest. And having shaken it twice, in a most unfriendly manner— Debbie was reminded of the pig baby and the Duchess in *Alice*—she thrust the baby into Debbie's arms, saying crossly: 'If you're so concerned with the little bugger, you can hang on to it whiles I have a word with the marshal. I can't abide bloody kids, and if it starts bellering I won't be responsible for me actions.'

She stomped off to the far end of the shelter where the marshal sat behind a small gate-legged table, writing in a ledger, and Gwen took advantage of her absence to lean across and take a good look at the baby. 'Ain't she the prettiest little thing?' she said softly. 'I don't reckon she's any kin to the old witch; what d'you think?'

Debbie, who had already examined the baby closely and noticed the blue eyes and the mossy down on its small round head, so different from the old woman's snapping black eyes and greasy black locks, agreed. 'If you ask me, the old 'un's a gypsy and I reckon she stole the baby out of a pram and means to sell it to someone who wants a child badly,' she said. 'Did you see the way she shook the poor little mite? If she hadn't handed it to me and waddled off, I'd have told her she was no fit person to be in charge of a kid. When she comes back, I may say something.'

'I don't think you should. If you start a ruckus down here, someone's going to get turned out, and—'

An enormous explosion from outside cut across her words. Gwen stopped speaking for a moment, then put her mouth close to Debbie's ear. 'Remember, we can't just get up and walk out,' she shouted. 'Save whatever you want to say to her until the All Clear goes; agreed?'

It was still too noisy to hear much so Debbie just nodded. She knew Gwen was right. Once or twice, rows and quarrels had started in their shelter but wiser counsels usually prevailed and folk sank their differences.

When the old woman returned bearing a small celluloid cup, Debbie held out the baby, expecting her to take it, but she shook her head. 'I ain't gorra bottle an' nor's that bleedin' marshal,' she said gruffly. 'I dare say it ain't never drunk out of a cup in its whole life, so it'll need two of us to get this down it.' She seated herself and pushed the cup, which proved to be half full of conny-onny and water, against the baby's mouth just as another explosion rent the air, and actually made the benches tilt.

The baby, finding the hard rim of the cup suddenly crashed against its soft little lips, began to weep in earnest and Debbie snatched the mug from the old woman, glaring. 'I'd better feed it myself, as you don't seem too handy at it,' she said, biting back the much more honest remark she would have liked to make. She cradled the baby softly against her breast, rocking it a little and holding the cup gently close and tilting it so that only a tiny amount of liquid entered the baby's open, crying mouth. 'There you are, my little love, a lovely warm drink which the kind marshal has made specially for you.' She turned to look at the old woman. 'What's its name?' she enquired baldly. 'Come to that, I don't know whether it's a boy or a girl.'

The old woman hesitated, looking unsure of herself for the first time. 'What do it matter? A baby's a baby when all's said and done,' and now there was a distinct whine in her voice. 'It ain't mine—even you must have guessed that much— and I disremember whether it's a boy or a girl. Kids is all the same to me.'

Debbie might have retorted sharply but at that moment the baby's crying ceased, the big blue eyes opened, and the tiny thing began to drink, gulping and coughing a little, but definitely taking the mixture which Debbie was trickling into its mouth, and clearly both enjoying it and anxious for more.

The sight of the baby's eager little face and, it must be admitted, the cessation of its wails gave Debbie a very real thrill. She had always loved babies, had longed for a little brother or sister, but she did not even have the satisfaction of having younger cousins, and now she determined that she

236

would look after this baby until the All Clear went. She said as much to the old woman, half expecting a dusty answer, but instead the first smile she had seen crossed the woman's face. 'Aye, that'll be best. I can see it's more at home wi' you than it were wi' me,' the old woman said. She added, almost apologetically: 'I didn't know it were hungry else I might ha' looked round for a bottle or summat, but I gorra clean nappy . . . it were hung over the side of the cradle.'

Debbie, cooing over the baby as it finished the last drop of milk, said nothing to this, but Gwen leaned forward eagerly. 'Are you the baby's gran?' she asked. 'Else I don't see how you come to get the clean nappy off of the cradle.'

The old woman's eyes had been closed as she leaned back against the wall, but they snapped open at Gwen's words. 'Mind your own bleedin' business, you cocky little tart,' she said, and Gwen was so shocked that she said nothing more, whereupon the old woman closed her eyes and leaned back again, taking up even more room than she had before. And then, with astonishing rapidity, she began to snore and to lean against Debbie's shoulder. Debbie tried to move away, for the old woman was heavy, and presently succeeded in extricating herself. Then, with the baby in her arms and Gwen beside her, she made a sort of nest of the blankets and the three of them cuddled up in it, trying to ignore the horrendous racket from outside.

Astonishingly, the old woman continued to sleep heavily. Her mouth fell open, her head fell sideways, and she snored and snored, now and then snuffling wetly, but not waking up even when a shock reverberated through the shelter.

'They're gettin' it real bad out there,' Gwen said apprehensively, her round brown eyes going towards the roof of the shelter as though she were trying to see through the solid concrete blocks. 'Mind you, every night since this lot started we've come out in the morning expecting to find nothing left standing, but there always is.' She looked appealingly at Debbie. 'It can't go on for ever, can it? They'll get sick of bombing Liverpool soon, surely? I'm warning you, Deb, if it goes on like this I'm going to tell 'em at work that I'm sick and go and stay with Mam and the kids for a few days.'

Debbie settled the baby, which seemed to be sleeping soundly, more comfortably in the crook of her arm, and put her other arm round Gwen. They had hoped to get some sleep but it was too noisy and there was too much going on around them. Women were leading children to and from the curtained-off area at the end of the shelter, and someone had started a sing-song in a brave attempt to take folks' minds off what was happening above ground. Some women, clearly better prepared than their sisters, were cutting chunks off homemade loaves, spreading the slices with margarine, and handing them out to friends and relatives. Debbie squeezed Gwen's shoulders comfortingly and put her mouth to her friend's ear. 'I might join you at that,' she said. 'An' I reckon my mam might come as well. She's worked all the hours God sends on those bleedin' wards; it's time she had a break. Uncle Max was telling her so only yesterday, and for once I think he was talking sense. Nursing is hard physical work, lifting great heavy patients, lugging them up in bed when it's

238

time for a meal, carting great trays of food and medicine around . . . and then all the cleaning and sterilising and that, as well as running the house. She could do with a break all right.'

Gwen nodded vigorously just as another bomb came screaming to earth nearby, and both girls clapped their hands over their ears as the roar of its impact and the crash of falling masonry made the shelter shake once more. 'That were a close one,' Gwen muttered. She leaned her head against Debbie's shoulder and Debbie realised for the first time that her friend was white and exhausted. She looked round at the people nearest her and saw that they, too, were beginning to show the strain. Many of the faces were grey; she was beginning to grow used to washing off a film of dust every time she entered her home from the streets outside. I reckon the whole of Liverpool could do with a break, if we aren't all to be ill, she told herself. I know everyone says London has had it worse but what could be worse than this?

In her arms the baby stirred, then snuggled against her once more. It was wrapped in a ragged pink shawl, and for the first time Debbie really looked into its small fair face, noting the long lashes and the clear pale skin with the faintest flush of rose on its cheeks. The shawl the child was wrapped in might be ragged but it was clean, and what Debbie could see of the gown beneath it— which was not much—was clean as well. Someone, and it's not that nasty old woman, is taking good care of you, Debbie told it silently, then she turned to Gwen. 'I wonder what we ought to do, Gwenny? When we get out of here, I mean. If the old woman is a gypsy, and she does look like one, then I don't

239

think we ought to hand the baby back to her, do you? I mean, if she stole it, which seems quite likely, we should try to find its rightful parents.'

She had spoken softly, or as softly as one could speak against the noise from outside, for the ack-ack battery stationed nearby was seldom silent for long, but nevertheless she had been overheard. An elderly man lying on the floor, wrapped in his blanket and cradling a dirty old sack in both arms, cocked a bright eye at her. 'You talkin' about Miz O'Shea? She ain't no gypsy, though I'll grant you she looks like one. When she were younger, she used to wear a pair o' them great big hoop earrings because she wanted to look mysterious like, but she ain't no gypsy, not really. She used to sell flowers in Clayton Square but then she reckoned she was too old to gerrup there an' back each day, so she got 'erself a bit of a house in one of them courts off the Scottie, an' let rooms.' He sat up and jerked a thumb at the child in Debbie's arms. 'That'll be a kid from one of them dockside prossies what she's took in,' he said knowledgeably. 'In the old days, sailors used to come to her house for a bit o' fun whenever they had a few coppers to spare. But the scuffers got on to her, made her life a misery she said, so now she only has three or four gals livin' in the house and they has to conduc' their business elsewhere.' He chuckled coarsely. 'I reckon they're the only people what are glad of the blackout 'cos they can earn a bob or two in any dark alley or back jigger these days. Why, even a scuffer thinks twice about flashin' a torch where Jerry might see it an' drop a bomb on 'im.'

The two girls leaned against one another, trying

to sleep, but of course it was impossible. A man with an accordion struck up a cheerful, jigging tune and a small girl, no more than three or four, began to dance. Debbie was watching her, laughing and clapping, though with some difficulty because the baby slumbered still in the curve of her arm, when Gwen nudged her. 'Debbie, can you keep a secret?'

Debbie stared at her. What a daft question! She and Gwen had been pals ever since she started at Daisy Street School. They had defended one another against would-be bullies, helped each other with their homework, walked to and from school with their arms linked whilst they discussed the doings of each day. They had cut and curled each other's hair, criticised each other's clothing, slept in each other's beds. They had, in fact, lived in one another's pockets, and, until this moment, Debbie had thought she knew Gwen as well as she knew herself. Yet here was Gwen intimating that she had a secret to share; what on earth could it be? Why, even now that they were almost grown-up and working in the factory, she and Gwen shared everything: thoughts, feelings and desires. So the face that Debbie turned to her friend was astonished as well as curious. 'Can I keep a secret? How can you ask such a question? Did I ever tell my mam that it were you who caught your skipping rope round my ankle and brought me crashing to the ground so's I cracked a bone in me wrist? When you were milk monitor, same as me, and tripped on the loose tile in the cloakroom, did I tell Miss Watkins which one of us went over first? Course I never.'

'Oh I know, really,' Gwen said hastily. 'I know

you'd never tell a soul nothing that I wanted kept quiet. What I *should* have said was, do you want to hear a secret?'

'Course I do,' Debbie said promptly. 'Spit it out!'

'Well, you know Dicky, the boy who gave us a lift to Prince's Park this morning?'

'Of course I know him,' Debbie said impatiently. 'He's nice, isn't he? I thought it was really kind of him to pick us up and take us to the good old Forum. But so what? I mean, there's nothing secret about that, is there?'

'No-o-o,' Gwen said. 'But you know you joined the queue and he called me back to the van for a moment? Well, he—he asked me if I was doing anything tomorrow evening. And when I said no, not as I knew, he—he went a bit red and said would I like to go dancin' with him.' She looked shyly at her friend, a rosy flush beginning to colour her cheeks. 'I—I said that would be lovely, so he's goin' to pick me up after work tomorrow!'

Debbie gazed at Gwen, almost unable to believe her ears, and realised, suddenly, how very much Gwen had changed over the course of the last year. When they had left school, Gwen had been a mousy little thing, skinny as a rake and with nothing to commend her but a pair of large brown eyes fringed with light brown lashes. Her hair had been lank and straight, like her figure, and she had been almost unbearably shy. Now, Gwen's hair was fashionably cut, the ends curled under in a pageboy. She darkened her lashes, which made her eyes appear larger than ever, and despite the shortages she had filled out so that Jess had remarked, only a few days earlier, that Gwen was

242

getting a very pretty figure.

The factory had cured her of her shyness; now she would chatter away happily in any company, and the fact that she was good at her job had given her self-confidence. No wonder Dicky wants to take her out, Debbie found herself thinking. I've always known she was a lovely person; I've often wished she were my sister, but I simply hadn't noticed how pretty she'd grown.

'Well? What d'you think? And why are you starin' at me as if I'd got two heads?' Gwen said plaintively. 'Would you call it a date, Debbie? Oh, I know he's not a stranger, I've known him for ever, but I've never been out with him alone before.'

Debbie leaned across and kissed her friend's cheek. 'Of *course* it's a date and I think it's grand,' she said jubilantly. 'I hope you're going to tell me everything when you get home because I've never been out with a feller and I want to know what it's like. Oh, Gwen, are you excited? Does it make you feel grown-up?'

'It scares me a bit,' Gwen admitted. 'Suppose—suppose he tries to kiss me goodnight? Should I let him or will he think I'm fast?'

Debbie, who had not the faintest idea of what constituted fastness, shook her head wisely. 'I see what you mean. I reckon he can kiss your cheek without anyone thinking the worse of you,' she said. 'It's all this first date business, isn't it? All the magazines tell you what you should and shouldn't do on a first date because that's the one the feller will judge you by for ever after. Tell you what, why don't you say you'd prefer a walk in the park? It 'ud be safer.'

'That's a good idea. And in fact, if it's another

lovely fine evening, I'd rather go for a walk than go dancing,' Gwen said. 'I say, the baby's waking up; do you want me to take it for a bit?'

Debbie was about to hand the baby over when an interruption occurred. From outside there came a loud crash and the tinkle of breaking glass, and then the heavy curtain which shielded them from the outside world was pushed to one side, and a wild-eyed mongrel dog with one fly-away ear dripping blood came hurtling into the shelter. Several people cried out that dogs were not allowed, that it should be evicted, but the marshal vetoed this suggestion and his voice was echoed by several others. 'Poor critter, it ain't his war, why should he have to face what's up there?' 'Have a heart, the poor bugger's wounded; part of his ear's been blown off.' 'How'd you like to find yourself in the street with all this here noise a-goin' on an' buildin's crashin' about your ears? Lerr'im stay.'

As Gwen took the baby from her, Debbie reached out to the dog. Someone warned her that the terrified animal might snap but, on the contrary, it came to her at once, wedged its trembling body as close to her as it could get, and reached up to lick the side of her face. Debbie got out her hanky and mopped the blood from its ear. 'I reckon it were hit by flying glass,' she said to Gwen. 'Poor thing. I wonder who owns it. But when the raid's over I dare say it'll make its way home.' She chuckled. 'Dogs are cleverer'n babies; that poor little mite . . .' she indicated the child, now wriggling and beginning to make small, discontented noises in her friend's arms, 'couldn't tell you who its mother is, let alone where it lives.'

Gwen laughed. 'A fat lot you know about

babies,' she observed. 'Come to that, we neither of us know much about dogs, either. But this here baby could do with another mug of that milk mixture. It must be a good four hours since it was last fed . . . oh! Oh God, it's been and gone and pee'd all over me. Did you say there were a clean nappy somewhere?'

She stood up, holding the baby away from herself, and Debbie took back the small, wriggling body. 'Yes, it's on the bench beside the old wom— beside Mrs O'Shea, I mean,' she said. 'Tell you what, Gwen, I'll take it up to the far end of the shelter, behind the curtain, clean it up and put on the new nappy whilst you can fetch another cup of the milk mixture.'

'I'll change the nappy if you'd rather,' Gwen said. She pulled the shawl aside and rolled up the child's long nightdress, then stepped back quickly, wrinkling her nose. 'Phew, the poor little blighter's dirty as well as wet! Look, if you want me to change it . . .'

For a moment Debbie was tempted. She had never changed a baby's nappy in her life but knew that Gwen had probably done so when her brothers and sisters were small. But Gwen had already taken a big step ahead of her by getting her first date; it was clearly time that she, Debbie, asserted herself. Besides, she would take careful note how the baby was pinned into its nappy when she removed the dirty one, so the task should not be beyond her. 'No, it's all right, Gwen, I'll do it,' she said airily. 'You get the milk. I shan't be a tick.'

She headed for the curtain which screened the privy buckets. There wasn't a lot of room back here but she sat herself down on one of the

245

benches and began to remove the dirty nappy. The dog had accompanied her and was gazing, curiously, at the baby as it kicked its little legs. She saw that the small bottom was scarlet and sore and looked round for some water. There was an enamel jug nearby so she dipped her hanky into the liquid and did her best to clean it up, noticing as she swabbed away that it was a girl. It took her rather longer than she had anticipated to get the baby comfortable but she managed it, pleased to see that the nappies were both fairly new and that the safety pin which anchored the new one into position was neither rusty nor bent.

Debbie had finished her task and was rewrapping the baby in its shawl when she heard the scream of a descending bomb. Instinctively, she clutched the baby and the dog to her, thinking that it sounded close. Then there was a tremendous explosion. Debbie was hurled off her feet by the blast, and descended into total darkness.

CHAPTER NINE

Debbie came round groggily. The darkness was total and she found she was freezing cold. She reached for her blankets, believing herself to be in bed, and turned her head to glance towards where the window should have been. It was not there, and neither were the blankets, but as she moved she felt someone touch her face very gently with something which was both warm and damp. A flannel? Had she been ill? Was it her mother gently stroking her cheek with a warm, wet

246

flannel? She tried to speak, but at first no words would come. Instead, a tiny moan escaped her parched lips and was immediately echoed by someone near at hand. Debbie frowned. Where the devil was she? She had no recollection of what had happened, or where she was, but she knew now that she was not in bed, or even in her own room.

She put out a tentative hand and felt someone move against her, and all of a sudden memory came flooding back. She had been in the shelter, changing a baby's nappy—she even remembered it was a baby girl—and then there had been a tremendous crash and she had felt as though a giant had picked her up, squeezed all the breath out of her, and hurled her into a dark pit.

Against her side, someone moved and gave a little whining moan. 'Gwen? Gwen, are you all right?' Debbie said tremulously. This time the words came out, but there was no answer. 'Gwen, have you got the baby? I can't . . . hang on a minute! Oh no, it's all right, I've got her.' She lifted up a bundle which had been sheltered in the curve of her body, and felt immeasurable relief as the child moved and then began a hiccuping cry. 'Oh, and there was a dog . . .' Despite the cold, the dark and the fear, Debbie chuckled. 'I thought someone was wiping my face with a damp cloth, but of course it was the perishing dog licking my cheek.' She was sitting up now, cradling the baby, and could feel the dog pressing against her. She put a comforting arm round its shaggy neck. 'Are you all right, old feller? I wish I had a torch, but if we can find the curtain we can get back into the rest of the shelter and someone out there is bound to have a

247

light.'

However, as soon as she began to move towards where she thought the curtain hung, she realised she had lost all sense of direction, for her seeking hand—she had the baby in one arm—found only concrete. Sighing, she called once more: 'Gwen? Are you there, Gwenny? Mrs O'Shea? Has the blast sent you all deaf? It's bloody dark here among the privies. Can't one of you show a light to guide me back?'

*   *   *

It was some time before Debbie could face the terrible truth that she, the dog and the baby were completely cut off from the other inhabitants of the shelter. Using only her hands, for her eyes were useless in the complete dark, she realised that the roof, and some of the walls of the shelter, had caved in, leaving the three of them in a tiny space probably no more than four feet wide in any direction. By the time she had discovered this, she had called herself hoarse to absolutely no avail. All that happened was that the inside of her mouth and throat began to feel as though they had been sandpapered, because every time she shouted she inhaled more dust.

At first, she had cried rather a lot, and the dog, who could probably sense if not see her tears, had licked her face, making her laugh in a choked and miserable sort of way. As time passed, she began to worry about the baby. It had been crying and Debbie's heart had bled for it, because it had been hungry when she had been changing its nappy and now it must be very hungry indeed. But now its

248

cries had stopped and its breathing had become uneven. Now and then it coughed; a pathetic little sound that worried Debbie. She knew she must get the baby out as soon as she possibly could if it was to survive, and she had no idea how to do so.

She thought she had explored every avenue in the small space but realised she had not done so when she heard the dog lapping. Hesitantly, she made her way towards the sound, shuffling along on her bottom with the baby against her shoulder, and moving very slowly. If the dog had found the jug of water, which seemed likely, then the last thing she wanted to do was discover it herself by kicking it over.

But it was all right. She found the jug, still about half full of water, and gave a gasp of relief. She took a small drink herself and felt immeasurably better for it, then removed the skimpy waist petticoat she was wearing, dipped it into the water and began to move the wet cotton around the baby's face, searching for the mouth. The baby co-operated eagerly, seizing the wet cloth between her lips and sucking enthusiastically. Debbie recklessly plunged more of the petticoat into the water, then tilted the jug so that the cloth was really wet. After a while the child stopped sucking and Debbie's heart gave a frightened leap, but very soon the child's even breathing told her that she slept.

Debbie settled herself against a block of concrete which seemed a little smoother than the others and began to rock the baby gently, murmuring to her that they would soon be rescued because Gwen knew where she was and would tell someone. She wondered whether it was daytime yet, whether rescuers were already digging their way down to the shelter. She refused to allow herself to think about the ominous silence on the other side of the fallen masonry. Why, there must have been nearly a hundred people in the shelter. It was clearly impossible that she, the baby and the dog were the only survivors. No, the marshal was a clever and resourceful man. He would have guided everyone to safety, and very soon rescuers would reach the end of the shelter and daylight—or torchlight—would begin to filter through to Debbie's tiny prison.

She began to get drowsy, but she fought against it at first, thinking that she would hear sounds of rescue presently, and must be awake to inform whoever came of their whereabouts. But she was very tired and it was difficult to fight sleep when the darkness was so complete and the air so horribly stuffy. So she settled herself as comfortably as she could, with the dog warm against her side and the baby cradled in her arms, and addressed her two companions. 'I shall call you Dusty, because you are dusty, I expect,' she told her shaggy companion, 'and I shall call you Baby, because I don't know your real name.' She tickled the dog beneath his chin as she spoke. 'Now, Dusty, listen to me; Baby and I are going to have a nap because babies need an awful lot of sleep and I'm tired out, and that means we're relying on you. D'you remember my friend, Gwen? She was going to fetch a mug of milk for Baby here when the bomb landed, so she knows where we are and she'll tell everyone, and that means you can't go to sleep like me and Baby here. You've got to sit up straight and listen with all your might, and as

250

soon as you hear folk beginning to search for us you must bark. Understood?'

The dog licked her cheek as if he had understood every word, and presently Debbie slept.

*   *   *

Pete had arrived in Liverpool because of a misunderstanding. He and Sammy had stayed in Devonshire until the end of their furlough, and had then got on a train to go back to Norfolk. When they changed trains, however, Sammy had decided to ring the air force station to say that they were on their way back and had been told that their aircraft was still not fit for flying so they could take a further three days' leave. Sammy decided he would return to the station anyway, but Pete had heard on the news that morning that Liverpool had had more than a week of intensive bombing raids and so announced that he would go to that city, just to make sure that his mother's friend was all right. He had her address tucked away in his wallet but, better than that, knew that Jess worked in a big hospital on the Stanley Road. He concluded that it would be easier to find the hospital than a tiny side street, so he would go there first. In her last letter, Nancy had laughed at herself for telling him that Jess's daughter Debbie was just a child. *Other people's time passes differently from one's own*, she had written. *Jess tells me that Debbie has been working in a big factory, assembling the radio sets you chaps use in your kites as you call them, which means, I suppose, that she's got to be at least fourteen, and possibly more. Yes, come to think of it,*

251

she's fifteen, quite a young lady. So remember what I said to you the last time we met! Pete, remembering that long-ago conversation, grinned to himself.

'I know you're only nineteen and your dad didn't even think of marriage until he was pushing thirty,' she had said, 'but women is rare in the outback even now and I guess you'll be posted to England sooner or later. English girls are the salt of the earth, son—look at Aunt Anne and myself!—so it would be a grand thing for you if you were to meet a girl over there and want to bring her back.'

Two years ago, the young Pete had laughed and thought his ma was joking, especially as she had laughed too before reaching up to kiss his cheek. 'And if you don't fancy an English girl yourself, then put a couple in your pocket for your brothers,' she had said lightly. 'Because if none of you marry, where shall I get grandchildren from?'

He had laughed aloud at that idea. 'Oh, Ma, ain't you jumping the gun a bit? Jamie's only sixteen and Jacko's not fourteen yet. Still, I'll do my best to provide you with a daughter-in-law.'

The two of them had laughed again at the absurdity of it and changed the subject and he had not given the matter another thought until today, when he might actually meet the Ryans at last.

Pete arrived in Liverpool early on a sunny May morning. His first view of the city had stunned him, for he had never before seen the results of a week of heavy bombing and was appalled by the scene before him. Everywhere, there was chaos and destruction. Buildings still smouldered, black smoke hung like a pall over what he assumed to be the dock area, and there was rubble and brick dust everywhere. Stepping down from the large lorry

252

whose driver had given him a lift for the last twenty-five miles, he thanked the man and wondered how on earth he was going to get anywhere or find anyone. People were doing their best—men were shifting rubble from the roadway as fast as they could—but it reminded Pete of an old poem he had read somewhere: *'If seven maids with seven mops / Swept it for half a year, / Do you suppose,' the Walrus said, / 'That they could get it clear?' / 'I doubt it,' said the Carpenter, / And shed a bitter tear*.

Grinning wryly to himself, Pete approached the nearest workman and asked for directions to the Stanley Hospital. One of the men pushed his dusty cap to the back of his head and scratched the tuft of hair which stuck out over his forehead. 'Once I'd ha' told you to jump aboard a number twenty-four tram, or I suppose you could ha' got a taxi, but now . . . I dunno. Wharrabout walking? It ain't that far, mebbe a couple o' miles, and a feller on foot can skirt round obstacles, or dive down a side street, whereas if you're on four wheels you could be stuck for hours.'

'Right, I'll walk,' Pete said equably. He glanced round him rather helplessly. 'But which way? Which way?' Once more he realised he was thinking of Alice, standing with her hand on the top of her head to feel whether she was growing taller or shorter after nibbling a bit of the EAT ME cake, anxiously saying to herself: 'Which way? Which way?' before finishing the rest.

His informant, however, had probably never read Lewis Carroll and certainly would not query the quotation. Instead, he indicated the direction Pete should take, saying prosaically: 'Keep straight on the main road, 'cept where there's buildings or bomb craters that won't let you pass, when you'll have to take to the side streets. You can ask anyone—everyone knows the Stanley.'

As he traversed the ruined streets, Pete saw broken water mains jetting their contents into the roadways, barricades and danger signs erected round fractured gas pipes, split tramlines rearing up like angry snakes, and electricity cables torn from their places, whilst more barricades were hastily erected to stop the public from getting too close. Grim-faced men laboured ceaselessly at the myriad tasks that faced them, but Pete realised that for most of the people of Liverpool life was simply going on. Two women stood on either side of a bomb crater, one shouting to the other that Sample's hadn't been touched and they'd got some bread, plain cake, and even a few ginger nuts. The other woman, large, shawled and cheery, called back that she didn't think she'd bother with Sample's since Mr O'Neil's storeroom had been hit. 'It ain't got no glass in the windows and one of them 'cendiaries set fire to some sacks of provisions, so mebbe he'll sell me some damaged goods cheap,' she bawled. 'I'll bet a pound to a penny they've got broken biscuits 'n' all, broke by the Jerries!'

Pete grinned to himself and continued on his way, and presently he reached the Stanley Hospital and went inside.

The reception hall was crowded with nurses in uniform and worried civilians and Pete guessed that all the hospitals would be run off their feet. He wondered whether it was fair to enquire for Jess before he had even visited her home and was turning away when one of the nurses came over. 'Can I help you?' she asked briskly. 'I can see you aren't hurt, but perhaps you're searching for someone?'

'Yes, I am. I'm trying to find a Mrs Jess Ryan; she nurses here and I thought—I wondered—oh, nurse, I can see you're busy . . .'

The nurse nodded. She was an attractive woman, dark-haired, dark-eyed and neat, probably in her mid-thirties, but there was a smear of dirt on her crisp white apron, and another on her forehead, and she looked pale and hollow-eyed, as though she had been working for many hours and would continue for many hours more. However, she consulted a clipboard which she held under her arm and told him: 'Oh, yes, she's in ward eight. That's straight down the corridor there and first turning on the right.'

'Thank you, nurse,' Pete said. 'It's awfully good of you to take the trouble . . .' But the nurse had turned away and was already hurrying in the opposite direction.

Pete made his way to the ward in question and as soon as he entered the swing doors a nurse hurried towards him. Like his previous informant, she carried a clipboard and she was consulting it even as she said: 'Yes? Who are you looking for? Most of these patients are in here as a result of last night's bombing.'

'It's all right, nurse, I'm looking for you,' Pete said, giving the woman a tentative smile. He had no idea what Jess actually looked like for his mother had no more recent photograph than one taken on Jess's wedding day, which had shown a slim, dark-haired, dark-eyed girl, perhaps not

255

pretty but certainly not plain, and the woman standing before him looked as he imagined that bride might look now. 'You are Nurse Jessica Ryan?'

The woman looked puzzled. 'No, I'm Nurse Berringer,' she said. 'But oddly enough, you've found the right ward. Nurse Ryan was brought in earlier.' She jerked her head at someone further down the ward. 'Are you a relative or just a friend? Only she's pretty bad and I'm not sure . . .'

'I've never met Nurse Ryan, but she and my mother were close friends when my mother lived in England,' Pete said. 'I promised my ma I'd make sure she was all right . . . how bad is she?'

The nurse shrugged slightly and began to lead him down the long ward. 'She's terribly worried about her daughter,' she said. 'In the middle of the raid—when she should have been having a meal break actually—she decided to go home and check that the girl was all right. She'd been intending to go to the cinema with a friend in the evening, apparently, and she hadn't got back by the time Nurse Ryan came on shift. But somewhere on the road—she doesn't seem to know where—she was hit both by flying glass and by blast, so she never did find out what had happened to her daughter. I think if you could promise to check the house and the local shelter and come back here with news, then she might rest easier.'

As she spoke, she stopped beside a bed and Pete saw Jess Ryan for the first time. She looked terrible. She had a huge face wound, stretching from her hairline across brow, nose and cheek right down to her jaw. It had been cleaned and stitched but he could see that placing a concealing

256

dressing across it would have been very difficult. Two tubes led from her arm, one to a bottle of what he assumed was saline solution and the other, unmistakably, to blood. The nurse bent over the bed and touched Jess's hollow cheek, and after a moment the older woman's eyes opened. She stared vacantly about her and then she saw Pete. It was as though she recognised in him some likeness, perhaps to his mother. 'Pete?' she said questioningly. 'Nancy's boy?'

Pete nodded dumbly; how the devil had she known? But she was speaking still, in a halting, breathy voice, and he bent close, the better to hear.

'She's alive, but she's in the dark,' the thin thread of a voice was murmuring. 'They don't know she's there; they think everybody's dead. Oh, Pete, I prayed someone would come, someone who could tell 'em she's buried under all that stuff. Will you fetch her out for me?'

The nurse had moved away and Pete bent closer over the wan figure. 'How do you know?' he asked quietly. 'And where is she? Which shelter? Under which building? I'll do everything I can, but I don't know the area. Don't know where to start?'

'She'd gone to the flicks with her friend Gwen; it'll be somewhere in the city centre,' Jess whispered, after a long pause. 'Please find her and look after her; she's so afraid, so alone.'

'I'll do my best,' Pete said softly. 'Can you think of anything else, anything else at all, that would help me to find her?'

He waited a few moments until it became all too clear that Jess, having passed her message on, had lapsed into unconsciousness once more. Then he turned and left the ward, walking with long,

257

impatient strides. He would check the house first, then ask the way to the nearest shelter. If it had not been bombed, then he supposed it was possible the girl might have made her way to the factory in which she worked. He remembered that it made radio parts so surely it would be easy to find. If she did not know her mother had been injured, she might easily have gone off to work, none the wiser.

Pete had to ask directions to Wykeham Street, but when he found it he realised almost at once that the house was simply a shattered shell. From a distance it had looked fairly respectable, but when he got closer he saw that this was an illusion. The back of the house had been sheared off, as though with a gigantic pair of scissors, and the frontage was already leaning to one side as though it longed to dive into the enormous bomb crater there. Curiously, he peered through a glassless front window, checking as he did so that it really was the right number. It was, and he found himself reluctant to look into the crater, dreading that he might see a girl's body there. But look he must, and all it seemed to contain was a variety of domestic furniture and fittings many of which, so far as he could see, were still all in one piece. Glancing up, he saw an old-fashioned double bed hanging by its back legs from the front wall, and hastily withdrew. That bed might crash down at any minute; indeed, the wall itself looked pretty shaky.

As he moved away from the house, an ARP warden came running up. 'Don't go near any of the buildings,' he shouted. 'They ain't been made safe; there's leakin' gas pipes, live electricity cables, and enough broken glass to have a whole army bleedin' to death if they was to make their way amongst it.

Besides, there's looters . . . you don't come from round here. Just what are you doin' hangin' round the Ryans' place?'

'I'm a friend and I'm searching for Jess's daughter Debbie,' Pete said. It was clearly not the moment to keep his own counsel. 'Jess is my—my godmother. She's badly injured, and when I saw her just now in the Stanley Hospital she explained that Debbie had gone to the cinema last night and asked me to try to find her.' He looked at the man, wondering how to phrase the next question. 'I don't suppose you know . . . her mother was afraid she might have been hurt . . .'

'She weren't in the house. I met her Uncle Max when I came down the road last night, checking that everyone was in the shelter. He went to the one down the Stanley Road, same as he always does. Later, I checked the shelter and spoke to him; he were worried because young Debbie hadn't joined him down there. So I reckon you'll have to go up to the city centre. If she were on her way home from a cinema when the raid started, I reckon she'd have been coming up the Scotland Road.' He looked at Pete under his brows and said thoughtfully: 'You from down south? I can tell you ain't from these parts.'

'I'm Australian,' Pete said briefly. 'My mam and Mrs Ryan nursed together in the last war. My mam asked me to make sure her pal was all right; that's why I'm here.'

'Oh aye? Look, lad, one of the shelters along the Scottie took a direct hit last night. I'm awful sorry, mate, but if she were in that shelter . . . well, as I said, it were a direct hit, so they're not expectin' many survivors. They'll be bringin' bodies out once they've made the site safe—cut the electrics and gas off—so if she's still missing you'd best go down there.'

Pete read pity in the older man's eyes and swallowed uneasily. He had seen death, of course, but he didn't fancy watching bodies being brought out and perhaps being asked to identify a girl he had never laid eyes on, save in a blurred snapshot taken half a dozen years ago. And the thought of having to tell Jess that her daughter was dead horrified him. The warden must have read his expression for he gave Pete a heartening thump on the back. 'Mebbe I'm wrong, mebbe they'll find dozens of survivors, or mebbe young Debbie weren't in that shelter,' he said. 'But you'd best cut along now.' He looked Pete over shrewdly. 'Once they've made the site safe, they'll need as many husky young fellers as they can lay hands on to help 'em move the rubble. They're afraid of using machinery in case they cause more damage, like. When they've moved the loose stuff, then it's a matter of burrowing through at some spot where it's safe to do so.'

'Thanks very much,' Pete said gratefully. 'But the thing is . . . well, I've never actually met Debbie, or not for years,' he amended, not wanting to admit that he did not know the girl. 'I doubt I'd recognise her. This Uncle Max . . . is he around? He might want to come with me . . .'

'No, he went off to work; he's something quite important in one of the ministries, I believe,' the man said vaguely. 'He thought Mrs Ryan was working her usual shift at the hospital, so naturally he assumed she was all right, knowing the hospital was still standing. But it'll be evening by the time

260

they begin to bring people out, so if I see him I'll send him along to the Scottie. You don't know which cinema they was at, I suppose?'

Pete admitted he did not, whereupon the warden said thoughtfully: 'Two young gals out on the spree . . . what would they want to see, d'you think?'

'Something all lovey dovey and romantic,' Pete said promptly. 'What was showing last night?'

The warden shrugged. 'Not sure, but the Forum is a popular cinema. It's just been reopened and I believe it were showin' a romance, so likely they went there.' He cocked a grizzled eyebrow at Pete. 'And don't you go lookin' for the Metropole 'cos it were burned to the ground last night,' he added gruffly. 'But they got everyone out as soon as Moaning Minnie started, so no one were hurt in the blaze.'

'Thanks very much,' Pete repeated. To himself he added, as he walked away, crunching over broken glass and skirting mounds of rubble, I'm going to find that kid whether she's dead or alive, but I reckon she's alive. I've seen the mothering instinct at work on the cattle station . . . oh, countless times . . . and if Jess says her daughter's alive and alone in the dark, then I reckon she's right and I'm the feller to find her.

* * *

Debbie awoke to total darkness once more, but this time she knew at once where she was. In her arms the baby slumbered though she was soaking wet, and the dog was curled up beside her. She thought he was asleep but he woke moments after

261

she did, and somehow there was something comforting in the fact that he stretched and yawned hugely before getting to his feet and nuzzling her hair aside so that he could lick her ear.

'Oh, Dusty, I do love you,' Debbie said gratefully, and was oddly heartened by the sound of her own voice. It was steady and showed no sign of the awful panic which had beset her on her previous awakening. In fact, she realised that she felt a little better, though she could not imagine why. The darkness was still absolute, and the silence . . . the silence was different! In fact it was not silence at all. She could hear a distant rumbling and, when she strained her ears, even more distant shouts.

She felt the dog's head turn and knew he was listening intently, as she was herself. Moving carefully, she reached out for the enamel jug, took a small drink of water, then tipped it so that the dog could drink too. She moved her hand over the baby's face with infinite care, but the child still slept, so cradling the small warm body she shuffled carefully across the floor and pressed her ear to the concrete block that she imagined separated her from the rest of the shelter. Softly, so as not to wake the baby, she began to call her friend's name. 'Gwen? Gwenny? Are you there? Are you hurt, queen? Only me and the baby and the dog, we're trapped like and it seems as if the roof's fallen between us and we can't get out. Gwenny?'

Beside her, she felt the dog's body tense, felt his excitement, and knew that his ears, so much sharper than her own, had heard something or somebody either stirring in the other part of the

262

shelter or beginning a rescue attempt somewhere above them. She put her free arm round the dog's shaggy shoulders. 'What can you hear?' she murmured into his flapping ear. 'What is it, Dusty? Has Gwen told 'em where we are? I dare say there's a lot of digging to be done to reach us, so we must be patient, but as soon as they get near enough you must bark your head off, and I'll shout, and we'll give Baby a little shake so she screams. Until then, we'd best preserve our strength.'

*   *   *

When Pete had first seen the jumble of masonry which he had been told was once a great six-storey department store, and knew it had fallen on top of the shelter, he almost gave up hope of ever seeing Debbie Ryan alive, but he had come here to help, so as soon as the engineer in charge said it was safe to begin moving some of the rubble he joined the human chain. They worked for hours, stripping down to trousers and singlets as the heat of the day increased. Soon they grew so grimed and filthy that Pete wondered, apprehensively, whether he would ever be able to wear his uniform again.

One young man who toiled beside him informed Pete that he had had his call-up papers and would be joining the air force himself in a couple of weeks. 'Me name's Dicky. I drive a delivery van and last night I dropped a couple of girls off at a cinema in the city centre,' he explained. 'I knew they'd be walking home about the time the raid started, so when I heard a shelter had been bombed I come straight down. You can imagine how my heart sank, only I'm tellin' meself these

263

shelters is built to withstand all sorts, tellin' meself they're goin' to come out of it alive, if not exactly laughin'.'

'I'm telling myself the same,' Pete said grimly as, between them, they staggered to the roadway bearing an enormous chunk of solid concrete. 'But you can't be sure your girls were in this shelter, can you, any more than I can? I mean, all sorts of things could have happened. They could be anywhere.' A thought struck him. 'These two girls, the ones you dropped off, is one of them called Debbie, by any chance? Do they work at a factory on Long Lane, assembling radio parts?'

He had asked the question as the two of them bent to pick up another chunk of concrete, but at his words the other straightened, staring at him round-eyed. 'Yes, she bleedin' well is,' he said slowly. 'And my girl's Gwen; Gwenny Soames. I don't know Debbie very well—met her for the first time yesterday morning. I gave them a lift to the Seffy 'cos they were going there for a picnic. Then I picked 'em up and took 'em back to the Forum.'

'Have you checked the factory?' Pete said suddenly, as they bent to their task once more. 'I couldn't 'cos I don't know where Long Lane is, but you've got transport. God, wouldn't it be a relief if they were both in work?'

But even as he spoke Dicky was shaking his head. 'I thought of that first go off. Checked Gwen's house—no one were there—then went to Long Lane, only they'd not gone in today. I couldn't check Debbie's house 'cos I don't know where she lives, but I reckon you've done that, eh?'

'Yup,' Pete said briefly. 'The house has gone and her ma is in the Stanley Hospital, pretty badly injured. So we'd best get this lot shifted as quickly as we can while I tell you what Mrs Ryan said to me—that's Debbie's mother—when I visited her this morning.'

*   *   *

The next time Debbie awoke it was because her chest was so tight that it hurt her, and also because she was suddenly conscious of a scraping noise. Wildly, she felt around, and her hands met Dusty's rear end. As he felt her touch, his tail wagged quickly twice, but then stopped, and Debbie realised that he was digging. Even as the thought occurred to her, she felt something cool against her cheek. It was fresh air, penetrating into their tiny prison cell, from somewhere outside. So there were people trying to dig their way down to them! She longed to lay the baby down so that she might help the dog in his efforts, but she was afraid either she or Dusty might inadvertently step on her and do her some mortal harm. However, she moved the child from her right arm to her left and tried to discover exactly where the dog was digging. The baby gave a little choking gasp and moved her head, and Debbie thought, fearfully, that they simply must get out soon. She remembered her mother telling her that babies are tough little things, but she also remembered that even tough little things need food and fresh air to stay alive. Carefully, she resisted the urge to hold the baby even tighter, and moved her free hand back to Dusty. He had discovered a seam of earth, no more than six inches wide, between two concrete blocks and was scraping away vigorously, and now

Debbie could hear, faint and far away, men's voices and, once, a distant shout.

Hope, which had almost died, reasserted itself and the urge to shout and yell, to make some effort to draw the rescuers towards her, was almost unbearable. Debbie resisted it. No point in wasting what little energy she had left; she would wait until she could see the whites of their eyes—that was what they always said in cowboy films—before beginning to bellow. She did try to help Dusty in his excavations, but this was not a success and he elbowed her aside impatiently, then thrust his nose deep into the hole he was making, and inhaled noisily. Then he sat back on his haunches, panting, and she could imagine the brightness of his eyes and the earth with which his face must be smeared. Tentatively, she put her face closer to the crack between the concrete blocks, and as she breathed in the clean air she felt the tightness in her chest ease, and told herself that rescue would definitely come, that all she needed was patience. As soon as she could make out an individual voice she would start shouting, but until then she, Baby and Dusty must simply wait.

*   *   *

It was late afternoon before the rescuers were able to enter what was left of the shelter and begin to bring bodies out. Grim-faced, they laid their grisly burdens in rows along the pavement and it was not long before Dicky grabbed Pete's arm. 'Gwen were wearin' a pink dress and she had a pink celluloid hair slide,' he said hoarsely. 'Can you look for me, old mate? Only some of 'em's in such a state I

266

wouldn't be no wiser, if you know what I mean.'

Pete nodded. He went along the road slowly and returned to Dicky within a very few minutes. Dicky's face was pale and his eyes were haunted by the horrors he had already seen. 'I think I've found her,' Pete told him quietly. 'Her face isn't touched. She looks to be around fifteen and she's wearing a pink cotton frock—at least I guess it's cotton—and there's a pink slide in her hair. Look, old chap, I truly think you should come. After all, someone's got to tell her parents and you're the only one around here who can actually identify her.' He led Dicky over to where the girl lay and Dicky looked down at her, almost with disbelief, for as Pete had said there was no outward sign of what had caused her death; she simply looked as though she was sleeping.

Dicky bent down and stroked the hair from her forehead, then straightened up. 'Goodbye, old girl,' he said huskily and Pete saw that he was crying, but he rubbed his eyes with the heels of both hands and then turned his dirt-smeared face to his companion. 'Sorry, sorry,' he muttered. 'But she were a good kid and I were fond of her. The other gal . . . Debbie, weren't it . . . was wearing pink as well, I think. You say you've never met her? Well, she had real lovely hair, with a sort of reddish tinge . . . no, now I come to think she were wearing a green frock, that stuff with a pattern of tiny little squares—gingham, ain't it? And she had a ribbon of the same material tying back her hair from her face.' He glanced quickly, shrinkingly almost, along the row of bodies. 'She ain't here, but there's still more down below. We'd best keep on helping until they've gorr'em all out. One of the wardens said

267

this shelter holds around a hundred and they've only brought forty out so far.' He turned a suddenly desperate face to Pete. 'Oh, gawd, I've just remembered. Gwen's mam's spendin' a few days in North Wales with the little 'uns; someone's goin' to have to find her and I reckon it'll have to be me.'

*   *   *

Debbie sat in the darkness, which was no longer total, and waited. The dog had dug and dug, occasionally whining and coming over to her as though he longed to be able to speak, to tell her what he saw or sensed ahead. But still the voices had not come near enough to make out so much as a single word. Things in the prison cell were better, however, for the prisoners had both fresh air, though it was dusty and smelt of brick rubble and soot, and a little light. It was just sufficient for Debbie to make out the baby lying in her lap and the great tangled mass of reinforced concrete, bricks, pipes and earth that had cut her off from the rest of the shelter. But suddenly the light grew less because Dusty was jamming himself into the impossibly small space between the two concrete blocks. He struggled and whined, and suddenly he barked sharply, twice, and Debbie could almost imagine the words he was saying. 'Give me a push, you stupid girl; I'm almost there, I just need a bit of help.' Debbie put her shoulder against the dog's rump and gave a rather half-hearted push. Dusty barked again, and almost as though she had understood the meaning behind the bark Debbie twisted round, put both hands against his rear, and

268

shoved with all her might. For a moment, nothing happened, then the dog gave a wriggle and disappeared into the cavity he had excavated, doing it so suddenly that Debbie, taken by surprise, fell forward and clouted her head on one of the concrete blocks. Ruefully rubbing what would doubtless turn out to be a tremendous bruise, she sat back on her haunches and let sheer relief wash over her. Dusty was a good dog; she knew he would never desert her and the baby. And he was intelligent; he would make those outside understand that there were people buried in the shelter. He would bring help. She hoped it would be soon, because now that light was filtering into their prison cell once more she could see that the baby was distressed. Carefully, she dipped her slip into the enamel jug—the water was now filthy, or perhaps it always had been—and pushed a corner of the material into the baby's mouth. The little creature sucked vigorously for a moment, then stopped and stared up at Debbie with wide reproachful eyes. She wants milk and all I'm offering is dirty water, Debbie thought despairingly. Oh, please God, let someone find Dusty soon and come searching. Don't let Baby and me die down here in the dark!

*　　　*　　　*

Pete had owned a dog ever since his seventh birthday when his dad had bought him a blue roan hunting dog as a present. He had named it Bluey, rather unoriginally, and had loved it devotedly. When Bluey had died of a snake bite, his father had expected him to want another dog, but Pete

269

had known that he would soon be leaving the Walleroo and would not be able to take the animal with him. He still missed Bluey, though, and thought of him often. His squadron leader had a golden retriever; a large and handsome beast with melting dark eyes and a curly coat which needed constant grooming. But Pete rather despised it because it was everyone's friend, especially if one had food about one's person. Bluey, on the other hand, had been a one-man dog and Pete thought that it was perhaps fortunate that he had died before his owner had left the Walleroo; Bluey would never have acknowledged another master.

So now, when Pete heard a couple of faint—very faint—barks, he immediately pricked up his ears and nudged Dicky. 'Hear that?' he demanded. 'There's a dog under all this stuff . . . did you hear it?'

'No, and there ain't, because they don't allow dogs in shelters,' Dicky said. 'Well, not in the big public ones, anyway. What you heard was a dog barking somewhere on the Scotland Road and the sound being bounced back by one of the tall buildings what's still standing.' He sighed heavily, wiping the sweat off his brow. 'Sound is very deceivin'. Well-known fact, that.'

'Oh,' Pete said, digesting this. He bent to his work once more. The two of them were making their way down to what had once been the entrance of the shelter every time more bodies were brought up, just to check, but so far there had been no girl dressed in a green frock with a green ribbon in her hair, and as the rescuers probed deeper into the shelter Pete's stubborn belief in what Jess had told him began to falter. The men emerged, stony-faced, with their pitiful burdens, reporting that the scene below was one of complete carnage. They were sure everyone in the shelter must be dead.

'How long do you want to stay here, old pal?' Dicky said some while later, coming back after another fruitless visit to the line of bodies laid out on the pavement. 'They believe they've cleared the shelter now. They think everyone's accounted for. Of course they'll go on digging in case . . . but all they're going to find is more of the same, if there's any left, that is.' Dicky looked awkwardly across at the other young man. 'Look, Pete, you've never even met the girl, and the truth is, I can't hang about no longer. I live a good way out of the city an' I've gorrer get home or me mam will start to worry. And some o' them bodies . . . well, the state they're in makes recognising anyone difficult, if not damn near impossible. So you see, there's just a chance that they've already got young Debbie out and we've neither of us realised . . .'

'But surely you'd have recognised the dress? A green frock and a green hair ribbon . . . that's all I've been looking for,' Pete pointed out.

'I'm beginning to wonder if she was wearing a green frock,' Dicky said gloomily. 'But if she is— was, I mean—you're as likely to recognise it as meself. As I said, I've really gorrer get back before this evening's trouble starts. You're very welcome to come home with me, if . . .'

'It's very kind of you to offer, mate, but I think I'll hang around here until they've excavated the whole of the shelter,' Pete said. 'And I've got to go back to the hospital as soon as I've found Debbie, so I can let her mother know what's happened.'

Dicky sighed but picked up the jacket he had cast off earlier and struggled into it. 'Yes, I was forgetting; before I can go home I'll have to go back to the bakery and tell my boss I need tomorrow off. I'll have to drive down to Betws—wharr ever—to break the news to Gwen's mam.' He looked hopefully at Pete. 'I s'pose you wouldn't like to come with me?'

Pete shook his head. 'No can do, mate. Once I've sorted things here I'll have to get back to my station; my Wimpy should be back on active service by then.'

'Yeah, right,' Dicky said. 'Look, I'll give you my address, then if you change your mind . . . only I'll be in the force meself quite soon.' He pulled a receipt book from his pocket, scribbled his name and address on the back of the next sheet and handed it to Pete, who thrust it into his trouser pocket.

The two young men shook hands and Dicky had actually turned away when Pete cocked his head, listening once more. There it was again, a faint but definite bark, and he was sure that it came from the mass of rubble which he and Dicky had been slowly clearing from where they assumed the end of the shelter must be. 'What was that, if it wasn't a dog?' Pete said, as another faint bark came to his ears. 'You *must* have heard that, Dicky, it was clear as a bell.' He turned his head but Dicky was already out of hearing, hurrying in the direction of his delivery van. Pete looked round for someone else to confirm what he had heard, but even as he did so a movement caught his eye. Puzzled, he stared, and then saw, squiggling and wriggling from under a huge block of masonry, a dog: a scruffy mongrel with one ear almost torn off and a coat so filthy and matted that it was impossible to tell what colour it had once been. But its eyes were bright and when Pete moved towards it, and bent down to help it out of the tiny gap, it licked his face before giving one last tremendous heave, which brought its spindly hind legs and disgraceful tail into the open at last.

'Well I'll be blowed,' Pete said, almost reverentially. He had been right: the dog had been under the rubble all the time, trying to let them know that it was alive; possibly, that there were others alive too. Pete approached the place where the dog had emerged, but his new friend was before him. Shoving its head inside the cavity, the dog began to bark shrilly, whilst its tail rotated so fast it was almost a blur. Pete bent over the dog and shouted: 'Anybody in there?' and faintly, so faintly that he wondered if he had really heard anything, came an answering hail. Wildly excited, Pete began to heave at one of the big lumps of masonry, then saw with dismay that, had he been successful, he would have started a miniature landslide, doing more harm than good. Backing away, he picked the dog up and set off towards the group of men still working with infinite care on the tumbled wreckage. 'This dog just squeezed out from where me and my mate were working, up t'other end,' Pete said breathlessly. 'I shouted and someone answered, though the voice was awfully faint. Can you . . . ?'

There was no need to say any more. The man in charge shouted orders and some of the equipment they had been using was picked up bodily and carried to the spot Pete pointed out. The boss bent

273

over the cavity and began to shout instruct ions to whoever was within. Then, before Pete could do anything about it, the dog had wriggled out of his arms and disappeared into the pile of rubble once more. He made an ineffectual grab at it, but was stopped by one of the engineers. 'It's all right, mate,' the man said quietly. 'If the dog can keep coming and going—and it looks as though it can—then it'll be out again in a minute, and next time it goes down we can tie a message to its collar. Often, the mere knowledge that help is on its way is enough to keep a survivor hanging on.'

'I see; I understand,' Pete said humbly. 'I—I've been hoping that a—a friend of mine might be still alive down there. She's a young girl called Debbie Ryan. Her house was bombed last night and her mother's seriously injured; oh, God, I hope it's her, I hope she's not hurt too badly.'

*   *   *

Debbie heard the rescuers getting closer, heard their muffled instructions to her to 'keep away from the wall and crouch back'. The baby in her arms had been ominously silent for the past hour, or perhaps her silence was no longer so ominous, for, only half an hour before, the dog had squeezed back through the tiny passageway it had made and there had not only been a message around its neck. Dusty had brought a small container of milk and, weeping with gratitude, Debbie had fed every drop into the small eager mouth.

And now they were almost through, though the aperture was not yet sufficiently large to allow her to escape. Very soon, however, the three of them

274

would be able to emerge into the outside world together and Debbie was sure that her mother must be amongst those waiting to greet her. And Gwen, of course, unless she had been injured, in which case she would be in hospital, Debbie supposed.

The voice which had been giving her instructions advised her, cheerfully, that she should turn away from the source of light, hunch down, and keep very still, since they were about to break through into her prison. Debbie obeyed. There were more noises, then a sharp crack, and then—oh, the relief of it—real, honest daylight. Hands reached out to her, pulling her gently towards safety. Someone exclaimed, tried to take the baby, but Debbie hung on grimly. 'Don't!' she said sharply. 'My mam will take her, she'll look after her for me. Mam? Gwen?'

There were murmurs all round. A uniformed man tried to take her towards an ambulance but she pushed him away, insisting that she would not move until her mother came. She was very confused, as much by the fact that amongst this crowd of people she knew no one as by the memory of her recent ordeal. Still holding Baby tightly, she looked wildly about her and saw a tall, fair-haired man coming towards her, both hands held out. 'You're Debbie, aren't you?' he said gently. 'I'm awfully sorry to have to tell you, but your mother's in hospital. Can I take you to her?'

Debbie gave a tiny nod. 'Gwen?' she said and scarcely recognised her own voice. 'Is she in hospital too? Or has she gone home to Daisy Street? She was in the shelter with me, only I went to change Baby's nappy and I was still behind the

275

curtain when the bomb fell.'

'Let's get you to hospital, then you can see your mother, and get yourself cleaned up,' a cheerful voice said. It was an ARP warden. He took her arm and the tall young man offered once more to take the baby, but Debbie was having none of it. In the confusion of events which had preceded the bomb, she had a vague memory of a woman who looked like a gypsy, who had tried to lay claim to the infant. Debbie remembered how she and Gwen had decided to hang on to Baby so that they might return her to her real mother and clung desperately to her now. 'No, I can manage,' she said fiercely. 'She's—she's mine.'

They let her keep the baby but bundled her into an ambulance and the tall young man with fair hair got in as well and so did Dusty, because when the ambulance man tried to evict him Debbie and the tall young man became so vociferous that the dog was allowed to remain.

They reached the hospital. Debbie climbed down and found her legs collapsing beneath her, but the young man carried her to a wheelchair and then pushed her swiftly down a long corridor. A nurse and a doctor stopped them, tried to say that Debbie must be examined and cleaned up before she could be taken on to a ward, but the tall young man drew the doctor aside and said something that must have had considerable weight, for the doctor turned to go with them, and accompanied them to the ward where Debbie's mother lay.

*   *   *

One of the porters at the entrance of the hospital

had offered to look after Dusty while they were inside and when they reached the ward Pete took the child from her, saying he would wait in the foyer, so Debbie was alone when she reached her mother's bed. She thought Jess looked terrible, quite unlike herself. But when Debbie murmured, 'Mam?' her mother's eyes flickered open, and from somewhere she conjured up the travesty of a smile.

'I knew you were all right,' she whispered. 'I told the young man he must search for you because you were still alive.'

'Yes, I'm fine,' Debbie said impatiently. 'But you . . . oh, Mam, you've been hurt bad. Don't try to talk. You should conserve your strength.'

Jess's head gave a tiny, negative shake. 'No; I must tell you something before I go,' she whispered. 'When the war started I—I wrote you a letter. I put all sorts in it; me Post Office details, stuff like that. It's in the secret drawer of my little bureau along o' some money. And there's a name and address . . .'

Her voice trailed away and Debbie leaned closer still, smoothing the damp hair from her mother's forehead and holding very tightly to the cold hand which she had clasped as soon as she reached the bedside. 'All right, Mam, I'll see to it, but you mustn't worry yourself,' she said. 'We're both alive, you and me, and you're going to get better. That's the only thing that matters to me, you getting better . . .'

But Jess's lips were parting and her eyes, which had closed, flickered open once more. 'No, queen, what's important is that you go straight home now and get that letter,' she said urgently. 'This is no place for a young girl alone. I want you to . . .'

Her voice faded away and Debbie had just started to remind her that she was not alone, that she had Gwen, that even Uncle Max would no doubt keep an eye on her, when she felt the fingers in her own loosen their clasp and saw her mother's head fall sideways on the pillow. There was a rattling sound, then nothing. 'Mam!' Debbie screamed, then flew down the ward, shrieking, 'Nurse! Nurse!' at the top of her voice, but though several nurses, and a doctor, came running, they could only tell Debbie, with all the sympathy and gentleness at their command, that her mother was dead.

CHAPTER TEN

Despite her frequently expressed desire to be allowed to go back to her own home, the hospital insisted on keeping Debbie in overnight, though they warned her that she would probably have to spend it in the hospital basement, since there was bound to be another raid.

As soon as he was able, Pete visited Debbie on the ward, knowing that he would have to tell her how he had met Dicky and how the other young man had identified Gwen's body. Then, of course, he would have to tell her that her home in Wykeham Street had been bombed.

He walked up the ward, which was full of women all staring at him, and almost walked past Debbie's bed, for the difference between the dirty child who had emerged from the shelter and the young woman in the clean hospital nightgown, leaning against her pillows, was astonishing. Debbie had come out of the shelter literally caked with dust and dirt; tears had made clean tracks down her filthy cheeks, her eyes had been red with rubbing and her dress had been dark with dirt. The ribbon which Dicky had mentioned had been long gone, and her hair had hung about her face in tangled witch locks. Now, Pete could see her hair was thick and glossy, the colour of a ripe chestnut. Her skin was pale and clear, though there was an enormous bruise on her forehead and a scratch above one cheek. Her large eyes were dark blue, though deeply shadowed. Pete thought that a woman would say the small, pointy-chinned face held the promise of beauty to come, but he simply considered her looks appealing. He sat down on the seat beside the bed and smiled at her. 'You look a good deal better than you did when I last saw you,' he said. 'I hadn't realised you were quite such a young lady . . . you looked about twelve when you appeared out of the rubble.'

'Oh, it *is* you,' Debbie said. She sounded relieved, and Pete realised that she had not been the only one covered in filth and dust when they had met earlier. Once he had settled her in the hospital, in charge of people who knew best how to take care of her, he had collected his kitbag and found himself a lodging house. It was quite a decent place and the landlady, a motherly soul, had run him a hot bath and had taken his filthy clothing, assuring him that it would be clean and decent in next to no time.

He opened his mouth to explain this to Debbie but had no opportunity to do so. She began to bombard him with questions: had he seen the

279

baby? They had told her Baby was in a special baby unit but had refused to let her visit. Where was Dusty? Was he well? Did Pete realise the dog had saved their lives, hers and Baby's? Where was Pete himself staying? If he wanted a bed, he could go to Wykeham Street and use Debbie's own small room; they had a lodger whom she called Uncle Max, but though she did not like him he was not a bad man and would give any friend of the Ryans a decent enough welcome.

Pete tried to answer the questions patiently. He had not visited the baby yet, but would do so when he left Debbie. Dusty was still in the charge of the friendly hospital porter and had been given a large bowl of scraps which he had devoured with great enthusiasm. His hurts had been disinfected, stitched and bandaged, and the doctor who had done the work had assured Pete that Dusty would be as good as new in a couple of days. He was quite a hero, for Pete had told everyone how the dog had fought his way out of the shelter to bring help to his mistress and her baby.

'Good, good,' Debbie said. 'But you've not told me whether you're sleeping in Wykeham Street. Have you met Uncle Max? And . . . and . . .' her voice dropped, almost to a mumble, 'have you found Gwen?'

Pete nodded miserably. 'Yes. She . . . she was . . .'

Debbie gave Pete a quick glance and what she read in his eyes must have been the news she was dreading to hear, for she put out her hand and laid it over his own for a moment. And then she said, 'You needn't tell me about Gwen because I know. I guess I must always have known because she was in

280

the shelter with us and when I first came to myself and started shouting her name there was no answer. She's dead, isn't she?'

'I'm afraid so, my dear,' Pete said quietly. 'I'll expect you'll hear soon enough that you and the baby and the dog were the only survivors. You were very, very lucky to be right at the far end of the shelter when the bomb fell. It saved your lives.'

Debbie nodded. 'I was changing Baby's nappy,' she told him. 'Gwen offered to do it but I said it was okay, I'd manage, so in a way it's my fault that she died. You see, one of us had to go to the marshal for some more milk mixture, and I thought—I thought . . .' Her voice broke and she fished out her handkerchief to blow her nose, then spoke resolutely. 'I thought changing the nappy was dirty work so it was only fair that I should do it. I wish I'd let Gwen come with me . . . but it's too late for wishing, isn't it?'

'You're right there. Wishing won't bring anyone back,' Pete said. He was choked with pity but knew that nothing he could say or do could make things better, and he still had to tell her that the house in Wykeham Street no longer existed. He took her hand, rubbing his thumb gently across the small knuckles, longing passionately to be able to give her good news instead of having to see her facing up to losing everything. Apart from the clothing she had worn in the shelter, the baby and the dog, she now had nothing. But she was looking at him enquiringly. 'Have you been to Wykeham Street? Did you find Uncle Max at home?'

Pete cleared his throat. 'I'm afraid your home was bombed last night; there's really nothing left of it,' he said gently. 'But I saw a warden who said your Uncle Max had been fire-watching and was unharmed. I'm sure he'll see that you and your baby, and good old Dusty of course, all find somewhere else to live.'

For the first time, Debbie looked angry. 'I wouldn't live with Uncle Max if he were the last man on earth,' she said vehemently. 'He's horrible, really horrible. The sort of man who comes into your room without knocking and puts his beastly arm round you when he thinks your mam isn't looking, and . . .' Her voice faltered and stopped, and Pete saw that big tears were rolling down her cheeks and it occurred to him that the lodger might have fathered the child. Or was it possible that Jess was the baby's mother and Debbie had been looking after her little sister? The idea sent a wave of hope through him, for he had been horrified to think that a girl of her age had given birth to a baby; in his eyes she was still a child herself. He took a deep breath. That baby—Baby, didn't you say?—is she—is she your sister?'

Debbie had been staring at him, letting the tears fall unchecked, but now her eyes shifted uneasily, and she dabbed at them with the corner of the sheet. There was a longish pause before she said, still mopping her eyes, 'No, she's not my sister. She's mine, and nobody's going to take her away from me.'

'What about her father?' Pete asked. 'If you like him . . .'

Once again, Debbie cut across his stammered words. 'I don't care about her father,' she said fiercely. 'Me and Baby and Dusty will manage all right . . . oh, if only Mam was alive, she'd tell me what to do.'

Pete felt completely at a loss. If it had not been for the baby, he would have said, positively, that Debbie was innocent of the sort of knowledge which a woman with a child must have. As it was, he was sure that she must have been seduced, probably against her will, which was rape. He had let go her hand while she mopped her eyes, but now he took it again, feeling protectiveness and affection for this little creature who was so alone rise up in him. He longed to ask questions about the baby, and its father, to discover the truth, but knew this was not the moment, that perhaps the moment would never come. Instead, he held her hand within both his own and changed the subject. 'You asked me if I'd got somewhere to stay. Well, I have. It's a quiet house in Huskisson Street. I shall be able to keep my eye on you, make sure you've a roof over your head, before I return to my air force station.' He hesitated. 'You said your friend Gwen lived in Daisy Street and I took a look before coming in to visit you. There's a lot of dust and rubble about, but the houses are undamaged. Couldn't you stay there until . . . well, until something else turns up?' he finished lamely.

To his dismay, tears welled up once more in Debbie's eyes, but she fished under her pillow, withdrew a handkerchief and blew her nose resoundingly for the second time, furtively mopping up the tears as she did so. She waited a moment, and to Pete the silence seemed to stretch unbearably, but when she spoke her voice was steady. 'I don't know. You see, Mrs Soames only remained in Liverpool because G-Gwen works— worked, I mean—with me in the factory at Long Lane, assembling radio parts. Her mam said it weren't fair, going off to be safe in the country leaving Gwenny to soldier on alone. But things have changed. I reckon she'll move away now, stay with her other kids, and there won't be no shortage of folk wanting to take over the rent in Daisy Street because thousands of homes have been destroyed.'

'Oh,' Pete said, rather inadequately. 'If it weren't for the baby, I dare say you could move in with a few other girls. Or how about going to that place—Betws something or other—where the Soameses are staying?'

'I can't; I'm doing important work,' Debbie said briefly. Then she shot Pete a suspicious look. 'How did you know that the Soameses had gone to Betws-y-Coed? I never told you, I know I didn't.'

'I met a feller called Dicky at the shelter. Do you remember him? He gave you and—he gave you a lift to . . . Oh, Debbie, he was the person who identified your friend.'

Debbie's eyes filled with tears once more, but she blinked them away and made vigorous use of her handkerchief. 'He and Gwen were going to go steady; he asked her to go dancin' . . . oh, poor Dicky!'

As soon as he was able, Pete took hold of her hand once more. He had been meaning to ask her how she had managed a factory job whilst taking care of the baby, but guessed that she and her mother had both worked shifts and had managed to take turns attending to the child. Instead, he said: 'I don't see that your job at the factory can continue, with the way things are. I think you must go into the country where you and the baby—and Dusty of course—will be safe.'

284

Debbie shook her head. 'Can't; no money,' she said briefly. 'I get a really good wage at the factory, more than my mam did for working all the hours God sends in the hospital, and I don't mean to give that up. I might have to let Baby go to a childminder, but they won't charge much for a baby and at least we'll be self-supporting. Besides, I—I don't want to have time to think about all the dreadful things that have happened, which is all I would do if I left the 'Pool. Working in the factory, you have to keep your mind on your job.'

Pete opened his mouth to argue, then closed it again. Quite soon he would have to leave, since he had no desire to be posted AWOL and perhaps face a court martial for desertion. He would do his best to see Jess's daughter settled, but he could do little else. However, it occurred to him that his landlady would probably give Debbie, the baby and the dog his room when he moved out of it, provided of course that he paid the rent. So he got to his feet and smiled down at the small figure in the bed. 'Look, I've an idea. The sister told me you can leave hospital tomorrow, and to tell you the truth I ought to go back to Norfolk then as well. My landlady in Huskisson Street is a nice woman and I'm sure she'll let you take over my room, at least while you search for something more permanent. How would that suit you?'

Debbie smiled up at him. 'It would be a great help,' she admitted. 'But oh, do you have to go? I—I feel so dreadfully alone!'

Pete returned to the bed to give her hand another comforting squeeze. 'I'll give the station a ring this evening, see if they can extend my leave for another day or two,' he promised. 'And now just you get a good night's sleep. Sister told me to come back about ten in the morning, when she thinks that you and the baby will be allowed to leave. I'm going to pick Dusty up from the porter and I just hope he'll settle down quietly at Mrs Roberts's place—she's my landlady—because if he doesn't we really will have a problem.'

*   *   *

Debbie and Baby were dressed and waiting for him by the time Pete arrived at the hospital next morning. The authorities had provided Debbie with a brown frock which was rather too big for her, and a navy blue jacket, though she was still wearing her own shoes. They had also given her a towel and a toothbrush, though they had been unable to provide either toothpaste, soap, or a temporary ration card, a lack which would be made good at a nearby centre next day. Debbie had been delighted with the clothes that the hospital had provided for Baby, who now wore a clean pink dress and a neat little coat, and when the baby saw Pete she gave a delightful gurgle and held her arms out to him. Pete smiled and Debbie thought that he was flattered. 'She remembers me!' he exclaimed. 'Well, I never would have thought it!'

Debbie laughed at Pete's gratified expression. 'She does that to everyone,' she said merrily. 'She's ever such a friendly little soul, aren't you, Baby? They got really fond of her in the baby unit, which is why they found her such pretty clothes. Sister said babies' memories are very short and she probably won't remember the raid at all, which is a good thing, isn't it?'

'A very good thing,' Pete agreed. 'You both look very much better this morning, and though your frock is nowhere near as fine as Baby's, you look very neat; I like the plait. Let's go and collect Dusty, and then I'll take you to Huskisson Street.'

Debbie did feel very much better this morning and knew she looked it for she had examined her reflection as she had washed in the hospital ablutions. Her eyes were still shadowed and her cheeks were pale, but one of the nurses had plaited her hair into a thick braid, which fell across one shoulder. Debbie knew it probably made her look younger, but it was tidy and Pete clearly approved. She thought, rather ruefully, that it was already important to her that Pete should approve; after all, there was no one else now who mattered, no one else who cared whether she looked pretty or plain, happy or miserable. Tears welled up in her eyes at the thought but she blinked them away. Self-pity was a useless emotion and one in which she did not mean to indulge. Resolutely, she tilted her chin and tucked her free hand into Pete's arm. 'Lead on,' she said. 'Does that mean your landlady has agreed to let us stay with her for a bit? Oh, and I have to go back to Wykeham Street. There's something I have to do there.'

'Yes, Mrs Roberts will let you take my room, so you can move in right away because I'm afraid I have to catch a train later this morning to return to my station,' Pete told her. He hesitated. 'Look, Debbie, your house is a real mess. Are you sure you want to go back there?'

By now, they had emerged on to the Stanley Road, Dusty frisking along beside them, and Debbie turned into Fountains Road, pulling Pete

287

with her. 'I know it's been bombed, but it wasn't a direct hit, was it? Anyway, the wardens rescue anything they can get out all in one piece, and— and I have to look.'

Pete nodded. 'Yes, you'll want to see it,' he agreed. 'Only I don't suppose they'll manage to salvage much.'

They turned into Wykeham Street and Debbie gasped, then hurried forward. Someone had piled a number of things on the pavement outside her home. The wooden kitchen table, a couple of easy chairs, and a nest of occasional tables, sturdily built of oak, had survived. In addition, there were a number of pots and pans and clothing, though most of it was extremely dirty. She turned the clothes over gingerly, her lip trembling, for it all seemed to have belonged to her mother. She could see no sign of the bureau; nevertheless, she went through the pile, revealing a quantity of tins of various foodstuffs, but then she turned a dis appointed face up to Pete's. 'Mam's bureau isn't here,' she said blankly. 'It was old, but it was real sturdy. Hang on a minute, here comes one of the fellers who goes into bombed property to keep your stuff safe . . .' She jerked her head at the pile of goods on the pavement. 'He'll have got all that stuff out of our house.'

When questioned about the bureau, however, the man could only shake his head. 'Blast's a strange thing,' he told them. 'It can reduce a great heavy Welsh dresser to matchwood and leave a delicate little teapot standing right next to it, as perfect as the day it were made.' He scratched his head thoughtfully, tilting his tin hat back in order to do so. 'A little bureau, you say? No, I don't recall seeing such a thing.'

Debbie turned away, thanking him for his good offices in a rather flat voice. 'If you could put the stuff away for me until I've got somewhere to live, I'd be ever so grateful,' she said. 'We had a lodger called Max Williams; if he comes round, don't let him take anything, because he is only the lodger. I'm the householder now.'

'Right,' the man said. He hesitated. 'Do you want to take the tinned goods, though? We does our best, but believe it or not, some bombed houses get looted while the bleedin' Luftwaffe are still overhead. An' tins is awful easy to stick in your pocket an'steal.'

Debbie was so disappointed over the loss of the bureau that she felt indifferent to the fate of the tins, but Pete soon put her right. 'We'll take 'em,' he said, handing the baby back to her and picking up a pillow case covered in brick dust from the top of a pile of linen. 'You'll be glad of them when you do get a place of your own,' he told Debbie. 'And so will Baby. I remember my ma straining a tin of peaches through a sieve for my little brother; you could do that for her.'

'So I could,' Debbie said. She glanced round her wistfully. They had been happy here, she and her mam, but it was pretty clear that it would be many years before Wykeham Street rose from the ashes again. Through the shattered walls she could see the ruins of the shed in the back yard, and she sent up a brief but heartfelt prayer of thanks that the last of the hens had been killed outright, and had not been made to suffer, before their home had been so rudely torn asunder. She told herself, severely, that looking back could only lead to tears

289

and pain, and turned to thank the man for his help.

'That's all right, queen,' he said awkwardly. 'By the by, where did you get that baby? I disremember your mam havin' any kids other than yourself . . . or does it belong to the young feller?'

Debbie felt her cheeks grow hot; she should have realised that all the neighbours who had known herself and Jess would also know that neither of them had a baby. But if she admitted that the baby wasn't hers someone would take it away from her, and she didn't think she could bear that. She cast an appealing look at Pete and was surprised to see him looking relieved, though she could not imagine why. Quickly, she slid her hand into the crook of his arm, pinching him convulsively. 'That's right. Baby is Pete's little girl,' she said. 'I've been helping him to look after her because men don't know much about babies, but I'll be giving her back to his wife when—er—when we meet up.' She turned desperate eyes on Pete. 'Can you manage that great heavy pillow case full of tins? Only I can't help because of Baby here.'

'I can manage,' Pete said shortly. Debbie saw that he was looking annoyed and couldn't blame him. One minute the poor chap had been fancy-free and the next she had saddled him not only with a baby, but with a wife as well. Still, he had backed her up and she was grateful; so grateful that she supposed she would have to confide in him, which meant admitting that she did not know who Baby's mother was, that she had, in fact, stolen her . . . well, not exactly stolen, because of course she meant to give her back to her real mother, if the woman was still alive. Otherwise, I shall jolly well keep her, she told herself.

290

Briskly, she turned away. Pete had hefted the pillow case across one shoulder and as soon as they were out of earshot he pulled her to a halt, stopping so abruptly that the dog's cold nose bumped into the back of Debbie's knees. Then he turned and faced her and she saw that he was looking grim. 'Just what sort of game are you playing, young woman?' he asked angrily. 'You've been lying to me all along, haven't you? You said the baby was yours when it was no such thing, and now you've said it's mine. Do you intend to tell people you're my wife? Is that to be your next lie?'

Debbie stared at him, her own anger slowly mounting. 'I did *not* lie to you,' she said furiously. 'Oh, I said the baby was mine but she is, because the old woman who had her in the shelter didn't care tuppence for her. She handed her over to me and Gwen and then snored off to sleep. Why, it were me who fed her with the milk the shelter marshal gave us. Gwen and I worked out that she had probably stolen the baby—gypsies do steal babies—and we meant to find its real mother and hand it back.'

'Well, you never told me any of that,' Pete said. 'You said the baby was yours when you should have said that you were looking after it for someone else—or—or—that you didn't know whose it was. I thought it really *was* yours!'

'Stop calling her "it"; I've named her Baby. And she is mine because finders keepers, you know,' Debbie snapped. 'I don't see anything wrong in that. After all, I'm going to tell everyone Dusty is mine because I shall feed him and take care of him, and anyway, he wants to be mine. That's why he follows us without us having to put him on a

291

lead.'

'You still don't understand, do you, you silly little girl?' Pete said and Debbie realised that he was seriously annoyed with her. 'Can't you see what it looked like when you said the baby was mine? Why, even when you said you didn't know who the father was . . . Deborah Ryan, I thought you were its bloody mother!'

By now Debbie was really angry. 'Don't call her *it*,' she shouted. 'And how could you possibly have believed I was Baby's mother? I'm only fifteen, and I'm not married! Why, you must have thought I was a bad girl!'

'Yes, I did; it's what anyone would have thought,' Pete said crossly. He began to walk again, so fast that Debbie had to trot to keep up. 'Now you can just explain exactly what happened, how you got hold of the baby and why you said I was its father.'

'I don't see why I should,' Debbie said sulkily, after a long pause. 'It's none of your bleedin' business. You're going to catch a train in a little while and go back to your beastly aeroplane and your beastly friends. I've no doubt you'll forget all about me and Baby here, and I don't suppose I'll ever set eyes on you again. So why should I tell you anything?'

'Because if you don't tell me, then I shall take the baby to the police and say I think it's been stolen,' Pete said. He looked down at Debbie and grinned. It was not a friendly grin. 'You see, I've got my own reputation to think about. You told that feller it was my baby so I reckon I'm entitled to see it's properly looked after.'

Debbie stared at him, feeling tears rise to her

292

eyes. She had thought him her friend, the only friend she had left in a suddenly hostile world. And now he had turned on her. He had thought her a bad girl, the sort of girl who went with sailors down on the docks, and gave birth to bastard babies. He had called her a liar when she was no such thing and had threatened to tell the police that Baby was not hers. She knew, of course, that if the authorities knew that Baby wasn't hers they would take the child from her and put her in an orphanage, and that would be dreadful. But if she could just escape from him . . . no, better to tell him the whole story, promise faithfully to get in touch with the authorities, and then see him aboard his train. As soon as she was able, she would move out of the lodgings he had found for her, leaving no forwarding address. That would scotch his bright idea of going to the police!

'Well?' Pete said. 'Are you going to come clean, tell me the whole story?'

Debbie's shoulders sagged. 'All right, but is it far to Mrs What's-her-name's house? Only the baby is beginning to feel awfully heavy and I'm awfully tired,' she ended.

Pete looked down and she saw that his expression had softened. 'It's not far at all, so keep your pecker up,' he said encouragingly. 'In fact, I shan't be sorry to put this bloody bag of tins down, because if you think the baby's heavy, you want to try carting this!'

'It was your idea to bring them,' Debbie reminded him, but she did not speak critically. She knew she would be grateful for the tins when she was feeding herself once more. Presently they arrived at the lodging house, and Pete introduced her to Mrs Roberts, who proved to be a motherly, middle-aged woman with grey-streaked hair cut in an Eton crop and rather dreamy blue eyes. She greeted Debbie kindly and admired the baby, then led them into the house. Pete paused to readjust the pillow case across his shoulders, but Mrs Roberts ushered Debbie straight to the staircase, saying, 'Now come up and see your room. I've not give you Mr Solomon's since I reckon you'd rather pay a bit less for the back bedroom, which is nearer the bathroom. As it happens, I've another very nice gentleman interested in the front room, and being a widow I can't afford to turn down good money.' She smiled at Debbie. 'Now, Flying Officer Solomon was telling me you'd been bombed out, you poor thing, so you had nothing but what you stood up in. Mind, there's hundreds in the same boat, but it's hard for a young girl like yourself, especially wi' the baby. But when you go along to the centre for your ration card they'll give you clothing for yourself and nappies and such for the littl'un.'

'Oh!' Debbie said. She turned to look down at Pete, some steps below them. 'Will you have time to come with me to the centre, Pete?'

They reached the top of the stairs and Pete caught up with them as Mrs Roberts threw open the door of the back bedroom. It was a small, neat room with a cot in one corner and a small bed beside it, and Mrs Roberts pointed proudly to the large red cushion which she had placed on the floor for the dog to sleep on. Dusty, who had followed them up the stairs, seemed to approve, for he went over and sniffed the cushion before wagging his tail and grinning at them, with a great show of lolling red tongue and perfect white teeth.

Mrs Roberts laughed. 'He'll settle; mongrels what've never had much don't expect much,' she said. 'I'll leave you to stow your goods . . .' she glanced at the stack of tins which Pete had put down with a relieved sigh as they entered the room, 'but as soon as you're ready there'll be a nice cup of tea and a new-baked scone waiting for you in the kitchen, and I've found up an old bottle which I used when my own were small. I got a couple of new rubber teats from me neighbour and I've got plenty of conny-onny so you can make the little 'un up a feed as soon as you like.'

Debbie thanked her, and as soon as Mrs Roberts had left the room she perched on the bed and laid the baby, who was still fast asleep, in the cot, whilst Pete sat in the wicker chair by the window.

'Well, it was like this. Gwen and I came out of the flicks and had just reached the Scottie when Moaning Minnie started and a warden hustled us straight into a shelter . . .'

Debbie told the story slowly and carefully, anxious to get it right and to tell the absolute truth, and it was a good thing she did so for when she came to the bit about her suspicion that the old lady was a gypsy and had stolen the child she remembered something which she had previously completely forgotten. 'There was an old man, wrapped in a blanket, lying nearby,' she said excitedly. 'He knew the old woman, said her name was Mrs O'Shea. He reckoned she lived in one of the courts off the Scottie—I mean the Scotland Road—and took in lodgers. He said some of the girls she took in were—were no better than they should be, so Mrs O'Shea would have brought the baby down to the shelter whilst its mam were working.'

'So if the baby's mother is still alive, you'll find her living in a court off the Scotland Road,' Pete said thoughtfully. 'Well, that's some help, at any rate.' He had been leaning back in the chair, but now he sat forward, elbows on knees. 'What do you think is best? If you tell the police, they'll run the mother to earth. Or you can ask around the neighbourhood, see if anyone can tell you where Mrs O'Shea lived.'

'I'll try to find her myself first,' Debbie decided. 'The courts aren't a good place to live, but the folk in them are often decent people who help one another. If Baby's mother is still alive, I'll find her.'

Pete stared at her for a moment, his eyes hard, then they softened. 'I believe you,' he said, almost grudgingly. 'But I want a promise from you: you'll write to me in the next couple of days telling me what you've done and how successful or unsuccessful you've been. It isn't that I don't trust you, but I can tell that you're very fond of the baby and don't want to be parted from it. Only, if the mother really is alive, that would be kidnap, do you understand? Theft, in other words. You could be sent to prison, and when I saw your mother I promised I'd look after you. So . . . will you promise?'

Debbie agreed. 'All right, but it may take me more than a couple of days,' she warned him. 'And I never asked you—' She broke off as Pete suddenly lurched to his feet.

'Oh my God, look at the time,' he said, waving his wristwatch under Debbie's nose. 'I'm gasping

296

for a cup of tea, but unless I hurry I'll never get to the train.'

Debbie glanced towards the cot; the baby was stirring and murmuring, so whilst Pete thundered down the stairs she lifted the child from amongst its blankets and held it against her face, kissing the petal-soft cheek as she did so. 'I'm going to have to find your mam, if she's still alive, little Baby,' she murmured, as she descended the stairs. 'Pete was rather unkind but I suppose he's quite right; your mam must be desperate with worry and longing to see you again, and though I'd much rather keep you all to myself, it would be very wrong of me to do so.'

Entering the kitchen, she saw Pete gulping desperately at a hot cup of tea whilst Mrs Roberts wrapped four newly buttered scones in a piece of greaseproof paper and pushed them into his coat pocket. 'You can eat them on the train,' she said, as he began to thank her. 'And don't you fret, I'll take care of these little girls for you.'

'Thanks, Mrs Roberts,' Pete said gratefully. He picked up his kitbag and slung it over one shoulder, wagging an admonitory finger at Debbie as he did so. 'Debbie is looking after the baby for a friend,' he said rapidly. 'She'll explain . . . oh, hell, I dare not miss this train.' Quickly, he crossed the kitchen, put his arms round Debbie and kissed her cheek. 'Take care of yourself and don't forget you promised to write,' he said softly. 'And don't worry; everything will come right in the end, you'll see.'

Watching him disappear out of the door at a run, Debbie clicked her tongue in annoyance. 'Drat,' she said. 'I still haven't asked him how he came to visit my mam in hospital. And I've just realised he never gave me his address.'

*   *   *

Pete spent most of the cross-country journey thinking about Debbie. He had been angry with her because she had lied to him and because she had told the rescue worker that he had fathered the child, but now he felt quite ashamed. Poor kid, she had been in a pretty desperate situation, now he had leisure to consider it. All she was doing was trying to keep something for herself, and that was understandable when you thought how much she had lost: her mother, her best friend, her home and pretty well all her possessions. There was that lodger as well, Uncle Max she called him. This time the anger he felt was not turned on Debbie but on the unknown relation. Nasty old man, trying to take advantage of a pretty young girl, just because they lived under the same roof! Well, at least that was one thing she would not have to worry about whilst she lived with Mrs Roberts. He had paid the landlady the rent of the room for two weeks because that was all the money he had on him, but he had made it clear that he would get a money order to her for every additional week that Debbie spent under her roof. Flying officers were not paid enormous salaries, but he knew he could rely on his mother to help him somehow, if he told her he needed it.

Sitting in the train—or rather sitting on his kitbag in the corridor of the train—he realised that he felt responsible for Debbie. She was so young, so brave and so very alone. What was more, she was living in a city—a sea port—which had been

298

under constant enemy attack; she had already been buried alive for the best part of twenty-four hours, had been the only survivor of that particular tragedy. She could easily be killed or badly wounded . . . he had to stay in touch to know what was happening. But she's got her job, he reminded himself, and she said it was well paid, so she had no intention of leaving it. And I've paid the rent for the next two weeks; if necessary, I'll go on paying. Then it occurred to him that he himself could easily be killed, because aircraft were constantly being shot down. If that happened, how could he continue to protect her, make sure she did not want? He decided he must make a Will, leaving the money he had in the bank to Debbie Ryan, and write to his mother to say that he wanted his share of the Walleroo to go to her friend Jess's child should he be killed. After all, the bond between the two women, Nancy and Jess, had been strong enough to withstand the long separation, the distance between them, and their very different lives. He was sure his mother would be as keen as he to see that Jess's daughter did not starve. Having decided how best to help Debbie, he settled back on his uncomfortable perch and began to try to think about the Walleroo, imagining his father mustering the cattle astride his favourite mount, a tall roan with black mane and tail which answered to the unlikely name of Taffy. He knew that this was one of the best times of the year, when the wet had made the country productive and the drought had not yet dried up all the streams and lagoons. Crops would be growing well and the cattle would be fat and sleek.

He thought of the homestead, of his ma's flower

garden, and wondered, with an inward smile, what she would think of the little gardens he could see from the window of the train where, at the government's request, housewives had replaced petunias and marigolds, delphiniums and geraniums, with potatoes, carrots and onions. He could imagine Nancy's quick glance towards the acres of productive land which she, and many other members of the staff, planted, weeded and harvested yearly. No need to sacrifice your blooms in a country like Australia, where there was more virgin land than the inhabitants could possibly cultivate.

Still smiling to himself, he pictured his mother as he had last seen her, waving him off at the station, her primrose-fair hair pulled back from her face, her lovely blue eyes tear-filled, though her mouth was smiling. And then, suddenly, he realised that he was seeing, not his mother's face, but Debbie's, framed with smooth and shiny chestnut hair. He could see the beautiful shape of the winged eyebrows, the sweep of dark lashes on her cheek, the steady regard of her dark blue eyes. Every detail of her small face, from broad brow to pointed, determined chin, was as clear in his mind as though he had known her for months instead of hours. Those hours had not been spent in quiet amity either, he mused. He had got extremely cross with her, had been furious when she had pretended that the child was his. His anger had melted, however, when she had explained why she had lied, and fortunately neither was the type to bear a grudge. She had waved him off merrily, had thanked him very prettily for all the help he had given her, and despite the terrible experiences through which she had lived had been careful not to show him a perpetually sad face. Yes, she was a nice girl, he told himself, and that made him think of his mother's desire for a daughter-in-law and grandchildren. Pete grinned at the recollection. He had met plenty of girls—nice girls too—since joining the Royal Air Force, but he realised, with a small stab of shock, that none of them had made as good an impression upon him as Debbie. She was only a kid, far too young for him really, but she had courage and humour and tenacity; she would not give the baby up to an orphanage, he was suddenly sure of it, and instead of being angry he realised he admired her for it. She loved and needed Baby all right, but her main anxiety was for the child's happiness and well-being. Yes, Debbie wasn't just a pretty girl, she had character, which was even more important.

Sitting on his kitbag, going over the events of the last couple of days, he had almost nodded off to sleep when he suddenly remembered that he had never actually told her that he was Nancy's son and had come to Liverpool expressly to see the Ryans. But surely she would put two and two together? He could not remember whether he had ever mentioned his surname, but she must have recognised his Australian accent, surely? Though that ARP warden hadn't . . . But then he recollected her promise to write. He would write back and tell her everything, and, in the meantime, would listen with added interest to the wireless and read the newspapers with more attention than he had previously given them. And next time he visited Liverpool . . .

The train jerked to a stop and a porter's voice

301

came echoing along the corridor. 'All change, all change.'

Pete got wearily to his feet and headed for the station platform. Another bloody hold-up, he thought savagely; he'd be lucky if he reached the station before midnight.

*   *   *

At about the same time that Pete was changing trains, Mrs Roberts was serving an excellent meal of macaroni cheese, mashed potatoes and spring greens to her lodger. 'Your young man will be well on his way by now,' she said, heaping food on to Debbie's plate. 'When he first come here, I thought he were from Birmingham . . . from his voice, you know. Then I thought London, 'cos he sounded a bit like one of them cockneys.' She gazed inquisitively across at Debbie. 'Am I right?'

'I dunno,' Debbie said truthfully. 'I only met him yesterday . . . he knew my mum, not me.'

'Oh, well,' Mrs Roberts said. 'What was he sayin' about the baby?'

'I'm looking after her for a friend who—who should be back in the city to pick her up in a day or two,' Debbie said, improvising rapidly. 'She were left with me and Mam while Mrs—Mrs Elliot went to visit her other kids, who've been evacuated. So she won't be with me for long.' Even as she said the words, Debbie was making up her mind; if she didn't find Baby's mum then she would move out, take other digs, but she would not abandon her to an orphanage.

'I see,' Mrs Roberts said. 'Cabbage, m'dear?'

302

Debbie began her search for the baby's mother the very next day, when she went along to the centre to see what help could be given her. It was very busy, with crowds waiting to be attended to, but she was given a pile of nappies and a couple of dresses and cardigans for the baby, and some underwear for herself. She was also presented with emergency ration cards, having given the baby's name as Ryan, though she crossed her fingers whilst doing so and was glad everyone was too busy to ask for other particulars. Because of the lengthy queues it was mid-afternoon before she made her way back to the area of Scotland Road where she and the baby had met in the shelter. Surely someone round here would be able to help her to trace the baby's mother, if she were still alive?

As she walked along the Scotland Road, Debbie was horrified anew by the extent of the destruction. Paddy's Market and the Metropole, to say nothing of scores of small shops and dwellings, had been razed to the ground, though when Debbie enquired of a passing woman she was told that there had been fewer deaths than one might suppose. 'This here trekking they're talking about was getting to everyone after seven nights without sleep,' she said heavily, glancing curiously at the baby on Debbie's hip. 'I took off meself wi' most o' the 'habitants of Lavender Court. We didn't care where we went so long as we could get a good night's sleep an' still be alive in the mornin'. So we trekked off to Crosby.' She chuckled richly, but Debbie could see the strain in her eyes. 'Much sleep we got! We was fire-bombed from midnight till nigh on three in the morning, but at least when daylight come we were still alive. Our side of the court were flattened, norra dwellin' standin', so you see we done right to gerrout, wharrever them fellers in the government say.'

'I'm glad, and I'm sure you did do the right thing,' Debbie said sincerely. She noticed that the woman was still eyeing Baby and realised suddenly that asking about the baby's mother might be dangerous. If Debbie asked the wrong person, someone would realise that the baby was not hers.

She made to move away but was forestalled. 'That your baby?' the woman enquired. 'I dare say all babies look alike to some but me, I'm different. I never had none o' me own, you see, though hubby and me would ha' liked a fambly. So when the old lady opposite took in a young gal wi' a little new 'un, I took a bit of an interest, like. And that 'un . . .' she jerked a thumb towards the baby, 'looks awful like Clodagh. Outlandish name, but then you can trust the Irish for that.'

Debbie could feel a smile begin to creep across her face. What a piece of luck! She might have searched the entire city of Liverpool without finding anyone who recognised the baby, yet she had chanced upon this woman on the very first day of her search. 'Was—was the lady who lived opposite you sort of gypsyish-looking?' she enquired eagerly.

Once again, the older woman chuckled. 'That's her; Mrs O'Shea,' she said, nodding. 'Her house is still standing, though I doubt there's a pane of glass in the place; number four it is.'

'Number four Lavender Court,' Debbie said, memorising it. 'I'll go there at once.'

'Well, you might not find the old gal at home since she didn't come out to Crosby with the rest of us,' the old woman said. She glanced slyly at Debbie. 'But young Biddy will be in, likely. She—she works nights, you know.'

'Yes, I do know,' Debbie said, rather awkwardly. 'Can you point Lavender Court out to me, please?'

'It's off Lawrence Street, second court along,' the woman said at once. 'Lawrence Street goes through to Cazneau so it's a right handy place to live. You goin' to look for young Biddy?'

'Yes,' Debbie said. 'What did you say her surname was?'

'I dunno as I ever heard it,' the woman said, as Debbie turned away. 'But it weren't O'Shea, that's for sure.'

Debbie wondered whether to find Lavender Court before she returned to her lodgings, but the baby was growing fretful and she realised the child must need a bottle, so she set off once more for Huskisson Street. She was in the kitchen chatting idly to Mrs Roberts and feeding Baby with a bottle of warmed milk when the front door bell rang.

Mrs Roberts surged ponderously to her feet. 'That'll be me new lodger,' she said. 'Ever such a nice gentleman. He's like you; lost his home and the woman he meant to make his wife, poor feller.'

'Oh, right,' Debbie said vaguely. She was cradling the baby against her shoulder, watching lovingly as the level in the bottle dropped. Baby—she must remember to call her Clodagh now—certainly enjoyed her milk, and if the previous day's experience was anything to go by she would presently enjoy a helping of mashed potato and carrot mixed with gravy.

Debbie heard the front door open and half heard two voices, then felt her blood go cold. The man's deep voice was not merely familiar, it was heartily disliked, and to her horror she heard Mrs Roberts usher its owner into the front parlour, saying as she did so: 'We'd best talk in here, Mr Williams, if you've anything of a confidential nature to say. I'd ask you into the kitchen, but I've another lodger in there, a young lady, and she's feeding her baby, so we'd best talk in the parlour.'

The baby had finished her bottle and seemed inclined to sleep, so Debbie propped her up in the deep old armchair and then tiptoed across the hall. The parlour door was not properly closed and through it she could hear Mrs Roberts's voice. 'Well, Mr Williams? You know my terms and conditions; is owt worrying you?'

'Not exactly worrying, Mrs Roberts,' Uncle Max said. 'But I've been to my lady friend's solicitor, the lady I was telling you about, the one I should have married only she were killed. She's left me everything she possessed in trust for her daughter and she's left her daughter in my guardianship. That means I'll have to find the child, and if I do, would you be able to accommodate her? Just until I get a place of me own, of course.'

'Well, there's the attic,' Mrs Roberts said doubtfully. 'Of course, the young woman what's here at present may not be stayin' long. She's paid a fortnight in advance but for all I know she may move on at the end of that time. She's gorra dog, which ain't ideal . . . yes, I reckon I'll be able to accommodate your ward.'

'Thanks very much, Mrs Roberts,' Uncle Max said, his voice positively oozing sincerity. Debbie

306

heard the chair creak as he got heavily to his feet. 'I'm fond of me lady friend's girl so I shan't leave any stone unturned to find her, and it's a real comfort to know she can stay here with me.'

Oh, I bet it is, Debbie thought savagely, shooting back into the kitchen and picking Baby up once more. And it would all start over again, the pinching and patting, and pretending to be jolly old Uncle Max, whilst all the time he was really dirty old Uncle Max. Without her mother to protect her . . . but it did not bear thinking about. She must get away, and get away fast.

The two adults crossed the hall and began to mount the stairs, Mrs Roberts saying that she would show him his room. 'And then if you come down to the parlour again there'll be a nice cup of tea and a tray of biscuits waiting,' she said comfortably. 'And then I'll introduce you to me other lodger.'

But Debbie, heart thumping, was preparing to leave. She went to the dresser drawer in which Mrs Roberts had placed the emergency ration cards and tucked them into her pocket. Then she snatched her coat and Baby's from the hooks on the back of the door. She was halfway across the kitchen when she heard the landlady descending the stairs, alone. 'Mrs Roberts? I'm off to see if me pal's home yet; I dunno what time I'll be back. I might spend the night at her place if she's late, but I'll pop in tomorrow, around ten o'clock.'

Mrs Roberts's flushed face appeared round the door, looking doubtful. 'Tomorrow's me mornin' for the WI canteen,' she observed. 'I won't be in till noon, mebbe later, but the key's under the third plant pot on the left. Does this mean you're goin' to miss my evenin' meal?' She dropped her voice to a husky whisper. 'The butcher halfway up Heyworth Street is me brother-in-law an' he's slipped me a pound of liver this morning; I gorran onion, an' all. You don't want to miss liver 'n' onions.'

'Well, I'll do my best to get back,' Debbie said untruthfully, though her mouth watered at the mention of liver and onions. 'But you know how it is, Mrs Roberts; if Gwen misses the train . . . or if it's late . . .' The name had slipped out and Debbie felt a pang of pain and guilt, then scolded herself as she said goodbye to the landlady and headed, with Dusty at her heels, across the back yard into the jigger. It had been natural to use the name of her oldest and best friend; she had no need to reproach herself.

And presently, hurrying along towards the Scotland Road, Debbie began to feel less hunted and more optimistic. She would go back to the Roberts house very late and leave very early next morning, before Uncle Max could possibly be up. She was beginning to feel very angry with him, which was better than being terrified. How dared he say he had lost the woman he meant to marry; he could only mean Jess and it seemed doubly unfair that he should make such a claim when Jess was unable to refute it. And she was certain that it would never have occurred to her mother to make Uncle Max her guardian; why should it? Her mother had not expected to die and she was ten years younger than him. What was more, Jess knew Debbie disliked the man, and so far as Debbie knew her mother had never consulted a solicitor. No, it was just a ploy on Uncle Max's part to try to get her into his clutches, and she would have none of it. They had told her at the centre that she could return next day. Now that she had no lodgings, she would need all the help she could get.

In her arms, the baby began to wriggle and coo, and suddenly Debbie felt almost happy. Moving in with Mrs Roberts had been too easy; now she was learning how tough life could be and she decided it was better that way. Less time to think, less time to brood, and more time to be herself. Whistling beneath her breath, Debbie headed for Lavender Court. She glanced at a clock above a chemist's shop. It was already half past six and she had been told Biddy worked nights so she had best get a move on.

It was a fair way from Huskisson Street to Lavender Court and she might not have made it in time save for a fortunate coincidence. She had paused by the window of a baker's shop to gaze longingly at a display of cakes when the door opened and someone emerged eating a fat currant bun. Debbie was beginning to move away when a voice spoke her name. 'Debbie! Oh, my God, I thought you was dead! So you weren't in the shelter, after all? I come along to help in the rescue work . . . we found poor Gwen, but there weren't a sign of you.'

It was Dicky. Debbie gave him a tremulous smile and felt Dusty's nose bump into her calf. He always walked close and had not expected her to stop again so suddenly. 'Oh, Dicky, I'm awful sorry about Gwen,' she said. 'We were all in the shelter, Baby and Dusty and me. A great slab of concrete stopped us from getting squashed—and they managed to get us out, though it took ages. The dog saved us, to tell you the truth; he was a stray but he's mine now.'

'An' is the baby a stray, an' all?' Dicky said humorously. He put out a tentative finger and touched the baby's soft, pink cheek. 'I disremember you had a baby with you when I dropped you off at the cinema.'

'No. The baby was in the shelter, up the same end as me and the dog. I've kept her with me—the baby, I mean—because I didn't know what else to do, but I've found out who the mother is and I'm taking her round to Lavender Court right now. I—I don't live in Wykeham Street any more because the house was bombed; I'm lodging in Huskisson Street. If you could give me a lift to Lavender Court, I'd be awful grateful.'

'Sure I will,' Dicky said. 'I say, did you come across a feller called Pete when you gorrout of the shelter? He and meself were working together but I had to get back to the yard.'

'Yes, he helped to get us out,' Debbie exclaimed. 'In fact, Pete's a friend of my mam's . . .' Her eyes filled with tears despite her resolution not to cry in front of Dicky. 'I should say he *was* a friend of my mam's, I suppose. She—she died soon after they got me out. Pete took me to the hospital but there weren't nothing anyone could do.'

Dicky had taken her arm and was leading her towards his van but now he drew her to a halt and patted her hand. 'Debbie, I'm so sorry. I never met your mam but Gwen often talked about her; she sounded like a grand lady. But how will you manage? You're only a kid when all's said and done. If Gwen were alive . . . but it's no good wishin'.'

'I'll manage all right,' Debbie said, trying to sound brisk and self-confident and failing dismally. 'That feller, Pete Solomon, he's paid for my lodgings for the next two weeks and I'm sure by then I'll have sorted something out. I'm just praying that my factory on Long Lane, the one that makes wireless parts, hasn't been destroyed.'

'It hasn't; I were by there earlier and it's still standin', and the gals are still workin' away there,' Dicky said confidently. 'No need to get in a state, though—when you're ready to go back just tell 'em what happened. Experienced workers is gettin' rarer, what wi' kids being evacuated and parents trekkin' into the country. Oh aye, you'll be fine, just you see.'

By now they had reached the van. Dicky opened the door and ushered her, the baby and the dog into the passenger seat, then went round and slid behind the wheel. He went to pull the self-starter, then looked with distaste at the sticky bun he still held. 'Think your dog might fancy this? I can't drive and eat at the same time; the old van is temperamental, to say the least.'

Dusty's face, as the bun descended in his direction, wore a look of such blissful anticipation that both Dicky and Debbie laughed. 'I think he'd eat anything you offered him,' Debbie said, but was pleased when the dog took the bun with care and delicacy, then lay down in the well of the van to enjoy the treat.

They reached Lavender Court just before seven. Dicky dropped her and the dog off, then waved a cheery goodbye and drove away. Debbie found the house, but after repeated knocking realised that no one could be at home. As she turned away, the

311

door of the next house shot open and a fat young woman, with hair in paper curlers and a pronounced squint, asked her who she was after.

'I'm looking for someone called Biddy,' Debbie said carefully. 'I was told she'd probably be in around this time.'

The fat woman sniffed disparagingly. 'I ain't seen 'er for a couple o' days,' she said, sounding almost pleased. 'She were a bad girl, you know.' She sniffed again and Debbie longed to advise her to use a handkerchief. 'Well, I reckon the court's better off wi'out the likes of 'er. I reckon she and the brat were in that shelter on the Scottie what gorra direct hit. Miz O'Shea were there and she were killed; Mr Perkins told me so.'

Debbie stared at her, not knowing what to say. The callousness of it! Not a word of regret or pity, only a sort of smug satisfaction because the speaker herself was alive. She opened her mouth to say as much, then turned away, hugging the baby tightly as tears formed in her eyes. She took a couple of stumbling steps towards the arch through which she could see the sunlit street, then she heard a shriek like a steam engine's whistle, and stopped short. A girl was running towards her, a slim girl with thickly curling black hair and a face white as paper. She hurled herself at Debbie and clutched at the baby, saying as she did so: 'It *is*, it really is! Oh, my darling, my little darling, I never t'ought to see you alive again! They said . . . oh, dear God, they said everyone in that shelter was kill't stone dead! Oh, Clodagh, Clodagh, your mammy loves you more'n anything else in the whole world, so she does!'

Debbie had handed the baby over—well, Biddy

312

had more or less snatched her—as soon as she realised who the girl was, and now felt herself being violently hugged. 'Oh, alannah, I'm so grateful to you, I just don't know what to say,' Biddy said, rubbing ineffectually at the tears streaming down her cheeks. 'I've spent the whole day searching, an' I were just turnin' into the court when I see'd someone standin' on Miz O'Shea's doorstep. Me heart began to beat double time and then I saw you turnin' away wit' the baby in your arms, and I just knew it were my little girl and you'd saved her. Oh, me darlin', I dunno who you are or how you come by Clodagh, but Mary, Mother of Jesus, you're a saint, so you are!' She glanced towards the door. 'Will you come in, so's I can thank you proper? I'll make you a meal if there's anything in the place that you fancy. Miz O'Shea were kill't so there won't be no one to object, and maybe you can tell me what happened and how you saved my baby . . .'

Debbie was suddenly filled with happiness. She had somehow imagined that Biddy would be an over-dressed, over-painted, smart woman, like the ones who paraded up and down outside Lime Street station. But this was a girl very little older than herself, with clear skin and bright eyes. And she was so fond of the baby! Debbie had known she must leave Clodagh with her natural mother whether she liked her or not, but having met Biddy she had no qualms. Even Dusty seemed to approve, for he sniffed at the girl's skirt then wagged his tail, grinning up at her as though he had known her all his life.

'It's awful kind of you,' Debbie said. 'But now that we've met I've—I've a sort of proposition to

313

put to you. It's—it's a bit of a favour . . . I dare say I've got a nerve to ask, but . . .'

'Oh, alannah, if there's anything I can do for you . . . but I don't know your name, and you've done me the best turn anyone could! I'm Biddy Callaghan. Who's you?'

'I'm Debbie Ryan, and the truth is I need somewhere to live. My home was flattened and my mother was killed during the last raid, and though I'm in temporary lodgings I thought . . . well, your house is still standing and poor Mrs O'Shea's room will be vacant right now, so . . .'

'You want to move in! Sure and we'd welcome you wit' open arms, me and Siobhan and Eanna. As you can see, a bomb has blowed all the glass out of the windows but there's a feller comin' to fix that tomorrow or the day after and the weather 'tis fine, so it is. As for rent, don't bother about that, the t'ree of us will put a bit extra in the kitty. After all, you saved me baby's life, and we'd already decided not to tell Mr Capper that t'ings had changed. Why, so long as we pay the rent every Monday mornin', I'm sure he'll be satisfied. So you needn't worry about your share, not after what you did for my baby.'

'I can pay my way; I'm in a good job and earning a good wage,' Debbie said quickly. 'And I can move in right away because I—I paid my landlady in advance, so there'll be nothing owing. So if it really is all right with you and your friends I'll get my stuff and be with you later this evening.'

Even as she said the words, it occurred to Debbie that she might be moving into what her mother had always called 'a house of ill repute'. The old man in the shelter had said Mrs O'Shea let

314

her rooms to bad girls, and the woman who had recognised Clodagh had said that Biddy worked nights, which Debbie had supposed meant that she . . . well, that she walked the streets looking for likely fellers. Suppose she, Debbie, moved in and the other girls brought sailors into the house and expected her to—to do whatever it was that bad girls did? On the other hand, however, she simply dared not remain under the same roof as Uncle Max. She was still mulling over the problem when Biddy looked at her enquiringly. 'What's up?' the Irish girl said baldly. 'If you're scared me pals won't agree to your moving in, no need to worry about that. We meant to find another lodger anyway so if you really can pay a share of the rent—well, that would be just grand, so it would.'

Debbie took a deep breath. It was time to make some enquiries of her own. 'Biddy, the old man in the shelter who told me about Mrs O'Shea said she let her rooms to bad girls. I can see you aren't a bad girl, but—but what about the other two? And—and do they bring sailors back to the house? The woman who recognised Clodagh and told me where you lived said you worked nights, and I'd guessed Mrs O'Shea had the baby with her because you were working, and I sort of got the idea . . .'

Biddy stared at her, round-eyed, then a wide smile spread across her face. 'Well, if that don't beat the Dutch,' she said. 'I'm an usherette at the Forum cinema up on Lime Street.' She clapped her hand over her mouth, then began to giggle through her fingers. 'When I first come over to Liverpool it were because Eanna—she's me cousin—said she could find me a job, which she did. I worked in a laundry until the baby came, then I took the job as

315

an usherette so's I could be wit' Clodagh during the day and Eanna or Siobhan or even the old 'un—Mrs O'Shea, I mean—could give an eye to her, evenings. I expect you t'ink I'm a bad girl 'cos Clodagh's a love child, but I'm not . . . I've never earned me livin' from goin' wit' sailors and that. As for Siobhan and Eanna, they'd be shocked if they knew what you've been thinkin'. Eanna works—or worked rather—at the Bryant & May factory, making matches, only that went up in flames t'other night, and Siobhan, she's the oldest of us— she's twenty-two—works in the laundry on Smithdown Road. Honest to God, alannah, they're real respectable girls. As for me, I didn't ought to ha' gone wit' Padraig, but he swore we'd get wed . . . then he joined the army as soon as he knew I were in the family way and left me to manage as best I could. My mam and dad are country folk, real respectable, so I dussent go home . . . but that's enough about me. Are you going to move in? Oh, you aren't in any sort of trouble, are you?'

'Yes please, I'd like to move in, and I'm not in any sort of trouble, not really,' Debbie said immediately, feeling ashamed of her suspicions yet reluctant to admit to her own difficulties. 'Only my landlady doesn't like the dog and I'm only fifteen . . . I'd rather leave quietly without any argument.'

'Ah, now I understand everythin',' Biddy said wisely. 'Aye, I know the type: make you pay double up front, take your ration book and feed you on scrapings, then turn nasty when you moves out and try to say you've robbed 'em. Want any help wit' getting your stuff out?'

Debbie laughed as she remembered her meagre possessions. 'I don't have much stuff to get, just half a dozen nappies, some undies, and a pillow case full of tinned fruit and veg.' She looked hopefully at Biddy. 'Know anyone who'd be willing to lend me a wheelbarrow? Or an old pram?'

'I've got an old pram meself; picked it up a week ago in Paddy's Market. You can borrow that,' Biddy said. 'And I'll come along wit' you to see there's no trouble.'

Poor Debbie was beginning to feel guilty over the things she had hinted about Mrs Roberts. She told Biddy that she could manage perfectly well, but was glad of the older girl's help when they reached the house. It was locked up, but she found the key in its hiding place and let herself in. Then she and Biddy packed all her possessions into the old perambulator, locked the door and pushed the key through the letter box. Then she scribbled a quick note saying that she had found a cousin who was going to give her a room, thanked Mrs Roberts for her hospitality, and set off once more for Lavender Court.

*　　　*　　　*

By the time summer was declining into autumn, Debbie felt as though she had lived in Lavender Court all her life. Originally, the girls had had a room each, but with more than seventy thousand people made homeless during the May blitz things had speedily changed and by the beginning of June six girls, all aged between fifteen and twenty-five, occupied the house. Biddy's attic room contained herself and Debbie as well as Baby Clodagh and Dusty. To her mother's initial dismay, the name Clodagh had been speedily shortened by the

English girls to Chloe, for no Liverpudlian could resist the urge to simplify, but Biddy comforted herself with the reflection that Chloe would doubtless prefer the shorter version when she was in school and had to write her name on all her exercise books.

The girls thought themselves fortunate indeed, both to have a roof over their heads and to be in pleasant company. But at the beginning of September a new tenant came forward and, after discussing it, the girls agreed that Mrs Batley, a fat and friendly woman, should join their number. She suggested that she should act as a sort of house mother, doing the marketing, preparing the meals, laundering clothing, and of course looking after Chloe when her mother was working. She would pay a token rent since she had no means of support other than the small sum she earned as an evening cook in a nearby café, and very soon all the girls realised that they had found a treasure. Mrs Batley was a Geordie from Tyneside, whose accent had baffled the girls at first, though they soon grew accustomed. When a Liverpudlian would have said 'chuck', or 'queen', and Biddy would have said 'alannah', Mrs Batley would say 'pet'. She had a laugh as raucous as a parrot's screech, though her speaking voice had a pleasant lilt, and she had a good sense of humour, sharing many a laugh with the girls in her care, who soon began to look on Mrs Batley as a mother substitute, confiding both worries and small triumphs, and knowing that the older woman would do her best to advise them.

Debbie's factory had not been hit. The firm were short of workers, so when Debbie introduced Eanna to her boss he was only too happy to take her on. In fact, by early September, several of the girls who shared the house in Lavender Court were assembling wirelesses alongside Debbie. Getting to and from work was becoming easier, too. Many roads were still cordoned off, but because of the number of factories on Long Lane, sufficient clearing had been done to allow the buses to ply to and from the city centre.

Debbie missed her mother dreadfully but her loss had forced independence upon her, and she found there was even satisfaction in deciding for herself what she should do with her day off, or upon which garment to spend her precious clothing coupons.

She speedily realised, however, that her hasty flight from Mrs Roberts's home had been unfortunate in one respect, at least. Without the name of his airfield, she had been unable to fulfil her promise to write to Pete Solomon, and although she was certain he would have written to her as soon as he realised she couldn't get in touch with him, she had removed herself from the only address he had for her. She determined to return to Huskisson Street at a time when Uncle Max was certain to be at work, and ask whether they had received any post addressed to herself. She was sure that they would have done so; after all, he had seemed very anxious to know what was going to happen to the baby, at least.

Accordingly, she and Biddy went round to Huskisson Street one quiet afternoon and knocked on the door. An old woman answered, telling them that she was Mrs Roberts's mother, come on a visit, and was giving an eye to the premises while her daughter attended a meeting of the local WVS.

Debbie explained her errand and the old woman asked them into the kitchen and fished half a dozen envelopes out of the dresser drawer. She threw them down on the table, rather ungraciously, telling Debbie to go through them, 'because if I tells you there's nothing for you, you'll likely think I'm too old to know what's what,' she said nastily. Debbie muttered a disclaimer but went through the envelopes, none of which was addressed to her. Then she gave the old woman her most conciliating smile, saying as she did so: 'No, there's nothing here for me, and it's been three months . . . perhaps I'll try again in a few weeks' time.'

'If he ain't written in three months, then likely he's dead,' the old woman said with spiteful frankness. 'Well, that's that then; good afternoon, both.'

The girls left; there was nothing else they could do, though Debbie could not help tears forming at the corners of her eyes and slipping down her cheeks. Pete had helped her at a bad time, and he had known her mother. She could not help feeling that there must have been a letter and that, had she remained with Mrs Roberts, she would have been able to keep in touch with her rescuer.

As they made their way slowly back down the street, Biddy gave Debbie's arm a squeeze, then leaned over to chuck Baby Chloe under the chin. 'Never mind, Deb,' she said consolingly. 'I'm a great believer in fate, I am, an' I reckon that feller didn't save you and my baby for nothin'. You'll find each other one of these days, see if I ain't right.' And against all the odds, this cheered Debbie immeasurably. She smiled at Biddy and began to help her to push the perambulator, which was

320

quite heavy since they had done a good deal of shopping as they went along.

'I guess you're right and we will meet again, because I won't believe he's dead,' she said firmly. 'Hey-ho, Chloe, your mammy and me's bought apples so you'll be having apple and custard for your dinner.'

*   *   *

In the kitchen of the house on Huskisson Street, Mrs Roberts's mother pulled open the dresser drawer and fished out the three letters it still contained, opened the envelopes one by one, and began to read the contents. She had hoped for love letters so that she could despise the young girl with the baby even more than she did already, but they did not seem to be any such thing. In fact, she did not even read the last letter but simply pushed it into the stove with the others and smiled to herself as the flames devoured it. Me daughter ain't a bleedin' post office, she told herself grimly, sinking into the fireside chair. And when, presently, Mrs Roberts returned, the old woman regaled her with the story of her two visitors who had come for 'them letters what you keep in the end drawer of the dresser'.

Mrs Roberts gave a relieved smile. 'I'm that glad to be rid of the responsibility,' she said. 'I were rare bothered that I didn't have no forwarding address so I couldn't send 'em on. He were a nice young feller . . . yes, I'm glad she's got her letters at last.'

CHAPTER ELEVEN

MAY 1943

It was a hot day, presaging what was to come, Nancy thought, wiping perspiration off her forehead with the piece of clean rag which she had tucked into the belt of her large striped overall. The month of May was well advanced, the rainy season was over and for a few blessed days or weeks, before the dry really got going, the temperature, though never cool or particularly pleasant, was easier to bear. A good time for visiting other stations, inviting friends over, even bathing without too much worry, for Andy had constructed a lagoon not too far from the house which filled up in the wet and did not dry out until the drought really got into its stride.

Nancy was making beef patties in the kitchen because Andy should be back from his latest muster this evening and the following day she had invited the McGuires over for a picnic, a swim in the lovely new lagoon, and then dinner and a chat. Like themselves, the McGuires had grown-up children, two boys who were in the army and were she believed in Italy, though Becky and Liz McGuire were still at home. Nancy had an eye on Becky, the older of the two, for her son Jacko; she knew they corresponded and she and Evie McGuire had often discussed how nice it would be if the two should fall in love and eventually marry. Jacko was only a year older than Becky and the two had always been good pals. Nancy sighed and began to cut large circles out of the huge sheet of pastry she had just made. The trouble was, no one could live another's life for them, and lately Jacko's letters had included casual references to some other girl with whom he was exchanging what appeared to be a lively correspondence.

Nancy began to pile the cooked beef and onions on to the pastry circles. Then she dipped her brush into the pot of water which stood ready, swiftly damped the edges of each circle, doubled them over and pinched them closed. After that, she stabbed each patty twice to let the steam emerge as they cooked, slid them on to a baking tray and was putting them into the oven when Aggie came into the room, flourishing a bundle of letters and newspapers. 'Mail's come, missus,' the woman said cheerfully. 'And the *Sydney Herald*, as well as that English paper you gets from time to time.' She jerked her head at the remaining pastry. 'Want me to finish these here patties whilst you read your mail and that? I know I ain't no good with pastry, but you've done all the work so I don't see as how I *could* mess things up, no matter what.'

Nancy smiled but shook her head. Past bitter experience had taught her that Aggie could, indeed, ruin the beef patties simply by over or underfilling the pastry, or by handling it too much. 'Thanks, Aggie, but I've made enough patties to feed a fighting army, so the rest of the pastry can be rolled into a ball for making apple pies later. What you could do is peel all the apples in that big brown paper bag, and if you wouldn't mind keeping an eye on the oven, I'll nip across to the house and deal with the mail there. I take it Bullwhip is waiting.'

323

Aggie nodded and, picking up the paper bag, selected a sharp knife from the cutlery drawer and began to peel the first of the apples. 'I put him on the veranda and gave him a pint of beer,' she informed her mistress. 'How long before I take a look at the patties, missus?'

Nancy, heading for the doorway, having already scooped up the mail, said airily: 'The first lot should be done any time. Thanks, Aggie. And when you've taken the last batch of beef patties out, you'd best bring the apples on to the veranda; it'll be cooler out there. But do keep an eye on the patties. Remember, there's a war on and we mustn't waste food.'

Aggie tutted. 'No one don't need to be reminded of that there war,' she said reproachfully. 'Mind, we ain't affected like our poor fellers what are doin' the actual fighting. Mr Paul and Mr Jerome from the Four Cross station, they're in Burma with them bloody Japs treatin' 'em worse than cattle. An' then there's Mr Pete, flying planes from England, and everyone knows the English have next to nothing to fill their bellies. Did you send Mr Pete another parcel, missus?'

'I send one whenever I'm allowed,' Nancy said, pausing in the doorway and feeling great relief at leaving the fierce heat of the kitchen, 'only you can't just send them whenever you want, you know. Still, in Pete's last letter he said the food was dull but there was plenty of it. And he's not as badly off as my poor Jamie. He gets Red Cross parcels and of course I write and he writes back. Well, I gather there isn't a lot to do except write letters, once you're a prisoner of war.'

Nancy headed for the veranda, reflecting as she

324

did so how odd it was that one felt less concern for the son who was a prisoner of war than for the two others who were still actively fighting for their country. She supposed it was because Jamie had, so to speak, been taken off the board, whereas the other two were still very much in play. They were both in the air force but Jacko was in North Africa whilst Pete, of course, was in Britain. He wrote whenever he could but his letters were brief and she knew she only received about half of those he sent. However, she understood that as the war progressed and the allies probed deeper into Germany, his time for letter writing grew more limited.

'Mornin', missus!'

'Morning, Bullwhip,' Nancy said, smiling at the mailman. He had changed very little over the years though the hair which had once been brown was now streaked with grey and his stomach, never small, had reached gigantic proportions. She sank into the long cane chair opposite the mailman's. 'If you fancy a cheese sandwich, you can nip over to the kitchen and get Aggie to make one for you. She's watching the beef patties so she'll be there a while yet.'

Bullwhip grinned but patted his huge stomach reflectively. 'I had the best part of half a fruit cake at the Four Cross, to say nothin' of enough bacon and eggs to feed every mailman in Queensland,' he said expansively. 'They'd killed a pig.' He smacked his lips appreciatively. 'I reckon Four Cross bacon is just about the best. Still an' all, thanks for the offer.' He took a long pull at his beer. 'You got any mail to go?'

'Yes, I've several airmail letters,' Nancy said,

beginning to slit open the envelopes. 'If you don't mind waiting I'll just make sure there's nothing urgent in any of these which needs a reply. I've not sealed any of mine yet, just in case.'

Bullwhip intimated that he had no objection to waiting, would quite enjoy a bit of a break, in fact, so Nancy read all the letters, spreading the thin, crackly airmail paper on to her lap and taking her time. All three of the boys had written. Jamie thanked her for her latest letter and talked of a sporting event which was to take place the following week. He was in an old castle which had been converted to house prisoners of war and from what he said, though always in a veiled manner, the occupants were chiefly prisoners who had tried to escape from other camps.

She opened Jacko's letter next. He appeared to be having a grand time but she knew her sons too well to think that they would worry her by relating the unpleasant face of war.

She had saved Pete's letter till last because in his previous letter he had told her that he and his crew would soon have completed sufficient sorties to allow them a long break from active service, and she knew that he intended to revisit Liverpool in order to try to trace Jess's daughter.

Nancy had been devastated by the news of Jess's death and delighted that her son had helped to rescue Debbie. She was glad, too, that Pete had actually met Jess and had promised to keep an eye on Debbie, even though it very soon transpired that he had not been able to do so. When he had written to explain that he had lodged Debbie in a respectable household, had paid the landlady two weeks in advance and meant to continue to pay for

326

the girl until he was sure she could manage alone, Nancy had immediately driven to their bank and sent Pete a money order, reminding him that since the Walleroo would belong to the boys one day, they were perfectly entitled to money from the station whenever they needed it. But then Pete had written to say that, having received no reply from Debbie to his letters, he had spent a four-day leave returning to Liverpool. He had gone to her lodgings, where he had been informed by the landlady that Debbie had left after spending only one night in the room he had hired for her. 'She met a cousin who offered her a room,' she had explained. 'She didn't leave no forwarding address but, of course, I put all her mail aside for her, and after a few weeks she called round and fetched it.' She had looked anxiously at her visitor. 'I couldn't return the money you'd paid me 'cos I didn't have no address but I kept the room vacant for the whole two weeks, honest to God I did, though folk was queuin' up to move in.'

Pete had told her she had done right and had gone back to his station, expecting to receive a letter from Debbie telling him her new address. But there had been nothing. And though Pete tried to make light of the whole business, it was clear to both Andy and Nancy that he worried a good deal over what had happened to Debbie and intended to do his utmost to trace her when he had the opportunity to return to the city.

So Nancy opened Pete's letter and read it eagerly, but was disappointed. He had not yet visited Liverpool and talked airily about members of his crew, of a dance at which he had met a pretty WAAF called Linda and of a trip to take a look at

Sandringham, where the royal family spent a good deal of their time. Then Nancy glanced at the date at the top of the page and realised that this letter had been en route for a considerable while—was, in fact, old news. Sighing, she put the mail down on a cane table between herself and Bullwhip, and went to fetch the letters which she had written.

When Andy came home later in the morning, she handed him the letters to read, then poured him a cool beer, thinking how very little he had changed, despite the extra work and responsibility that the war had brought. Because he was so blond, any white hairs which he might have had did not show, and though he was deeply tanned his skin did not have the seamed, leathery look which made many cattle owners seem older than their years. Nancy smiled to herself at the thought that not all her good cooking had given Andy a pot belly like Bullwhip's, for he still had the whipcord leanness of a man who spent most of his time doing hard physical work, and when he looked at her and grinned, his teeth white against the tan, she felt her heart give a little lurch of pure pleasure. She loved him so much, respected and admired him, could think of no one with whom she would rather spend her time. Because of the nature of his work, she saw very much less of him than an English housewife would expect to see of her man, though of course the war had wrenched people apart even more conclusively than cattle droving. Sometimes, she thought of the little Devonshire village she had left, thought about the life she might have lived had she stayed at home and married one of the local farmers, but she soon found that Devon, and her life there, no longer had any reality. When she

328

discussed it with Anne, she found that her sister felt exactly the same. The Devon vicarage was part of a different world which no longer had any meaning for either of them; Australia, and their lives with the Sullivan brothers, occupied them completely.

Nancy was still thinking about Jess's daughter when Andy finished Pete's letter—he had saved it till last as she had—and placed it on top of the others on the table. Then he turned to her, his blue eyes kind. 'It's an old letter, as you say,' he commented. 'But things are looking up, darling. I glanced at the papers just now and there was a report saying that the North African campaign is over—that's official—and the English government have lifted the ban on church bells, which must mean that the fear of invasion has retreated. But you are worrying about your Jess's daughter, aren't you? Well, don't. If she needs help, she'll find Pete somehow, and besides, there's that cousin of hers who's taken her in. Blood's thicker than water; a relative won't let her down.'

'Oh, I know, but anything could have happened to her—it's been two years almost to the day since Pete saw her last—and if only we had an address, I could send her a parcel. No matter how cheerfully Pete writes, it's different for the armed forces. Ordinary civilians are having a lean time of it. Can you imagine, Andy, trying to get by on two ounces of butter each a week? And four of bacon? You eat three times that amount every morning, and several eggs. I know they have dried eggs—horrid stuff—but I gather from what I've read in the newspapers that real eggs are almost unobtainable unless you keep hens of your own and I doubt they

329

can do that in the middle of Liverpool.'

Andy came round the table, put both arms round her and kissed her resoundingly, and as it always did, Nancy's heart gave a joyous bound; she loved him so much!

'I know what you're saying,' Andy said, giving her an extra squeeze. 'But believe me, honey, the government won't let its people starve, and they're a resourceful lot, the British. You've read all about the special recipes the government are putting out, and how housewives are learning to use any food that comes to hand. Rabbit isn't rationed and they put it into pies, fricassee it, curry it . . . for all I know, they might make rabbit trifle out of it.' He sighed, pulling a comical face. 'Wish they'd come over here and attack our rabbit population the way they're attacking their own! And remember, Debbie isn't a child any longer. She must be, oh, seventeen or eighteen, I suppose. Why, she's probably in the forces herself by now and eating three good meals each day, at the government's expense.'

Nancy sighed and leaned against his broad and comfortable chest. 'You're right, of course, and even if you weren't there'd be no point in my worrying,' she admitted. 'Because Pete will find her one of these days, I just know he will, and when he does, he'll see she's all right. I know my boy. He won't let anyone down.'

'There you are, then,' Andy said, releasing her and taking an apple from the bowl on the table. 'And if you want to know what I think, if she's anything like your friend Jess, she'll be pretty capable. And now how about you trotting over to the kitchen and frying me some of that bacon you were talking about earlier?'

* * *

'Hey, Bid, if you've finished with the *Echo*, pass it to me, will you?' Debbie said. It was a warm September evening and she and Biddy were sitting on the doorstep whilst she darned stockings; a task she hated but which had to be done since she needed them for work the next day, having run out of leg paint. 'Remember who bought the paper this evening, and I've scarcely glanced at it, since it was my turn to cook the supper.'

Biddy, knitting industriously away at what one day would be a jumper for her small daughter, picked up the newspaper which lay beside her and glanced at the headlines. 'Looks like things are goin' a bit better,' she observed. 'The Eyeties have surrendered.' She handed the paper to Debbie as she spoke, then held up her knitting. 'Oh, I'm never goin' to have enough wool to finish this . . . unless I do the cuffs and the collar in blue or white instead of pink. Curse it, and I've followed the pattern like a bleedin' slave, so I have.'

'The trouble is, babies turn into toddlers and toddlers gobble their groats and guzzle their rusks and get bigger and bigger,' Debbie pointed out. 'Where is she, by the way?'

'Who, Chloe? In bed, of course; where else should she be at past seven o'clock?' Biddy said a trifle defensively, getting up and going into the kitchen. She knew that Debbie disapproved of the somewhat erratic hours the child kept, but Biddy, though she adored her little girl, did not intend to give up her social life entirely. She had left her job

331

at the cinema the previous year and now worked in the munitions factory, earning a great deal more money than she had ever done as an usherette. However, it meant working shifts, so she and Debbie tried to arrange it so that one of them was always free to babysit. Biddy, with her lilting Irish accent, quick smile and neat figure, was popular with young men and enjoyed their company, and saw no reason why she should not have a social life just because of the child. So Debbie had discovered, with some dismay, that her friend was wrapping the baby in a shawl and taking her off to the cinema, or even to a dance hall. This had been fairly acceptable when Chloe was small, but now that she was almost three Debbie knew it was a bad idea, and had persuaded Biddy that a reliable babysitter might be paid a small sum to mind the child whilst Biddy went off to a dance or the cinema.

Then had come the incident when Biddy, unable to find a responsible adult to look after her daughter, had engaged a couple of twelve-year-olds to babysit. Debbie had returned from her late shift to find Chloe, red-faced and screaming, tied to one of the kitchen chairs whilst the two 'babysitters' clumped round the house in the residents' best dresses and high-heeled shoes, completely ignoring the little girl. When Debbie began to tell them off, however, it soon became apparent that it was not only clothing and shoes that had been 'borrowed'. Both girls had helped themselves to the bottled beer they had discovered in Biddy's wardrobe, and were exceedingly drunk.

Biddy had been as horrified as Debbie, but it had not prevented her from leaving Chloe again with some very unsuitable sitters, and it was this, more than anything, that had led to a coolness between the two girls. Debbie adored the child and could not bear to see her being treated so casually, and Biddy, who to be fair also adored Chloe, could not see that such treatment was not perfectly normal and acceptable. Debbie supposed that the difference in their outlooks was due to their very different upbringings, but, even so, found it hard to accept.

Now, however, sensing the challenge in Biddy's tone, she followed her into the kitchen and said placatingly: 'Yes, of course. Only didn't you say Paddy was going to take you dancing tonight? I did think I'd like to see the film at the Forum since I'm on earlies this week, but if he is I can always put off my cinema trip until some time when you can stay with Chloe.'

'Oh, that would be just grand, so it would,' Biddy said eagerly. 'I was going to ask Mrs Rushton if she'd give an eye to Chloe until one or other of the girls gets back, but if you could go to the cinema another night, it 'ud be even better.'

Debbie gave an inward sigh; she had looked forward to having a night out and would have to tell her friend Millie that the cinema trip was off, for now at any rate. Fortunately, Millie meant to call for her so she would not have to leave the house in order to change her plans, but she guessed the other girl would not be best pleased. After all, this was by no means the first time that Debbie had had to cancel a date, and though Millie understood the situation she was apt to remark, waspishly, that it was high time Biddy stopped being so flighty and settled down to being

333

a mam.

'Heavens, is that the time?' Biddy said suddenly, glancing at the clock on the mantel. Dusty, who had been asleep, curled up on the cool linoleum in the hallway, leapt to his feet and barked, then realised that it was only Biddy and sank down again, looking embarrassed. 'I'd best go and start putting on me glad rags, 'cos Paddy said he'd be here at eight o'clock and he hates being kept waiting.' She smiled beguilingly at Debbie. 'Be a darlin' an' put the kettle on. Paddy won't mind waiting five minutes if you give him a cup of tea and one of them nice scones Mrs Batley made earlier. Oh, how I bless that woman! If it weren't for her I dunno how we'd go on.'

'Very true; she's worth her weight in gold . . .' Debbie began, but found herself speaking to the dog; Biddy had disappeared, though the sound of her feet clattering up the stairs could still be heard. The wretched girl made no concession to the fact that Chloe was asleep up there, but that was Biddy all over. If she woke the child she'd be full of remorse, would pluck her from her blankets and give her a loving cuddle, and then go happily off with Paddy, leaving someone else to persuade Chloe that it was not yet morning and that she should go back to sleep.

Sighing, Debbie lit the gas under the kettle and got out the tin in which Mrs Batley's scones reposed. The older woman kept the house in excellent order, did all the marketing and cooking, and was always on hand from six in the morning until around five o'clock in the evening. After that, however, she went off to her evening job, which meant that she could never babysit. Debbie thought this was quite a good thing because the older woman worked quite hard enough without adding childminding to her other duties. And fond though she was of Biddy, Debbie knew that the Irish girl would take advantage of anyone soft enough to offer help.

By the time Biddy clattered downstairs, clad in someone else's best dance dress and Debbie's black high-heeled pumps, Paddy, a young seaman home for a week's leave, had drunk two cups of tea and eaten as much of a scone as Dusty allowed him, for the dog sat close, eyes bright with hope and mouth watering, until Paddy had given him a share. Having thanked Debbie politely for her hospitality he whisked Biddy out just as Millie arrived at the door. Thankfully, Millie was philosophical about the change of plan, but refused Debbie's invitation to spend the evening at No. 4 and to go to the cinema the following night instead. 'Me cousin Ted is home on a forty-eight, so seeing as Biddy's upset all our plans once again, I'll go round to Aunt Ethel's and have a chat wi' Ted,' she said, rather reproachfully. 'Honest to God, Debbie, it's no wonder to me that you don't have a feller if you'd treat him the way you treat your other friends. Why can't you tell Biddy to look after her own brat? Or she could pay some really respectable woman to come in . . .'

'Oh, I don't mind really,' Debbie said vaguely. 'I'm ever so fond of the kid, that's my trouble. Sometimes I think I'd make a better mother to her than poor Biddy does and it worries me to see her left with strangers. The trouble with Biddy is she leaves everything to the last moment. She always hopes someone in the house will be planning a quiet evening at home so they can give an eye to Chloe, and when it turns out everyone's either working or has a date she rushes round the neighbours, only to find they've got their own plans. So then . . . well, she'll get some kid or other to come in and that's not fair on Chloe.'

'The reason she leaves it till the last minute is because she don't like payin' for a decent baby sitter,' Millie said bluntly. 'I don't understand her; she's earning good money at the munitions factory, so she could afford proper childcare. I mean, Mrs Batley looks after Chloe all day, doesn't she?'

'Yes, but Biddy sends money home, you know— to her parents in Ireland, I mean—and she's saving up so that when the war's over and she goes back to Dublin she'll be able to afford a place of her own,' Debbie said glibly. She did not know if this was true, in fact she doubted it, but it was what Biddy had said one day when questioned by Mrs Batley and it was a much more acceptable explanation for Biddy's behaviour than the fact that she spent every penny she earned on buying clothing coupons on the black market, or going to the flicks.

Millie sniffed. 'We all give our mams as much as we can,' she said grudgingly, and then apparently remembered Debbie's circumstances and flushed. 'Sorry, queen, I weren't thinking. See you tomorrow mornin' in work, then.'

'But what about the film?' Debbie asked, dismayed. 'Won't you come with me tomorrow evening?'

'Can't,' Millie said briefly. 'I *told* you. I'm going to me nephew's birthday party.'

'Yes, of course. I remember. Well, never mind.

I'll go by myself; it'll serve me right for ruining your cinema trip,' Debbie said remorsefully. 'T.T.F.N. then, queen.'

Once Millie had gone, Debbie settled down to a lonely evening. She had finished darning her stockings so she picked up the knitting which Biddy had cast down, intending to add a few rows, but then changed her mind. She did quite enough for Biddy as it was, and though she was always glad to lend Biddy clothing she had been annoyed that Biddy had taken her brand new shoes without so much as a by your leave, and she knew that Sandra, the girl whose dance dress had been borrowed, would never have consented to lending it had she been in the house at the time. Biddy's riding for a fall, she told herself, pouring a cup of tea. She's very sweet and charming when she wants something from you but she's not yet learned to give as well as to take, and she jolly well should. She's three years older than me but you'd never think it because she's so irresponsible. Oh, dear, I know I shouldn't criticise her because most of the time I really love her; she's kind, easy-going and good fun. I suppose I didn't like her taking my shoes without asking, which is rather petty but I can't help it. And I *did* want to see *Now Voyager*. Still, perhaps one of the other girls might be free to come with me tomorrow night . . .

At this stage in her musings, somebody knocked on the front door. Dusty shot into the hallway, barking madly, and Debbie, who had just settled herself in the most comfortable of the fireside chairs, groaned and got to her feet. If it was someone trying to persuade her to hand over savings stamps in the 'Wings for Victory' campaign, then she would tell them to find someone who hadn't already contributed heavily. And if it was someone else trying to collect saucepans to make a Spitfire she would remind them, caustically, that all her personal saucepans had been lost in the Blitz and they had better go elsewhere. Armed with this intention, she snatched the front door open, saying belligerently: 'Yes? What is it?'

The young man standing on the doorstep looked startled, to say the least. He began to speak, was halfway through a hesitant sentence, when Debbie gave a squeak of joy and almost jumped into his arms. Fortunately, as she did so, a broad smile swept across his face and he picked her up and whirled her round, then gave her a smacking kiss on the cheek. 'Debbie! My, but haven't you grown! I were about to ask if you remembered me, but it's pretty plain you do. How *are* you, queen? Oh, but it's grand to see you again.'

'Oh, Dicky, it's grand to see you as well,' Debbie said breathlessly. 'But where have you been? And how did you find out where I lived? Oh, listen to me rabbitin' on. I'm forgetting me manners . . . do come in. I've just brewed a pot of tea and there's some scones . . . Oh, Dicky, it's just so good to see you after all this time!'

Dusty was dancing round him as though they had known one another all their lives and Debbie wondered, fleetingly, whether the dog could possibly remember that gift of a sticky bun, all that time ago. But Dusty, she reminded herself, was a very remarkable animal . . . and very fond of sticky buns. It was quite possible that the incident had remained in his doggy mind.

However, she was glad the dog had not barked and woken Chloe. She led Dicky into the kitchen, poured him a cup of tea, and was amused when he produced a small phial of saccharin tablets, waving away her offer of sugar. 'No one takes sugar no more, but I've a sweet tooth so I carry me saccharin tablets everywhere,' he told her. 'As for finding you . . . well, I asked around, and when I mentioned the baby, they said to try number four. So I did, and here I am.'

'Oh yes, of course; you must have guessed that I'd found the baby's mother because you dropped me off here, as I recall,' Debbie said, remembering. 'But where have you been all this time, Dicky, and why are you here now?'

He put his arm round her shoulders and gave her a brotherly hug. 'I were on the east coast but they've moved me up here, so I thought I'd see if I could find you, and here I am. I went round to Daisy Street but the Soameses weren't there.'

'Oh, they're in North Wales and mean to stay there after the war. I keep in touch with Mrs Soames by letter, though she's not too good at answering back.' As she talked Debbie had been pouring a second cup of tea and now she pushed Dicky into one of the fireside chairs, spread margarine rather thinly on a scone and handed it to him. Then she sank into her own chair and let her eyes rove approvingly over him. 'The uniform suits you—but why haven't you called before?'

'I have popped round a couple of times, only you were' never in. I didn't leave me name because I wasn't certain exactly who did live here. The woman who answered my knock the first time said there were six young ladies all living under this one roof and for the life of me I couldn't bring your name to mind—I thought it were Dolly—but the minute I set eyes on you just now, I remembered the lot. Debbie Ryan, I thought, that's the girl; little Debbie Ryan! And I take it from what you've just said that you *did* find the baby's mother and that she lives here with you.'

'That's right; her name's Biddy Callaghan and the baby's called Chloe. Biddy's probably my best pal; she's Irish and very pretty. To tell you the truth, she reminds me of Gwen in lots of ways . . . particularly to look at. She's small and dark and very lively and vivacious. She works in the munitions factory.'

Dicky's eyebrows shot up. 'You mean she's working right now? Oh, I suppose she must be, since she's obviously not here.'

'No, actually she's gone dancing at the Grafton with a chap called Paddy,' Debbie told him. 'Do you remember Dusty, Dicky? I'm pretty sure he remembers you because he barks like mad at strangers and he's not uttered a peep. We did think, Biddy and myself, of sending him into the country with the Soameses, but we couldn't bring ourselves to part with him.'

Dicky nodded. 'Yes, I can understand that, though the country's the best place for dogs, and for kids,' he said. 'Why didn't you and this Biddy join the Land Army? I'm sure they'd welcome the baby, only I suppose she's not a baby any more, not really.'

'No, she isn't really a baby, she's going on for three and a gorgeous little girl. As for joining up, we tried, but the authorities wouldn't let us because we're doing essential war work,' Debbie

340

explained. 'We're experienced as well, you see, and perhaps we wouldn't make very good land girls. Anyway, it seems we're stuck here for the duration so we must make the best of it. And now tell me a bit about yourself, Dicky. Where are you stationed? Why did they send you home?'

Dicky laughed. 'We're protecting an airfield not far from Wrexham in North Wales . . . pretty convenient for Liverpool, really,' he said. 'And it's grand to be so near home.' He looked at her hopefully. 'Deb, can you give me your working hours? What about tomorrow, for instance? There's a flick on at the Forum I wouldn't mind seeing, and if you're free tomorrow evening . . .'

'I am; I'm on earlies tomorrow,' Debbie said eagerly. 'And I intended to go to the Forum tonight, only Biddy was going dancing and I didn't want to leave Chloe to the tender mercies of—of someone she didn't know very well, so it would be a real treat to go with you tomorrow instead. I'd pay for myself,' she added quickly. 'I earn quite a lot of money now, what with shift work and overtime and so on.'

Dicky laughed. 'I'll pay for us both. When I ask a girl out on a date I don't expect her to fork out,' he said, getting to his feet. 'Tell you what, though, can we meet outside the Forum to save me coming all the way to Lavender Court . . . and if we could go to the early performance then I can be sure of catching the train back to my station in good time.'

Debbie agreed to this and waved him off at the door feeling truly glad that she had given up her evening with Millie. She might be seventeen—well, she was seventeen—but this would be her very first date and she was excited and thrilled that it was

Dicky who had asked her out. Oh, she had been asked out before, once or twice, but she had never felt tempted to accept such invitations, because she had never forgotten Pete, who had saved her life and that of Dusty and Chloe, and she was still convinced would find her one day. She had liked him very much and was sure he had liked her, young though she had been at the time. However, she knew that he could have been posted anywhere, to any theatre of war, and now, quite suddenly, she decided it was time to stop mooning over Pete Solomon, whom she might never see again, and to start living the sort of life which Biddy and the other girls took for granted. Debbie was rather shy with strangers and often felt uneasy when young men asked her to dance. With Dicky, though, it would be different, because he was Gwen's cousin's friend—would have been her boyfriend—and he and Debbie had a host of acquaintances in common. Why, they had talked for an hour this evening without Debbie's once feeling awkward or self-conscious. Yes, a date with Dicky would be fun and it would help her to erase, at last, the memory of a tall, fair-haired young man with a tanned face and steady eyes, who had obviously never given her a second thought.

When the other girls returned, Biddy with a love bite on her neck, Debbie made everyone cocoa and they all thoroughly chewed over the evening's events before making their way to bed. Debbie slid between the sheets and lay there thinking pleasant thoughts, and presently Dusty sneaked on to her bed and curled up against her back, as he always did. I hope I dream about Dicky, Debbie thought, as she settled down to sleep, but dreams are contrary things and do not come for the asking. Instead, she dreamed of a tall, fair-haired figure, with a teasing, affectionate smile, who came calling in Lavender Court but always turned away and left before she could run down the stairs and greet him.

Next morning, when she awoke, there were tears on her cheeks.

*   *   *

By the time winter arrived, Debbie and Dicky were thoroughly at ease in one another's company. They had gone several times to the cinema together, had enjoyed picnics in the park, and had also gone dancing at the Daulby Hall, though for some reason which she could not fathom Dicky had refused, at first, to take her to the Grafton.

'But everyone goes there,' Debbie had wailed when she had suggested they might join up with the other girls. 'They're a nice crowd, Dicky, honest to God they are. And the fellers are nice, too . . . well, they must be or Biddy and Sandy and Ruth wouldn't go out with them.'

'Aye, that's just my point,' Dicky had said at once. 'Everyone does go there, all the fellers from my unit, all the seamen from the ships in the docks, every perishin' girl who's got two pennies to rub together, including both my sisters and a heap o' cousins. I want to be with *you*, Debbie. I want to dance with you, not have to do the polite with half of Liverpool.'

Debbie had been forced to see his point and had stopped trying to persuade him to go out in a group, but she had insisted that he come back to

Lavender Court so that she could introduce him to Biddy, to Mrs Batley, and to anyone else who was home on a Sunday evening. She thought that everyone had thoroughly approved of him, though Biddy had been a bit odd, now she came to think of it. Debbie, Dicky and Chloe had spent a pleasant afternoon in Prince's Park and had returned to No. 4 with Chloe in her pushchair longing to tell everyone how she had fed the ducks, and Dusty bouncing at their heels and greeting everyone with flattened ears, a furiously waving tail, and white teeth displayed in an ingratiating grin. 'Hello, girls! This is Dicky Barnes,' Debbie had said to the assembled company. 'We've just had a grand afternoon . . .' She had looked around the room. 'But where's Biddy?'

At this point, Biddy had entered the kitchen, singing as she did so, but had stopped short when she saw them. 'Hello, stranger!' she had said, staring at Dicky with no very friendly expression on her small, lively face. 'Just what . . .'

'Oh, Biddy, this is my friend Dicky Barnes, the one I told you about,' Debbie had said earnestly. 'We've just got back from Prince's Park and we've had a splendid tea, haven't we, Dicky? Speaking for myself, I shan't be wanting to eat again for a week, and I bet Chloe feels the same.' She had turned to her companion. 'Dicky, this is Biddy Callaghan, young Chloe's mam.'

'How do you do, Mrs Callaghan,' Dicky had said at once. 'Nice to meet you. I don't mind admitting I've fallen in love with your daughter. She's a real charmer; she'll break some hearts one o' these days.'

Biddy had given a rather ungracious sniff and

344

bent over the pushchair to unfasten the straps and lift the child out. 'How do ye do, Mr Barnes; and I'm Miss Callaghan, not Mrs,' Biddy had said, rather crossly. She had turned to Debbie. 'If you're right, and she's got a full belly, then she'd best go straight to bed. I'm goin' out later . . . all right for you to babysit, or does Mr Barnes intend to tek you off out again?'

Debbie, puzzled by her friend's apparent animosity, had been about to reply that Biddy could jolly well look elsewhere for a sitter when Chloe set up a wail. 'Me belly ain't full and I want me supper,' she had said. 'Where's Auntie Batley? She says good lickle girls have warm bread and milk to gerr'em to sleep, and I want some now.'

This demand had broken the ice. Biddy had laughed and apologised for her daughter, and Mrs Batley, who did not work on Sunday evenings, had produced a bowl of bread and milk, and told the girls, briskly, to get the table laid for a supper of farmhouse scramble, followed by blackberry pie and custard. She had invited Dicky to join them but he had courteously refused, assuring Mrs Batley that the meal both smelt and looked delicious, but that he had to get back to his airfield before the witching hour of ten o'clock, and would be hard pressed to do so unless he left them at once.

But now, as she popped the last carrot into the large pan of cold water, Debbie reflected that the situation was far easier. Dicky often came to the house—sometimes she returned from a shift to find him sitting cross-legged on the hearthrug, playing with Chloe and the dog, or helping Mrs Batley to put away her shopping, or simply leaning

345

against the sink, chatting to Biddy whilst she prepared vegetables or washed the crocks. The previous week he had actually gone along to the Grafton ballroom and had danced twice with Biddy and once with Sandra, though the rest of the time he had spent with Debbie.

By now, he was accepted by everyone at No. 4 as Debbie's boyfriend, and she was beginning to worry a little as his attentions grew warmer. It was nice having someone who would take you to the cinema or the theatre, out for picnics, or even for long dreamy walks beside the river, but she had no desire to end up in Biddy's situation, and always called a halt to Dicky's love-making far sooner than he wished. She supposed she would have to tell him that she was saving herself for marriage, but this sounded both priggish and forward, particularly as she had no wish, as yet, to marry anyone.

Debbie lugged the heavy pan across the kitchen and stood it on the stove. Rationing was bad enough, but shortages were worse for there were a number of unrationed goods which were simply unobtainable, and even Mrs Batley, with her genius for making a meal out of nothing, was finding it difficult to feed her brood and herself, to say nothing of Dusty. Tonight, however, Mrs Batley had cooked one of her specialities. She had managed to get some fish and had made a glorious fish pie, so all Debbie had to do was pop it in the oven at around six o'clock and pull the vegetables over the flame. Humming to herself, Debbie made a pot of tea, poured a cup, and then remembered that it was Chloe's day with the childminder who lived a couple of hundred yards along the road from Lavender Court. She knew that Biddy was on a late, so she had best run along there herself and try to get back before the vegetables boiled over. She grabbed her coat and draped it round her shoulders, then hurried along the passage to the door, crossed the court, and ran hard until she reached the childminder's house on Horatio Street. She would have knocked on the door, but as she approached it shot open and the childminder stood framed in the doorway, looking harassed. 'I'm glad you've come, Miss Ryan,' she said agitatedly. 'Miss Callaghan promised she'd fetch the littl'un early when I told her me cousin's eldest is going to give me a home perm, but she's not come near nor by.'

'She's on a late,' Debbie said, rather puzzled. She picked Chloe up and sat her on her hip. 'Still, I'm here now. Thanks very much for taking care of her.'

Once again, she set off at a brisk trot, the child bumping on her hip, and was about to turn into Lavender Court when Chloe squeaked: 'Mammy! There's my mammy, Deb, and she's wit' me friend Dicky.'

Startled, Debbie stared in the direction of the child's pointing finger, then laughed and shook her head. 'No, darling, that's not your mammy and it's not Dicky either. It's a lady wearing a coat and headscarf just like your mammy's. Wait till they turn the corner, and then you'll see.'

The child stared, then sagged against Debbie's shoulder. 'No, it ain't my mammy,' she agreed mournfully, then brightened. 'But I doesn't care, Debbie, 'cos I love you best of anyone in the whole world . . . well, next to Dusty, that is.'

Debbie was touched by this remark but assured her small friend, as they turned into Lavender Court, that she could not possibly mean what she had said. 'Children love their mammies best, then their aunties, and then their friends,' she told her. 'And I'm very sure your mammy loves you best.'

'No she don't,' the small realist said obstinately. 'She loves Uncle Freddy, Uncle Padraig and Uncle Roddy best. She'd far rather be wit' one of them than wit' me.'

Debbie was horrified. She had not realised that Chloe watched her mother's antics so closely, for she had to admit that Biddy did indeed play the field. However, it would not do to let the child suspect that she had hit the nail on the head, so she laughed, kissed Chloe's round, pink cheek, and told her that she was much mistaken. 'Mammy loves you best of all, but she does like to go dancing and to see a flick occasionally,' she said. 'You can't take her to the cinema, can you, or to a dance? So the fellers you mention are like workmates, really; pals to go about with when you're tucked up in bed.'

Chloe seemed about to argue, but at this point they entered the kitchen and Debbie had to put her down and rush over to lower the gas, for the vegetables were beginning to boil briskly. Behind her, Chloe pattered over to the pantry and stood on tiptoe to examine the food on the lower shelf. 'Can I have a butty, Auntie Deb?' she asked hopefully. 'I can see a big bowl of dripping; I loves bread and drippin', so I does.'

And Debbie, spreading dripping on a thick slice of bread and handing it to her small companion, could only be thankful that the subject of 'uncles'

348

seemed to have been forgotten.

CHAPTER TWELVE

MAY 1945

Debbie and Millie stood side by side at their bench, doing the work which they had done almost every day now for five long years. Debbie reflected that she truly believed she could assemble a wireless set in her sleep and thought that Millie could probably do the same. But now, suddenly, it no longer seemed important, because the war was officially over and tomorrow was VE Day—Victory in Europe—though the troops in the Far East still fought on, for it was only the Germans who had surrendered, and not the Japanese.

'What'll you do tomorrow, Deb?' Millie said presently, pausing for a moment in the constant repetitive work. 'There's to be a street party down our way but it's mainly for the kids. I reckon me and Mam will go up to St George's Plateau 'cos there'll be fireworks there and all sorts; want to come along?'

'We're having a street party . . . or rather a Lavender Court party, with everyone providing as much food as they can spare,' Debbie told her. 'The school kids have made masses of paper hats and one of the neighbours got a roll of newsprint to cover the tables with. Me and some of the other girls have made crackers with bits of stuff inside, only we couldn't get anything to make them pop when they're pulled, which was a bit disappointing.

Still, I reckon the kids aren't going to complain. Most of us have hoarded tins of fruit, and some have had parcels from folk in the States with tinned ham, tinned salmon and that, so there'll be quite a spread.'

'Yes, it's the same for us,' Millie said. 'I wonder when rationing will actually stop, though? I was talkin' to one o' me neighbours yesterday and she said she didn't see how it could stop, not all of a sudden like, because there just ain't the food to hand round, is there? And I reckon it'll be a while before the merchant fleet can stand down as fighting ships and turn themselves back into food carriers.'

Debbie pulled a face. 'Considering they've just cut the bacon ration and we only get one measly ounce of lard a week, I don't imagine things will get better for a while,' she observed. 'It's a good thing summer's starting because the troops will be coming home soon and they'll have to be fed. Dicky says they get plenty to eat in the forces, though it isn't very exciting food. Apparently the canteens go in for lots of potatoes and sawdust sausages, and suet puddings and stuff like that. So I imagine the fellers will be pretty dismayed when they see the sort of rations the rest of us get.'

'And when they get home we'll lose our jobs,' Millie said gloomily. 'Come to that, I s'pose a good few of the factories will close down altogether. No one's going to want uniforms now the war's over, and since the wireless sets we make go into aeroplanes, they aren't going to need them either. I know the government is promising to build new houses, or repair bomb-damaged ones, but that'll take ages, so where'll all these fellers live, eh? Oh,

I know lots of women have crammed in with their mums or grandmas, and farmed their kids out, but now we're at peace folks are goin' to expect that things will go back to normal. Men like to be the boss in their own homes and I've not met one yet who got on with his mother-in-law well enough to want to live under the same roof.'

The woman working on the other side of Debbie shook an admonitory finger at the two girls. 'Don't be so bleedin' miserable,' she said bracingly. 'We've won the bleedin' war, haven't we? Then everything's bound to be all right. Old Winnie promised us blood, toil, tears and sweat, and God knows, we've had them in plenty. But now we've won the good time will start, 'cos if it don't . . .'

'Good old Allie,' Debbie said, beaming at the other woman. 'You're right, of course, we must all look on the bright side. It'll be grand to have the men back, even if they do want to take our jobs!'

*　　　*　　　*

'If you aren't going to wear your pink dress, then I wouldn't mind a borrow of it. I'm that fed up wit' my own blue one that I could scream. Well? Are you wearin' it or aren't you?'

Debbie raised her eyebrows in mild surprise. Biddy sounded truculent, not at all like her usual, happy-go-lucky self, and why on earth should she want to borrow her pink dress? It was a fairly new garment and she said as much, adding: 'And anyway, I mean to wear it myself. For once the weather is really good and Millie bought a length of pink ribbon the other day and gave me half, so I can tie back my hair with that. I'll look quite presentable for a change; I just hope Dicky is impressed.'

Biddy shot her a quick glance out of the corners of her eyes. 'Are you serious about Dicky?' she asked curiously. 'If he asked you, would you marry him? Only sometimes you don't seem all that keen.'

Debbie had managed to acquire a small lipstick which she was guarding jealously from the other residents of No. 4. Now she got it out of her cracked and elderly handbag and began to apply it gingerly to her lips, gazing at herself earnestly in the small mirror as she did so. She thought the lipstick improved her and she rather admired the shine on her long chestnut hair, though she envied Biddy her mop of dark curls.

'Well? Didn't you hear what I said?'

'Yes, I heard,' Debbie said mildly. 'Dicky's very nice but he's the only boy I've ever been out with and because I only see him when he's on leave I don't know him awfully well. I don't think he'll ask me—to marry him, I mean—but if he did I reckon I'd say it were a bit soon and I'd like time to make up my mind.'

As Debbie turned away from the mirror, Biddy took her place. Both girls were wearing old clothes since there was a deal of preparation to do before the party in the Court could start. Biddy had on a dress which had once been cream but after countless washings had degenerated to a sort of dirty grey. The hem dipped and the bodice was far too tight, but with Biddy clothes seemed scarcely to matter. Everyone's attention always focused on her bright, vivacious little face, and Debbie thought, enviously, that her friend could go to a party in rags and still be the belle of the ball. Putting away her lipstick, she went over to the window and peered out, then turned back with a chuckle. 'Chloe's out there playing hopscotch with two or three of her friends. I can see her wagging her finger, laying down the law, even though she must be the youngest.'

This won a grin from Biddy. 'Aye, she's bossy, just like I were meself at her age,' she said, turning towards the bedroom door. 'Better go down and start making sandwiches else we shan't have the tea prepared by four o'clock.'

As the two girls hurried down the stairs and crossed the hall, Debbie asked: 'Is that young feller you're so keen on coming to the street party, or can't he get away? Padraig, isn't it?'

'Oh, him! I dunno what he's doin' but I dare say he'll turn up some time,' Biddy said airily as they entered the kitchen. 'And I'm not particularly keen on him, though he is on me, poor sap.' She raised her voice, addressing Mrs Batley, who was masterminding the kitchen activities. 'What'll we do, Mrs B? I'm a dab hand at making sandwiches, or shellin' hard boiled eggs, or chopping cress. So what'll it be?'

*   *   *

By half past three the trestle tables borrowed from the school were laid with the long rolls of newsprint, which looked very like a nice tablecloth, and had the plates of food set out on them. A couple of boys had been provided with leafy branches and told to wave them across the food to discourage flies, but not until the net curtains with

353

which Mrs Batley had covered everything edible were removed. By now, Biddy and Debbie were dressed in their best, and Chloe looked positively angelic in a white cotton dress covered in pink roses. She was terribly excited, hopping from one foot to the other and declaring over and over that she wanted to sit next to Freddy Miller, and to have the red cracker for her very own. Mrs Batley, passing with a huge platter of sausage rolls, overheard this pronouncement and dug her elbow into Debbie's ribs. 'She's going to be just like her mam: a real devil for the lads,' she hissed. 'Any feller who takes those two on will have his work cut out, I'm tellin' you.'

Debbie smiled. Sometimes she wondered if Biddy would take her daughter to Ireland one day to visit her grandparents and all those uncles and aunts to whom Biddy occasionally referred, but she thought it unlikely. Biddy never mentioned doing such a thing, and when Debbie had said it was unfair to deprive grandparents of their grandchild's company she had stared at her for a moment looking honestly puzzled before replying airily: 'Me parents have a grosh o' grandchilder and don't even know that Chloe exists. In fact, since I've never writ home once, they probably think I'm dead 'n' all. And a fat lot they'd care,' she had ended.

Debbie had been shocked, but on thinking it over had decided that Biddy had probably not spoken the truth. After all, only a couple of years before, her friend had claimed to be sending her parents money. And I'm sure she did send them something, Debbie told herself, returning to the kitchen to carry out one of the great enamel jugs of homemade lemonade. It was not, of course, made with real lemons—citrus fruit was just a name to most folk—and contained no sugar, but was made up of a virulent yellow substance known as lemon powder and a good few crushed saccharin tablets. Ah well, Biddy does like to dramatise herself, and Mrs Batley's right: darling Chloe gets more like her mam every day.

By the time four o'clock arrived, the children were taking their places round the table, whilst the adults milled around making sure that everyone got their fair share. Dusty, who adored Chloe, sat very close to the child, and she fed him scraps whenever she thought no one was looking. One of the men had a mouth organ and another an old ukulele, and when it was suggested that the children might like to contribute to the entertainment Chloe stood up at once and, accompanied by the mouth organ, sang an old Irish ballad which Biddy had taught her. After that, several other children recited poems or sang songs, and this kept them happily occupied whilst the adults cleared away the empty plates, disposed of the spotted and stained newsprint, and folded away the trestle tables so that they might organise some games. Dicky turned up with a couple of pals from his airfield just as the games were starting and the three of them were a great help, organising races and providing threepenny bits for the winners.

When at last the children's party was over, Mrs Batley agreed to babysit and everyone surged out of the court in a happy, laughing crowd, making their way on to Scotland Road. Chloe had objected strongly to being left behind, only consenting to go up to bed when Debbie said that

355

she might take Dusty with her. 'You can have a little party, just the two of you,' she said, slipping a couple of sausage rolls and some iced fairy cakes into a bag and handing it to the little girl. 'And when you've finished the food you can both sleep in my bed, for a special treat. I'll share with your mammy, love.'

Dicky linked arms with Biddy and Debbie and led them into the shouting, flag-waving throng, but the crowd was too thick to allow speedy progress and dusk was already falling before they reached the vicinity of St George's Hall and saw the first of the fireworks burst in many-coloured splendour above the plateau. Presently, Debbie realised that she was alone, for the constant movement of the crowd had separated her from her friends, and when she spotted Millie, clutching her mam's arm and waving a gloriously large Union Jack, she fought her way across to her to exchange greetings and news of their respective parties.

Debbie had met Millie's mam several times and knew how close an interest she took in her daughter's friends, so she was not surprised when Mrs Grimble said curiously: 'Why's you all on your lonesome, Deb? Where's that nice young Mr Barnes I see'd you with when we met outside the Derby cinema? I thought you'd be with 'im on such a day.'

'I was, only we got separated by the crowd,' Debbie explained. 'Isn't it grand to see the street lights? And St George's Hall, all lit up? Dicky and his pals have a share in an old banger—it's an Austin Seven, actually—and he told us earlier how they had ripped the cardboard shutters off the lights and how grand it made them feel to drive along the country roads with the beams revealing every little rabbit who crossed their path.'

Mrs Grimble smiled at her. 'You're right, it's a real treat to be able to see where you're going,' she said. 'Now, how about coming back to our place for some fish and chips? I've got a cousin what fishes out of Seaforth Sands an' he give me a rare big old cod and a pile o' spuds from his allotment. He and his wife will come round if they can get, but there's plenty for all and you'd be very welcome.'

'That would be lovely,' Debbie said, meaning it. When she had left the house Chloe had still been extremely excited, and Debbie realised that the longer she stayed out the more likely she was to find the child asleep in her bed on her return, and no longer bouncing up and down and shouting. She thought, furthermore, that if Biddy got home first it would do her good to have to cope with the child, though she knew it was likelier that Biddy would be back even later than herself. She did feel a twinge of conscience as she left the plateau with the Grimbles, for when all was said and done she supposed that since she had arrived here with Biddy and Dick she should also have left with them. But one glance at the huge crowd, everyone linking arms as they sang *There'll be blue birds over / The white cliffs of Dover / Tomorrow, just you wait and see*, told her that searching would be fruitless. She clung tightly to Millie's arm, therefore, determined to enjoy herself, despite feeling somewhat aggrieved. After all, Dicky was meant to be *her* friend, yet she had a shrewd suspicion that he would have managed to hang on to pretty, vivacious Biddy, even though he had let go of

357

herself.

The family fish supper to which Mrs Grimble had invited her turned out to be a very large party indeed. There were several young men who had come ashore from the various ships lying in the docks and one of these set Debbie's heart thumping, for as soon as she heard him speak she thought she knew him. 'How you doin', cobber?' he said in a slow, easy drawl, addressing another man. 'I've not set eyes on you for a while. Anything new?'

Debbie's heart missed a beat, then went into overtime. The young man was tall and fair, and very tanned, and for one giddy, enchanting moment Debbie thought that Pete Solomon had found her at last. Then the young man, who had had his back to her, turned round and she saw at once that he was not her one-time rescuer. Nevertheless, she introduced herself, intrigued by his accent which, even after four years, she recognised as being the same as Pete's. He told her his name was Ralph Middleton, and that he came from somewhere called Canberra.

'Is that in the south of England?' Debbie asked politely, and then felt foolish when he grinned quizzically at her and told her that she was only about six thousand miles out; he came from Australia.

As soon as he said it, Debbie felt a surge of excitement. Australia! For the first time, she began to put two and two together. She had wondered how Pete had come to know her mother but had simply thought he must have met her through her work at the hospital; perhaps he had been visiting a patient on her ward, perhaps he had even been a patient himself. Now, however, her brain was trying to tell her that Australia was the link . . . but there was so much going on, so many people who wanted to celebrate . . . oh, if only she could think straight!

For some reason Ralph Middleton attached himself to her, and she was glad of it, because every time he spoke images of Pete danced in her mind, and other images too: a great river in whose depths strange creatures—crocodiles and water snakes—lurked; a house made of timber with a wide veranda on which a family sat to eat their meals, read their letters, discuss their problems. Letters! Of course, why had she never thought of the letters? All through her childhood and adolescence, letters had winged their way between Australia and Liverpool as two old friends shared both triumphs and disasters, described their lives, their loves, their families.

Beside her, Ralph took her hand. He examined her fingers as though searching for some clue. 'You aren't a land girl because your nails are clean; you ain't in the catering business because if you had your hands in water half the day your fingers would have a spongy look.' He put her hand down and smiled at her. 'You're somebody's secretary,' he said triumphantly. 'Unless you're one of those mannequins who walk up and down the big stores, showing off the pretty frocks.'

'I'm a wireless assembler,' Debbie told him. 'But never mind what I do. I've just been wondering if you could help me? You see, my mam's greatest friend lives in Australia, but I've lost her address . . . well, not lost exactly. My home was bombed and everything in it was destroyed. But there was a young fellow . . . he arrived in Liverpool on the worst night of the bombing and he was actually there when I was dug out of the ruins . . . and I think he might have been her son. My mam was killed in the raid but Pete—his name was Pete—got me lodgings and was most awfully kind. He had my address but I never had his, and since I moved in with friends within a couple of days of Pete's returning to his airfield, we lost touch. Is there any way that I could find him, do you suppose?'

'What's his name?' Ralph said immediately. 'And have you any idea whereabouts in Britain he was stationed?'

'I think his name is Pete Sullivan,' Debbie said slowly. 'You see, someone told me he was Pete Solomon—or I thought that was what she said—so I didn't connect him with my mam's old friend. Well, to tell you the truth, I didn't even know he was an Australian. He never said and I simply didn't guess, or perhaps I just didn't put two and two together. I haven't made much attempt to find him, though I've asked a lot of RAF types if they've come across a Peter Solomon. But since I never said he was Australian I suppose I might have been speaking to his best friend without either of us realising who I meant.'

The young man nodded thoughtfully. 'Your best bet would be to write to the Air Ministry, I guess,' he said. 'It'll take months, because such enquiries tend to be handed from one department to another, but I'm sure you'll get some satisfaction in the end. I suppose you don't know where Mrs Sullivan lives? Most Australians live round the coast—Sydney would be your best bet. Did the family live in New South Wales?'

'I don't know,' Debbie wailed dismally. 'Oh, they had a cattle station. When I was little, I used to think they must be royal. Is there somewhere with "king" in the name?'

Ralph began to shake his head, then said triumphantly: 'Queensland! Could it have been Queensland?'

Debbie gave an excited little bounce in her seat. 'I'm sure it was . . . is, I mean,' she said. 'Would Mrs Sullivan, Queensland, Australia find her, do you suppose?'

Ralph laughed. 'I've never been to Queensland but I know it's enormous—ten times the size of Great Britain. But it's very sparsely populated,' he told her. 'You could try writing; it just might come off.'

Soon after this, Debbie left the party. She had intended to go home unaccompanied, but her new friend would not hear of it. 'There's fellers out there, mad with excitement and foolish with drink, just looking for a pretty little sheila like you,' he said. And in the face of this information, Debbie felt obliged to accept his escort. Presently she was glad she had done so, for as he had said the crowds outside were still wild with excitement and they were continually being bumped and jostled. People were good natured, to be sure, but Debbie realised that had she been unaccompanied she would have been very frightened indeed.

Ralph went with her to the door of No. 4 Lavender Court and accepted her invitation to come in for a cup of cocoa. Two of the other girls were still up, so they all had cocoa together and then Ralph asked Debbie, very shyly, if he might see her again. Debbie looked at him thoughtfully.

He had a round, freckled face, hazel green eyes and a snub nose, and she was aware that he had done her a very good turn; had it not been for Ralph she might never have realised that Pete's name was Sullivan, not Solomon, and that he was most probably the son of her mother's best friend. So she agreed to meet him again next time he had some leave, and then waved him off and turned, thankfully, back into the kitchen. Sandy and Ruth were still there, preparing their sandwiches for the next day, chatting busily as they did so. Debbie considered making her own snap but then decided to check on Chloe first, unless Biddy was in already, of course. She turned to the two girls. 'Is Biddy back yet? Only we got separated when we reached the firework display and didn't manage to meet up again.'

Sandy grinned at her. 'Well, you didn't waste much time in replacing Dicky,' she observed. 'He's nice, that Ralph of yours. Known him long?'

'As if you didn't know,' Debbie scoffed, returning the grin. 'I met him for the first time this evening. A pal from work asked me to go back to her house, and when we got there we found quite a party going on. Ralph was one of the guests. Is Biddy in yet?'

To her surprise, the girls exchanged a quick glance and then Ruth muttered, 'I dunno; I think . . . but you'd best go up and see for yourself.'

Something in the way she spoke alarmed Debbie and she flew up the stairs, then went quietly into the bedroom, her heart thumping. As soon as she entered the room, she knew it was empty. There was no Biddy curled up in her small bed; no Chloe starfished in Debbie's, no Dusty either, but there

362

was a brown manila envelope propped up on her pillow. Debbie grabbed it, then lit the candle on the washstand, her hands trembling so much that she had to make three attempts before the wick caught. Then she sat heavily down on her bed, opened the envelope and read the blotched and ill-spelt letter within.

Dear Debbie,

Me and Dicky have decided to take Chloe back to Ireland. I reckon we'll get wed in Dublin. I knew if I told you you'd be really angry with me, so I've not said nothing. If you loved Dicky, I wouldn't have tried to take him off you, but you don't, do you? I always have, ever since the first time we met, though he didn't treat me too good, one way and another. That time he come to the court and you threw yourself into his arms (he told me how it were) he were after me—didn't you guess? No, you're too nice, but there's some chaps aren't content with one woman, and Dicky's a bit like that.

He says to tell you he's sorry, and that he isn't Chloe's dad, whatever folk may think, but he's mortal fond of her and will do right by her.

I'll write when we've got a place of our own and mebbe you'll visit. Don't be too angry with me but I reckon it's for the best. A kid shouldn't have two mams, and it were getting that way, weren't it?

All the best, queen,
Biddy
PS We've took Dusty becos Chloe wouldn't come with us, else. She loves him you know. Sorry but she wouldn't leave him.

363

Debbie read the letter through several times, almost unable to believe the words she was reading. Then she went heavily downstairs, knowing that she must face the other girls sooner or later and deciding it had better be sooner. She went into the kitchen, still holding the letter, and saw at once that both girls knew. Sandy dropped the knife she was holding and came over, giving Debbie a spontaneous hug. 'You're going to miss Chloe because you were more like a mother to her than ever that Biddy was,' she observed, 'but don't you go missing *her*. She were a bad lot, though no one ever said so to you because she were your pal. Only a real pal doesn't treat folk the way Biddy treated you.'

Debbie straightened her shoulders and tried to smile. 'I suppose I always knew that Biddy wasn't a terribly nice person,' she admitted. 'But, oh, I love Chloe so much! As for Dicky . . . well, I must have been blind. I had no idea he even knew Biddy. Why, I thought I introduced them.'

Ruth looked up from carefully wrapping her sandwiches in greaseproof paper and sliding a rubber band round them. 'Think back,' she urged. 'Think back to the very first time you brought Dicky into this kitchen.'

Frowning, Debbie cast her mind back, and for the first time she realised why Biddy's initial reaction to Dicky had struck her as odd. 'Hello, stranger,' she had said—not because she did not know him, as Debbie had assumed at the time, but because she *did* know him and was reproaching him for not coming to see her more often. And Dicky was as guilty of deceit as Biddy had been, for he had never let Debbie know that he and Biddy were old friends, had certainly never admitted that he was fond of the other girl. But now Sandy was speaking, her voice gentle but frank. 'Didn't you ever notice how often Biddy went off on some spree or other, leaving you in charge of Chloe, when she knew perfectly well you'd planned an outing with Dicky? Oh, Debbie, it happened over and over and you never fought back, never insisted that she should look after her own child for once.'

'And I never put two and two together and realised what was going on,' Debbie said. 'But perhaps it was because I never was terribly interested in a future with Dicky. At any rate, I hope it's taught me a lesson not to take people at their face value.'

Ruth and Sandy both nodded. 'You'll get over it, queen,' Sandy told her. 'It's a horrible thing to have happened and I know you're going to miss Chloe dreadfully, but, you know, she was her mother's daughter; one day she would have given you real grief. As it is, you'll have to put all three of them out of your mind and get on with your own life.' She came over to Debbie and gave her another hug. 'That feller you brought in tonight, he seemed really nice. And when you first moved in, you talked about some chap called Pete . . .'

Debbie returned the hug. 'Yes, I always meant to track Pete down,' she said. 'Oddly enough, this very evening I got a clue which I mean to follow up. And thank you both for your support and understanding; you're a couple of *real* friends and I reckon I'm going to need you to keep me cheerful in the days to come.'

A week later, Debbie returned home to find Mrs Batley waiting for her. The older woman was dressed for work and greeted Debbie with some relief. 'There's a feller been round asking for you,' she said, heading for the back door. 'He says he found out where you lived quite by chance and will call again. Sorry, love, he didn't leave no name, but I reckon he'll be back. He said he'd come round later this evening, and he seemed a reliable type.'

Debbie's heart gave a joyful bound; who could it be but Pete? She supposed he must have sufficient leave, now that the war was over, to come back to Liverpool and search for her. But Mrs Batley was saying rapidly: 'I've got to go, hinny, 'cos I don't want to be late or I'll mebbe lose me job. I hung on just to make sure you knew you'd be having a caller later on.'

'Thanks ever so much, Mrs B. What have I got to do for tea, since I'm first in?' Debbie shouted, as the other woman began to hurry down the hall. 'I know it's not my turn but I might as well get things started.'

'Well, I've done me best to buy whatever's available, but the truth is, the shops is nigh on empty. The butcher's were the worst; I didn't spend half the money I'm allowed because there weren't nothing to spend it on. Still, there's plenty of potatoes and a fair number of other vegetables, so you could make a blind scouse.'

'Thanks, Mrs B,' Debbie said, going over to the pantry to collect the vegetables. If the caller had been Pete, and she couldn't think of anyone else it could be, then she would want to ask him to share their meal. It was just hard luck that he should arrive on the day a meatless tea was planned, though such days were becoming more and more frequent as supplies dwindled.

Debbie had prepared half the vegetables before the girls began to trickle back and Lucy, whose turn it was to cook, took over. Only then did she grab a jug of water and race up the stairs to her own room, which seemed almost spacious now that it contained only one bed and no cot. Debbie was sure she would have to share again some day, but no would-be lodger had yet presented herself, and in the meantime, though she felt a little ashamed of the fact, Debbie found herself enjoying having a room of her own. She missed Chloe, but she had to admit that of late the child had been increasingly demanding. Bedtime stories, tales of her own childhood and games of I Spy might have been fun for the child, but after a long day at work Debbie now felt only relief that she was free of a responsibility that had fallen increasingly on her shoulders.

She had a strip-down wash and selected her only decent frock, the pink cotton one she had worn on VE Day. She undid the ribbon which tied back her hair, brushed it into a gleaming curtain, and decided to leave it loose for once. Then she checked her appearance in the mirror, noticing with approval how excitement had brought a faint flush to her cheeks and made her large, dark blue eyes sparkle.

She made her way downstairs and helped the girls to lay the table, make the tea, and cut a plateful of bread and margarine. 'Goin' out?' Lucy asked. 'You look very pretty this evening!'

Debbie dropped her a mock curtsy. 'Thank you, kind lady,' she said. 'And I might be going out; I'm not sure. Apparently, some feller came round this afternoon wanting to see me and Mrs Batley told him to try again this evening, when I'd be at home.'

Sandy, getting bottles of sauce and a jar of pickled onions out of the cupboard, gave Debbie an approving smile. 'That's right, queen, you make the best of yourself,' she said. 'I reckon it'll be that feller who saw you home on Victory night. Now don't look so disappointed . . . you weren't hoping it would be Dicky, were you?'

'No, not Dicky; another friend,' Debbie mumbled. 'Are the spuds done? If so, I'll mash 'em. And the scouse must be just about ready.'

Presently the girls settled down to their meal, but Debbie didn't join in the chatter. She was wondering how on earth she'd been so daft as to forget all about Ralph Middleton; it would be him, of course it would. But then she remembered that Mrs Batley had said that the caller had found out where she lived quite by chance, so it could not possibly be Ralph, and she had never imagined it was Dicky, because Mrs Batley knew Dicky as well as she did. Cheering up, Debbie began to join in the conversation, though she could not help shooting hopeful glances at the door every few minutes. The meal was long over, however, before someone rapped and the kitchen was empty save for Debbie herself and Phyllis, whose turn it was to wash up.

'I'll go,' Debbie said unnecessarily, since Phyllis, up to her elbows in greasy washing-up water, could scarcely have done so. She shot down the hall and opened the door. Then she simply stared, eyes and mouth both rounding with sheer incredulity. Standing on the doorstep as large as life, and staring at her, was Uncle Max!

Debbie actually fell back a pace, but then she remembered her manners; remembered, too, that her mother had been fond of this man. She tried to smile. 'Uncle Max! Well, fancy seeing you! Would you like to come in?'

Uncle Max hesitated. 'Is there somewhere we could talk, somewhere private like?' he asked diffidently. 'I reckon I've a deal of explaining to do and I'd rather do it without strangers listenin' in.'

For a moment, Debbie almost panicked. Once, she had been afraid to be alone with Uncle Max because of his tendency to grab and cuddle, but that had been years ago, when she was little more than a child. Now she was a young woman, quite capable of defending herself against an unwanted handshake, let alone anything more intimate. And giving Uncle Max a long, hard look, she saw that she was not the only one who had changed. In the intervening period, Uncle Max had grown old. He was a great deal thinner than she remembered, and when he took off his hat to enter the house she saw that the thick thatch of hair, of which he had once been so proud, had shrunk to a white, monk-like nimbus around his bald crown. Suddenly, she felt sorry for him. After all, she had acknowledged to herself some time ago that he had been genuinely fond of her mother, which must mean that he was not all bad.

As Uncle Max entered the kitchen, Phyllis was turning away from the sink and moving over to dry her hands on the roller towel behind the door. Debbie introduced them, explaining that she and

Uncle Max would go into the front room for a chat and asking Phyllis if she could possibly make a tray of tea and bring it through. Then she led Uncle Max across the hall into the front room and settled him in one of the fireside chairs. When Phyllis entered the room bearing a tray upon which rested two enamel mugs of tea Uncle Max began to protest, to say that he did not mean to trespass upon their hospitality, but Debbie shook her head chidingly at him as Phyllis left the room. He was clearly nervous; his big-knuckled, heavily veined hands were actually shaking. 'A cup of tea will do us both good,' she said firmly. 'Besides, I'm thirsty even if you aren't.' She settled herself in the chair opposite and took a sip of tea. 'I suspect we've both got some explaining to do,' she said, after a moment, as her visitor did not seem anxious to start. 'I'm afraid I made no attempt to find you after Mam died. It might have been different if the house hadn't been flattened, but once that was gone I simply searched for somewhere else to live. I wanted young company, I think, because my friend was killed in the same raid that killed Mam, you know. To be honest, Uncle Max, I think I was rather jealous of Mam's affection for you. And I was never one for a lot of cuddling.'

'I know, I know. Your mam ticked me off good 'n' proper a couple of times, but I meant no harm. I were real fond of you and just wanted to show how I felt,' Uncle Max said humbly. 'When I gave you presents—and they weren't much, just a few sweets, a couple of apples, some cigarette cards— you seemed to think I was trying to bribe you, but I weren't, you know. I've always been fond of kids— why, I give your friend Gwen such things and she

370

were grateful, seemed to like me. But I could tell you never really took to me, no matter how hard I tried to please you.'

'Well, as I said, I was jealous, which I'm sure didn't help. Now I'm older, I can see it was wrong of me not to contact you. But I knew you were all right and hadn't been hurt because, like everyone else, I checked the casualty lists after every raid and your name was never on 'em,' Debbie said.

Uncle Max grinned wryly. 'Don't say you weren't disappointed,' he said. 'I checked the lists, too, for a mention of you. It was horrible, because I felt guilty, felt I'd driven you away from your home and your friends. But at least you weren't on the casualty lists, so I comforted myself that you'd probably gone off to that village where the Soameses went. I told meself you'd be safe there, but that you'd come back to the city when the war was over, and then I could make my peace with you.' He heaved a sigh so gusty that it lifted a wing of Debbie's soft hair from her forehead. 'But then VE Day came and I couldn't help thinking how upset your mam would be that I'd lost touch with you, particularly as me circumstances have changed.' He looked imploringly across at Debbie. 'After the May blitz, I moved into lodgings with a very nice landlady. She were good to me and I did me best to be an ideal lodger. But then I had the chance of buyin' a little place of me own. I'd saved up, you know, quite a tidy sum, and I've always wanted to own property. Oh, it ain't a palace, by any means; it needed a lot of work doing, but I knew it would be a decent enough home once I'd finished with the decoratin' and that. I bought it a year ago, just about the time of the Normandy landings, and moved in two months back. But a couple of days ago I—I went round to Wykeham Street. I don't really know why except for old times' sake. I walked up and down the road a couple of times—I won't deny there were tears in me eyes—then turned back towards Fountains Road and bumped slap bang into Mrs Bingham, that friend of your mam's who lived on Howley Street and worked in the Stanley as a cleaner. Well, she saw I were upset and she asked me back to her place so's we could chat about old times.'

'Yes, I remember Mrs Bingham; Mam always had a soft spot for her, though she said she often suspected that the old girl was a bit light-fingered. She used to warn the patients on her ward to keep an eye on their possessions whilst the cleaner was around,' Debbie said with a chuckle. 'So you went back to her place and she gave you a cup of tea and told you all the gossip; is that right?'

Uncle Max grinned again but Debbie thought he looked rather shifty. 'Ye-es,' he said slowly. 'We sat in the kitchen but the door to the hall was open and I could see the parlour. And suddenly, just as I were explaining that I'd lost touch with you, she saw where I were lookin' and got up to shut the kitchen door, only that just confirmed what I'd been thinkin'. I got to me feet, opened the door, and crossed the hallway into the parlour. And there were the brass fire irons which always stood in the parlour grate and the little roll-topped bureau which Jess was so fond of.'

'The wicked old woman!' Debbie said. 'Oh, Uncle Max, I went and searched for that bureau and asked around, but of course it never occurred to me that it had been stolen. You see, my mam left a letter in that bureau, and the last thing she said to me was to go and find it, because it was important. So what did Mrs Bingham say when you accused her?'

Uncle Max gave a short laugh. 'She said she'd rescued the stuff for her old friend Jess, 'cos she couldn't bear to see such nice furniture took by looters,' he said. 'Then when she heard Jess had died, she said she'd hung on to it for you. So I said you were my responsibility and since I now had a house of me own, I'd take the stuff right away. I even thanked her for looking after it so nicely, 'cos it were all polished up a treat,' he ended.

'I suppose I can't blame you for lying to her, but I'm not your responsibility and never were,' Debbie said firmly. 'So what happened next? I take it you now have the bureau and the fire irons in your new house?'

Uncle Max sighed. 'You could have purrit better; you've made me sound like a perishin' thief meself. But yes, I borrowed a van from a pal and the stuff is in my house right now. But of course, I didn't mean to take it for myself. So the very next day I gorron a train and went into North Wales; the village is pretty small so I found the Soameses right away. Mrs Soames told me you'd never moved in with them but that you wrote regular. So she gave me your address and here I am.'

'Gosh,' Debbie said inadequately. 'After all this time! I don't mind telling you, Uncle Max, that I never thought I'd see Mam's bureau again. But what did the old devil do with Mam's papers and that?'

'She said there weren't nothing in it but bills and receipts and two half-used ration books,' Uncle

Max said. 'I didn't believe her for a moment because I know your mam bought war bonds and had at least one Post Office savings account, but the old girl probably stripped that lot within a week of getting her hands on the bureau. I'm afraid all I can offer you is what I took from Mrs Bingham, but you're very welcome to it, seein' as it's yours anyway.'

'I thought you said everything was left to you in Mam's Will . . .' Debbie began, then could have cursed herself. She had never intended to let Uncle Max know that it had been she in Mrs Roberts's kitchen the day he took up residence in Huskisson Street. And now, looking into his once-hated face, she realised that the knowledge would give him pain and that all her old bitterness against him had faded. She might never want to live under the same roof as Uncle Max, but she realised that her mother, Gwen, and a good many other people had been right and she had been wrong. She had been prejudiced against him from the start, had seen him as an enemy, but, after all, he was under no real obligation to find her and hand the furniture over; he had done it because it was the right thing to do. And he had gone to a lot of trouble to find her, trekking out to Betws-y-Coed, asking a lot of questions, and finally, with her address in his possession, calling on her and telling her about the furniture when he could easily have kept quiet. And if Mrs Bingham had failed to find the secret drawer, then Uncle Max deserved Debbie's thanks and not her condemnation.

'Who the devil told you that?' Uncle Max said, very red in the face. 'It were wrong of me, of course it were, but I did tell folk as your mam had left a will, leaving you in my charge. After all, you were only fourteen or so and I knew your mam wouldn't want you landed in an orphanage. Honest to God, queen, I meant to offer to let you lodge wi' Mrs Roberts—me old landlady—just so's we could mourn your mam together.'

Suddenly, unexpectedly, his eyes filled with tears and Debbie watched, horrified and conscience-stricken, as they ran down his face.

*   *   *

When Debbie saw Uncle Max off, late that night, they had reached what she felt was a comfortable compromise. He was to keep the fire irons, as a memento of Jess, and she would take the bureau, which she would collect from him as soon as she was able, since there was plenty of space in her bedroom for such an item. 'I'll hire a cart, or something, and come round after work. See you soon, Uncle Max,' she said.

CHAPTER THIRTEEN

In fact, it was a week before the bureau stood in Debbie's small bedroom. It looked extremely large and shiny, and Debbie acknowledged that, whatever her faults, Mrs Bingham had treasured it. She must have waxed it at least once a week, and now here it stood in Debbie's sparsely furnished room looking, if the truth were known, somewhat out of place.

Debbie had hired a handcart from a nearby

shop, together with a stout young man who had done all the heavy work of getting the bureau on and off the cart, and up the stairs of No. 4. Uncle Max had offered to do it but Debbie had explained that the young man had come with the cart for the humble sum of half a crown, and Uncle Max had probably been glad enough to give way, for the bureau was heavy.

Now, Debbie regarded her new possession almost shyly. It was as clean as a new pin and totally empty, though she had not yet tried the secret drawer. She knew where it was but found herself reluctant to slide it open because the more she looked at the bureau, fairly glowing with polish and elbow grease, the more certain she became that Mrs Bingham must have discovered—and emptied—the drawer long ago. However, nothing venture, nothing gain, she told herself, and pulled out the top drawer, laying it carefully on the bed behind her. Cautiously, she slid her hand into the aperture, fumbled around for a moment, found the slight indentation and pressed downward, then pulled. The false bottom came away smoothly, revealing another drawer, shallower than the first, and containing—oh joy!—several thin sheets of paper and a large white envelope with her own name written neatly on the front in her mother's well-remembered handwriting.

Debbie took the papers and the envelope out with a trembling hand, and sat down heavily on the bed. She could see at a glance that the loose sheets—and there were more of them than she had at first supposed—were letters from her Aunt Nancy. She glanced quickly at the address in the top right-hand corner of the first page of the letter

376

and saw the address, neatly printed. The Walleroo! How could she have forgotten such a strange and interesting name? Yet she had done so totally. She was tempted to begin reading the letters, saving the one from her mother until later, but realised that this was sheer cowardice. It was easy to talk about a voice from beyond the grave, but she found she was frightened of what the envelope might contain. If her mother had written the letter at the beginning of the war, she would have been addressing a thirteen-year-old child, and what she said might in no way be what her nineteen-year-old daughter wanted to hear. Hesitantly, she opened the white envelope, drew out the pages within, and began to read.

My darling Debbie,

If you are reading this, it means that I'm no longer with you, but even so, I want the best for you. Poor old Debbie, I'm afraid I haven't managed to amass very much for you to inherit, but there is some money in my Post Office savings account, and also some war bonds, though you won't be able to change them until the war is over. I've talked to Uncle Max and he will give you all the help he can, because, having thought the matter over, I think the wisest thing you can do is to go to your Aunt Nancy in Australia. As you know, queen, she's been the best of good friends. We would have done anything for one another and I'm sure Nancy will see that you are well and happy. I know you won't be able to go until the war is over, and all sorts of things may happen which I can't possibly guess at, but please write to her

*immediately and tell her I'm gone and explain
that I have left you, so to speak, in her charge.*

*It seems to me that this isn't going to be a
short war and when it ends, whatever the
outcome, Britain will be weary and beaten
down by it. I don't mean beaten because I
know, already, that we shall triumph—who
could believe anything else with Winnie in
charge—but I do think Britain will run out of
money and be in a pretty poor state. Australia is
a young country, for young people. I had my
chance of going out there years ago, when
Nancy did, in fact, and I turned it down. I was
afraid, Debbie, scared of the challenge, but not
wanting to admit it. Of course, I'm glad now
that I didn't go, because if I had I'd never have
met and married your father, and you would
not have been born. No, I wouldn't swap my
memories of Ken and the pleasures of having a
daughter, darling Debbie, for all Nancy's
mansion, if she has a mansion, that is.*

*But just because I couldn't face leaving the
only life I knew, that doesn't mean that you
should do the same. You are much braver than
I ever was, and I hope with all my heart that
you'll give your Aunt Nancy the chance to help
you to a new life. If you show Uncle Max this
letter, and I'm assuming that he is still alive and
well, then he's promised to see you right until
you are able to take care of yourself and I'm
sure that he will pay your passage to Australia.
Though of course if it's not what you want . . .*

*Debbie, my love, this has been a horribly
hard letter to write because it is peering through
a glass darkly, as it says in the Bible. I long to*

be able to give you some security, but if I am killed—and I am writing this whilst sheltering in the hospital basement during a very heavy raid—then your going to Nancy seems the only possible solution.

Take care of yourself, darling Debbie; I know you'll never forget me as I shall never forget you. Remember I love you,
Mam

By the time Debbie had finished reading, she could scarcely see the writing through the tears welling up in her eyes. Poor Mam! As she said, it must have been a dreadfully difficult letter to write, because she had no idea when—or even if—it would be read; no idea whether she was addressing a thirteen-year-old child or a grown woman. And, Debbie realised, her mother could not have known which way the war would go; not in 1941, when the raids were at their height.

Carefully, she laid the letter upon the others in the pile, and began to dry her eyes. Then she read it again and knew that she would do just as her mother had suggested. She had sufficient money in her own savings account to pay for a passage to Australia, or so she imagined, but if she had not she would sell the bureau, her bed and anything else she owned in order to get to Australia and Aunt Nancy. This time, however, she did not intend to keep her plans a secret from anyone. She would tell the girls where she was going, give in her notice at the factory, and tell her boss and all her friends whither she was bound. And last, but not least, she would tell Uncle Max. He had not lied when he had said that Jess had left Debbie in his charge, for the letter had more or less said the same. Furthermore, she would give Uncle Max the Sullivans' address, would promise to write both on the journey to the Walleroo cattle station and on her arrival there. She thought, guiltily, that it might easily have been she who had contributed to his ageing, because she admitted to herself now that he really had loved her mother, and would have felt miserably responsible when he had lost touch with Debbie herself.

Downstairs, she could hear the girls assembling in the kitchen and presently one of them erupted into the hall. 'Supper! Come to the cookhouse door, boys, come to the cookhouse door!' a voice trilled, and Debbie gathered up all the letters and left the bedroom. She would tell them the whole story as they ate their meal, from the time she and Pete Sullivan had stood on the pavement in Wykeham Street, thinking that the bureau had been blown to bits, until the marvellous moment when she had opened the secret drawer and found the documents within.

Smiling to herself, she began to descend the stairs. She would not tell them that her real reason for making the epic journey was because she now believed that Pete would be at the Walleroo before her. You can't fall in love with someone after only two or three meetings, particularly when you are only fifteen and he is twenty-one, she told herself, but she did not believe a word of it. His face had remained absolutely clear in her mind for more than four years: the way his hair grew, the gentleness of his smile, the way his eyes could harden when he was cross and soften when he was pleased. And there was no accounting for the way her stomach turned over every time she heard an Australian accent, or allowed herself to relive the brief hours she had spent in his company.

As she entered the kitchen, she reminded herself that this love—which might, after all, be just imagination—was very unlikely to be reciprocated. They had not set eyes on one another for four years, and for all she knew it might have been, for him, out of sight, out of mind. For despite his apparent concern, he had never written.

Yet she was certain sure she would have known had he been killed, certain sure that he had really liked her. So it was with a smile on her face that she entered the kitchen and beamed round at the assembled company. 'Guess what, girls? I'm off on the longest journey of my life. First of all, though, I've a story to tell you . . .'

*   *   *

In the end, unlikely though it seemed, it was Uncle Max who actually got Debbie moving. She had decided that since he had been the one to find the bureau, it was only right that she should share its secrets with him. She went round to his house in Gregson Street the very next evening and took both Jess's letter and the ones from Nancy with her.

He had been delighted to see her, had invited her into a small but cosy kitchen, had plied her with homemade scones, richly buttered, some delicious ginger biscuits and a small dish of strawberries which, he told her proudly, he had grown himself on the allotment he had recently acquired. 'And the scones were made for me by my old landlady,' he confided. 'To tell the truth, queen, her 'n' me's thinking of getting hitched. She reckons her house is too big for her now she's gettin' on a bit, so she'd sell up in Huskisson Street and move in here wi' me.'

'Congratulations. I'm sure it's the best thing for you,' Debbie said warmly. 'But is this house big enough?'

Uncle Max grinned sheepishly. 'That's one of the advantages, chuck. The fact is, Sarah—that's her name—has a rare nasty old mother what landed herself on her daughter, oh, it must be three years or more ago. You may think I'm prejudiced but I'm not and my Sarah is desperate to get the old girl off her back.' He chuckled reminiscently. 'She's full of courage, my Sarah, but she's kind 'n' all, and couldn't bring 'erself to turn the old woman out. But this house only has the one decent bedroom and the old girl knows I'd not have her under my roof so she's goin' to her other daughter what lives up in Scotland, and good riddance! I'm tellin' you, Sarah lost more lodgers through her mam than you'd ever believe, so you can imagine how glad we are to see the back of the old harridan.'

'Yes, I can,' Debbie said eagerly; she remembered her own confrontation with Mrs Roberts's mother. 'I've met people like that, who really enjoy making trouble.'

Uncle Max nodded heavily. 'That's her all right! Have another scone,' he urged. 'And now tell me about yourself. Is everything all right? Happy with the bureau?'

'Yes, very happy,' Debbie said, producing the

382

letters from her bag. 'I didn't tell you before because I was afraid Mrs Bingham might have found it, but there's a secret drawer in the bureau and these were still in it, quite intact and obviously unread. I brought them round to show you because I'm sure it's what my mam would have wished me to do. Go on, read them. The first one was addressed to me and Mam meant it as a sort of last Will and Testament, I think. It—it made me cry, but it made me happy, too, and I guess you'll feel the same when you've read it.' Settling back in her chair, she sipped her tea, keeping her eyes tactfully fixed on the patterned rug at her feet.

Presently, Uncle Max handed back the letters, his eyes very bright and shiny, and his hands trembling a little. 'Thank you, Debbie. You're a kind girl, and I appreciate you bringin' the stuff to me, 'cos it's made me feel a good deal better,' he said humbly. 'I told you your mam wanted me to look after you but I never guessed she'd purrit in writing, so to speak.' He got to his feet and offered her another scone, and, when she refused, took another himself before sitting down again. 'What'll you do, queen? Australia's a devil of a long way off but this here Nancy woman sounds a really grand person and there's no doubt about it, things is going to be difficult in England for a long while yet. The Yanks will want their lease-lend money back, you can be sure of that, and there'll be no end of rebuilding to be done and precious little money to do it with. Folk here is worn out from the struggle and sad from the losses we've suffered, and now that we've won, there ain't much fight left in us. If you can get out of it, then I reckon your mam was right and you should do what she wants.

After all, if you hate it, you can always come home again.'

'Oh, Uncle Max, I hoped you'd say that,' Debbie said eagerly. 'Because I really want to go. Of course I'll be leaving heaps of friends behind, but I hope to make friends there as well. And I'll write to you, nice long letters, so you'll know what's happening to me.'

'I'll write back, I promise,' Uncle Max assured her. 'And I'll pay your passage as your mother asked.' Debbie began to protest but he cut her short. 'I know, queen, you want to be independent, but remember it's a long way and you'll have to feed and clothe yourself for weeks—maybe months for all I know—so at least let me do something for you.' He wagged an admonitory finger, then reached out and very gently chucked her under the chin. 'There's only you an' me left now, old girl, so don't deny me the pleasure of helping you,' he said huskily. 'After all, your mam asked me to take care of you and I couldn't do it 'cos I didn't know where you were, so now let me give what help I can.'

It would have been churlish to refuse, and anyway Debbie saw the force of his argument. So she said that she would be very grateful for his help and presently they parted, on the best of terms. Debbie left the house with a light step, happy on two counts, one that she had truly made friends with Uncle Max at last, and the second that he had never once suggested accompanying her to the other side of the world. Had he done so, she would have felt obliged to agree to it, but she had guessed as soon as he revealed his plan to marry that their new-found friendship would not be put to the test.

Naturally enough, actually leaving for Australia

384

was not as simple as it had at first appeared. By the time Victory in Japan came round on 15 August, Debbie had resigned from the factory and was working out a month's notice. She had also managed to get another tenant for her room, since the rent had increased steadily due to the shortage of accommodation caused by the enormous bomb damage the city had suffered, and the other girls would have been hard put to it to make up her share. The woman who took her place was a friend of Mrs Batley's, a stout and cheerful person in her forties, who had been a cook in the ATS and needed accommodation in the city since she was now cooking at a British Restaurant and needed to be near her work.

Naturally, Debbie had meant to write to Nancy as soon as all her arrangements were made, but her passage itself was constantly under review, for the powers-that-be had decided to repatriate their allies before allowing emigration to start in earnest. Debbie began the letter several times, but the story was so involved that each time she wrote she decided to tear it up and start again, to make it simpler. Also, she found herself reluctant to write too soon in case Aunt Nancy advised her to stay where she was for the time being. The fact that she had given up her job and her place at No. 4 Lavender Court meant that she intended to go to Australia as soon as she could, even if Aunt Nancy considered it unwise. Best to write at the last moment, giving details of her voyage, her port of arrival, and the date and time at which she expected to dock. She was hopeful that someone would be able to meet her, but prolonged study of books and maps told her that this was unlikely.

Australia was an unbelievably vast country; she doubted that anyone would be prepared to travel thousands of miles to meet an uninvited guest whom they had never met.

Debbie had voiced these fears to Millie as they worked side by side at their bench, and Millie had reminded her of one of the letters from Nancy which she had been allowed to read. 'She went all that way alone to meet a complete stranger, with a view to the most intimate relationship of all, marriage,' she said reprovingly. 'And Andy came thousands of miles from his cattle station to Sydney harbour, just so that she wouldn't feel alone and afraid. One of the sons might meet you. Is the eldest one married? If so, he could bring his wife.'

The thought that Pete might be married had not occurred to Debbie before and a cold spasm of fear clutched at her heart. Why had she never thought of that? She had seen photographs in the papers of the girls they called the GI brides, crowding aboard the American-bound liners which would take them to their fiancés or husbands. And she had watched the numbers of weddings taking place at register offices and churches of all denominations in her own city. She had found Pete very attractive and guessed that his height and blond good looks would have made him a target for many an eager WAAF on his own station, let alone the girls he must have met at the dances and socials which had grown more frequent as the war neared its end. She stared at Millie, dismay welling up within her, then realised that her friend had noticed nothing, was continuing with her assembly work, eyes down, attention elsewhere. Hastily,

Debbie pulled herself together. She could, of course, write to Aunt Nancy this very day, or even telegraph her, but how could she possibly ask the question now uppermost in her mind? It was unthinkable that she should say, baldly: 'Is your son Pete married or engaged to some young female, or is he still fancy free?' The very thought of posing such a question brought the hot blood rushing to her cheeks. No, she would rather die than ask such a thing. And anyway, she reminded herself, people change. The man I thought I was in love with may not be the man I shall meet at the Walleroo station; come to that, the young girl Pete took under his wing isn't the same either. Goodness, I was a child then and now I'm a woman, and Pete, of course, has had four years of horrendous war.

Despite her hopes, it was November before Debbie found herself on board the SS *South Pacific* with her letter to Nancy posted, and those friends who had managed to get to Southampton standing on the quayside waving her off.

*   *   *

Nancy and Andy were sitting on the veranda, eating their midday meal, when they heard the mailman's whistle. Andy looked up and grimaced. Outside, the rain was coming down in torrents, but both he and Nancy knew that if they wanted their letters he would have to get the boat out, for during the wet it was impossible for Bullwhip to cross the river. Indeed, he often did not get this far, so the fact that he was blowing his whistle to get their attention was really a cause for rejoicing, since it meant that the letters for which they longed would be in their possession as soon as one of the hands—or Andy himself—could cross the water.

The whistle sounded again and Andy got to his feet. 'I'll go myself,' he said, as Nancy began to ask him which of the men he would send. 'After all, there might be a letter from one of the lads, telling us when he's coming home.'

He picked up his wide-brimmed hat and jammed it down over his curls, which were still more blond than white. He did not bother with a waterproof, but Nancy took down her own from where it hung near the screen door and struggled into it as she hurried to catch him up. Thunder rumbled overhead and an occasional spear of lightning darted to earth, and Nancy wished she had stopped to put on her wellingtons for the water was already lapping at the tops of her shoes. Ahead of her she could just make out the river through the driving rain, and she could see what she imagined must be Bullwhip on the further bank. Habit had brought him to where, in the dry, he would have forded the water, and it was a good place for Andy to cross now, since it was more shallow and less dangerous than other parts of the mighty river.

The boat was drawn well up on the bank and securely tethered to a gum tree. By the time Nancy reached him, Andy had untied the craft and was pulling it down towards the water. Nancy seized the oars and Andy looked round. 'What on earth are you doing here, old girl?' He had to shout to be heard above the roaring of the river, the pelting of the rain, and the rumbling of the thunder above

388

their heads. 'I can manage, you know; you go back to the house.'

Nancy snorted and glanced meaningly at the yellow flood water, flecked with foam, tumbling past. The river in flood was an awe-inspiring sight and she thought it would take both of them to get the boat safely across. 'You row and I'll steer,' she shrieked. 'What's happened to the rope?' Usually, a double length of stout rope was slung across the river at this point and tied securely to strong, well-rooted trees on either bank, but today, despite the heavy downfall, Nancy had seen at once that the rope was missing.

'The tree on the further bank has gone,' Andy roared back. 'Reckon it weren't strongly rooted enough to withstand the storm . . . it might even have been struck by lightning. Anyhow, it's gone. But we can still get across if we're careful.'

Andy launched the boat and jumped in, then gestured to Nancy to follow suit, seizing one oar as he did so. 'I'll pole her across,' he shouted. 'You do the same if you can.'

The short crossing, which with the aid of the rope would have taken them perhaps two minutes, now took more like twenty, and despite their most strenuous efforts the boat was carried a good forty yards down the river before they managed to bring her close enough to the opposite bank for Bullwhip to grab the bows. He clung on grimly until Andy jumped out of their small craft and heaved it on to comparatively dry land, then he stood back, grinning with relief and rubbing the wet—and the sweat—off his face with muddy hands. 'I thought you were goners for a minute there. What's happened to the rope?' he said gruffly. 'I dunno as it's worth riskin' your life for a few letters. But then, you cattle folk risk your lives a dozen times a week, I dare say. Do you want to take the McGuire mail while you're at it? I shan't be able to get through to them for weeks, mebbe.'

'Give it to me, Bullwhip,' Nancy said breathlessly, taking the fat bundle of letters and tucking them into the neck of her once crisp white blouse. 'Nellie McGuire's eldest boy was in Burma when Japan surrendered. I know she's as desperate for news as we are, and since this is the first time you've got as far as this for a month, she'll be downright grateful for any letters at all.'

'There's one from her boy . . . no, two, I believe . . . a couple of seed catalogues, some official-looking envelopes, and the rest from relatives in England,' Bullwhip announced. 'You've got one from your sister, three or four from them lads of yours, an' two or three from England . . . didn't recognise the handwriting on one of 'em.'

Nancy saw Andy's lurking grin appear and could not help smiling herself. Andy had once remarked that Bullwhip was as curious as a woman, and she had countered by saying that she was always grateful that the mailman did not have access to a boiling kettle, or she was sure he would have steamed open all their mail and shamelessly read every word. Now, however, she simply accepted the batch of letters and pushed them into her blouse, thanked Bullwhip, and cautiously climbed back into the boat, which they had pulled along the bank until it was once more level with their embarkation point. Andy jumped down as well, causing the craft to lurch dangerously, then they both seized their oars and began to pole their way

390

back through the raging waters.

In fact, the journey back was easier than the journey out had been, and in a remarkably short time Nancy and Andy were settled once more on the veranda. Nancy divided the mail, placing the McGuires' in the drawer of the cane table, and spreading their own letters out on the top of it. The boys had already told her that the armed forces would repatriate them, even though Jamie had warned them that since he intended to marry a Canadian girl and to make his home in that country he was unlikely to remain with them for long. Jacko, on the other hand, intended to stay in Australia, though not on the cattle station. He meant to qualify as an accountant—he had always been good at figures—and would take up a post in Sydney as soon as his disembarkation leave had finished.

Pete had not said much about the future. His parents knew that he had been searching for Jess's daughter whenever he had the opportunity, but Nancy assumed he must have given up by now and would very soon be home. She flicked through the pile of letters. None from Jamie or Jacko, which probably meant they were already on their way, but she seized upon the letter from Pete, opening the envelope so rapidly that she tore the page within and tutted at her own carelessness before beginning to read it aloud.

Dear Ma and Pa,

Not long now and I'll be back on the old homestead, giving you both a huge hug. First thing I'll do, after I've ate the biggest steak you can provide, is to get on board that lanky

391

*chestnut stallion and go for a gallop, because
I've not ridden since I left the Walleroo and I
miss the horses almost as much as I miss my
family.*

*As you know, I've been trying to contact
Jess's daughter—we lost touch after only a
couple of meetings back in May '41—but no
luck so far. I feel kind of responsible for her
because she was so alone and such a bonza kid.
Liverpool's a big city and the bomb damage is
unbelievable. Folk have moved around a good
deal, searching for accommodation, so it's
possible she's left the area altogether. However,
I'll have one more try before I leave here, which
looks like being some time in December, if I'm
one of the lucky ones. You see, I suddenly
remembered her telling me she worked in a
factory assembling radio parts; I'm pretty sure
that's what it was. So next time I go to
Liverpool, I won't just look for Debbie Ryan,
but for a wireless assembly factory. If I can't
find her there I guess I'll give up, but I'm
hoping.*

*Must go; there's a lecture on life in Civvy
Street this evening, and I reckon I ought to
attend, though my life in the peace is already
mapped out, if the Walleroo will have me, that
is! Can't wait to see the old place—and you old
folk!—again.*

Much love,
Pete

Nancy laid the letter down and smiled rather
mistily at Andy. 'Old folk indeed!' she said
indignantly. 'We're young enough to have run the

station with only the hands to help ever since the boys went off to the war. Still, I suppose when you're in your mid-twenties, someone in their fifties seems as old as the hills. But oh, Andy, it'll be so good to see them again! Of course, it isn't done to have favourites—I'm sure we both love all our sons equally—but I've always had a soft spot for our Pete. The other two never were interested in the cattle or the station, for that matter never wanted to help with the muster, hankered after city life, shops, theatres and so on. But Pete just wanted to be like you. Do you remember when he was about three, finding him wearing your hat and carrying one of your guns, and heading out across the paddocks? I remember he said he was going to shoot crocs . . .'

Andy laughed with her. 'Yeah, and when I asked him where he thought he was going, he said he wasn't too sure because the hat had fallen down over his eyes so he could only see his little gum boots.' He sighed and reached for the next letter on the pile and handed it to his wife. 'Go on, you open it. You can read it to me whilst I finish my coffee,' he added, reaching for his mug.

Nancy took the envelope, a frown creasing her brow. The letter had been sent from England but she did not recognise the handwriting; perhaps one of the boys was hurt and had got someone else to address it for him. Hastily, and with thumping heart, she opened the envelope and spread out the contents. She read the first few lines, her frown gradually clearing, then turned to the last page and smiled with relief. 'Oh, Andy, you'll never believe this! It's from Debbie Ryan, Jess's daughter; the child that our Pete has been trying to find. Well, by

393

all that's wonderful . . . oh!'

Just as she spoke the wind changed direction and the rain suddenly swirled on to the veranda, the heavy drops soaking everything they reached and the draught lifting Nancy's skirt above her knees.

Andy stood up, grabbed the pile of mail and headed for the living room. 'We'd best read the rest indoors,' he shouted. Nancy scuttled after him, then exclaimed again as the thunder crashed almost directly overhead, making her flinch and lose her hold for a moment on the letter in her hand. Spitefully, the wind whipped the first page up into the air, and even as Nancy cried out in dismay some trick of the air currents caused the page to swirl beneath the veranda.

'Oh, oh, oh!' Nancy shrieked. 'Can you get it, Andy? It's gone right under the bloody veranda.' Andy dumped the mail he was carrying down on the nearest chair and dived outside once more. He paused for a moment, peering at the board beneath his feet, and Nancy jerked his arm and pointed. 'There! I can just see it through the floor,' she shouted, raising her voice above the thunder. 'Oh, Andy, do be careful.'

Andy, however, ignored her warning and dived beneath the veranda. There was a short scuffle, then a grunt and a stream of swear words, some of which made Nancy blink for Andy seldom swore in front of his wife. Then he emerged, with the page in his left hand and something else in his right; something which squirmed and wriggled and lashed about until he threw it on the ground and stamped on its head with one heavy leather boot. Nancy gasped; it was a snake, and she saw at once

394

that Andy had been bitten, for the moment the snake stopped wriggling he held up his arm so that she could see the fang marks and would know what she must do. He came slowly up on to the veranda. Beneath the tan, his face was white, and for a moment Nancy could not think what her next move must be. Then, in a rush, all that she had been told about snake bites came into her mind and she straightened her back, took Andy gently by the hand and helped him into the long cane chair. 'Stay there and don't move, don't sneeze, don't smile, don't do anything,' she said rapidly. 'I'll fetch the medical box.' She flew for the box, calling out to anyone within hearing as she did so. 'The boss has been bit—a snake. I'll radio for the doc as soon as I've done what I can. Oh, pray heaven that the plane is at Cloncurry and not answering a call in the other direction.'

Seconds later, she was back on the veranda, her heart thumping like a trip hammer. Carefully, remembering that even the slightest movement could cause the venom to spread further into the blood stream, she bandaged the blue-edged fang marks with their little ooze of blood firmly, remembering the instructions she had been given when she had attended a first-aid class at the Cloncurry hospital. Never use a tourniquet, they had been told. Such a thing might trap the venom but it could result in the loss of the limb below it.

She finished the bandage off neatly and looked anxiously into her husband's face. He was still pale, but gave her a reassuring smile as she stood up. 'I'm going to contact the Flying Doc, darling,' she said gently. 'D'you know what sort of snake it was? Only they're bound to ask and I can never tell one from t'other.'

'Not sure,' Andy mumbled. 'There are so many of them. This one may be harmless—well, not harmless, but not as venomous as some. The doc'll know when he sees the body; he's got a book . . .' His voice trailed into silence and as she hurried out of the room, turning to give Andy one more glance, Nancy saw that he had closed his eyes.

The radio was kept in the living room, and glancing at the clock on the mantel she realised that it was the galah hour, when most of the women in the outback enjoyed a chat and some idle gossip amongst themselves. Someone, almost certainly a man, had nicknamed it the galah hour after the pink and grey galah parrots that chattered incessantly all over the country. Nancy sat down in front of the radio, flicked on the switch and immediately heard a babble of voices. A woman was repeating a recipe but Nancy cut across her words. 'Urgent! This is the Walleroo. Andy's been bit by a snake and I need the Flying Doc. Calling Cloncurry; calling Dr Mitchell. Over.' She flicked the switch on to receiver mode.

At her words, the radio went eerily silent for a moment, then a voice came from the receiver. 'That you, Nancy? Doc Mitchell here. I've been at the Partiger place so I can be with you in thirty minutes. You've immobilised the bite area? Don't let him move and keep your head. What was the snake? Remember, no guessing, you either know or you don't. Over.'

At the very sound of the doctor's voice, relief had flooded over Nancy in waves, and some of the sheer terror which had caused her hands to shake and her voice to tremble left her. She took a deep

396

breath. 'We're not sure, doc, but Andy killed it and we've got the body,' she said. 'Yes, I bandaged the wound and Andy's lying down and keeping still. Over.'

'Good, good. Stay calm and tell Andy to do the same. What sort of state is your airstrip in? Over.'

Nancy thought hard. 'It's muddy, but apart from that, not too bad,' she said, and was grateful for Andy's insistence that the strip should be checked every two or three days. She had often thought he was too fussy; now she blessed his thoroughness. But best to make sure. 'I'll get Aggie to go to the nearest humpy and fetch a few of the fellers over. One of them can drive the truck up and down the strip and the rest can help clear away as much water as they can. Did you say thirty minutes, doc? Over.'

'I did, but I'll mebbe make it in less,' the doctor said cheerfully. 'Andy will be good, you'll see. I'm in the air an' headin' for the Walleroo but you might take time out to fetch the snake over to the radio. Then you can describe the markings to me, which will give me some idea. Over.'

Nancy flew outside and snatched up the snake's limp body, glancing at Andy as she did so. His eyes were still closed and she fancied she saw a bluish tinge round his mouth. Oh, God, she prayed, running back across the living room and sliding on to the chair in front of the radio set. Oh, God, let the doc arrive in time. Don't let my Andy die!

*   *   *

Dr Mitchell was as good as his word, better in fact. Twenty minutes after Nancy had described the

397

snake, she heard the buzz of the plane's engine approaching and looked up into the cloud-filled sky to see the small machine beginning to descend. The pilot, skilled at landing in the bush, brought the plane to a halt with scarcely a wobble and almost before it had stopped the doctor had jumped down and was running towards the house. He arrived on the veranda closely followed by half the Walleroo staff, and even in her terrified state Nancy could read the anxiety in the men's eyes and was grateful for it. They were truly fond of 'the boss' and would do anything they could to help him.

However, their presence alone was not much use at present, so Nancy shooed them away, promising to send Aggie or Violet over to the camp with news as soon as she had something to report.

Nancy had expected the doctor to perform some sort of operation, but in the event he consulted his book and then came to her, clearly worried but trying not to let his anxiety show. 'I've given him a shot of something which should help,' he said, 'but I want him in hospital.' He indicated the snake. 'The head's too badly mangled to identify it for certain, but I guess it could carry diseases other than its venom, so I want Andy under my eye for a few days.' He looked keenly at Nancy. He was a tall, rangy man, with thinning fair hair, steady blue-grey eyes and a large, drooping moustache. He put a hand on her arm. 'Can you leave the station? It's not as if you'll be wanting to muster the cattle in this weather, and anyway'—he grinned suddenly, boyishly—'I doubt if you'd be much use on a muster. Andy would say it was men's work.'

'I'll go with Andy,' Nancy said at once. 'I'll radio the McGuires; their Phil is home again so I reckon they'll spare him to us for a few days, just until . . .' her voice wobbled and she hesitated until she could control it once more, 'until Andy's well again,' she finished firmly.

'Right. I'll give you five minutes to get a few things together while the boys and myself carry Andy out to the plane and make him comfortable,' the doctor said. 'Five minutes, mind; that do you?'

Nancy did not need to reply. She hurried through to the bedroom, flung her washing things and Andy's into an old knapsack, added some underwear and a change of clothes, and ran out to where Violet and Aggie were watching as the men carried Andy, on a stretcher which had been brought from the plane, to the airstrip.

'Violet, Aggie, I'm going to the hospital with the boss,' Nancy said rapidly. 'I'll radio the McGuires as soon as we reach Cloncurry, and ask them to send young Phil over to keep an eye on the cattle. He's a good lad and his mum was saying he's bored with kicking his heels about the station 'cos Bob and Alf had to manage without him during the war and they can manage without him now. If he can't come, I dare say the stockmen will cope for a few days, but I don't think it'll come to that. If you need me, use the radio to get a message to Cloncurry. Oh, and check the batteries, though I think they're all right for a while. D'you know how to use the set, Aggie?'

Aggie nodded seriously. 'Course I does, missus. I uses it when the boss takes you to town. But I guess you won't be gone long, eh?'

Nancy saw that Andy's stretcher had been

399

loaded on to the plane, Dr Mitchell was swinging himself aboard and the pilot had started the engine. Hastily, she grabbed her bag and set off towards the airstrip at a smart trot. 'I dunno, but I'll stay for as long as it takes,' she shouted over her shoulder. 'If I'm going to be gone long, I'll send someone to hold the fort.'

Behind her she heard the women murmuring that they would manage, and then she reached the plane and was hauled unceremoniously aboard by the doctor's strong hands. She looked anxiously at Andy, lying very still on the stretcher; his tanned face looking yellowish, his eyes still closed. For a moment, he reminded her of someone, but she could not think who, and then the doctor was settling her in a small bucket seat, telling her that they would soon have Andy in the hospital and regaining some colour. 'Sleep's the best thing for him right now,' he shouted above the roar of the engines. 'And it wouldn't hurt you to have a bit of a rest. Just try to relax or you won't be much good to Andy when we reach Cloncurry. The nursing staff there won't want an extra patient.'

Nancy nodded and presently fell into an uneasy doze, for though she had thought sleep was out of the question exhaustion claimed her the moment she relaxed, and she did not fully awaken until the plane landed on the Cloncurry airstrip.

*   *   *

The next week was one of the worst of Nancy's life, but at the end of it even her anxious eyes could see that Andy had turned the corner and was going to get better. For the first three or four days, she had

400

stayed constantly by his bed, even though he had been in a sort of coma, unable to speak to her, not even aware of her presence, she thought. She knew that the doctor who was treating him here, a Dr Leandro, had been as worried as she, but on the fifth day he began to look a little more hopeful, on the sixth he became almost cheery, and on the seventh, when Andy had sat up and demanded bacon and egg for breakfast, he assured Nancy that her husband would make a full recovery. He was a small man of Italian origin, with thick black hair swept back from a broad lined forehead, bright eyes dark as sloes and a full-lipped mouth which revealed very even white teeth when he smiled. His English was far from perfect, though he had lived in Australia for twenty years, but Nancy soon realised that the nurses thought him a first-rate doctor and, as Andy began to improve, found she agreed with them. He was a quiet man but he was always willing to explain to Nancy what he was doing and why, particularly when she told him that she had nursed in France during the First World War. She also appreciated the fact that, when Andy tried to say he must be allowed to leave the hospital and go back to the Walleroo since he felt so much better, the doctor was able to dissuade him without shaking his confidence in his recovery.

'I admeet you are very much better, Mr Sullivan,' Dr Leandro had said seriously, 'but the Walleroo is a cattle station, is it not? And such places are not of the healthiest. I trust you have been pleased with the attention we have given you at the Cloncurry? Well, we in our turn are pleased with your progress. If you stay here, under our eyes, for another week or so, we can send you home as fit as

401

you were before the snake bite. But if you go home now, and have a relapse . . .' he had shrugged and rolled his eyes, a peculiarly Italian gesture, 'then you would be making work for us and misery for yourself. No?'

Nancy had waited for Andy to rip up but instead he had grinned at the doctor. 'I guess you're right, doc,' he had admitted. 'Getting myself out to the dunny took just about all my strength this morning so mebbe I'll hang around in here for a while longer.'

Later in the day, Nancy sat beside his bed and passed on all the news from the Walleroo she had gleaned when she radioed them to say they would be staying in Cloncurry for a while yet. 'Violet and Aggie are managing just fine and young Phil McGuire is downright enjoying himself,' she reported. 'Why, he's even got some of the fellers together and they've cleaned out under the veranda, killed a dozen snakes and a great heap of creepy crawlies. But I'm telling you, Andy Sullivan, that if you ever try to go under that veranda again . . .' She gasped, a hand flying to her mouth. 'Oh, Andy, the letter! How absolutely awful, but it went completely out of my head!' She looked frantically round the ward. 'Can you remember what you did with the page you rescued after the wind blew it away?'

Andy thought for a moment, brow furrowed. Then his face cleared. 'I'm pretty sure I crumpled it up and pushed it into my trouser pocket,' he said slowly. 'I was still wearing them when I came in here so I guess if you find the trousers, you'll find the letter. What about the second page—the one you had?'

'I did just what you did; shoved it into my skirt pocket,' Nancy said. She was still wearing the skirt and now she plunged a hand into the pocket. She withdrew the page triumphantly, smoothed it out and began to read, then turned a worried face towards her husband. 'Darn it, we'll have to find that first sheet. This one doesn't make sense by itself, and it doesn't even have her address on, so I can't reply.' She got to her feet and crossed to Andy's bedside locker. Pulling it open, she extracted the drill trousers he had been wearing when he arrived at the hospital. 'Oh, Andy, what a fool I am! Sister said I might make use of their laundry to get the mud cleaned off your shirt and trousers, so I did. I never thought to check the pockets . . .' She plunged a hand into both pockets of the trousers, pulling the lining out to prove that they were empty. 'Oh, whatever shall we do?'

'There isn't much we can do . . .' Andy was beginning, when Sister's round and rosy face appeared round the door at the end of the ward and she trotted towards them. She was starting to say that it was time Nancy took herself off for her daily walk when Nancy interrupted her. 'Sister, the most awful thing . . .'

She was only halfway through her explanation, however, when the sister cut across her words. 'Well, what a fuss about nothing, Mrs Sullivan,' she said reprovingly. 'I guess all hospitals have the same rules about patients' property, or have you forgotten? As soon as we got Mr Sullivan into hospital pyjamas, the contents of his pockets were emptied by the almoner and placed in a stout envelope, which was then sealed and put in the hospital safe. On your way out, just ask for

Miss Brown—that's the almoner—and she will hand it over.'

Nancy could have hugged her. She had been as worried as Pete over the disappearance of Jess's daughter and knew her son would be delighted if she could write and give him Debbie Ryan's address. So she gave Andy a quick kiss and hurried off the ward, and very soon she was pacing the pavement, walking a little less swiftly than usual, since she was reading as she went. At first she was disappointed that there was no address on top of the letter, but she soon realised why. Debbie Ryan was coming to Australia to visit them! It was wonderful, more than she had ever dared hope. And she knew that Andy—and Pete of course— would be equally delighted. Pete had told her how guilty he had felt over losing touch with Jess's child, though Nancy had always maintained that it was as much Debbie's fault as Pete's. Or perhaps it was no one's fault; in wartime, no one could be sure of anything. But at any rate, it looked as though Pete and Debbie would meet up again after all, and in Pete's very own home, what was more.

Nancy continued her walk, her pace quickening joyously as she neared the hospital again. Andy would be so thrilled to hear the news! She knew better than to run once she entered the hospital but hurried nevertheless, beaming as she arrived at the bedside. 'You'll never guess . . . but I'll read the letter aloud to you, then you'll have an excellent reason for getting better,' she said breathlessly. 'Oh, Andy, she's coming to visit us at the Walleroo.'

She read him the letter from start to finish, saying as she ended: 'So we must send someone to meet the SS *South Pacific*, because the upcountry journey is better tackled in company, don't you think?'

She smiled hopefully at her husband but he was shaking his head at her. 'Nancy, didn't you notice the date? She must have arrived in Australia a week ago; she could be anywhere by now, because as she says in her letter she'll need to earn the money to pay for the journey as she goes along.'

'Oh, Andy,' Nancy wailed. 'She'll think—she's bound to think—that we didn't care enough about her to meet the ship!'

'She won't think that; she'll just think we're too busy to spare the time,' Andy said comfortingly. 'But there's no help for it, so we'll just have to wait till she turns up and then give her a grand welcome. We're bound to be home before she arrives.'

'Yes, I guess you're right. And I'm sure she'll stay for a good while because it's the heck of a journey,' Nancy said. 'It'll be lovely to have Jess's daughter here. Do you know, darling, I still miss Jess.'

'Of course you do,' Andy said heartily. 'You've never said much, Nan, but I know how much you would have liked a daughter. This child is an orphan; I reckon she'll be happy to stay for a good long time.'

'I hope you're right,' Nancy said absently. She was stroking his arm as she spoke, looking idly at the scars which she knew he had received when he had been struck by shell fragments during the First World War. Now, she saw one she had never noticed before. It was a thin straight line, three or four inches long, with stitch marks on either side,

405

and for a moment she stared at it, puzzled, tracing it with her forefinger. 'What on earth . . .' she was beginning, when suddenly the truth burst upon her. 'Well, I never did . . . you never told me you had a blood transfusion when you were injured, Andy.' She looked across at him and saw the lurking smile she loved dawn on his face. 'This scar is from a blood transfusion, isn't it? I'm sure I can't be mistaken.'

'Too right,' Andy said. He was still smiling. 'I reckon my life's been saved twice, don't you? The first time, this little blonde nurse took one look at me and realised I was bleeding internally and needed a blood transfusion. Lucky, wasn't I?'

'I don't know why I never noticed it before,' Nancy said slowly, only half listening to her husband's words. 'I suppose it was because your arms are covered with fair hair and there are several scars on them. Andy, why are you laughing? Why are you looking at me like that?'

Andy shrugged, but he was still smiling. 'I've waited twenty-five years for you to remark on that scar. I guess I didn't make much of an impression on you, though you made a hell of a one on me, you little blonde nurse, you! When I got your letter and photograph in answer to my advert, I was almost sure you were the nurse who'd saved my life out in France . . . almost sure, but not certain. Then, when you came down the gangway . . . well, I knew at once, of course. At first, I was a bit hurt that you didn't recognise me—I'd recognised you, after all—but then I remembered the number of patients who must have passed through your hands, and I remembered how thin and pale I had been after losing all that blood, not a bit like my usual self.' He grinned at her shyly, then slid his hand up her arm, across her shoulder and round the back of her neck, until his fingers were buried in the soft golden floss of her hair. 'I guess I fell in love with you that very first time, when you bent over the bed and said, "You'll be fine, soldier, but I think maybe your bandage is loosening."'

Nancy gasped and turned to stare into her husband's familiar, much-loved face. Her mind flew back to that makeshift hospital in France, to tent No. 3, and the young soldier bleeding to death from an internal haemorrhage, needing help, needing her. For a moment, she could only stare at him as tears welled up in her eyes and began to fall down her cheeks. Then, heedless of her surroundings, of the other men on the ward, she cast herself on his chest, her arms round his neck, and began desperately kissing everything she could reach. 'I love you, love you, love you,' she said wildly. 'When we first married, I was ashamed of the way I felt about you, because it made me seem fickle and shallow, but how different it would have been if I'd recognised you! Oh, Andy, you've made me feel such a fool.'

Andy sat up straighter in his bed and smoothed her hair back from her damp face with a gentle hand. 'It don't matter,' he said gruffly. 'Nothing matters except that you love me and I love you.' He chuckled deep in his chest. 'What do twenty-five years matter when all's said and done? Oh, Nancy Sullivan, you've spent twenty-five years making me the happiest man on earth, and that's all that matters.'

CHAPTER FOURTEEN

Debbie arrived in Sydney on an extremely hot day in early February. She was enchanted by her first view of the great modern city, but it would be idle to pretend she was not disappointed when she examined the crowds who had come to meet the ship and was unable to see the tall, blond figure she had half expected amongst them. Once she got on to the quayside, she saw that there were several people holding up placards with names written across them, but hard though she stared she could not see her own name anywhere. Plainly, none of the Sullivans, not only Pete, thought it necessary to undertake the tremendous journey just to meet a young girl whom they did not really know.

However, she told herself that she understood. Pete could not have been back on the Walleroo very long and doubtless had a great many demands on his time. Besides, despite her first intention to work en route, she had been advised by a young officer on the SS *South Pacific* that this was not a good idea. He said she should catch a train which would take her most of the way, and then finish her journey by 'cadging a lift'—his words—with someone delivering mail or goods to the cattle stations. 'Get to your friends first, then see what they advise,' he told her. 'Remember, they want your company . . . and I believe there's work enough for dozens on most cattle stations.'

Right now, however, the young seaman who had carried her trunk down the gangway was saying that he was prepared to carry it all the way to the railway station if she was willing to pay him a few bob. 'I mean to buy a present for me girlfriend,' he explained. 'But I spent up at the last port, so any money I can earn is welcome.'

They reached the railway station and found the train for Queensland already waiting by the platform. So whilst Debbie bought her ticket, the young seaman stood guard over her trunk, then bade her a hasty goodbye and set off for what he described as 'a poke around the shops'.

It was a pity in a way, Debbie thought, as she climbed aboard the train, that she had decided not to get a job right here in Sydney, and then to make her way up to Queensland by slow degrees, because she would have seen more of the country that way. But the young officer had been right. No one would want to employ a waitress, or a shop assistant, or a barmaid for a matter of days, so she would have had to work perhaps for several weeks before moving on. That would have prolonged the journey ridiculously, and besides, the train fare was not yet beyond her means. In any case, the truth was that she was longing to reach the Walleroo. She kept telling herself that Pete would have changed, that he might be married or at least engaged, that she must not place any reliance upon his feeling for her as she felt for him. But such good sense made no impression on her hopeful heart. What was more, once aboard the train, she soon realised that the countryside trundling past the windows only seemed strange and wonderful for a short period. The small towns through which they passed were all rather similar and the bush was mainly gum trees, brush and a tangle of undergrowth interspersed by stretches of desert where almost nothing grew. Long before they reached Queensland, she had grown weary of the journey and was eager to reach her destination. There was no dining car aboard the train, and when they stopped at small wayside stations she was invariably offered the same food in the refreshment room, so that as well as growing weary of the journey she also grew extremely tired of being presented with a large—and tough—beef steak topped by two greasy fried eggs and surrounded by flabby chipped potatoes. Then, of course, she had left Sydney in hot, dry sunshine, but as she travelled further north the weather changed. It became sultry and humid, and the scenes outside the windows of her carriage were more often than not obscured by sudden downpours: tropical rainstorms accompanied by thunder and lightning which seemed intent on ripping the sky apart whilst Debbie watched, awed, as much impressed as frightened by the display.

She got on well with her fellow travellers, all of whom were extremely friendly and helpful, and as they scuttled aboard the train through swirling rain and collapsed into their seats she asked her neighbour, a tousle-headed youth called Mick, about the change in the weather which had started a couple of days before.

'Oh my word, didn't no one tell you about the wet in Queensland and the Territories?' the young man said, staring at her incredulously. 'This is a durned big country and there's two completely different types o' weather. As you get further north, I reckon it becomes more tropical like; there's rain forests and that, and you get what they call the wet. Right now we're in February and that's often the worst month, with storms and torrential rain every few days. Why, the folk runnin' cattle an' sheep stations can be cut off for weeks at a time.'

'Oh!' Debbie said, considerably startled. She had assumed that the whole country would follow a similar weather pattern and had congratulated herself, on board the ship, on her wisdom in choosing what she had thought of as the Australian summer in which to arrive. Most of the books she had read, now she came to think of it, had concentrated upon New South Wales and Victoria, with a sideways glance at Perth, and had said very little about Queensland. So she gazed with new interest at her companion, who had already informed her that he had been born and bred on a cattle station a hundred miles from Cairns and knew the whole area well. 'Then I've come in the monsoon season, have I?'

The young man shook his head indulgently. 'It ain't as bad as that,' he told her. 'Sure, we get plenty of rain and sometimes the floods get real serious, but it don't just rain for four or five months like it does in some countries. We can have a fortnight of decent weather, with sunshine every day, and the cattle's coats steamin', then the dark clouds begin to pile up and you can hear the thunder rolling, and you'll have a downpour and storms for another couple of days.' He chuckled. 'You ought to have come in the dry if you wanted to see much of the country while it's not under water.'

This conversation gave Debbie fresh heart. So there was a perfectly reasonable explanation for the absence of the Sullivan family when her ship had docked. From what Mick said, the Walleroo could have been cut off by floods, or they might never have received her letter. There had been sacks of mail aboard the train which she had watched being deposited on small station platforms as they made their way steadily north, but now she realised that much of the mail contained in the sacks might not arrive at its destination for many weeks. So it was perfectly possible that she and her letter might arrive simultaneously at the Walleroo.

From the moment of learning about the havoc wrought by the wet, Debbie cheered up immeasurably. Subconsciously, she had actually begun to doubt her welcome at the Walleroo. If Pete had married, then it was not impossible that his parents—and his new wife—might see her as an unwanted intruder, and if so, whatever would she do? But if they had never received her letter, or had been cut off by floods, their failure to come and meet her was perfectly understandable.

After Mick's revelations regarding the wet, Debbie began to enjoy the journey once more, and by the time she and her trunk were deposited on the station platform at Mungana her natural optimism had reasserted itself and she was looking forward to her arrival at the Walleroo.

Mick had also been bound for Mungana, though from there he would travel a hundred miles in the opposite direction to the Walleroo. He went with her to see if he could find her some sort of vehicle to take her out to the cattle station, then booked her into a small hotel for the night and bade her a cheery farewell. 'You'll be good. You'll get there, and it's a bonza homestead,' he said earnestly, though Debbie knew perfectly well that he had never set eyes on the Walleroo. 'Just remember there's precious few pretty girls in the outback, so everyone will want to help you. So long, Debbie.'

Since the young man had found several drivers willing to take her at least part of the way to her destination, Debbie went to bed with an unworried mind, and despite the sudden drumming of rain on the roof in the early hours slept soundly till morning.

*   *   *

Debbie arrived at the Walleroo during one of the fine spells which Mick had told her about. The last stage of her journey had been accomplished in a truck and the driver had gone out of his way to set her down within feet of the veranda, so she bade him a grateful farewell, heaved her trunk off the ground with considerable difficulty, and began to climb the veranda steps. She was still struggling with the trunk when two things happened simultaneously. The screen door burst open to reveal a very large and very black woman with a watermelon smile and small, sparkling black eyes. And at the same moment a hand reached over Debbie's shoulder, lifted the trunk as if it weighed no more than a feather, and deposited it upon the veranda itself. Debbie squeaked and glanced up to find a tall young man grinning down at her. He had clumpy brown hair and a great many freckles, but her heart dropped for this was most definitely not Pete. However, it would be rude to let her dis appointment show so she said timidly: 'Jamie? I don't think you can be Jacko because Mrs Sullivan always called him the baby of the family, and I know you aren't Pete . . .'

The young man took her elbow and guided her up on to the veranda whilst the large woman surged out of the house, flung both arms round Debbie, and gave her an affectionate hug. 'D'you know who I is?' she said, in a rich, friendly voice. 'I's Violet and you must be little Debbie Ryan what the missus said on the radio that we was to look out for and make welcome. The missus said you'd come all the way from England which must be a million miles, so I reckon a cup of tea would go down well.'

This rush of words almost bowled Debbie over but she responded immediately. 'Oh, Violet, I've heard all about you in Mrs Sullivan's letters. How d'you do? It's lovely to meet you and a cup of tea would be wonderful. I don't know about a million miles, but I've certainly had an awfully long journey and I'm very glad to be here at last.' She turned to the young man who was about to carry her trunk into the house. 'Hang on a minute, Jamie; I guess your mother did get my letter. I'm longing to meet her in the flesh . . . if she's here, that is?'

The young man put her trunk down and turned towards her. 'I'm afraid she's not here and I'm not Jamie. I'm Phil McGuire and I'm looking after the Walleroo while the Sullivans are in Cloncurry. But it's a long story so if you don't mind I'll take your trunk to your room and then come back and explain, over that cup of tea Violet mentioned. She has made up the bed in Jamie's room since he won't be coming back for a while yet.'

'And—and Pete?' Debbie asked, unable to

414

remain in ignorance any longer. 'Is Pete back? I was sure he would have been demobbed some time ago.'

Phil, who had picked up her trunk once more, turned back. 'He was demobbed all right, but he got a deferred passage home because he was worried about a young lady he'd lost touch with. He wanted to meet up with her again, make sure she was all right before leaving her half a world away.'

'Oh, right,' Debbie said feebly, feeling the hot blood rush to her cheeks. She was certain that Pete must have been searching for her and it was just her luck that she had decided to search for him at the same time. But she had told everyone in Lavender Court where she was bound, had even told Uncle Max, so if Pete did manage to trace her he would realise at once whereabouts in Australia she was to be found. She felt herself beginning to smile and said, idiotically, to Phil's receding back: 'He's not married then? Not engaged, or anything like that?'

Phil laughed. 'Not that I've heard,' he said. 'But if he finds his young lady, I reckon that's just what he'll do; marry her, I mean. You don't go deferring your return home for a girl you don't care about.'

By now, Debbie's grin must be positively Cheshire Cat like, she thought, but she simply could not help it. So this delightful young man believed that Pete really liked her; if, of course, it was she for whom he was searching. She felt joy bubbling within her and was still trying to sober up when Violet came heavily on to the veranda, bearing a huge tray upon which stood teapot, sugar bowl, milk jug and cups, as well as an enormous fruit cake and a plate of delicious-looking biscuits.

'Here y'are, missy,' she said heartily, setting the tray down on a cane table. 'Now I reckon Mr Phil will tell you what's been happenin' and why the boss and the missus ain't at home right now.'

* * *

It did not take long for Debbie to be told all about the arrival of the mail, the dropping of the letter, Andy's dive under the veranda, and the sub sequent snake bite. When she heard, Debbie could not help shooting a quick glance at the veranda beneath her feet. Phil saw it and smiled. 'It's all right, Debbie; I organised some of the staff to go under there and clear everything out. They put down a deal of Jeyes fluid, which will discourage the critters, we hope. But Andy didn't stop to think, that was the trouble. He just saw the page of the letter go under the veranda and dived after it. It's not like Andy to act impulsively, but he's crazy about Nancy and never gave the danger a second thought, I reckon.'

'And is he going to be all right?' Debbie asked anxiously. 'When did all this happen? And where is this Cloncurry place you spoke of?'

Phil explained, adding that the Sullivans should be back soon, but assuring her that Violet and Aggie would look after her until Nancy could take over. 'They're grand women and know the ropes,' he told her. 'I reckon the Sullivans will be back here in a week or so because Andy is very much better, quite like his old self. And if you want to use the radio, either myself or one of the gins will show you what to do. Everyone on the Walleroo

416

will help you to settle in and understand our ways. If you need anything, you only have to ask. Can you ride?'

Debbie admitted that she could not and did not know whether to be pleased or apprehensive when Phil said he would get one of the stockmen to teach her. 'You never know when you may need to get somewhere fast, and since you can't drive Andy's truck you'd be better off learning to ride,' he pointed out.

After a week of watery sunshine, the storms set in again but by now Debbie was growing accustomed to the vagaries of the weather. Together with Violet and Aggie, she began to plan a party for the Sullivans' return. 'If the rain eases off and the storms give us a break, then I reckon most of the neighbours will come,' Phil said. 'But of course if the weather's real bad it'll be just us and the staff. They're planning a corroboree to end all corroborees.'

'What exactly is a corroboree? Just a specially good sort of party?' Debbie asked curiously, but Phil just grinned and would not enlighten her.

'It's a good deal more than that,' he said. 'But I won't spoil the surprise. Now tell me, how are you getting on with the riding?'

*   *   *

Pete went straight to Long Lane and almost immediately was directed to the factory where they assembled radio sets for aircraft. Pete asked to see the manager and presently found himself seated in a tiny office opposite a small, elderly man who looked tired to death but nevertheless gave him a warm smile and held out his hand. 'Ah, Mr Sullivan, how can I help you?'

Pete explained his errand and the manager pulled an enormous book out of the top drawer of his desk and spread it out upon the blotter. 'Deborah Ryan, Deborah Ryan,' he murmured. 'I remember her; a thoroughly nice girl, hard working and reliable. Her address will be . . . ah, here it is! Number four Lavender Court, off Lawrence Street.'

'I suppose I couldn't see her for a moment, could I?' Pete asked, rather surprised that he had been given her address and no other information. 'You see, I don't have much time . . .'

'But I thought you must know that Miss Ryan had left the factory . . . oh, some while ago,' the little man said. 'However, if you go round to Lavender Court, and if she's still in the city, I'm sure you'll find her. But there was talk of her going abroad.'

Pete thanked him and stood up, feeling distinctly uneasy. Going abroad? If she was in France, or Spain, or Germany, however would he find her? And why should she go abroad? But he was being foolish. She would have left a forwarding address with the landlady in Lavender Court—he assumed that she must have been in lodgings—and once he had her address he would find her, no matter how long it took.

He was about to leave the factory when a stream of girls and a few young men began to push past him and one of them tapped him on the arm. 'Excuse me, sir,' she said shyly. 'But the manager spotted me as I were leaving me bench and said a young feller had come enquirin' after me old mate

Debbie. Were it you, sir?'

'Yes, it were—was, I mean,' Pete said quickly, his heart giving a hopeful lurch. 'Do you happen to know where she's gone? Only we lost touch and I'm very anxious to meet up with her again.'

'Well, you ain't likely to do that, unless you was thinkin' of emigrating,' the girl said cheerfully. 'She's gone to visit an old pal of her mam's what lives in Australia. She meant to work her way across the country, she said, to some place with a queer sort of address, a sort of mixture of wallabies and kangaroos, I thought, when she told me.'

Pete stared at her for one unbelieving moment, then he gave a whoop and lifted her off her feet and kissed her resoundingly. 'I don't know who you are but you're the nicest girl I've ever set eyes on,' he found himself babbling. 'She's gone to the Walleroo! Why, she might be aboard the very ship I'm booked on next week. Oh, my word, I've as good as found her!'

Millie gazed at him open-mouthed, but she had no opportunity to ask him just what he meant by his last remark, for he plonked her down on the ground, pushed his way out of the crowd and made off down the road at what she could only describe as a fast gallop.

She turned back to her friend Tess, who was staring at her open-mouthed. 'What were all that about?' Tess asked, round-eyed. 'Who were he? And what did he want with Debbie? And fancy kissin' you in front of everyone!' She giggled. 'You're a shameless hussy, you! I always suspected it but now I know for sure.'

Millie shook her head and took her friend's arm, and together they began to make their way towards

419

the tram stop. 'I dunno,' she said, hearing the puzzlement in her own voice, and frowning over it. Then her brow cleared. 'Oh, of course; wharran idiot I am! Debbie were keen on some young Australian feller what looked after her for a few days after her mam died, only they lost touch. I reckon it were him . . . come to think of it, I'm almost sure Debbie said he were her Aunt Nancy's son.'

'Then he must be her cousin,' Tess said, having wrestled with the problem for a moment. 'And they'll meet up again when he gets back home, I suppose. But I thought her cousin was called Max.'

'Oh, you!' Millie said, giving her friend's arm an affectionate shake. 'That were her uncle, the one she didn't like much. And now let's drop it. Are you comin' to the flicks this evening, or have you other plans?'

*   *   *

Andy and Nancy arrived home during a lull in the bad weather and were welcomed rapturously by everyone on the Walleroo. They drove up in a battered old truck and were immediately surrounded. Debbie, standing on the veranda, went hesitantly down the steps, but the moment Andy caught sight of her he looped an arm round his wife's waist and fought his way through the crowd until they reached her. She opened her mouth to explain who she was and found herself being seized and kissed. 'Even if I'd not known you had arrived, I'd have recognised you as Jess's daughter,' Nancy said, holding Debbie back from her whilst her eyes filled with tears. 'Oh, my love,

420

you are the very image of your mother. She had just such beautiful chestnut hair, the same dark blue eyes . . . but I mustn't be foolish. I'm just so glad that you came to me, as your mother wished.'

Debbie found herself blinking back tears as well but said in a rallying tone: 'Now that isn't quite right, Aunt Nancy, because my mother's hair was a mass of curls, and mine is straight as any poker. But you are just as she described you and I'm sure you look young enough to be my sister. And Mam would be so happy if she could see us now, because I think, in her heart, she wished she had had the courage to accompany you to Australia—at first, that is,' she added hastily. 'Afterwards, when she met my dad, she was glad she'd not gone away.'

Then it was Andy's turn. He shook her hand, then laughed and kissed her cheek. 'What a diplomat,' he said, with mock admiration, 'saying she looks young enough to be your sister! But you aren't far off; I always tell people Nancy was a child bride, but then she goes and spoils it by admitting that she was a nurse throughout the First World War. But we'd better go inside because that big black cloud is coming closer every minute and we don't want to get soaked.'

Debbie, climbing the veranda steps and re-entering the homestead, thought they were both delightful, though it also occurred to her that a stranger might easily have taken them for brother and sister. They were both tall, both very fair indeed, and both tanned, though Nancy's skin was pale gold and Andy's a rich russet brown. Both were blue-eyed with even features and beautifully white teeth, but when they spoke the resemblance ended, for Andy had the typical Australian twang whilst Nancy had retained the soft tones of middle-class England.

As they entered the living room, Nancy turned to Debbie once more. 'Aggie tells me that tucker will be ready in half an hour so Andy and I will go and wash and get into some clean clothes,' she said. 'I dare say you could do with a cool shower, so if you'd like to use the bathroom first . . .'

Debbie laughed. 'I've not wasted my time here; I'm quite a useful member of the household now,' she said. 'I helped in the preparation of the meal and I mean to go on helping because it's some small return for the hospitality I've already received. But one thing before you disappear. Have—have you heard from Pete?'

Nancy pulled a wry face. 'Not for weeks; in fact, he doesn't know his father's been in hospital,' she admitted. 'We had the mail intercepted so it came straight to Cloncurry instead of the Walleroo, but there was nothing from Pete. Andy and I believe it's because he's already on his way home, so he may turn up at any moment.' She looked curiously at Debbie. 'You only met him the once, didn't you?' She chuckled. 'And if I remember rightly, you were only fourteen or fifteen at the time, so he'll get quite a shock to find the child he knew has turned into a young woman, and a very pretty one at that.'

Debbie felt her cheeks grow warm but she was spared the necessity of replying when Aggie appeared in the doorway. 'Missy Deb, is it time to take that fluffy stuff you made out of the icebox?' she asked. 'Violet says it is but I ain't so sure; can you come?'

Saved by the bell, Debbie thought, hurrying

gratefully in Aggie's wake. She had no idea what Pete had said to his parents regarding herself and no wish, she realised, to be asked questions which she might find difficult to answer. At one time, Pete had believed her to be Chloe's mother, had thought her a bad girl, and though she had disabused him on this score, Nancy might still believe Debbie was not the sort of person she wanted her son to be involved with. Then she chided herself for being foolish. At the time of the bombing, Pete must have had a good many things on his mind more important than one young girl whom he scarcely knew. Obviously, he would have told his mother that her friend had been killed, described how he had helped rescue Debbie from the shelter, but other than that . . .

By now, she and Aggie had reached the kitchen and they hurried into its steamy heat to begin the task of serving out the huge beef stew with dumplings and carting it across to the veranda whilst Violet mashed potatoes into a snowy heap. The beef was followed by Debbie's apple mousse. When the meal was finished, everyone would go along to the camp for the corroboree which the staff had planned. Debbie glanced up at the sky, dreading rain, which would ruin everything, but the black clouds had passed them by this time and pale sunshine glinted off the water in the lagoons, whilst steam rose gently from the backs of the cattle grazing nearby.

By the time the staff had been fed and the family were sitting down to their own meal, Debbie had remembered that Andy had been in hospital and was profuse in her apologies for not enquiring about his health before.

423

Andy laughed. 'It's the biggest compliment you could pay me, because I'm obviously looking like a healthy man and not an invalid,' he told her. 'As for myself, I've forgotten the snake bite except that I'll be a good deal more careful in future. And now let's change the subject. Ever been to a corroboree before?'

Debbie admitted that she had not but told him that there had been great excitement and carryings-on amongst the stockmen and their families ever since the date of the Sullivans' arrival home had become known. 'Frankie and Porky seem to have made themselves wigs out of dried grass and Slim was all done up in green leaves, ever so cleverly sewn together,' she told him. 'I didn't get the significance but I'm sure it's something to do with the corroboree.'

Andy and Nancy both laughed. 'I know,' Nancy crowed. 'I've seen at least a part of it before. The grass wigs are Andy and myself . . .'

She would have gone on but Andy interrupted her. 'That's enough, old lady,' he said chidingly. 'Half the fun is in gradually realising just what's happening.' He turned to Debbie. 'And if you were responsible for that apple mousse, then I hope you mean to stay with us for a good long time.'

*　　　*　　　*

Pete had docked in Sydney but after that he had not followed the same route as Debbie. Instead, he had taken a berth aboard a steamer making its way up the coast. It was cooler at sea than it would have been in the train, yet he found himself im patiently pacing the deck and longing for the

424

moment when the voyage would end and he could begin the cross-country journey to the Walleroo. Also, he found himself thinking, increasingly, of Debbie. He had left Liverpool within hours of Millie's telling him that her friend had gone to Australia, and had travelled straight down to Southampton to claim his berth on the ship that would take him home. Afterwards, he had regretted not questioning Millie more closely because he realised that Debbie could have left England weeks before, or could have delayed her departure for various reasons and might even have been in England still, though he did not think this likely. He wondered about the baby, too—not that she would be a baby any more . . . my word, she would probably be at school. But he found he trusted Debbie; she had said she would find the child's mother and hand her over, and he was sure she would have done just that. Then there was the dog; she had loved that dog. He could not imagine her abandoning it. But a dog could be left with someone reliable; he was pretty sure that the shipping line would not undertake the carriage of a dog with much enthusiasm.

He kept reminding himself, of course, that it was no use becoming obsessive over a girl he had not seen for nearly five years. She would have changed as he had, and they had met only briefly, but the memory of her small pale face, wide eyes and straight, shining hair had remained crystal clear in his mind. He thought this a good sign since, when he tried to remember the faces of various girls he had taken out whilst stationed in Norfolk, he could not do so. Oh, he could say one was blonde, one brunette, one small and plump, another tall and thin, but that was about it; their actual features he could not bring to mind, no matter how hard he tried.

The ship docked at last and Pete hurried ashore. He caught a train, then hired an ancient truck. For a wonder, the weather had cleared and he thought there was a good chance that he might actually arrive home in a matter of a few hours, though he would probably have to abandon the truck by the river's edge and holler until he got someone's attention, since he doubted that the river would be fordable at this time of year, even after a spell of dryish weather.

The old truck rattled and plunged, and Pete's excitement and impatience grew. The journey was never-ending and it gave him too much time to think. For all he knew, Debbie might have a boyfriend back in England . . . no, that was unlikely; if she had had a boyfriend, she would scarcely have abandoned him to visit her mother's old friend in Australia. But of course she might have met someone since, a young officer aboard the ship which had brought her to Sydney, or someone en route. Good God, he was being downright ridiculous, fretting like a fool over imaginary situations. He slowed to negotiate a pothole in the dirt track and told himself to stop making mount ains out of molehills. Half a mile on, it occurred to him that Debbie might have arrived at the Walleroo and fallen in love with Jamie, or Jacko. The truck lurched and he spun the wheel with such force that he narrowly missed a gum tree. He must keep his mind on the road and not allow himself even to think about Debbie. Determinedly, he drove onwards.

*   *   *

The corroboree was everything that Debbie had imagined and more. She and the Sullivans were escorted to a raised platform, upon which had been placed the cane chairs from the veranda. Then the men treated them to a display of war dancing; brandishing spears, stamping and yelling. After that came what was obviously the high spot of the corroboree, a faithful enactment of Andy's being bitten by the snake. It was at once hilarious and carefully rehearsed, for they began at the very beginning with Porky, white grass wig in place, clutching some sheets of paper. One of the men, clearly representing the wind, danced around, whirling leaves up into the air and shaking the branches of a nearby tree, before pouncing upon the man representing Nancy and carrying the paper across the compound and into one of the humpies. And then 'Nancy' shrieked and began to gabble that this was an important letter from an important person and must be retrieved at once, whereupon Frankie, representing Andy, rushed across the compound and dived into the humpy, emerging immediately and wrestling wildly with Slim, clad in green leaves and taking the part of the snake. The two actors were obviously enjoying themselves immensely and strung out the fight until someone shouted, 'Get on with it!' whereupon the snake grabbed Andy's arm and Andy gesticulated dramatically before crawling over to the veranda and collapsing at his wife's feet.

Debbie watched, fascinated, as the men went

427

right through every aspect of the episode. The doctor was deliberately funny, wearing a stethoscope made of vine stems, and chasing Andy round and round the ward to give him an inject ion. Then, of course, there was her own arrival, the stranger from England, and finally the corroboree came to an end with the feast which Debbie had helped to make, and now helped to serve to the chattering, laughing, excitable crowd.

When it was over, the three of them walked back towards the homestead and Nancy put her arm lightly round Debbie's shoulders. 'I'm going to let my old man go straight to bed now, because though he's nearly as good as new, he still needs his rest. But you and I will sit on the veranda a while and watch the moon come up, because the corroboree made me remember something you might not know. I'll make us a cup of tea and explain as we drink it.'

*   *   *

Pete reached the river and abandoned the truck as he had planned. He went to the river's edge and hollered, but nobody came. He was wondering why when he heard a tremendous roar coming from the camp and groaned aloud. It was just his luck that they should be holding a corroboree when he needed someone to row the boat across the river. No one would hear him, not if he hollered for hours, so unless he wanted to spend the night in the truck he had better start testing the water. Cautiously, he began to wade across, being careful to feel for potholes as he went. The light was fading in the west but it made little difference to his progress since the water was always muddy in the wet, and anyway, if he plunged into a pothole he could always swim.

Another roar, this time definitely of laughter, came from the direction of the camp, just as Pete's foot found a deep hole and he began to swim. The water was welcoming, like cool silk against his hot skin. Pete swam steadily on.

*　　　*　　　*

'. . . so you see, my dear, it was the first page of your letter which blew away and sent Andy scuttling under the veranda,' Nancy was saying. 'I didn't mention it before because I was afraid you might think we blamed you for the accident. But that was why the letter never even got read until a week or ten days after we received it. I wouldn't have said anything, but watching the re-enactment just now it occurred to me that either Aggie or Violet might refer to it as "your letter", which would have been unfortunate, to say the least.'

'I'm glad you told me, and I feel more honoured than guilty,' Debbie said honestly. 'After all, Andy must have thought it was important otherwise he wouldn't have taken such a dreadful risk. But did he know, at that point, that the letter was from me?'

'Oh yes, most definitely. You see, I . . .' Nancy was beginning to explain how she had read the first few words and then turned to the last page to read the signature when she realised that Debbie was not listening. She was half out of her chair and leaning forward, like a runner waiting for the start of a race. Nancy turned to gaze in the same direction and saw that Debbie's eyes were fixed on a tall figure approaching the homestead from the direction of the river. Immediately, her heart gave a joyful bound; it would be one of the boys, and judging by what she could see in the fading light, it was her dear Pete. She started to her feet, but Debbie was ahead of her. She flew down the steps and halfway across the compound, then drew to a halt within a yard of the tall figure, and Nancy saw that it was indeed her eldest son.

'Debbie?' Pete's voice was low and husky.

And there was a long pause before Debbie spoke. 'Hello, Pete.'

'I had to swim the river. I'm awful wet.'

'So I see. Oh, Pete, it's been a long time!'

'Yeah. You been here for a while?'

There was another silence and Nancy realised that the two young people were simply staring at each other. She moved nearer until she could see their faces and thought, with a stab of something very like pain, that she had never seen such hunger expressed merely by a glance. Hesitantly she cleared her throat, wanting to break the silence which was suddenly so charged with emotion that she felt tears prick behind her eyelids. 'Pete, my dear, it's good to see you . . .' she began, then realised that neither Debbie nor Pete had heard a word.

'I arrived two weeks ago.' That was Debbie, her voice a little shaky. 'It's a grand place, Pete.'

'Yeah.'

*   *   *

Andy woke as Nancy climbed into bed beside him.

430

He said huskily: 'Everythin' all right? Young Debbie wasn't too upset about the letter?'

'Oh, the letter,' Nancy said. 'Andy, darling, Pete's home, and it's the weirdest thing. Debbie saw him before I did and she just flew across the compound, then stopped short. They exchanged a few words, nothing very much, but the way they stared at one another . . . oh, Andy, it was weird, truly it was. I tried to tell Pete how wonderful it was to see him after all this time, but I don't think he heard me at all. He'd asked Debbie how long she'd been at the Walleroo and she told him a couple of weeks. And then he said, "You staying?" and she said, "Would you like me to?" and he gave a sort of grunt and took hold of her hand—it was the first time he'd touched her—and they just walked away together. They didn't take the slightest notice of me. I don't believe they even knew I was there.'

CHIVERS
LARGE PRINT
-direct-

If you have enjoyed this Large Print book
and would like to build up your own
collection of Large Print books, please
contact

Chivers Large Print Direct

Chivers Large Print Direct offers you
a full service:

• Prompt mail order service

• Easy-to-read type

• The very best authors

• Special low prices

For further details either call
Customer Services on (01225) 336552
or write to us at Chivers Large Print Direct,
FREEPOST, Bath BA1 3ZZ

Telephone Orders:
FREEPHONE 08081 72 74 75